TRAVLERS
OF THE GRAY DAWN

A NOVEL

BY

PAUL GRIMSHAW

CHART HOUSE PUBLISHING

SOUTH CAROLINA

CHART HOUSE PUBLISHING, JUNE 2013

Grimshaw, Paul, 1960-

ISBN–13: 978-0615820453
Library of Congress LCCN Pending

First Edition June, 2013   1234567890

Chart House Publishing Web address: www.charthousepublishing.com

Cover design: William Craven

Editorial Consultant: Patrick LoBrutto

- for all the countless soldiers who fought in countless wars, on every continent, on every planet, in every universe, who sacrificed everything for causes just and unjust.

Acknowledgements

Special thanks go to my family, friends and associates who listened with real or feigned enthusiasm to my ramblings, especially the ramblings over the past 25 years since the 125th Anniversary of the Battle of Franklin. It was at that December 1989 Civil War reenactment, on a Tennessee hillside, that I was first convinced I had a story to tell.

To Mom, David, Dad, Mary & Popo, Grandaddy (who all loved history and helped me love history), the Simpsons, Molly & Dave, the cousins, Glenda M. (thanks for your invaluable service and enthusiasm!). Robin T., Kent K, Jody M.,Troy N., Stephen M., DVL, TVL, PGB (current and former). To Matt "Tater Tot" R., Tom J., Becca B., Alice M., Chad M., the 7th S.C. / 4th N.H past and present: (Buddy & Beth). Gary W., Doc, Paul L., The Horry Boys. To those who've listened to me discuss this book and sent me clippings, ideas and encouragement: Charlie C., Uncle Jessie J., BJ C., Chuck B., Mark & Sharon, Lenny & Joanne, Tom & Ros, Marc & Christine, Cathy W., the Forever Friends Birthday Crew, and the many, many, many unnamed others.

And finally to my editorial consultant, Patrick LoBrutto, who loves this stuff, and who helped make this a better book.

"Fellow citizens, we cannot escape history." — Abraham Lincoln

"There is a terrible war coming, and these young men who have never seen war cannot wait for it to happen, but I tell you, I wish that I owned every slave in the South, for I would free them all to avoid this war." — Robert E. Lee

"The distinction between past, present and future is only an illusion." — Albert Einstein

TRAVELERS
OF THE GRAY DAWN

Chapter 1

5:33 a.m. July 6, 2013
Gettysburg, Pa.

In the kitchen of his small converted row house apartment, just south of downtown Gettysburg, Tommy Fuller chugged a glass of orange juice and put a can of Coke and an apple in his canvas haversack. The reproduction haversack was worn on the hip with a long strap from the neck and shoulder. It was a small, flattened satchel, used by nearly every soldier, both Confederate and Union, during the American Civil War. He had purchased his online from an outfitter that catered to American Civil War reenactors. All reenactors needed these accoutrements (or, "cooters" as they were more commonly known) to participate in events large and small throughout the U.S.

He checked himself one last time in the hall mirror and managed a slight smile. As he left, he quietly locked and closed the door behind him, leaving his wife, Susan, still asleep, and altogether disinterested in his "hobby," as she called it. Tommy Fuller saw it as something much more important. Born in Montgomery, Alabama, he and his family moved north to Gettysburg when he was nine, but his love of the South was already deeply and permanently ingrained. On this particular day, the last day of the four-day 150th anniversary remembrance of the Battle of Gettysburg, and on every other day, the 23-year-old thought himself a true Southerner, with a capital "S."

The streets were quiet in his neighborhood on the edge of town, and he felt uneasy walking to his Nissan pickup truck dressed in full Confederate soldier regalia, complete with a working 1853 Enfield musket, but had no choice. He'd been unable to camp with the rest of his unit and was to arrive at the Gettysburg Battlefield ready to fight.

Still dark, only a distant street lamp shed a dim, yellow-orange glow over the deserted streets. The city had installed these 'crime lights' as a supposed deterrent after a spate of beatings, gang initiated drive-by shootings, and burglaries in recent years. Tommy hadn't noticed the lights making much difference. For the moment he wouldn't worry about his troubles; they were mostly behind him, he hoped, and there was fun ahead.

With every step on the cracked sidewalk his excitement grew as he looked forward to the biggest Civil War reenactment he'd ever been a part of, the 150th anniversary of the Battle of Gettysburg. This was to be the best attended Civil War reenactment ever held. For nearly a week some 14,000 reenactors from all over the U.S., and 12 foreign countries, along with 90,000 spectators, would all converge on the little Pennsylvania tourist town to experience the live-action drama. The reenactment represented the battle most historians say turned the tide of the War; a battle that ended the South's incursion into northern territory, the so-called "high water mark."

Already a block away from his apartment Tommy relaxed slightly and smiled, though he felt out of place in his Confederate get-up, while not also out on a battlefield. In the stillness of early morning the out-of-synch gait of his walk echoed through the streets in an unusual pattern. He moved efficiently, though with a slight limp, his left leg not completely healed from a brutal attack he had barely survived three months earlier. Although the physical pain was waning, the emotional scars would take longer to heal. Alone, before sunrise on the dimly lit street, he took in the pleasant coolness of what had, so far, been a sweltering summer. An unusual quiet and stillness hung in the air. He liked his neighborhood this way.

At first, the thumping, like that of a faint heartbeat, could be felt more than heard. Tommy cocked his ear. A few restless birds chirped, and from a block or two away he heard the yap from some poor, chained dog barking at phantoms. Still walking toward his truck he heard the unsettling noise again and he stopped. Only the cicadas kept up their clamor.

...boom, ba-boom, boom...

The thumping was louder this time and he realized he was hearing the all too recognizable, nearly subsonic bass notes that come from amplified subwoofer speakers, the pride of many hip-hop and rap enthusiasts who install them in the backs of their vehicles.

"It's still a good bit off," Tommy whispered to himself, fearing that it wasn't. He tensed a little and picked up his pace. The thumping got steadily louder and he spoke aloud again.

"Please, not now. Not dressed like this."

His truck was still a block-and-a-half away. He picked up speed. The thumping – Boom! Ba-boom! Boom! was like the unwanted approach of

2

an evil giant's footsteps and it was growing louder and coming closer at an alarming speed. Before he could run into the shadows to hide, the enemy was upon him.

A late-model Honda Accord zoomed around the corner toward him, its motor buzzing like an angry wasp. The car was customized, chopped and low to the ground. Shiny from countless coats of wax, the small, white sedan reflected and amplified any light touching it. The windows were tinted so dark they were as black as the night, and probably not legal. Flashing neon license plate holders and ultraviolet purple-hued blacklights, glowing from underneath, gave the small car an evil aura that chilled him to the bone.

Tommy stared straight ahead as the menacing machine roared by him, leaves and dirt swirling at his feet. The sounds of hardcore rap shook the otherwise quiet neighborhood.

Boom! Ba-boom! Boom!

He didn't dare turn around to look. Still some distance from his truck, he kept his quickened pace steady. Screeching brakes behind him sent a fresh wave of adrenaline flowing through his body to the point of nausea. Without daring to look, he heard behind the constant drone of the music the frightening laughter of young men who seemed hell-bent for trouble. They laughed and looked hard at Tommy, mocking him and his wardrobe, while yelling over the thumping bass.

"What the fuck?" one of the teenagers yelled out, while the others laughed, heads stuck out of the car's windows. This was the young reenactor's worst nightmare. He searched his pockets frantically and he yelled aloud, desperate.

"Where are they? Where are my keys?"

Behind him he heard the turbo-charged Honda burn its tires in a 180-degree spin, creating a cloud of choking, black smoke. He was in trouble. He thought maybe he'd left his keys at home on the kitchen counter. He was sure he had taken them but where were they? The young Rebel soldier was now 80 yards from a truck, which he wouldn't be able to get into, and a quarter-mile from an apartment from which he was locked out.

At 5:30 in the morning, with gang-bangers on his heels looking to have some fun, he fought off flashbacks of all the previous traumatic encounters he had suffered in this very neighborhood. His small automotive repair shop, less than two miles away, had been burglarized and vandalized a half-dozen times in the previous 15 months. In a particularly brutal attack, just after closing one night, he'd been robbed of the day's receipts, was badly beaten, and left for dead.

Once again, in these early morning hours, he found himself on the receiving end of more unwanted and criminal attention. He felt cursed and dreamed of a place where he could live in peace, where bleeding-heart liberal judges wouldn't set gang-bangers free to harass law-abiding citizens, and a place where cops could mete out instant justice with the end of a baton without fear of video cameras recording and judging their every move.

The menacing car sped up to within 20 feet of him and screeched to a stop. When the doors opened the pounding bass was so loud it made him blink every time a new beat came his way. He kept walking. He didn't dare turn around.

"Yo! Johnny Reb!" called one of the boys, yelling over the relentless thumping. Tommy heard laughter. "The war's over. Ain't you heard?"

He was closer to his truck now, but without keys still had no way inside. Beads of sweat formed on his brow and his heart seemed to beat out of his chest in time with the unyielding music. He reached for his cell phone, also not there.

"Yo! Muthafucka! We talkin' to you!" another voice taunted with an amplified malevolence.

"This bitch dissin us? He finna learn a little history lesson. He sure ain't no Yankee fan in that gear."

Tommy was surprised the youth recognized his Confederate gray, and apparently knew the difference between uniforms, and between North and South, but he couldn't take the time to be impressed.

"Yeah," added another voice, "did'n the Yankees kick them redneck asses?"

Their mocking had moved from bullying to sinister, and like a pack of wolves they circled their quarry. Despite the cool early-morning air, sweat poured off Tommy's forehead and he could feel his hands sticky, moist and cold as he desperately, frantically searched for his keys.

BANG!

A single metallic whack punctuated the air above the ceaseless drone of the thumping music, and Tommy's heart leapt into his throat. Instinctively, he turned. He saw one boy holding an aluminum baseball bat that he had just slammed into a post-office mailbox. Just twenty feet away, two black youths, one holding the baseball bat, approached. Another teenager, a white kid, used one hand to hold up his sagging pants, and another to flash a gleaming knife blade.

"Not again...," he thought. "Please, not again."

Desperately Tommy felt for his keys and put his hand on a piece of infantry gear. Slung over one shoulder, his haversack contained only an apple and can of Coke. His leather cartridge box was slung from his other shoulder and rested on his right hip. He opened it thinking he may have put his keys inside. Instead he found 40 black powder-filled paper cartridges,

4

for his musket, that he had rolled himself without including the lead Minié ball bullet. Reenactors, after all, fired blanks at one another, and bullets were strictly forbidden at reenactments.

But wedged in the corner of the cartridge box he felt something like a steel marble with a dull point. He grasped what he immediately realized to be a Minié ball rifle bullet. Weeks earlier he and his friends had enjoyed a little live-fire target shooting, testing the steadiness of their hands and the accuracy of their muskets. This singular Minié ball was a potentially lethal leftover from the target practice, and it gave Tommy Fuller a fighting chance.

The youths took a few tentative steps forward, eyeing the antique rifle, and shouting vulgarities of all sorts. The blaring urban music continued its ceaseless, thumping taunts.

Boom! Ba-boom! Boom!

Tommy knew what he had to do and moved with practiced efficiency. His training and experience were about to be tested. Silently he went over the steps, called a "load in nine," not missing a beat. He could almost hear his sergeant call out the commands.

"Load!" He slung the nine-pound 1853 Enfield musket from his shoulder, and placed the stock on the ground.

"Handle cartridge!" From his cartridge box he retrieved a small tube of gunpowder, and brought it to his mouth.

"Tear cartridge!" He ripped open the paper tube with his teeth and tasted the black powder on his tongue.

"Charge cartridge!" The soldier poured the black powder down the barrel of his musket, followed by the Minié ball and the empty tube of paper.

"Draw rammer!" He pulled the slender ramrod from beneath the barrel.

"Ram cartridge!" He tamped the paper, bullet, and gunpowder into a tight, deadly package.

"Return rammer!" The ramrod was brought back to its resting place under the barrel of the Enfield.

"Prime!" With the hammer half-cocked, he reached into his cap box and placed a tiny brass percussion cap on the firing nipple.

"Ready!" With his right thumb he pulled the hammer back one more click. This final step would turn his antique musket into a lethal weapon, as deadly as any modern gun, ready to fire.

He backed away from the youths who stopped their approach, sizing up the situation. His technique was dead-on, and right up to military standards.

"Affix bayonet!" Tommy pulled the bayonet from its sheath and twisted it into place on the end of the rifle. The boys howled with nervous laughter, still uncertain of the gun's validity. One of them urged his friends to back off.

"Come on. This cracker crazy," he said. "We ain't packin'. Let's bounce."

Two of the boys ignored the wise council of their friend and the one with the bat made two quick steps forward swinging the aluminum weapon at Tommy's head. The duel was on. The whizzing bat sounded like a light saber slicing through air, narrowly missing him, connecting with the bayonet's edge, sparking. They stepped backward laughing at the terror on the Rebel soldier's face. The music continued.

Boom! Ba-boom! Boom!

"Leave me alone! I'll shoot!" said Tommy as he tightened his Kepi, the French-designed hat that nearly all Civil War privates wore.

The smallest of the three attackers tossed his knife back and forth between his hands, almost losing his pants in the process. Tommy would have laughed at the struggling sagger had he not feared for his life. His head pounded with adrenaline and he felt dizzy. As he took one step forward he thought he saw the sky flash, as if from distant lightning. Pain shot through his bad leg and he rocked back on his right to relieve the pressure. The streetlights disappeared and reappeared, only to again disappear with another flash of light.

Without the aid of the streetlights he could just see the three Yankee soldiers, two from a colored unit, jeering at him, while the sounds of war raged around him. He took a single step back and the sky flashed again, the streetlights returning. One of the Yanks was swinging his gun like a huge stick and another tossed a silver bayonet playfully from hand to hand. Cannons blasted all around him in a strange musical rhythm.

Boom! Ba-boom! Boom!

The Reb soldier checked and tightened the small percussion cap placed on the firing mechanism of his rifle. Now just 15 feet and closing, the Yanks continued their advance. The one with the big gun charged him. In an instant Private Tommy Fuller dropped to one knee, settled the stock of the rifle in his shoulder, aimed at the colored Yank's chest and pulled the trigger.

In a millisecond he heard the blast in his ear, felt a strong kick to his shoulder, and witnessed a two-foot long orange flame issuing forth from the barrel. The round was off. Traveling at 1000 feet-per-second, the soft lead bullet partially melted and expanded in the barrel as it spun, continuing its expansion in the air so that when it reached its target it was a mass of bone-crushing lead. The hot metal shattered the breastbone and ripped through the chest of the colored soldier in front of him. Blood sprayed the young Yanks standing just behind their comrade and they screamed in horror - high-pitched adolescent screams of those who were not quite men, but no longer boys.

"Just kids," thought Private Fuller, who was not much more than a kid himself. He felt an instant revulsion of the act, and a wave of nausea coursed through his body. They may have been just kids, but they were "damn Yankees, just the same, and in a man's war."

The distant moon cast a yellowish-orange glow over the street-turned-battlefield. Surrounding him, the cannons still blasted in a mocking, steady, sickening beat. Fuller covered his ears. The noise was maddening.

Boom! Ba-boom! Boom...

Then the pounding stopped.

One Yank soldier lay dead on the ground while two others backed away. The Rebel soldier stood up, his musket barrel still hot to the touch, the bayonet extended. He heard something fall to the ground as he stood. He looked down and stooped to pick up a set of keys. The pre-dawn sky flashed around him, as the street changed from cobblestone to pavement, and back again, several times. Holding the keys and looking at the largest one, the soldier's mind struggled to connect to a word that was both familiar and strange: *Nissan*.

Chapter 2

9 p.m., July 2, 1863
Gettysburg, Pa.

Blue-white smoke from hundreds of small campfires mixed with the night's cool mist and hovered over a valley on the outskirts of Gettysburg, Pennsylvania. A fog rolled in mingling with the smoke, and with the struggling light of a nearly full moon, created an eerie, softly glowing cloak of hazy white that partially hid the army encamped within.

Surrounded by the western woods of Seminary Ridge, some of the 65,000 of General Lee's war-weary, Confederate troops not killed, injured, or captured from two disastrous days of fighting, slept fitfully. Those who couldn't sleep wrote farewell letters to families and lovers. Some spoke quietly in small groups, while others, in shifts, fortified earthworks and bunkers expecting to work through the night. Some gathered in prayer, certain God was on their side. A smaller number practiced the age-old tradition of storytelling and sang songs of the South, desperate to remember happier times when promises of a sure and rapid close to the War were made by overly optimistic Southern leaders. Those despondent and hopeless few who had lost all their will to fight another fight slipped quietly away in the shadows. Military tribunals called them deserters. History looks on them with less harsh judgment; not all men are born to fight.

From a distance, the gathering, with its thousands of white canvas A-frame tents erected in perfect rows, might have looked like a 1950s-era Boy Scout Jamboree. The morning light, however, would not usher in the smell of eggs and bacon cooked over open campfires and the laughter of teenagers, but instead, one of the bloodiest battles of the deadliest war in American history.

Less than three miles to the west, 41-year-old Major General George G. Meade was encamped with his corps of almost 80,000 troops. Better fed and better equipped than Lee's soldiers, this group, though also bloodied and tired, had a more confident disposition than its enemy over the ridge.

Though Lee's Army was well into northern territory, Federal troops felt the almost imperceptible tide of the battle and of the War turning in their favor. Some dared to express cautious optimism about what lay ahead. General Meade kept his opinions close and dared not show any hopefulness; it was not his way. He and his fellow Federal commanders were fighting a war of attrition and though they were gaining ground, their losses were staggering. And worse still, Lee was in Pennsylvania, bolstered by his victory at Chancellorsville. For weeks Lee's army had been occupying parts of Maryland, all of Virginia, and had Washington D.C. nearly surrounded.

But like an arm wrestling match where neither side would give, the War dragged on. It had already been two-and-a-half bloody years, with each side having been on the verge of victory many times, only to have Fate turn the tide back toward the underdog.

Neither Meade nor Grant were strangers to these kinds of losses. Grant, busy with the Western War, was in Vicksburg, Mississippi, leaving Meade to defend the U.S. Capitol. At battles such as Bull Run, Antietam, and Stone's River, the advantage shifted back and forth in the course of an afternoon, like a bloody football game that left the field strewn with the dead and dying. The same was true of lesser battles and skirmishes, in which one side or the other would have the clear advantage only to have the disadvantaged side inexplicably turn things around.

On September 8, 1863, at Sabine Pass, Texas, 44 Confederate gunners effectively repelled a flotilla of Federal ships and troops numbering 15,000. Not a single Confederate soldier was lost and the small unit of Rebels captured a Union gunboat and 200 prisoners. Anything and everything could and did happen during this war.

On this particular night of this particular war, neither side could have known they were less than twelve hours away from THE pivotal battle, the final day of fighting at Gettysburg. One side or the other would parlay the win toward the conflict's ultimate conclusion. Without the advantage of hindsight, to the men on the field this night was just like so many countless others: a culmination of days and weeks of marching, re-supplying, strategic planning, dangerous occupations of towns that didn't want them, back and forth shelling, advancing, retreating, and waiting to strike, while both sides prayed to the same God for victory.

All wars have their heroes. Some are well known with monuments erected in honor of their sacrifice and bravery, but many heroes are lost to wars' fog and remain anonymous subtext whose deeds are remembered by few. No one was likely to erect statues honoring Thomas and William Grissom. The brothers were both members of newly promoted Confederate Brigadier General Jordan's unnamed, rudimentary spy ring.

Jordan, a former U.S. Army officer turned Confederate, led a band of spies and scouts. The Grissom brothers had been recruited, shortly after they enlisted, to act as scouts for the A.N.V., the Army of Northern Virginia. Theirs was an untested, elite band, not attached to any particular unit, and the Gettysburg Campaign had called them to a part of the country they'd never before visited.

"Whoa, horse," said Thomas Grissom, approaching a ridge and pulling a monocular from his satchel. His brother, Billy, was close behind.

Younger by 11 months, Billy Grissom, in happier times, had shared his brother's good looks and rogue-ish disposition. His curly, dark hair was receding in the front, and long in the back. He didn't possess the will or motivation to keep it neat. The brothers' once bright blue eyes had grown cold and callous after two years of war, and had turned the color of the CSA's uniform jackets, lifeless gray.

"Whacha lookin' for?" asked Billy, a little too loudly.

"Hush," admonished his brother. "Shut yer big bazoo. There's snipers out yonder."

"You an old croaker, Tom Grissom. Worry 'bout everything."

Both men were in their early twenties, though, at this point in the conflict, looked to be twice that age. Tom Grissom's thinning hair was turning prematurely gray. A small bandage covered a wound on his chin caused by a fall from his horse a week earlier. Gaunt and shallow eyes were deep set and rested above protruding cheekbones. The beginning stages of malnourishment hid otherwise handsome, youthful features. Both men were unusually tall, and yet each weighed less than 140 pounds. Being underweight was not an uncommon malady among soldiers from both sides of the conflict.

Their physical condition, as bad as it was, was far better than most. They enjoyed a few privileges that not even those with higher rank were afforded. New boots were delivered regularly, as a spy with bad feet was useless. They were on horseback a great deal of the time and were spared the endless marches that sometimes killed other men. Fresh horses were often saved for scouting parties, as speed and reliable transportation were essential for the timely delivery of information. Avoiding capture and gathering intelligence were the scouts' specialties, and they were among the best at their trade. Protecting their way of life, pride in their Southern Heritage, and revenge acted as motivation to fight what many had been calling "the lost cause" since before the War started.

Under the partial cover of haze and night, the two men sat upon their horses gazing from the rock-strewn slopes of Seminary Ridge toward

Cemetery Hill. When the patchy fog would separate long enough, the bright glow of a nearly full moon afforded them a brief, crystal-clear view of what would again become a battlefield. Looking behind them, into the woods, they viewed some of their fellow Confederates, quiet and somber.

Looking ahead, through the mist, they could just make out a faint glow made by fires from the enemy's largest camp less than three miles away. As they rested upon their horses, an occasional rush of mid-summer wind would carry to their ears the vile sound of singing from their adversaries, and they felt hatred for them, and dread at what this battle's third morning might bring.

Billy Grissom spoke again, quieter this time. "How many Yanks ya' reckon are out there?"

His brother answered in their shared native Tennessee drawl, slightly annoyed at a question to which they both already knew the answer.

"Dunno for sure. Sixty... maybe eighty-thousand or so. We already reported that, 'member?"

Billy didn't comment right away.

"Well...by hook or crook, we'll clean their plows come 'morrow," he said, not sounding too sure. They both knew the odds were against them. Billy Grissom didn't possess the maturity and confidence of his older sibling; he never had, though he tried.

A bat swooped down and circled silently, darting back and forth, before disappearing into the blackness. Tom, looking through his monocular, struggled to focus on something in the distance he'd been trying to identify. What he saw, illuminated only by diffused moonlight a half-mile ahead, rising up out of the mist, started his wheels turning.

"Billy. Ya see that small rise in the middle there? Near Emmitsburg Road?" Tom questioned.

"Barely, but yeah. What about it?"

"I seen something that ain't on the map."

Tom looked down at the worn and frayed Federal map, one he'd stolen from a Yankee Major a week earlier, slipping it from his tent in the middle of the night. He looked again through his scope, struggling to see the feature when the moon offered a little more light.

"Before it got dark I seen it clearer. There's a boulder or rock in the middle of the field, and I swore I seen...like a cave or some sort of opening cut into the rock, facing East, toward us, just about slap-dab in the middle."

"Yeah, okay. I see it – I think. You lookin' for a place to hide?" whispered Billy, taunting.

Tom ignored the sarcasm. "I bet the Yanks don't know it's there 'cuz the cave ain't on any of these maps, ours or theirs, and the opening faces us. All they can see from their side is the little rise and a few rocks."

"Okay," said Billy. "What are you gettin' at?"

"I'm tryin' to think of a way we can avoid having *our* plows cleaned, come sun up."

Billy was silent.

"I got a plan, just might work. And I'm going to the Ol' Man with it," said Tom.

"Are you crazy?" said Billy. "General Lee's got better things to do. And besides, you'll never get in to see him. We already made our report to that jack-ass Commander of his, anyway." Billy's horse snorted and nodded in apparent agreement with its rider. He stroked the horse's muscular jaw in appreciation.

"Just might work..." Tom muttered under his breath, again ignoring his brother. With a quick flip of the reins, he turned his horse back into the woods at Seminary Ridge. Dutifully, Billy followed, and they disappeared into the hazy darkness.

Chapter 3

9:05 p.m., July 5, 2013
Gettysburg, Pa.

Less than nine hours prior to Tommy Fuller's bloody incident on the street, he'd been seated on a bar stool, attending a rare, mandatory reenactment meeting. This meeting, like most, was a friendly gathering at a favorite local pub, MacAuley's Tavern. They were there to run through a few logistics of the event's final day. As the stragglers trickled in, the Captain and his officers, in civilian clothes, chatted at a table in back.

An old TV was affixed to the ceiling and angled toward the bar. An inch of dust on its top, threatened to cascade onto the heads of the patrons below. A ballgame, pitting the Atlanta Braves against the New York Yankees, had been on for an hour and the Braves were ahead by one. There was some interest from the dozen or so regulars watching, though no one watched more intently than new reenactor recruit Greg Jackson. He was glad to have the diversion and an excuse to keep to himself. With some difficulty he hoisted his large frame closer to the bar and loosened his tie. He felt out of place–a well-dressed black man among mostly working-class whites, and he didn't know a soul except the bartender.

"Scotch, Mac," he called out to tavern owner Shay MacAuley, never taking his eyes from the TV.

The drink was delivered and Mac spoke.

"So when's this meeting of yours starting?" Mac recognized Jackson, and nodded in a greeting of sorts. The bar was a favorite after-work watering hole for area businessmen, and this was not his first time in.

"Umm...15 minutes," said Jackson, glancing at his Rolex and then back up to the game. He swirled his drink, the ice clinking in the glass.

Jackson, a Harvard-educated attorney, had been practicing in Gettysburg for nine months after moving from D.C. He was respected and well liked by his co-workers, and especially, by his boss, Mike Phillips, the only real friend he'd made since moving to the small, historic, tourist town. He didn't know Phillips very well outside of work, but still, a familiar face would ease his discomfort and he hoped his boss would arrive soon.

"Where the hell is he?" he asked himself, looking hopefully toward the door. He took a long sip from his Scotch and grimaced at the burn it caused in his throat. He worried if he'd ever "fit in" living in this "red neck little tourist town," as he described it to his friends in D.C., though in truth this "little tourist town" was growing on him. Filled with bikers and occasionally large numbers of Rebel flag-waving Civil War buffs, the town, especially in the summer, sometimes felt like a Confederate enclave though it was situated well into Yankee territory.

His big-city style only added to his anxiety while sitting at the bar. Though he wore thousand-dollar tailored Armani suits, and five thousand dollar watches, he was otherwise generally without effrontery. He liked looking good, and as a single attorney with few financial responsibilities, he could afford it. His grounding came, in part, from the fact that he had worked his way up through the trenches as a Public Defender in D.C. and knew, first hand, the precariously shaky tightrope between the haves and the have-nots.

Scouted by Phillips, Gilder, Bailey & Scott, a Gettysburg law firm, Jackson was promised a partnership and twice the money he was earning in D.C. He accepted, without hesitation, an offer to escape the D.C. rat race, relocate to Gettysburg, and join the firm.

Mac wiped down the bar and restocked the peanuts in a small ceramic dish.

"What's your wife say about this crazy club you're in?" he asked.

"My wife?" asked Jackson, smiling. "No worries there. I'm free, free at last." He raised his cocktail triumphantly in the air.

At 34-years-old he had recently divorced a woman he'd been married to for less than two years. "We were just a bad match," he'd tell people. "We knew when to cut our losses." In Gettysburg he was settling uncomfortably into the role of eligible bachelor, and while he was sure there must be some eligible women in town, the college girls were too young, and he'd yet to connect with any others. He thought the pickings were slim, especially slim that night at MacAuley's.

He glanced around the room and saw 30 or 40 men, ranging from late teens to men he guessed were in their 60s, a few even older. Some wore ball caps emblazoned with the Confederate battle flag. He couldn't help but notice the beer guts most of these guys carried proudly.

He'd never seen a more overweight, out-of-shape group of men ever gathered together in one place that wasn't also an all-you-can-eat buffet.

14

Though there were exceptions, Jackson would discover that Civil War reenactors, as a group, were not known for their svelte physiques, standing in almost comical contrast to actual Civil War soldiers, who were mostly malnourished and rail thin. One such exception sat at the other end of the bar; a kid who looked like he wandered in straight from 1863.

"You know this one down here?" asked the bartender, nodding to his left, where a sullen looking Tommy Fuller stared at his beer. "I been watchin' this one," he continued. "This lad looks troubled to me; one sandwich short of a picnic, if you know what I mean. Keep your eye on him, I would."

What no one, not even Fuller himself, could know was that he was less than 10 hours away from using his Civil War-era musket against a 17-year-old gang-banger blocks from his home. Whatever "troubles" Fuller was feeling at the end of the bar would pale in comparison to the new hell waiting around the corner.

Jackson smiled at the bartender's overly dramatic concern and lowered his gaze from the TV to the man he had just been made aware of, and Jackson agreed; he did look troubled. A furrowed brow put premature lines across the young man's forehead and his thinning, blond hair didn't help his odd appearance. He looked young and old simultaneously. Grease from his auto shop showed in dark spots on his hands and face. Curiously, he also appeared strong as an ox, for a smaller man, and was well proportioned from good genes and the hard physical labor of garage work. Tommy Fuller was a simple workingman, a mechanic, with a lot on his mind.

Owning a small, independent service station in the day of corporate giants was not easy and the experience had taken its toll, not to mention the "troubles." Fuller, though reserved by nature, had been growing angry and increasingly emotional from dealing with more than his share of hard knocks. Even his marriage was failing.

Once described as his "soul mate," his equally young wife, Susan, and he, had been high school sweethearts. They'd been together since before either of them had a driver's license, though Tommy Fuller had been driving since he was 13 and old enough to help in the family's side business, auto repair. While they had been madly in love, they'd grown apart. "We married too young," she told him. That, and the stress of their troubles drove a wedge of unhappiness, distance, and regret through their lives and neither knew what to do, so Tommy settled into work and his hobby, Civil War reenacting.

A true shade-tree mechanic, Tommy Fuller learned his trade by watching his father and twin uncles in their endless hours of tinkering on various automobiles. Nostalgic for better days, he often let his mind drift to his boyhood, his family's rural home, and a yard always littered with two or three vehicles in various states of disassembly. By age 12 he was accomplished with his own set of tools, and by 15 was regularly hiring himself out for tune-ups, brake jobs, and oil changes. That backyard training ground and early entrepreneurship led him to an obvious career choice. He could rip apart and put back together just about anything motorized put in front of him.

For six years he'd saved every penny he could, borrowed a few thousand dollars from his father in-law, combined the funds with a small inheritance from his twin uncles who had died in a tow truck accident, and he finally had enough to lease and equip a garage of his own.

He envied the Firestones, Pep Boys, and the Goodyear Service Centers in the suburban neighborhoods with their enormous buildings along with startup and working capital that he couldn't even imagine. The $20,000 he'd scraped together was just barely enough to open his business in a run-down, two-bay garage just outside of downtown, in a neighborhood that wasn't exactly known for its affluence or safety.

His business, *Fuller's Service*, had been open for fifteen months and had been vandalized and burglarized nine times; but that was the least of the trouble. His insurance company dropped all coverage except for the liability, which they were required by law to provide, and they would have dropped him altogether if they'd been allowed to. It was Greg Jackson's law firm that successfully argued the case against United Auto Service Insurers, Inc. It had cost Fuller $12,000 in heavily discounted legal fees, and took more than a year to settle. He was still paying on the firm's bills.

Attorney Greg Jackson didn't handle Fuller's case personally, but was familiar with it and he recognized him from frequent office visits. He looked down the bar toward the war-weary mechanic and considered the young man's troubles. Jackson would get to know Tommy Fuller better, as they were both fellow members of the 132nd Virginia Militia, a Civil War reenactment group whose meeting was just about to get underway.

•••••

MacAuley's filled quickly with twenty or so additional reenactors, all there to enjoy a late-night snack, a few beers, and to hear the details for the upcoming reenactment's final day.

Most of the unit had already set up at the battlefield, and would return to camp that night, but the meeting at MacAuley's was a last encounter with civilization before the anniversary event's biggest day. The next morning they would all trade bar stools for hay bales, and cute waitresses for self-service food cooked on an open fire.

With the meeting about to begin, Jackson again looked around for Mike Phillips, the guy who had begged him to join the group, and who now seemed to have stood him up.

This particular reenactment unit was more active than many, and followed a set of by-laws that would be too much trouble for most units. Here, the longevity of your membership had its benefits, mostly out in the field. Ben Holloway, a friend of Phillips' and an acquaintance of Jackson's, had just arrived, the stink of horse manure following him in. He was the historic district's only independent pharmacist and because he supplied 12 horses for the event from his own stable, was a Colonel in the Cavalry, part of a larger group from across three states.

Holloway had arrived with Brad Lake, who was the managing news editor at the *Seminary Ridge Tribune.* Lake, another new recruit, was also enlisted as a private, despite his age and standing in the town. In reenacting everyone starts at the bottom; unless you bear an uncanny resemblance to the face on a five or fifty-dollar bill.

The unit was a registered non-profit group and had been formed 25-years earlier, in 1988, just prior to the 125th anniversary of the battle. Reenactors from all over the U.S., even as far away as Hawaii, along with a few dozen from Europe participated in that reenactment. An even larger turnout was expected for this anniversary, with its biggest weekend commemoration less than a day away.

In the original battle, in 1863, nearly 155,000 men fought one another in what many scholars say was the pivotal conflict of the Civil War. The ultimately victorious Federal forces finally and permanently drove the South back and hastened Lee's formal surrender at the Appomattox Courthouse, though that was still a bloody two years away in 1865.

Though a reenactment was staged each year, on big anniversary years more reenactors than might usually show up, arrive en masse. These reenactors, their families, and interested public besieged the little town, filling every hotel and motel room for miles in every direction. Most reenactors camped, Yank and Reb, in separate fields, well apart. Those who didn't camp were forced to stay wherever they could. Some, in nearby towns, had to commute to the event.

The reenactment's press coverage turned into an unprecedented media circus, which promised to make this anniversary's battle better attended than any in history. The Discovery Channel, History Channel, National Geographic, CNN, independent filmmakers, documentarians, and local and national media already had positions on the battlefield, or were embedded as camouflaged journalists, and the 132nd Virginia was ready to play its part.

A friendly, but commanding, voice came from the end of MacAuley's small dining room.

"Okay fellas, listen up." The conversations in the crowd dwindled. "Most of you already know me, but for the new faces out there, I am Captain Joseph DiCarlo, and I'm the Commander of this unit; as long as I don't screw this up." A few hearty laughs and calls of 'good luck' lightened the mood.

"We're all very excited about this upcoming last day of the 150th Anniversary reenactment of the Battle of Gettysburg." The crowd whooped and yelled, clapping loudly, which pleased DiCarlo immensely. He took his leadership role seriously and referred to the several documents on the table behind him.

"Because of the size of this last fling, we've all agreed to live by the rules of the Park Service and the host unit out of D.C." He was interrupted by loud booing. The Army of the Potomac, a sizeable amalgamation of independent Federal reenactors, and DiCarlo's, a much smaller, usually Confederate, unit under the umbrella of the A.N.V. (Army of Northern Virginia), shared a friendly rivalry.

"Okay, come on now. They're bringing most of the horses and artillery, and they're going to feed us lunch and dinner tomorrow night... and throw a barn dance."

A musician and reenactor seated at the back of the room picked up his banjo and began plucking the melody from "Dueling Banjos," eliciting squealing pig imitations, delighting the crowd. DiCarlo hushed them before continuing.

"Alright, come on. Listen up so we can get out of here. For tomorrow's battle the Park Service and the host unit have this thing figured out pretty much to the minute," he said. "Assignments have been delivered to us and are "written in stone," so complaining about them won't help you. For those of you fresh fish who have never been to a reenactment, and weren't here for the 149th anniversary, and for those of you who seem to need constant reminding...let me brief you on how it works."

"First and foremost we're committed to absolute accuracy, to the best of our ability, based on the historical record. With all the TV coverage this year it's important we get this one right. A bunch of us are going to have to die early in this thing and wait it out. We want to give the spectators and fellow reenactors total realism, which brings me to another point. Your uniforms and cooters have to pass authenticity guidelines or you will not be allowed to participate."

He held up his hand and counted on his fingers. "No khakis, camouflage, Pizza Hut T-shirts, ball caps, wristwatches, Wrangler jeans, smartphones, cameras, or paintball guns allowed."

The men chuckled and Jackson took an opportunity to say hello to his constantly tardy boss, Mike Phillips, who'd just slipped in.

Jackson ribbed him under his breath.

"Glad you could make it, counselor. The Captain was just telling us the rules, and the details of our unfortunate demise." Phillips took an empty seat at the bar next to his friend and pointed to Jackson's drink, gesturing for another round from the bartender.

"Well, Greg, at how many battles can you die and then be well enough for dinner and a barn dance a couple of hours later?" asked Phillips with a smile. Jackson wasn't comforted by the notion. White, redneck barn dances were not his cup of tea.

DiCarlo continued: "Some of you have made your own uniforms, and that's great, and a few of you nut balls even own the real deal, actual period relics, and while the official line is that we think you're crazy to risk these valuable artifacts in the field... if you own 'em, it's entirely up to you."

Still seated at the far end of the bar, Tommy Fuller rubbed the hard bill of his Confederate Kepi, proud of its authenticity and rarity. It was no mere reproduction; this *was* the real deal. Fuller, like most reenactors, could have owned a reproduction for around $15, purchasing it from any one of hundreds of dealers catering to American Civil War reenactors. Only a handful owned and used the real thing.

"Remember, just don't show up in jeans and Nikes and expect to go into battle. Oh, yeah..." he added. "You know the drill on eyeglasses. Either wear period-friendly glasses or contacts. And don't walk on the field with your Wayfarers or your Oakley's. And for God's sake, no cell phones, please. I will personally run my saber through the first person whose cell phone goes off at the site. Leave 'em in your car. Oh, yeah, and about the site. The Park Service has roped off who knows how many acres of the original battlefield, which is, by the way, the most historically preserved battlefield in America."

Jackson finally smiled, and with some eager anticipation turned toward his friend. "This will be huge."

Phillips nodded. "Yep. This is the big, final day. The Holy Grail of reenactments, Greg. You couldn't have signed up at a better time."

"We'll see about that," said Jackson, sipping from his glass.

"Most of the reenactment is held on a large farm outside of town," continued DiCarlo, "but our part, for the 150th, it's right exactly where all the blood was spilled, and we should be grateful for that. Most reenactments around the country take place near their original battle sites, and that's because the actual battlefield sits under a shopping mall or a housing development. Because this reenactment is on and around the original battlefields this is one of the reasons we're getting so much press and having such a good turn out. Also, because of the historic importance of this battle and the press coverage it got, even in 1863, we know with relative certainty exactly how it went down," continued DiCarlo. "We will be re-enacting day three of this battle on the same exact spot, at the same time of day it happened and we'll orchestrate certain portions of the battle based on military record and press coverage of the day. Matthew Brady was even at this one taking pictures."

The Captain turned to the table behind him where most of his officers sat dutifully. He grabbed a stack of papers. "Okay, now, I received the reenactor attendance reports before the meeting today and it lists the following:" He adjusted his small, round-lens antique reading glasses. "Looks like...8,300 blue, 11,100 gray, around 300 mounted cavalry, and 200 pieces of artillery."

An electric excitement rushed through the room as the size and scope of the reenactment began to take form. Most reenactments around the country were lucky to have a few hundred participants, a dozen cannons, and ten horses. The biggest gatherings might draw more, but this was to be, by far, the largest and best-attended Civil War reenactment in recent history.

The filming of the movie "Gettysburg," in 1992, and the 135th Anniversary in 1998, both were unprecedented in size and scope, but 2013 was expected to be bigger yet. The "Great Reunion" of 1913 was said to have had more than 50,000 reenactors, some of whom were actual Civil War veterans.

"Okay, listen up please. Just a few more things." DiCarlo scratched his snow-white beard, and slid his glasses closer to his face. "I have orders and maps handed down to me from the higher-ups and I need the officers here to go over this stuff. Remember, before we break up here, and you guys go back to camp, accuracy is the final goal and if you're asked to lie dead on the battlefield for 45 minutes, realize you're doing your part for your fellow reenactors and the spectators. Don't move until you hear the call to "resurrect." Also, if you are asked to die early in this reenactment, you'll live longer in the next one. That's how we roll."

DiCarlo paused again, taking a long swig from a bottle of Budweiser. "Well, as you all well know, we lose this one, bad." The men again booed and laughed. "But it doesn't mean we can't scare the beJesus out of them damn Yankees with a Rebel yell before we die. So, let's hear it!"

He threw his fists in the air and MacAuley's was transformed into a sea of frothing Rebs, war-whooping with a frightening, authentic blood lust. Greg Jackson did not share in the revelry. He was seriously re-thinking his decision to join this organization, but it was too late. Mike Philips, also caught up in the excitement, patted him on the back and gave him an enthusiastic thumbs-up.

Captain DiCarlo delivered orders to each of the officers, including Phillips, who was a 1st Sergeant, and told them he'd see them all the next morning at the battlefield at 8:00 a.m. for Morning Parade. Audible groans could be heard from the younger reenactors as they considered the partying still ahead of them followed by early-morning bugle reveille.

Private Greg Jackson considered the very real possibility that he would be expected to lie in the summer sun, on the ground, wearing head-to-toe wool until the order to "resurrect" was given, and all the war dead miraculously got up to rejoin the living. At smaller reenactments soldiers might be resurrected three or four times in the course of an afternoon.

"Oh, great," Jackson said to his boss and Confederate recruiter. "How'd you talk me into this? Not only do I have to fight for the damn Klan, I might have to die in the first five minutes? This is embarrassing. What would my brothers think of me?"

Phillips laughed at his new charge and put a consoling hand on his shoulder. "Listen, I've been to 20 reenactments and I've been in this unit for four years. I know from experience, you should be happy to die; it's hard work out there, so quit yer bitchin'. It'll be fun, plus...don't worry. I've got a few surprises in mind. I promise you a battle like you've never seen." The sideways smile and twinkle in his eye put Jackson at ease. "Trust me."

The bar cleared out except for Jackson and a few fellow reenactors, including Phillips, Ken Holloway, Brad Lake, and the contemplative Tommy Fuller, who was nursing a beer, still seated at the end of the bar. Fuller was in no hurry to go home. He and Susan had been fighting more lately, and staying away was easier on both of them.

"Another Scotch, Mac," called Jackson, standing to stretch his legs. He'd been watching the baseball game as best he could during the meeting and it was now late in the 8th inning. His thoughts wandered to the city of Atlanta. Though it was now a thriving southern metropolis, the 11th largest city in the U.S., Atlanta had been devastated during Yankee General Sherman's brutal "March to the Sea," part of the Savannah Campaign 150 years earlier, but there at MacAuley's, live from Atlanta on network television, Yankees and Rebs played a friendly game of baseball. Both teams were made up of an ethnic soup of white, Hispanic, African-American, and Asian players and coaches.

He looked around the room and studied this club, or "unit" as they liked to call themselves, and noticed they were lacking in much diversity.

"Oh, well," he thought, "Big surprise there." He glanced back up at the game, and realized, for the most part, the country had moved on. But old wounds heal slowly, he thought, and for some, even after a century-and-a-half, the battle still rages.

"Last call," yelled Mac, delivering a final round of drinks. "What do you guys see in this Civil War soldier stuff, anyway?" he asked of anyone within earshot.

"It's living history. And it's a nice break from reality," said Phillips, both answering Mac and attempting to encourage the still cynical Jackson. "We're history buffs, and most of us can trace our ancestors to service during the War. You could spend a lifetime studying the Civil War and still not understand all its nuances, and what-ifs. Getting out on the battlefield brings it to life. It's like you're there. They call it 'seeing the elephant.' That's when you lose touch with the present and feel, only for a fleeting few moments, that you're actually in battle."

"My great, great, grandfather fought for the Union," said Mac, absentmindedly wiping and re-wiping the same spot on the bar. "As the story goes, he'd immigrated to Boston, from Ireland, ten months before the war started and was so gung-ho for America that, at 19, he and my great, great uncle enlisted in the 28th Massachusetts Volunteer Infantry, Company B, Irish Brigade - a bunch of Micks, all of 'em. They were all killed at Gettysburg before their 23rd birthdays leaving my great, great, grandmother with four kids and no husband."

The men at the bar were taken by surprise at Mac's disclosure and his knowledge of details surrounding his Civil War heritage, having never heard him mention it before. They all silently pondered the cruel reality of war, and of this war especially. It was hard to shake the sobering thought of how very many young men died. The best estimates, nearly 600,000 Americans dead, and at the War's close countless veterans chronically ill and disabled, many of whom died prematurely from their wounds and war-born disease. It's likely the War was responsible, directly or indirectly, for deaths of more than 1 million Americans, at a time when the entire population was just about 32 million. In terms of percentages, it would be as if the morning paper, circa 2013, were to report on 10-million American men, between the ages of 15 and 40, had died on U.S. soil over the previous four years.

Phillips re-started the conversation. "Well, some of us are not going to see much of this battle. The host unit has us dying off pretty quickly. But it's still going to be an amazing thing to be a part of."

"It's a nice way to take a nap, you mean," quipped Jackson. "Provided it's not raining. Why do I let you white devils talk me into this stuff?" The men at the bar laughed. He dropped into an urban affectation that was as authentic as his educated persona. Jackson had family from the "hood," as he called it, along with friends of great wealth and education in the D.C. suburbs, and was equally comfortable in both worlds. He knew his white friends loved it when he hammed it up for them.

"Damn crazy-ass crackers," he continued, enjoying the tease, while those at MacAuley's seemed to enjoy the attention as well. It made them all a bit more comfortable with the fact that he was the only black man in a sea of Southern-fried, white men. Jackson had always felt that so called "color-blindness" was a myth, that it was okay to acknowledge racial diversity. But anyone who dared venture into ethnocentric territory was looking at big trouble, from a big man.

Tommy Fuller took a sudden interest in the conversation and carried no intended malice with his remark. "You know the Rebels had bunches of niggers on their side. There was lots of …" He stopped himself and flushed at the horrifying realization of what he'd just said. "…blacks," he continued, "who fought for the South." He prayed his slip of the lip had escaped everyone's notice, though all heard it and all eyes avoided the only black man in the room.

"Nigger with a suit," Jackson thought. "That's how this redneck punk sees me. Some things will never change." The bar was quiet except for the sound of the game-winning run, and cheers coming from the TV mounted over the bar. The conversation picked up when Ben Holloway started to brag about his horses, one a retired thoroughbred he'd just bought in Saratoga Springs, New York.

Philips leaned over to Jackson and spoke quietly. "I'm not making any excuses for him, but these guys grow up this way. He didn't mean anything by it. He's really not a bad guy. He's just…he's not well educated and he's had it rough lately."

"Damn it, Mike," Jackson said under his breath. "Growing up "that way" is no excuse for being a racist redneck. I should be all over that little punk-ass. I'd like to pop him in the face."

Jackson was incensed and offended, but with his 34-years came a growing maturity and insight that allowed him, begrudgingly, to see the point his boss was trying to make. He knew of Fuller's troubles at the service station and that young black men had perpetrated most all of the crime against him. Though he was furious at the kid for using a racial slur in such a casual way, he knew that a surprisingly large number of whites regularly used the "N" word, and why "Nigger" might be a part of his vocabulary. As livid as he was, he bit his tongue and left it alone. It was just like so many times before. It seemed just the same, no matter where he lived.

"It ain't right," he said aloud, looking straight ahead, temper cooling, but only slightly.

Ben Holloway sat a few seats over and was watching the post game wrap-up. Like Jackson, he too was a big man, weathered and cracked from hard outdoor work. He looked like a cowboy in every way: thick, graying hair under a western styled hat, well worn blue jeans, and a pair of giant hands that looked like they could crush stone.

"Rank has its privileges, men, as does supplying 12 horses, I might add," said Holloway. My orders read: 'Part of Pickett's Charge, up to the ridge, holding position near Emmitsburg Road, shooting for 15 minutes and then…'" He looked closely again at the paper in his hands, showing mock disgust. "I get shot off my damn horse! How the hell am I going to do that without breaking my neck?"

Everyone laughed and Phillips took the opportunity to shoot a quick glance at Jackson, still stinging from Fuller's thoughtlessness. Jackson was glad to have had Mike Philips to whom he could vent. He admired his boss and though cognizant of his own entry-level rank at the office and the unusual fraternization, he counted Phillips among his few friends in town, in fact his only friend in town. He smiled back at his boss, shaking his head slightly and Phillips showed his appreciation by mouthing the words "I'm sorry," to which Jackson simply nodded and drained the last sip of Scotch from his glass.

•••••

The majority of less ideological reenactors played dual roles, owning replica uniforms from both North and South, ready to pitch in when one side or the other needed extra bodies for an accurate recreation of a battle; it was called "galvanizing." Tommy Fuller was not among them. He responded with a resounding 'Hell no!' when he was once asked to wear a Yankee uniform for a commercial being filmed in town. For most, reenacting was done out of a love of history and family ties, not a love of ideology, and though that was also true for most in the unit, Jackson suspected Fuller's motives for membership. He glanced back up at the TV. The final score: Atlanta 3, Yankees 2.

"Yankees were supposed to win that one easily. Wonder what happened?" he asked of the mostly disinterested crowd who were making motions toward leaving.

They were stopped from their exit when a pretty young woman with dyed jet-black hair, a half-dozen facial piercings and tattoos on nearly every inch of exposed skin entered the bar and began yelling.

"Stop! Please!"

With an enormous camera bag slung over one shoulder, flushed and exasperated, she fiddled with a gigantic camera and lighting equipment. "I'm sorry Mr. Lake," she said, "The traffic was unbelievable. I almost wrecked with a CNN truck. I can't believe how many people are in town. Did I miss the shot? I missed the shot, didn't I?"

Fortunately for her, Brad Lake was an easygoing news editor. He never had the stomach for barking out orders and pulling the *Lou Grant* or the *Daily Globe* act, requiring his staff to call him "Chief."

"Well, fellas," said Lake, "it looks like it's just us for the morning edition. Mind posing for a group photo?"

Nervous laughter and hair grooming filled MacAuley's as the five stragglers realized they would be highlighted in the newspaper's upcoming story of the final day of the biggest event the town had ever seen.

"Why not?" said Holloway. "Haven't had my mug in the paper in quite a while."

Mac suggested a spot with a clear view of the neon, MacAuley's sign

24

in the background and the men gathered, Tommy Fuller purposefully excusing himself out of the group. In a few minutes the photographer had her shot and left.

"Well, I guess I'd better get going, too," said Lake. "I have to get this piece together before midnight. Can I get just a few more quotes from you guys before I go?"

All were agreeable except Fuller.

"Keep me out of this if you would, Mr. Lake. I had three more windows busted out after that letter to the editor I wrote ran last month. I can't afford any more trouble."

"No problem, son. I understand what you're up against."

And he did understand as the paper had run several stories about declining property values and crime in Tommy Fuller's once prosperous neighborhood. Now impoverished and plagued by homes and businesses in obvious neglect, things were only getting worse.

Fuller, in his frustration, had written a fair, but pointed, letter to the editor. He implied that the trouble with his neighborhood came from "the bad influence of poorer families moving in, more established families moving out, and the lack of parental discipline among those newly arriving families toward their teenaged children." Though he hadn't said it in writing, everyone reading the piece knew he meant poor Black and Latino families. The demographics of the neighborhood had changed dramatically in less than a decade, from being mostly white, to a racially mixed middle-class, to a predominantly Black and Latino low-income area, and crime had gone up steadily.

The series of articles and Fuller's published letter were the catalyst for most of his troubles, and Lake, while not exactly feeling guilty, felt a twang of responsibility.

Months earlier four black youths waited outside the rear entrance to Fuller's garage and surrounded him after he had closed up shop. He'd tried to talk his way out of any serious confrontation, and offered them his wallet and the keys to his truck, but they were out for blood, and they got it. Three of the young men jumped him and held him down while the fourth robbed him, and then began beating him with a six-pound, truck-tire wrench. When they thought he was dead they left him, apparently lifeless, with a fractured jaw, six broken ribs, a broken femur, and a punctured lung.

If a tardy customer, late to pick up her car, hadn't miraculously arrived within ten minutes of the beating, he would have certainly died from the injuries. However, Fuller had a few things going for him. His youth and stubbornness helped him survive the beating, and after six weeks in the hospital and six more recuperating at home, he re-opened the garage.

No one was ever charged in the crime, though video surveillance confirmed the race and general description of the assailants. Over the next six months, he endured a gasoline bomb thrown through the window, two robberies at gunpoint, and one burglary where the thieves stole $5,000 in tools. His home had been vandalized, too, and he watched helplessly as businesses closed up around him. Some of his neighbors, fearing for their own lives and livelihoods, left the area. It saddened the editor that Tommy Fuller had reason to request a low profile, but he certainly understood.

As Lake put his quotes together and thanked his fellow reenactors, Buster, Mac's graying Golden Retriever, decided it was time to come out from behind the bar. The dog shared the same pleasant disposition, reddish-blond hair, and white muzzle as did his owner. No dog and its master could have looked more alike. Buster wandered in a serpentine search between the legs of the remaining patrons, begging head scratches and bar snacks. He got plenty of both.

The men finished their drinks and Tommy Fuller began to walk over toward Greg Jackson, stopped and turned on his heel, leaving the bar without a word to anyone. Mac pulled the chain turning off the neon "OPEN" sign, darkening the window. The rest of the men finally made their way out of the tavern and into the dark of night, full of anticipation for the next morning's battle.

Chapter 4

3:05 a.m. July 3, 1863
Gettysburg, Pa.

The pickets, guards posted near the officers' tents, barely looked up as Billy and Tom Grissom arrived back at the main Confederate encampment. The two men wandered through the rows of small tents, their horses softly clip-clopping through the well-trampled soil. The closer they moved to the small stone house General Lee had commandeered as the Confederate Headquarters, the more frequently they were stopped and questioned about their business.

"Why are you two out strolling around? Reveille will sound in less'n two hours," barked a high-ranking guard just outside the house.

The men stopped riding and dismounted, throwing the reins over a hitching post. Here within the small home, life and death decisions were made that would affect the lives of some 70,000 soldiers in the A.N.V. Lee also had a large, canvas wall tent, just behind the house. It was important to him that his quarters were no better than any other soldier's in the A.N.V. He could agonize equally well in either structure. No greater a burden had been felt by a commander in history.

In the middle of Lee's tent sat a simple oak desk that had accompanied him through nine states and five major campaigns. Kerosene lanterns hanging inside and outside the command tent were turned low, casting a yellowish hue and giving off a sweet, oily odor.

"Permission to see General Lee, Sir," said Thomas Grissom, saluting. It was the most military thing he'd done in days. Scouts were the forerunners of modern-day spies. They often acted independently and were sometimes above the rules and regulations that restricted other soldiers. Some officers and enlisted alike, resented them for their freedom to come and go, for their lack of protocol, and for their special treatment. Permission to see the General, however, was strictly by the book.

"We already have your report from an hour ago," said the Major, fiercely protective of Lee. He had little respect for these untrained lone-rangers, and it showed. "The General will not see anyone before the officer's meeting at..." He was interrupted.

"I have new information that the General would want," said Grissom. "We've just returned from the ridge at the front line."

"Well, unless you can tell me the Yanks have surrendered, no news is worth bothering the General at this hour. He's..." the Major stopped himself from saying that the General was not well, though most everyone knew it. "Dismissed," he barked, intending it to be the last word on the subject.

"But Sir..." Tom took an unwise step toward the guarded door.

The Major blocked his move and, in a flash, had his hand on the hilt of his knife and was standing an inch from Grissom's face.

"Soldier," he stated through gritted teeth. "I will personally disembowel you and hang you from the nearest tree if your next move isn't directly backward and out of here...you *and* your dog, now!" The Major sneered at Billy, who was standing just behind his brother.

"That's all right Major," said General Robert E. Lee, emerging in the doorway, half dressed. Everyone in his presence stood at immediate attention. "I wasn't sleeping anyway, and I want to hear what these boys have to report. Come inside." Lee moved slowly, declining health and the stress of war wreaking havoc on his body. He was suffering from a heart condition, and a particularly bad case of diarrhea, a common malady among Civil War soldiers, that caused dehydration, and in the worst cases, death.

With a sharp salute to Lee, the Major backed away from the scouts, and Billy and Tom couldn't help but smile, just slightly, as they brushed past him following the General into the headquarters.

Lee was wearing his uniform pants, an undershirt and his boots. Even in this uncharacteristic casual state he had a commanding presence. Lee was approaching 60, and was beginning to feel like the struggling Confederate Army would be better served by a younger man. Descended from Robert The Bruce, of Scotland and the son of Revolutionary war hero, "Light Horse Harry," the well-schooled Lee came by his military pedigree honestly, and was respected as a tactician by Confederates and Yankees, equally.

"I'm sorry to ask again," said Lee, remembering their faces. The brothers had offered a brief report a few hours earlier.

"What's your name, son?"

"Tom Grissom, Sir. And this is my brother Billy."

Lee raised the wick on the lantern by a quarter-inch, brightening the space.

"I hope you can report that those people would like to surrender," said the General, who nearly always referred to the Federal forces as "those people." "Is that it? Please tell me it's so," said Lee with a weary smile, allowing his mind to drift momentarily to happier times as a youth in Old Dominion, his beloved Virginia.

Midway through the War, Lee's snow-white hair and beard to match, became an iconic symbol of the Old South and its southern gentlemen. Had the South won the war it would likely be his image on the fifty-dollar bill, not Grant's. He was a good soldier, but he was weary of this War, and it was easy for him to imagine rocking on a wide porch, looking out over the Chesapeake Bay's tidal marshes with a litter of unruly grandchildren playing at his feet. He sat and rubbed his eyes while the two young men stood before him.

With a notable amount of nervousness in his voice, Tom answered Lee's rhetorical question about the Yanks having pulled up stakes and having left Gettysburg.

"'Fraid not, Sir. I hope I ain't wastin' your time, and I surely don't want to suggest that I know what's best in the upcomin'..."

Lee interrupted him.

"Spit it out, boy. Let's have it. There's no time to be shy. I won't hang you...probably."

"Well, Sir. A little more'n half way toward the Yank's central line, just at Emmitsburg Road, there's a small rise in the middle of the flattest field y'ever saw."

Lee got up from his chair and walked to his desk where a map lay unrolled, and weighted on its corners. He put on his reading glasses.

"In the middle of that rise, is a cave or an overhang of rock. It's a little hard to tell through the scope as far away as it is. But either way I reckon it's big enough for three or four wagons to fit in it side-b'-side, pretty well hidden from all directions but sure 'nuff invisible from the Yanks. It faces us."

"Go on," said Lee through a yawn that disguised his budding interest.

"What I was wonderin' is...why couldn't we plant a little explosive surprise for the Yanks in that cave? We could flank and force as many of them as we might hope to in front of it and blow a few thousand of 'em up in one shot."

Tom couldn't hide his enthusiasm as he was finally hearing his own plan spoken aloud for the first time. For a moment his eyes brightened and some of the vigor of his youth returned. He looked and sounded like a schoolboy planning his moves in a game of field-lot baseball.

Billy Grissom's eyebrows raised in disbelief at his brother's plan, having just then heard it. Lee did the same and they looked at each other before turning back to Tom, who cleared his throat.

"So, Sir, what I was wonderin'...."

The General interrupted him.

"I can smell that bastard Meade from here, you know." Lee looked over the men's heads as if he were staring directly at the Union Commander himself. "Meade will make no blunder in my front. And if I make one he will make haste to take advantage." He was quiet for a moment, lost in thought.

"Do you know how much explosive it would take to accomplish anything close to significant?" asked Lee. "Especially blasting through rock to get to those people?"

"Well, Sir, I ain't no munitions expert, but I seen the craters made when we blow a bridge or a railway track, and I seen the rock flying through the air like cannon balls, and that's when we only use a little. We've got to be a half-mile away when we blow those things. Imagine half the Yank army on top of two or three wagonloads of powder and nitro when it goes. We could get the wagons there under cover of dark and this haze. After the battle starts, the Yanks will head straight for Emmitsburg Road, if we make it easy for 'em, and give 'em reason to. What if we used everything we got and just blew those Yank bastards up?"

Lee sat back and rubbed his whiskers. Here was a scout, a spy barely a step above a foot soldier, brazen enough to come forward in the midst of a disastrous battle, thus far, with military strategies. Though there was plenty of impropriety in the air, Lee liked the boy and he was beginning to like his idea. He sent for the Major, who was instructed to gather Lee's commanding officers.

"To pull this off we'd have to sacrifice a good deal of what's left of our artillery powder," said Lee, "and what if it didn't work? We'd be at their mercy and would be slaughtered without enough cannon cover. It could spell our end."

Tom took a deep breath before answering.

"Sir, we just come from the field. There are maybe 60,000 fresh Yanks camped on the other side of Cemetery Ridge. There are probably more. They're not writin' good-bye letters. They're not meditatin' in prayer. They're carryin' on, singin' and dancin', Sir. We heard 'em, we seen 'em. They're actin' as if they already slaughtered us. We are already at their mercy."

Lee's eyes flashed in anger at the impertinence of this child who dared comment on the readiness of the greatest army ever assembled. "Only one desperate and without much hope would be so bold," thought Lee to himself. And that's when the realization sunk in. After two tragic days in this horrific battle, the scout's desperation and assessment was right, and his insolence proved it. Lee silently wished he'd never embarked on the Gettysburg Campaign, but it was too late, and hindsight, especially in war, is never of much use, except to historians.

Lee tapped his pen on the map in front of him and stared into space.

"You believe in this cause, don't you, son?"

"Yessir. Our Ma & Pa..." Tom started, nodding toward Billy whose head hung slightly "...were killed by the Yankee trash in Murfreesboro, Tennessee."

Lee looked at the boys and seemed to know of their pain and grief; he'd lost a daughter less than a year earlier.

"Rosecran's Rats, I suppose," said Lee, referring to the Brigadier General of the Army of the Cumberland, William S. Rosecran, who'd occupied most of Middle Tennessee.

"We swore by all that was in us that we'd avenge their deaths and we'll do it, by God, from here or beyond the grave if need be. We'll find a way."

"Revenge is never a recommended motivation to fight a war," said Lee in a fatherly tone, "but you seem to have your wits about you."

As Lt. Gen. James Longstreet, Lt. Gen. Richard Ewell, Maj. Gen George Pickett, and a half-dozen additional commanders arrived, Lee called out through the flaps of the tent. "Major Smith. Come here for a moment, would you?"

Smith entered the tent and stood at attention sneering slightly at the boys, waiting for Lee's orders to have them court-martialed or better, hung.

"I'm sorry," said Lee, looking at Tom. "What's your name, again?"

"Thomas Grissom, Sir."

Lee cleared his throat. "Thomas Grissom," he said, turning to the young man who'd been taken by surprise at the formal calling of his name. "According to the War Powers of the Confederate States of America and the authority given me by its President, Jefferson Davis, and in front of these witnesses, I am issuing a battlefield commission and promoting you to the rank of Aide-de-Camp for The Confederacy at Gettysburg, effective immediately, and to only be withdrawn by my order. Major Smith, you will assist Mr. Grissom in anyway he desires."

Smith's jaw dropped open when he realized this insolent kid, half his age, had in a moment achieved a superior rank in an unceremonious, but fully legal appointment.

Lee glanced at the clock sitting on his desk. It was almost 4 a.m. "My officers, advisors and I will work on your plan," said Lee engaging Tom Grissom with a look straight into his soul. "And I'll give you two hours to assemble your team and inventory your supplies. I want to see details and discuss this thoroughly. Then I'll decide." The brothers stood trying to absorb all that had just happened.

"That will be all," said Lee nodding toward the door of the tent.

"You've got a lot of work to do. Go!"

"Yes Sir!" shouted the Grissoms in unison, spirits rekindled. It was a hopelessly optimistic plan but one with some merit, they thought, and considering the current desperate situation, maybe the South's best hope for victory.

5 a.m. July 6, 2013
Gettysburg, Pa.

In a $1,500-a-month, one-bedroom, brownstone apartment in an affluent neighborhood just east of downtown Gettysburg, the 5 a.m. buzz of an alarm clock was an unwelcome intruder. Greg Jackson was becoming sorrier by the moment that he'd been talked into this silly game of pretend. He hit the snooze button with a closed fist, but dreams of the upcoming battle persisted. He had been a history major before law school and was especially interested in American history, the Civil War and Civil Rights, in particular. He reflected on Tommy Fuller's inappropriate, but accurate, observation from the night before at MacAuley's.

An estimated 30,000 blacks may have taken up arms for the South, though the written record and historical evidence is inconclusive. Memoirs and diary accounts suggest that many African and Caribbean slaves didn't even realize that their emancipation was one of the things the North was fighting for. For obvious reasons these slaves were kept in the dark, and among other lies, were told the Yankees wanted to kill them. Most were forced to fight, but a smaller number did so willingly and with a full knowledge of the circumstances surrounding the War, having been conditioned by the brutality of slavery.

After the Emancipation Proclamation was set forth in January, 1863, many more blacks fought for the North, though they found some difficulty when attempting to volunteer, as the reluctance to accept them was strong throughout the Union ranks and leadership. An estimated 200,000 blacks served in the U.S. Army and Navy during the Civil War, and by the War's end were receiving the same pay as their white counterparts: $13 a month.

Sixteen black men received the Medal of Honor for valor at the War's conclusion. Aside from the civil rights movement 100 years later, the American Civil War did more for the cause of non-white minorities than any other event in U.S. history, possibly in world history, effectively freeing more than 3 million slaves as the Union gained control of the Rebellious Southern states.

Just prior to the War, Georgia Senator Robert Toombs, boasted that one day he would "call the roll of his slaves at the foot of the Bunker Hill monument," in Massachusetts.

Jackson first heard of black reenactors when Hollywood came calling

32

during the filming of *Glory,* and then later the filming of *Gettysburg.* The call went out from the studios for thousands of reenactors and many still boast of their casting in one or both of these movies. Several members of the reenactment group Jackson had just joined had been extras in *Gettysburg* during the Pickett's Charge scene where almost 12,000 volunteer reenactors were engaged. Only after Jackson saw these movies, did it hit home how many black men actually fought in the Civil War.

The buzzing returned and Jackson rolled out of bed while simultaneously turning off the alarm. He rubbed his eyes with one hand and grabbed the TV remote with the other, turning to the Weather Channel.

"...unseasonably cool, with patches of heavy ground fog in low-lying areas expected," he spoke aloud reading the local forecast crawling along the bottom of the screen. "Just great," he muttered. A news headline flashed on the screen just moments after Jackson left the room.

"SHOOTING REPORTED IN GETTYSBURG, ONE TEENAGER DEAD, SUSPECT AT LARGE."

Most of his unit's reenactors, along with most of the out of town reenactors, stayed in encampments at the Park, which had made special provisions for the tens of thousands of reenactors and sutlers (those traveling vendors who, like the original sutlers, sold their wares to soldiers and a souvenir-hungry public). Camping was half of the fun for many reenactors, but wasn't an absolute requirement. Jackson had no intention of sleeping on the ground in the midst of that group. He picked up a flyer from his kitchen counter, and reread his instructions out loud.

"Meet at the battlefield at 7 a.m., Morning Parade at 8, open to the public at 9, blah, blah, blah, reenactment starts at 11...O.K....well...shit, here I go."

Jackson was trying to come to terms with his role in this historical play, and wasn't too bothered about portraying a Rebel soldier. He wasn't pledging his allegiance to the South. He was simply play-acting in an important battle in an important war. His boss at the firm belonged to this group so he belonged, too. The fact that he was the only black man in the group of 65 wasn't a big deal to him. He was used to being in a minority. In law school he was one of four blacks to graduate from his entire class. Still, self-doubt occasionally wandered into his thinking. While showering he again spoke aloud.

"What the hell am I doing this for? These crazy rednecks really don't want me around. Why am I even showering? I'm going to be rolling around in the dirt in a couple of hours. What a waste of a day off this is going to be..."

Chapter 5

5 a.m. July 3, 1863
Gettysburg, Pa.

The contentious meeting underway within the stone Confederate headquarters was on the verge of becoming a small war of its own. They could not agree that this plan of the "Grissom boy," as they'd begun calling Tom Grissom, was the best way to proceed. Frustration levels were high. The Gettysburg Campaign had started with so much promise that Lee and Confederate States' President Davis were certain the Yankees would yield to peace with the Confederate Army's northernmost incursion; the "High Watermark," as it was known. Philadelphia was to be Lee's next stop, but the first two days of fighting at Gettysburg had gone so horribly wrong, that bad tempers, accusations, exhaustion, and uncertainty dominated the conversations. It was virtually impossible to consider heading any further north. They had serious doubts about surviving the next half-day, let alone forcing Meade and President Lincoln to the cease-fire table.

"No, Sir, I don't like it one bit," said Longstreet. "Too risky. We've never seen an explosion like this before. We have no guarantee what it will do." This was about the only thing the eight men at the meeting could agree upon, but Lee thought the plan had merit, and wasn't ready to abandon it altogether.

"I'm waiting for an inventory update and final details of this plan," said Lee. "No decision will be made until then. Stay close by, gentlemen. You'll have my decision in an hour. Dismissed."

•••••

As the encampment was stirring, the Grissom brothers set about final development of a battle plan that was still vague, at best. Reveille had not

34

yet sounded but the officers were all up preparing for a battle they didn't want to fight. The air was moist and sticky, promising a hot day ahead as dawn slowly approached.

Tom Grissom, with Lee's approval, had made Billy his assistant in an impromptu ceremony, which pleased the younger man. Billy stuck close to his brother's side like a faithful Terrier, repeating orders and barking and nipping at the men just because he could. He was so pleased with himself and his sudden acquisition of power that he smiled and snickered every time a soldier responded to a command. Drunk with newfound authority, he seemed almost oblivious to the seriousness of the task at hand and the possibility that it might just be his last day on earth. Tom almost envied his brother's blissful ignorance and innocence. Billy stood near a tent where a shaving mirror hung by twine to a makeshift tripod of wood. In the waning moonlight he stood admiring his image, primping.

"Billy!" Tom Grissom yelled, breaking military protocol in an attempt to make contact with his daydreaming brother. "Billy! Damn it!" Still no response came from the younger man. "Grissom!" he finally yelled in his little brother's ear. This approach worked.

"Damn it, Tom. Whataya tryin' to do?" asked Billy, shaken from his dream world. "Is this 'Aide-de-camp' thing going to your head?"

"Do you know what's going on here?" Tom sighed. "I need your help, not for you to just walk around like a fool Mynah Bird, repeatin' everything I say. You sound like a damn canyon wall, echoing every word. The men are laughing at you and me both, so quit with the Army stuff and shut up and listen to me." This Billy understood.

"Get three large supply wagons and empty 'em where they sit. When you're done with that, attach a two-horse team, hook the three in a train and get 'em over to the Artillery Regiment. Do this quick, now, cuz we ain't got but an hour. Go!"

Tom Grissom, newly appointed aide-de-camp to General Robert E. Lee, was formulating details of the plan as he went, and taking some liberties Lee hadn't actually yet authorized. He was glad Lee hadn't asked for all the specifics back in the tent. He would have been hard pressed to come up with any.

"How are we gonna get to the cave?" he thought aloud. He ran through the course in his mind.

"Straight over to the ridge is no good, because Yank snipers would probably see us." The best course, he decided was out to the north and around the lowest point in the valley, using cover of the haze for as long as he could.

These questions and a hundred more flooded his head as he tried to put the plan together. He was walking toward Field Artillery Sergeant Henderson's tent. He'd been given a list of the officers' names from the various divisions he'd be utilizing. Most of these men he'd never met before and they certainly weren't aware of any new Aide-de-Camp of Lee's. For back up, he brought Major Smith with him.

Standing outside Henderson's tent, Grissom yelled inside and rapped on the dirty white canvas with his hand.

"Sergeant Henderson!" he yelled. No answer. "Sergeant Henderson. This is…", he hesitated, not sure what to call himself, "General Lee's Aide-de-Camp…Adjutant Grissom." The title was cumbersome, and he didn't like it, but he needed to get the man's attention.

Rustling came from inside the tent and the sleepy Sergeant stuck his head out the front flap. Henderson was by far the youngest officer that Grissom had ever come in contact with. He looked to be no older than himself, maybe even a teenager. Henderson was one of the fabled "Young Lions" of the South, young men who became cadets in southern academies and colleges that had been turned into de facto military institutions: Virginia Military Institute, The Citadel, The South Carolina Military Academy, The University of Alabama Corps of Cadets and others. They would play a vital part in the war effort and 21-year-old Henderson, was a recent graduate from one of the oldest schools in the nation, The Citadel of Charleston, South Carolina.

Henderson had close cropped, brown hair and small, sharp eyes, like a fox, Tom thought. The Sergeant fumbled for his round, thick-lens wire-rimmed glasses, and once attached to his head, finally focused on Tom and Major Smith standing just outside his tent in the still dark of late morning.

"Yes, Sir?" asked Henderson. This kid was not Tom's image of an artillery officer and he had to suppress his lack of confidence.

"Henderson," started Tom. "Major Smith and I are here on special orders of General Lee. I need you dressed and out here in two minutes - make that one minute."

Henderson looked quizzically back and forth between the two men. He'd seen Major Smith before, but this new man giving orders was a stranger to him.

"Henderson! You now have less than one minute!" Tom didn't normally yell, especially at men he didn't know, but there was no time to be cordial. The Sergeant slipped his head back inside the tent and hastily began to dress.

Major Smith was slowly softening his harsh opinion of Grissom; the kid was smart and that was plainly obvious. He was also a decent man, and under the stress of the situation, Smith thought, he was acting like a natural born leader.

"Major Smith," said Grissom quietly, looking toward the tent. "What can you tell me about Henderson? Do you know him?"

"Well," said Smith, clearing his throat, not used to being asked his opinion. "General Lee hand picked him from the Citadel's graduating class of '62. He's 20 or 21. Some've said he's like a sort of genius or something with chemicals and gunpowder, explosives, in particular."

Grissom smiled.

"You know those big holes we leave behind?" continued Smith. "The ones that you were talking to the Ol' Man about? Those were his doing." Smith was pleased with the amount of detail with which he'd been able to answer, and the information was good news to Tom. He was glad to hear about the Sergeant's qualifications.

In less than the two minutes given, the Sergeant emerged from his tent, disheveled and not looking at all like a soldier, though he stood straight at attention without protest.

"At ease, Sergeant." The words were new, and felt uncomfortable.

Tom told Henderson the outline of the plan and of the cave in the middle of the field. He needed detailed advice on preparing a charge big enough to do the job. Henderson actually rubbed his hands together maniacally and smiled. The young Sergeant loved the potential of simple chemistry. He loved big explosions more than anything, and this was his chance to play with literally tons of experimental high explosives.

"Well," he started, his eyes cast to the ground in thought. "Your first issue, Sir, is how big a bang do you want? On what scale? Mt. Vesuvius or something less spectacular?" Henderson spoke with a thick Charlestonian accent that betrayed both his southern heritage and his privilege. Charleston, South Carolina, had become the wealthiest port city in the southeast, and those of any affluence were well spoken and well educated. Like Henderson, they were slow, deliberate and gracious in their speech.

"The biggest bang possible," answered Tom. "Enough to cover half a square mile or more and blow up, knock down, or kill 30,000 Yanks."

Henderson's eyes grew wide with the terrible realization of what he was being asked to create; the world's first weapon of mass destruction - a WMD. He shared no deep hatred of the Yankees, and in fact was only two generations removed from New York where he still had cousins, most of whom fought for the North. His biggest fear was that one day he'd be involved in a battle with his own family; maybe this was that day, he thought.

Reading his mind, Grissom spoke up. "It's them or us, Henderson. There's 70 – maybe 80,000 Yanks with full bellies, new boots, new guns and a lot more rest than our half-dead, swollen-footed, half-starved Rebs. Don't go soft on me now."

The Sergeant shook off his hesitance and continued. "Of course, Sir. Ahh… well…we'll need something big to contain all the powder."

"How about three supply wagons?" Tom asked.

"That could do," said Henderson, nodding. "The other problem we'll have to deal with is getting all the powder to blow at once. Two or three, separate, smaller explosions won't do the trick."

He tapped his finger against his chin and spoke half to himself.

"Part of the problem is already taken care of. The cave, or whatever you say it is, will act as a compression device, of sorts, helping all the munitions to go at once, but because it's open on one side, three quarters of the blast will head out of the opening in one direction, toward us and the Confederate line. The force of the explosion will probably spread laterally, relevant to the shape of the cave. Depending on how thick the walls are, and what they're made of, will determine where the other 25 percent of the blast goes."

The direction of blast was a wrinkle Grissom hadn't thought through, but ideas were forming. "We'll have to make sure to lure the Yanks in front of the cave and wait until they're all almost on top of us to do the job. But it still could work."

"If we also load the wagons with grape and canister shot that will help insure greater..." Henderson chose the next word carefully, "...mortality. Another thing, Sir," he said with a finger in the air, as if asking permission to speak. "To cover the ground you're talking about...this will take most all our available stock of powder, including most all the cannon powder and even the men's back-up supply of musket powder. Begging your pardon, Sir...this is risky. There's no guarantee it will work exactly like we want it to. I've never seen an explosion as big as we're talking about. This is all very...theoretical."

"Don't tell me that, Sergeant," said Grissom in mock disgust. "Tell me it could work. Right? That's all I want to hear."

He thought for a moment before answering. "Yessir. It could work." Then he added, "And I have an extra little surprise that might help it along."

Chapter 6

6:19 a.m. July 6, 2013
Gettysburg National Military Park

Greg Jackson arrived at the Gettysburg National Military Park through heavy traffic. Hundreds of cars behind him were forced to park along the sides of the road leading to the main spectator entrance and Jackson felt privileged to have a special pass allowing him into the lot, though he still had a distance to go.

He parked his BMW, got out, locked it, and said to himself "Here goes nothin'." Already in full Rebel uniform, he joined other soldiers as they all walked with their guns and packs full of supplies to their respective meeting points. Yanks, Rebs, and civilians walked together across the parking lot sharing good-natured jabs at one another, laughing and talking. The patchy, heavy mist in the growing daylight, together with the circumstance of the gathering, painted a surrealistic picture as the two armies walked side-by-side toward the reenactors' gate. It was gradually becoming harder for Jackson, and many others, he guessed, to stay connected to the present. Disconnection and total immersion into the battle created the intended high hardcore reenactors lived for, and they were well on their way.

"Damn. This is weird," he said to a middle-aged Union Soldier walking beside him.

"Your first reenactment?" the Yank asked cheerfully.

"Yeah," answered Jackson. "Not yours, I'm assuming?"

"Naw. I've been in maybe 30 over the last 15 or so years. This is by far the biggest though. Except for the *Gettysburg* movie. That was huge. But I'm told this one will be bigger, the anniversary, and all."

The two men walked silently for a minute until a CNN reporter with a tag-along cameraman hurried up to Jackson and his new friend and asked for an interview. Jackson backed away. He wasn't wild about the kind of exposure his participation might bring. The Yankee, however, was thrilled at the prospect of a TV interview and took his place with the reporter gladly.

"Why is Civil War reenactment such a popular hobby?" asked the smartly dressed reporter. Jackson stopped to listen to the answer, one he was looking for himself.

"This War, more than all others, is a real American tragedy," the Yank started. "When you're out there in the middle of the battle, and all the guns are going off and the cannons are blasting behind you, and men are dropping like flies, it's as big a rush as you'll ever experience. It's like you're there."

"Can you describe what you feel out on the battlefield?" asked the reporter.

"I know you've heard this before, but it's true. You almost lose touch with reality. You know deep down it's not real, but your mind in the moment tells you that you are a soldier in the middle of a battle and people are shooting at you and your friends are dying all around you. A hundred other thoughts flood your head at the same time and it's exciting, and fun, and scary as hell, too. When it's all over, the sane among us can better imagine the horror of war and hope that we're never forced to be in a real one – I never had to serve in combat, and I sometimes feel guilty about that. But this War...we need to remember it, reenact it, and realize how lucky we are that our nation survived it. This thing could have gone either way. I can only imagine what the world would look like if the Union had crumbled."

"Besides the sobering part of the War itself, and the living history aspects, do you manage to have fun?"

"Fun?" laughed the Yank. "We party like teenagers every night. Really, we do. Campfires, way too much beer...it's a ton of fun."

The reporter asked a few more questions and scurried off to interview a small family of civilians dressed in period costumes, a woman in a hoop skirt, two boys in knickers, and a dandy gentlemen with a stovepipe hat and a Chihuahua dressed in a Confederate uniform under one arm. The unnamed Yankee and Jackson continued their walk toward the last gate separating reenactor from spectator. It would soon be show time.

"Well, ahh...good luck!" said the Yank as he turned toward the west and General Meade's Army of the Potomac.

Jackson laughed. "We'll need it."

"By the way..." the quizzical Yankee called out in an afterthought. "Aren't you fighting for the wrong side?" he asked with obvious reference to Jackson's race and his Confederate uniform.

"This is my boss's deal," Jackson yelled back. "I figured it might be good for my career. Plus, he's kind of a slave-driver, if you know what I mean." Both men laughed and they parted company.

The only open access to the Park was on the east side of the property, very near the Confederate encampment. For this, Jackson was relieved. The Union reenactors had a mile and a half to walk before they could settle in prior to battle.

Jackson pulled an event brochure out of his pocket. Looking at a small map he tried to orient himself to the Park entrance and the meeting point of his unit but found it difficult to figure out. Many of the landmarks were obscured from view by mist and fog, and he stood looking at the map, confused.

Additional groups of Confederate and Union soldiers walked by and he was sure he had heard disparaging remarks coming from among the Yankees about "dumb niggers" and the like. He seethed at their ignorance and bigotry and wanted to smash the butt of his gun across the side of one or two heads and get this battle started early, but managed not to let them know he'd been riled.

"You look lost, soldier," said Mike Phillips walking up behind him, punching him lightly in the back. "You can read your map, can't you?"

"Don't you start, too," said Jackson, feigning annoyance, but secretly relieved a friendly face had shown up.

"What's the matter?" Phillips asked, sensing his friend's foul mood.

"Just a couple of Yankee assholes," answered Jackson somewhat cryptically.

"That's the spirit!" laughed Phillips. "You're really starting to get into this."

'Whatever..."

A USA News truck rolled by and Philips saw an easy ride.

"That's where we're going," he said. "Found out last night that they're setting up twenty feet from our unit. Come on!" he shouted and hopped up on the rear deck of the slow-moving, giant news truck, waving for Jackson to join him. Jackson ran a few steps and joined his boss standing on the rear bumper enjoying the free ride to the encampment.

Though still early, the crowd was already growing at a serious pace and several thousand reenactors and their families, along with some hardcore spectators looking for the best positions, all seemed to be flooding into the Park's staging area at the same time. The heavy traffic on PA. Rt. 97 slowed to a crawl, still three miles before the entrance. Stuck in the traffic was Tommy Fuller.

•••••

Fuller's truck, emblazoned with two Confederate battle flag decals on the tailgate, sat still, idling in a miles-long line of cars. Tommy was numb and nauseous. Still in shock at what had happened an hour-and-a-half earlier, he stared straight ahead, unblinking, glassy-eyed. He was shaken to life by the sound of an involuntary gasp for breath, his own. Almost as if his soul and spirit were returning to their earthly vessel, mind and body were suddenly and violently reunited.

"Oh my God," he cried aloud, pounding his fists on the steering wheel. "What have I done?"

Tears welled up in his eyes. "It was self defense," he answered calmly. "But I killed that kid. Then I got in my truck and drove away. Nobody will believe me," he thought. He screamed something guttural, in terror of a thousand possible futures. He envisioned images of the police at the scene, the other boys crying over their dead companion, lying to the police about what happened. Then they would give the police a description of his truck, possibly even a license plate number.

In his mind's eye he saw his wife awakened by police at the door, asking for the whereabouts of Tommy Fuller. Then came visions of trials and unsympathetic jurors who heard weeks of testimony about Tommy's failing business, his letters to the editor with racist overtones, and other troubles in the neighborhood, and his "obsession" with the Confederacy. Then would come the sentence of 'Life without the possibility of parole.' Racially motivated hate crimes were taken seriously and after 15 years of appeals had finally failed, he would resign himself to die in prison. No call would come from the Governor. He sobbed uncontrollably as his future flashed before him in excruciating detail. A police siren wailed in the distance and grew closer with each passing moment.

Again gripped by fear and dread at what was coming, he glanced in the rearview mirror and saw flashing lights flying up the median of the highway through the stopped traffic. Tommy was in the inside lane and his truck would be in plain view of the police within seconds. He gripped the wheel tightly, unsure of what to do. Before he could make a move, the flashing lights were upon him.

The Gettysburg Fire Company's first response vehicle flew by. Not the police. Tommy breathed again. Seeing the ambulance reminded him of his Emergency Band scanner. He hadn't listened to it in months, but knew it carried fire bands and, more importantly, police bands. Technically illegal in civilian vehicles, lots of guys in the automotive service industry had one tweaked to hear police bands, and Tommy searched for his. He tried the glove box and between the seats and found nothing. Under the front seat he found his prize and actually smiled, a desperate man's smile. He turned it on and miraculously the batteries had held their charge. Loud intermittent static filled the inside of the cab as he found the police band and adjusted the tuning.

The stopped traffic finally began to move again. An accident between a tourist and a local news crew had been the cause of the hold up and as Tommy inched forward he could see the fire department vehicle parked with its rear doors wide open. Emergency med-techs hovered over the body of the most seriously hurt victim. As he slowly inched by the horrific scene, he looked into the eyes of the young black man who was being treated on a stretcher. The face of the accident victim morphed into that of the boy he had just shot, and it seemed to stare back accusingly. He thought about what must be unfolding in his own neighborhood. Susan was probably awake, looking out of the window at the dozens of police cars and ambulances that were certainly, by now, investigating the early-morning homicide.

The traffic inched forward and then stopped again. He was still two miles from the entrance to the Park and the sun would have been, now, just visible, except for the gray clouds in the sky and the mist that still hovered over the ground. He hated having been stopped so close to this accident and couldn't help staring at the carnage. The driver must have gone partially through the windshield of the small car and was being treated for head injuries. He was still alive as his hands moved in involuntary gestures, which had to be constrained by another EMT.

Tommy thought, hopefully, that maybe his victim might still be alive. Not likely though. He had been at nearly point blank range, and had aimed for the center of the boy's chest and had seen the blood and tissue splatter from his shot. A Minie ball was a deadly projectile that shattered bones and tore through flesh indiscriminately. The kid must have been killed instantly. Waves of sorrow, guilt, and fear once again consumed him.

Tommy just missed his chance to move forward as a fireman had stopped all traffic. He watched as the car in front of him was the last to move ahead freely. The fireman stood directly in the way of Tommy's progress, and, he thought, his escape. He rolled down the window to plead his case but his request fell on deaf ears.

"But sir," Tommy pleaded. "I'm a reenactor and I've got to get to my unit."

"Too bad," the officer replied unsympathetically. "There're plenty of reenactors behind you. They won't start the battle without you, soldier. Don't worry. We already know how this thing ends, anyway," he said sarcastically. "Spoiler alert...I'm pretty sure the South looses."

"Look," Tommy said, raising his voice. "You don't understand...."

"No. *You* don't understand, buddy," interrupted the fireman. "Take it up with State Troopers if you don't like it. They'll be here any minute."

Just then his scanner came to life and the monotone voice of a young woman confirmed his worst fear: "Seven-Larry-Niner, Seven-Larry-Niner... You're in response to the personal injury accident on PA. 97. Confirm?" She was talking about the accident not ten feet from Tommy's truck.

"Ahh, this is Seven-Larry-Niner. Copy that," answered the husky voice of a Pennsylvania State Trooper. "Dispatch, our approximate

ETA... about four to six minutes." The troopers were on their way.

"Dispatch out," answered the woman, her voice followed by a loud static click. Seconds later the static click returned. It was the same woman, but this time her voice was noticeably higher pitched, faster, and obviously agitated.

"All units. All units. APB for one Thomas, "Tommy" Fuller. White male, approximately 23-years-old, 5-foot 10, 160 pounds. The suspect is wanted for questioning in the fatal shooting of a black, male victim. Suspect is armed and considered very dangerous and was last seen driving an off-white 1995 Nissan Pathfinder pick-up truck, Pennsylvania State tag eight-four-three, Betty-David-Paul. Suspect is believed to be in... Confederate Civil War costume."

Well, there it was. He'd heard it with his own ears. Tommy sat stunned, and wondered how long it would be before the police arrived and his nightmare became reality. He stared blankly out into the mist until the fireman walked past the front of his truck. He thought he noticed a suspicious look from the officer and wondered if he had heard the same APB? There was no way to know for sure.

The wail of distant sirens growing closer sent a new wave of panic and adrenaline coursing through his veins. He was sure this time that the sirens had to be from Troopers en-route. There was no question that *they* had heard the APB and he assumed he was as good as caught. In his mind the judge had issued sentence and Susan was in the courtroom crying as they carted him off to a maximum security Federal prison.

Chapter 7

7:04 a.m. July 3, 1863
Gettysburg, Pa.

In the middle of the dining room of a commandeered home, now temporary Confederate Headquarters, Tom Grissom stood looking down upon a stolen Federal map of Gettysburg, unfurled upon a large table. Land features, with soon to be infamous names, were circled: *Little Round Top, Peach Orchard, Copse of Trees, Ziegler's Grove, Seminary Ridge, Cemetery Ridge,* and *Cemetery Hill.*

Major Smith, brother Billy, and Sergeant Henderson surrounded him and looked over his shoulder. The General had stepped out for a few moments of private thought, and to again visit the officers' latrine. Inside Tom Grissom attempted to sell his plan. Together, they had all pored over the map, and written down the strategies step by step. Though they didn't know it at the time, this unlikely coalition of soldiers had been thrown together to make war plans that would rival any previous plans in the History of Warfare. It was an awesome responsibility and it weighed heavily upon each man, especially 23-year-old Tom Grissom.

To keep the timing of the event on their side, they had decided that they had to make the first move. The Yank army wouldn't be tentative because they knew of the weakened condition of Lee's Army of Northern Virginia. They hoped, given an open invitation, that the Yank army would respond rapidly, en masse, in an attempt to finish them off, or send them scurrying south, out of Pennsylvania.

The Top Secret plan, dubbed the "Yankee Surprise," was laid out, this time with new detail and a timeline, but the officers present wasted no time voicing their opposition.

"This is insanity," said Longstreet, the most vocal of the leaders. "To pour most all of our resources into this effort…What if it doesn't work?"

Longstreet was saying aloud what everyone in the room was thinking. They all understood the criticism. So did Grissom. Maybe it was foolish, but it was a grand plan, of that there was no doubt.

The suggested battle plan had nearly all of the available Confederate troops converging, some flanking, all toward the main Union line, drawing them from their defensive positions. When the Yanks were at their heaviest concentration, on the Rebel side of the rock outcropping laden with explosives, the Confederate officers would order a retreat, hopefully with the bulk of the Yank army in pursuit. Then they would turn their troops to hold the Yanks in position in front of the hoped for blast. Once the Yanks were in position, the very heavens and earth would shake with the most powerful, manmade explosion the 19th century world ever witness.

Added to the 8,000 lbs of black powder and nitro already packed into the 3 wagons, Sergeant Henderson would add an additional 300 lbs of a new, experimental chemical formulation mixing nitrogen and ammonia. Once Henderson got started, his head was like a pomegranate full of exploding idea seeds. He had worked and re-worked formulas on paper until he finally announced he could increase the power of the over-all blast by at least 30 percent. Even Henderson couldn't say for sure how far away would be far enough to survive.

They would surround the charges with 200 canister shots, each a 12-pound, thin metal cannon cartridge filled with powder and dozens of bullet-sized steel balls, spent ammo, or whatever they could find to inflict damage. Whoever or whatever not at least a mile-and-a-half away, would be mowed down in a hail of hot metal.

Those near ground zero would be vaporized instantly. Their ashes, if there were any, would eventually float down out of the black mushroom cloud into a crater a half-mile wide and 50-feet deep. Those a quarter to a half-mile away could have limbs blown off and would likely be killed directly. At three quarters of a mile the shock wave and concussion would destroy the air sacks in the lining of the lungs, causing death by drowning in blood.

If it didn't kill, the shock wave would likely cause brain damage, and knock anybody in its path unconscious. Up to two miles away the ground would shake and the shock wave could still have enough power to knock a soldier or a horse off its feet. The tremor from an explosion of that magnitude would be felt a hundred or more miles away.

All this power would emanate from the small cave in an ever-widening, pie-shaped arc, like the pattern of a shotgun blast, spreading as it goes. Behind the cave, up to a few hundred yards away, the earth and anything on it would turn to fine rubble. The process was called 'liquefaction.' The material would rise thousands of feet and fall back under the shadow of a black cloud so immense that it would block sunlight for a mile and rain down hot ash and debris over three square miles.

The lethal power they planned to unleash was frightening to contemplate. The explosion could decimate the Yanks, but also posed considerable risk for the Confederate Army, especially those too close to the blast arc. With too much collateral damage and friendly fire injuries, the Southern cause wouldn't be helped. They would have to keep the Confederate army to the extreme edges of the battlefield, but this would likely confuse the Union army and make it difficult to predict exactly how they'd respond. Flawed as it was, that was the blueprint for the "Yankee Surprise" in the waning hours just prior to the Battle of Gettysburg, day three.

"I think that's about as much of the plan as we can put together," said Grissom, rubbing his eyes, exhausted. "I guess we're ready for the Ol' Man...er...General Lee. Did I leave anything out?"

The other men looked at one another and Henderson nervously adjusted his glasses. "Well, Sir, there's still the issue of detonation."

Tom gazed straight ahead with unblinking eyes. "Tell me my options."

"A fuse is the surest way we'll get proper detonation," said the Sergeant. "The problem is, it would have to be 30 feet long and burn for ten minutes in order to allow a man enough time to light it, mount his horse and ride like hell in the opposite direction of the expected blast path. But he'd be riding directly toward the Yankees and probably wouldn't make it 10 feet before he was shot dead. Plus, a fuse that long could run into trouble. They quit sometimes and have to be re-lit. If the powder in the fuse is at all damp, it might go out. Also, with a ten-minute fuse the Yankee Army could move a considerable distance if we didn't hold 'em just so. They might be off the rise or discover the explosives and disable the bomb before it ever went off."

"Any more good news?" asked Grissom. He was annoyed by Henderson's pessimism and attention to details, but he also appreciated the thoroughness of the young officer. He was at least confident in the advice he was given, even if he didn't like what he heard.

"The other option is detonation from a well-placed, exploding cannon ball. If we planted one dead center of the wagons and it went off like it's supposed to, that would work, but generally it takes three to five shots from one mile to hit the target, that is, on a good day. If one of the first few shots gets close, but misses, it could spread the powder around without igniting it and then even if we did hit it we'd loose the intensity of our blast."

"Shit!" Grissom said, disgusted. "How could we be so close and get stuck now?" He sat for a moment. "Listen," he said to Henderson out of

47

earshot of the officers in the room, "no mention of detonation to the Ol' Man. I'll work this thing out. He's expecting a report and a plan, and we're going to give him the best one we've got, without causin'...unnecessary doubts."

Major Smith spoke up, having overheard Grissom's comments. "Begging your pardon, Sir. But I don't like the idea of presenting a partial plan as if it's complete. These aren't 'unnecessary doubts.' If we can't get the thing to go off then that's something the Ol' Man needs to know about, in my opinion, Sir."

"Oh it'll go off, Captain." said Grissom. "With me riding the blast straight into the sunrise if need be." His brother, who hadn't been paying close attention, heard the remark.

"Tom! I know what you're thinkin'," said Billy. He stepped closer and grabbed his brother's arm. "I won't let you do that. You are not gonna blow yourself up just to prove out a plan. That don't make a lick of sense."

"I don't want to, Billy, and hopefully it won't come to that, but I'm willing to strike the flint on the whole damn thing if that's what it takes. Remember being chased out of Murfreesboro? Remember Ma and Pa? Remember how they was murdered by the Yankee scum? Remember we couldn't even bury 'em proper 'cuz the Yanks was on our ass, shootin' at our backs. And remember what you and me swore to?"

Billy looked down. He didn't answer. He didn't have to. Both brothers had sworn an oath of allegiance to one another and to a cause they hoped would avenge the brutal deaths of their parents. "This may be our last chance and I'm gonna make damn sure this works," continued Tom. "The entire Confederacy and our way of life is depending on it. General Lee is depending on it and God wants it, too. We've got a score to settle and I'll settle it from the grave if I got to."

"If you go out there," said Billy, tears forming, "then I'm going with you, and that's all there is to it. No orders could keep me away so don't even try." Tom smiled at the loyalty and courage of the best friend he'd ever known. Trying to stop him would be useless, so he smiled and acquiesced.

"Well, then...all agreed?" asked Tom. Each man reluctantly nodded.

"Major Smith. Please inform the General that we've got a plan ready to show him."

•••••

Not far from the headquarters, General Lee patted the nose of his horse, Traveller, tied beneath a large oak tree. He put his other hand on the tree's massive trunk. It was tall, strong and quiet, like Lee himself. His thoughts wandered to his mother, Ann Carter Lee, who had instilled in her son a strong sense of duty and loyalty. Lee had hated the very thought of this War. His resignation from the U.S. Army, just after Virginia had seceded, had come only after long, hard personal deliberation. Once again he found himself faced with imponderable circumstances, and impossible choices.

Still mourning the death of his daughter, 23-year-old Anne Carter Lee, who had died the previous October, the General was not well, emotionally or physically. The effects of dysentery were rendering him weak and foggy-minded. All too clear, however, was the reality of a campaign gone wrong. By the end of the second day of battle, some 35,000 troops lay dead or dying. He had also lost Thomas Jonathon "Stonewall" Jackson, his most trusted officer and close friend, his "War Horse." Jackson had been killed by friendly fire at Chancellorsville just two months earlier.

The Confederacy had placed nearly all of its resources and faith in the aging General and the burden was taking its toll. But still he held out hope. As a trained engineer, Lee saw the real possibilities in Grissom's bold plan, and strategic maneuvering. He wasn't afraid to divide his army. He'd done it before to great effect, but time for pondering was over, and he rejoined the others and listened quietly and thoughtfully.

"It's daring and well thought out, gentlemen," said Lee, finally. "If it works, we'll be in the history books as the craftiest army ever to fight a war. If it doesn't...I don't like to even think about that."

"I don't like it," said Longstreet, "too many ways this can go wrong," he continued.

Lee stroked his beard and stared thoughtfully at the map.

"General Longstreet," said Lee. "Soldiering has one great trap. To be a good soldier, you must love the army. To be a good commander, you must be willing to order the death of the thing you love. When you attack you must hold nothing back; you must commit yourself totally. We are adrift here in a sea of blood, and I want it to end. I want this to be the final battle."

When Lee again asked his advisors what they thought, all he received back were pessimistic grumbles, but no serious rebuttal or alternate plan came, and so the army's fate was set in that moment.

"That's it then," said Lee, turning toward his Aide-de-Camp. "You've done it, my boy. You've earned a battlefield commission, and managed to convince me to place the entire Army of Northern Virginia and the hopes of the Confederacy in your hands. God help us all." As he rose from the table, reveille sounded as the camp readied itself for the unknown.

Chapter 8

7:30 a.m. July 6, 2013
Gettysburg National Military Park

The USA News truck made its way along the winding access road leading to the eastern-most side of Gettysburg National Military Park and to the heart of the Confederate encampment. Jackson and Phillips watched the surreal scene unfolding a few hundred yards ahead. Along the way scores of civilian reenactors occupied makeshift camps and were depicting life as War refugees. The 1000 or so were doing a good job depicting the lamentable conditions. Women, very young children, and disabled War veterans made up the group. Boys over the age of 13, and men under the age of 50, on both sides of the conflict were hard to find anywhere but in battle, and this held true at the reenactment as well.

Not all civilian reenactors represented the threadbare, beleaguered masses. Some young women, mostly the daughters and friends of reenactors, dressed in hoop skirts and packed picnic lunches to take to the edge of the battlefield. The wealthy from both sides often congregated at the War's edge, just to watch, cheering for one side or another as if spectators at a college football game – attendees of the first, gruesome tailgate parties.

Jackson took note of several divisions of soldiers readying themselves for battle and he noticed for the first time how many children were involved. He knew from his study of the war that indeed many thousands of children as young as 13, and probably younger, fought for both sides.

Fewer children fought for the North, but even there, 11, 12 and 13 year-old soldiers were on record as having fought and died in the infantry. The youngest were usually drummers and pipers, which was extremely hazardous duty. They were there to bolster the morale of the infantry as they made their way into battle from the front lines. Many young, unarmed musicians were wounded and killed on both sides.

Older and stronger boys, ages 12-14, often served as Powder Monkeys, supplying gun crews in the Navy and were also used on the front lines as infantrymen. Seeing these kids, even though they were reenactors, was a sobering reminder of just who are the greatest victims of all war—the very young. Using child soldiers in combat was not a new phenomenon, Jackson realized, limited to Sierra Leone, the Congo, and Darfur, and it made him sick to think about it.

Except for the officers, most of the original soldiers, both Confederate and Union, were from among the poorer working classes. In the North, for $300, a young man could purchase his way out of the draft. This policy caused rioting in New York City. This was a rich man's war but a poor man's fight. Thanks to the reenactors, all the nuances of a war 150 years removed were on display.

The news truck rolled to a stop and Jackson and Phillips hopped off, thanking the driver for the lift. They could just see the rest of their company through the mist. Holloway was there, on horseback, and he was talking to Brad Lake, ever the mindful journalist, writing feverishly in his pad. The rest of the 65-member Company were all there, except Tommy Fuller. From not too far away, they heard sirens, and Lake shook his head. "Someone's screwed up already."

●●●●●

Tommy Fuller looked in his rear-view mirror and saw the unmistakable low profile of Pennsylvania State Trooper patrol cars moving quickly up the median and inside lane of Highway 97. He figured he had two minutes, tops. He spied just enough room between ambulances and fire trucks to make his move.

Jerking the steering wheel hard to the right, he floored the gas pedal, sending gravel, mud, and grass high into the air behind him. He drove off the median and halfway down the embankment to get around the remnants of the accident and was then just barely able to maneuver the truck back up on the road. The fireman yelled curses at him and jumped back to avoid being hit. The road ahead was without traffic as far as he could see, which wasn't too far. Thick patches of fog made visibility poor at best. He sped down the two-lane as fast as he dared, while the scene behind him quickly

51

disappeared out of his sight.

The troopers arrived at the accident and parked in the same spot Tommy had just vacated. Unaware of what had just transpired, they took their time gathering up report papers, clipboards and other paraphernalia, expecting to be writing up a fairly straightforward accident report. The trooper in the first car got out, and while surveying the scene, walked to the Fire Chief.

"First response?" asked the youngish trooper, rhetorically, snapping his gum, clicking his pen.

"Yeah. No life-threatening injuries. A few facial lacerations and a possible concussion. Got it just about wrapped up here." They both looked down at the victims, one a young black male, the other a reenactor dressed in a Yankee uniform, his collar caked with real blood, looking more authentic than expected. "The news van that hit them was a little anxious to get to this battle, I guess," said one of the EMTs. "There are some real winners out here. I'm afraid it's gonna be a long day."

"Got that right," answered the rookie Trooper. "Had a shooting in town, about an hour ago. A black kid is dead and his buddies said a crazy Rebel soldier pulled out his musket and shot him, point blank. Drove off in a little Nissan pick-up truck. Probably a hundred miles from here by now."

The color drained from the Chief's face. He searched his recent memory for clearer details and answers to the ringing bells inside his head.

"No shit...," he said to the trooper. "Off-white Nissan, '93 or '94 model, with two confederate flags on the tailgate?"

The trooper stopped snapping his gum and looked up at him attentively. "Yeah. White male, mid twenties, Civil War outfit."

"Well, Trooper, if I'm not mistaken, your boy just tore off down the road less than three minutes ago. He was nervous and jumpy as hell, and very anxious to get out of here. Could be your man."

The Trooper ran back to his car, filled in the other patrolman on the details of the conversation and both cars began a pursuit.

Every policeman, fireman, and dog catcher within 50 miles heard the news over their radios: the possible murder suspect had just been spotted and was speeding down Route 97, heading straight for Gettysburg National Park Battlefield. The first guns of the reenactment were now just 40 minutes from firing their opening volleys.

Tommy Fuller's scanner broadcast the same news also, and he knew the Troopers had to be close behind. With the traffic ahead cleared, Tommy was alone on the road for the first two minutes of his escape. He estimated he was less than a mile or so from the Park entrance and the parking lot. He was in flight mode and his mind fired in a hundred directions as he carried on a conversation with himself.

"What the hell am I doing?" he screamed aloud as he sped down the road, tires whining with the excessive speed. "I just need some time," he thought, trying to calm down. "You've got to remember exactly what happened. When you get your story straight and you can figure this thing out, you'll give yourself up."

He tried to remember details, but they were all so cloudy. Images of teenagers in baggy clothing and baseball caps were mixed with images of Yankee soldiers with bayonets and guns. He could remember hearing the loud, thumping bass from their stereo, or was it cannon fire? He was on the verge of a complete breakdown when the stopped traffic in front of him came suddenly into focus. He didn't realize how fast he'd been driving. He slammed on the brakes in an attempt to avoid hitting the giant Cadillac Escalade SUV, in front of him. He turned the wheel sharply to the left, but the damp road surface was like ice and he skidded straight for this tank of a vehicle and could do nothing, but brace for impact.

The crash was deafening, and though his arms had been locked tightly against the wheel, the violent force of the impact sent him up over the steering wheel into the windshield, smashing it, his body thrown around inside the small truck before being deposited back down into the driver's seat. He sat motionless and stunned for a moment and felt something warm dripping from his chin. He had hit the rear-view mirror with his face and cut himself badly. In shock, he stumbled out of the truck, which had turned 180-degrees and was pointing in the wrong direction. The smell of burning tire rubber choked the air. He looked for the SUV he had just plowed into but only saw empty road and mist. He heard car doors and yelling behind him and he turned to see a great, fat man push his way from behind a deployed air-bag and step, apparently unhurt, out of his slightly damaged vehicle.

"You all-right?" asked the big Yankee soldier, walking up to Tommy.

"Yeah...yeah. I think so," he stuttered. "I didn't see you stopped there— the fog..." He nearly fainted. The Yankee propped him up against the mangled fender of his Nissan.

"You're bleeding pretty bad from your chin." he said and walked back to his SUV. He pulled his pack from the backseat and returned to Tommy, who was now sitting on the tailgate of his Nissan, sprung open from the impact.

"I'm a doctor, and a reenactor, 34th Pennsylvania. What the hell was your hurry? Hope you've got good insurance." He fished in his pack for some sterile gauze and antibiotic spray. "Let me see that," he said, as he leaned in towards Tommy.

"Get the fuck away from me, Yankee!" Tommy screamed, arms flying, pushing away the big man. Tears began to roll from his eyes. The suppressed emotions brought on by the trauma of his last few years and last few hours had caught up with him.

"Whoa, buddy. Calm down," the man said. "For starters, I'm from South Carolina. Look, you're in shock. I'm a real doctor, for real, a heart surgeon, to be exact. I'm not the enemy here."

Through sobs, Tommy gave in and let the big Yankee tend his wounds. "It's not too bad, but you need stitches. For now let me put these steri-strips on your chin to help close up that gash."

As he finished the bandaging and did a little clean-up on his face they both heard sirens and speeding cars headed their way.

"Shit. Not again!" said the Yankee, fearing another imminent wreck. "They won't see us through this fog. We're both gonna get hit if we don't move." The big man attempted to take Fuller by the elbow and get them both out of the way, but Tommy shook free and dove for the cab of his truck.

The first patrol car appeared out of the mist less than 50 feet away and, considering the conditions, was flying at about 60 or 70 miles an hour. The big Ford Crown Victoria slammed into Tommy's Nissan, narrowly missing the Doctor. The impact sent Tommy, now back inside his truck, careening down a 10-foot embankment, just missing a large oak tree. The second patrol car was close behind. Too close. The trooper slammed into the first car, spinning them both in two complete 360s.

Only the steam venting from Fuller's cracked and bleeding radiator made any noise. Tommy got out of his truck, partially buried in the wet ditch. Above him, on the shoulder of the road, a few witnesses stood by, stunned. The sweet and sickening stench of sputtering antifreeze filled the air. Tommy doubled over and vomited. A moment later, as he looked up, he watched the bewildered patrolmen work their way out from behind airbags and out of their seat belts. They hadn't seen him below. They wrenched their patrol car doors open and as they started to get out, Tommy made his move.

He reached through the driver's window, which had been rolled down, and grabbed his Rebel cap from the dashboard, and his musket from behind the seat. He felt for his portable scanner, but couldn't find it. He heard voices from the road and realized the Yankee was talking to the patrolman and must have filled him in on what was going on. He had to move quickly. Where was that damned scanner? He needed it. He heard the static come simultaneously from the radio in one of the patrol cars above him on the road and from his own scanner somewhere in his truck.

"Seven-Larry-Niner, Seven-Larry-Niner, - we're on Route 97, one mile south of the Gettysburg Battlefield entrance...and while in pursuit of a shooting suspect, have been involved in a 10-50. Calling for immediate back up and two tow trucks. Suspect is believed to be armed and has fled the scene on foot. We're in pursuit."

A loud static pulse from his scanner allowed Tommy to zero in on the source and find it under the front seat. As he moved within the truck, the entire vehicle slid a few inches in the wet grass, and he thought he saw lightening, as the sky seemed to flash. He picked up the radio, turned its volume low, stuffed it into his cartridge box and slipped into the woods and looked up at another odd flash. He never heard the troopers make their way down the embankment. They followed the truck's tire marks in the wet grass until they stopped abruptly.

"What the…" said one trooper, unable to finish his sentence.

"Where is it? Where's the goddamn truck?" He could not explain why Tommy's truck, the one they'd hit and knocked down the embankment minutes earlier, was gone. Along with their suspect, it had simply vanished.

Chapter 9

July 3, 1863 8:00 a.m.
Gettysburg Pa.

Step one of the "Yankee Surprise" was to sneak three, horse-drawn wagons loaded with highly explosive materials, undetected, to a cave that only one man had seen, and even that, just through a scope from almost a mile away. Confidence was not at an all-time high, but the men under him were good soldiers and followed orders. Under Sergeant Henderson's watchful eye, the three large supply wagons were filled with an estimated 60-percent of the powder Lee's tattered Army of Northern Virginia had. Several men within the Artillery Battalion had to be physically restrained at the sight of so much of their powder being taken. They left only enough for half the cannons to fire five or six times each. Nearby, soldiers watched in disbelief as the loading took place.

Five of Henderson's men appeared, each carrying a two-gallon glass container filled with an opaque, thick, paste. Henderson reminded them that they were carrying nitroglycerin, an unstable compound, and that it might be in everyone's best interest to walk a little slower. He carefully took each bottle from the shaking men and placed it in the center of each wagon in a nest made from Army blankets and hay.

Henderson had also mixed 10 barrels of nitro with diatomaceous earth, a soft, powdery residue formed of ancient algae. This same fossilized clay particulate would later play an important role in society, cat litter. He had discovered the mixture quite by accident while studying chemistry at the Citadel in Charleston, South Carolina. Henderson found himself still trying to figure out the exact formula and was reluctant to send the men off with this experimental mixture, but he knew it would do the trick if detonated.

Though he didn't realize it at the time, Henderson had invented dynamite, a full three years before Alfred Nobel, the Swedish inventor, would discover the same formula and use his vast fortunes to offer 'Prizes' in his name. Additionally, 12 kegs of kerosene were mixed with saltpeter, ammonia, and chlorine in another experimental cocktail that had proven potent in the laboratory. The contents of the wagons were covered with great sheets of canvas and tied in place. The combination of explosives was dangerous and lethal and word spread through the camp to steer clear. Except for the fuse, Henderson's work was done.

The world's largest bomb was prepared and ready to go, except for one final morbid step, the placement of three dead bodies atop the wagons. They would disguise the bomb beneath the corpses of fallen enemy, re-dressed in Confederate uniforms, making it look as if they were recovering bodies from the battlefield. Any Federals spying them would likely leave them to their gruesome task, unmolested; it was a civil war, after all.

·····

Pickett and Longstreet were going over details of the battle plan with several field officers, noting that they were about two hours away from First Strike, the part of the plan which had the entire Confederate army pouring down off Seminary Ridge from both north and south extremes. General Lee's orders were simple and clear. He felt his men had a right to know the plan and the inherent dangers it contained, so he was unusually forthcoming with the details. From atop Traveller, and in full battle dress, he addressed the silent encampment, yelling so as to be heard by as many as possible.

"You have served your country well," he started. "I feel Fate hanging heavily in the air this morning. What her winds may bring us, I do not know. I do know that boys will become men today and that men will be lost. But this great Army of Northern Virginia is not ready to yield to those people over there, those northern aggressors!"

The men cheered loudly and Lee was forced to wait before he could continue.

"Today...we will go into battle with only God ... and our little surprise that I believe most of you know about. So much for secrecy." The men laughed and appreciated the General's levity, but their smiles were short-lived.

"Your commanders should have, by now, told you that we will unleash the very fires of hell upon the battlefield in a terrible blast that I'm told will burn the sky and shake the earth to the very steps of Washington!" Again, the men cheered loudly and started their familiar Rebel yell. "We may lose many today, but our opponents will lose more. May God grant us victory over tyranny, and put an end to this awful conflict."

An "Amen" in unison could be heard from the thousands in the ranks able to hear, underpinning the words of their beloved General. "Fall-in and wait for your orders!" These were the final words to his troops on that morning of July 3, 1863. The men shouted with anticipation as the army split in half, like the parting of the Red Sea, with around 14,500 troops to the east and 18,000 to the west and, when fully in formation, nearly a mile in the middle separating them.

Scouts on the flanks of the ridge had not detected any move of the Yankee army, except for some early morning Federal fire at Culp's Hill, but it was certainly possible to come at any time. Sitting atop a makeshift buckboard of the first wagon in the train of three, the two brothers made their way toward a small gap in the line. The wagons were loaded beyond capacity and the horses struggled to pull them. The sides of each wagon were reinforced with circles of rope, like 19th Century duct tape, to keep the overstuffed contents from bursting out through the side rails. Sergeant Henderson rode beside them, giving last minute instructions on how and where to set the fuse. Infantrymen called out "Good luck!" and "Godspeed" as they rode past.

"The wagons need to be side by side, as close as possible and as far inside the cave as they'll go," said Henderson. "Remember, we don't want the blast to go up into the open air, but out, and the further in and under the overhang those wagons are, the better." He instructed the Grissoms like a nervous football coach.

"Yes, Sergeant." Tom smiled at him. "We understand what we need to do." With that, the two brothers and their horse-drawn apocalypse disappeared into the warm haze of an early July morning.

Henderson had also rigged a flare system that would alert Lee and his officers of various stages in the operation, including when the explosives were in place, and when to start the charge. They would not move until they saw the first red flare, high in the sky. The Yankees would see it too, but wouldn't understand its significance. In fact, they needed the Yankee Army to charge at about the same time, so it was hoped they actually would sense it as a charge signal and begin their own move.

There were also spotters with flares, atop Seminary Ridge. They would, with the help of additional spotters, approximate the time it would take for the maximum number of Union troops to be within ten minutes of being in place. Then they would send up two flares. This would be the signal to the Grissom brothers to light the fuse and attempt their escape, as unlikely as that possibility seemed.

There were so many things that could go wrong, the brothers didn't dare even think about it. With a compass setting in hand, they moved forward, careful of the added admonition about the Nitro. *"If even one wagon wheel goes into a ditch, or small hole, or anything, you'll be the first to know about it,"* Henderson had scolded earlier, *"and we'll know half a second later. The mix is highly unstable and any good jarring of the containers will send the whole package up. Sirs, this you'll want to see from a safe distance, not a front-row seat."*

Their escape from harm's way would be upon the two horses used to transport the wagons. Hopefully, there would be enough time for the men to slip past the oncoming Yankees. They would probably be hanged as deserters or spies, instead of shot as enemies, but at least, they hoped, it might buy them enough time to mount an escape in the confusion.

Thick underbrush had been harvested from the woods, tied in bundles and placed on top of one of the wagons. It would be used to hide and disguise the bomb from early, advancing infantry and Cavalry. The morning haze was rapidly burning off, and they found themselves vulnerable in sudden and unexpected clear air. They could only hope that Yankee scouts wouldn't spot them, or if they did, think they were on a humanitarian recovery mission.

Their travel was smooth over the flat, hard soil and was made easier when they reached a farm road that seemed to be pointing in the exact direction they were headed. This was a stroke of luck they hadn't anticipated because the narrow road had not been seen through the mist, and didn't appear on any map. They traveled slowly for fifteen minutes before they were compelled by the compass needle to veer off the road and back on to rougher, unknown terrain.

They spoke in whispers, passing the time as they made their methodical, slow approach to the rise, a mere mile in front of the bulk of the entire Union Army of the Potomac.

"Tom?" asked Billy. "Remember that pretty Robbins girl from back in Murfreesboro?"

"Yeah. She moved to Nashville, didn't she…or was it Franklin?"

"Can't remember, but I know she was lit up for me."

Tom laughed at his brother. "Billy, you always thought every pretty girl you saw was lit up for you. Don't you suppose that at least a few of them mighta been lit up for me?"

"Well, big brother," answered Billy, "The ones that mighta been interested told me they thought you was too high on yourself, and that they liked a younger, stronger, more sensitive man…like me."

"Is that so? Well, then how do you explain when me and that pretty Robbins girl both disappeared for the night after the Harvest Fair, three years ago?"

"Why you dog. I don't believe you."

"Believe it."

"I won't."

"Well, then how would I know about that heart shaped birth mark on her..."

Before he could finish his ribald sentence, the horses snorted and reared back, spooked by a small animal underfoot. They whinnied wildly and bolted forward, attempting to gallop, struggling to pull the heavy and dangerous cargo. The wagon and its hitches groaned under the stresses caused by the nervous horses.

"Whoa!" Tom shouted, pulling back the reins, not as concerned about accidentally alerting the Yanks as he was of stopping a potential runaway wagon train.

"Tom! Stop them! Them damn horses'll kill us!" yelled Billy in an earnest, if not obvious, appeal.

The horses had gained speed, and were now running wildly, still shaken by whatever had spooked them, and Tom had lost his bearing with the compass. He tried to stop the advance of the team and find his compass heading, but couldn't handle both tasks.

"Billy! Take the compass!"

He had to regain use of both hands to slow the horses. As Billy grabbed the small brass compass, the lead wagon hit a rock with its right front wheel and both men bounced into the air and in the process, the compass flew out of Billy's hand out into the morning haze.

"No!" Tom yelled, sure the wagons were about to blow, and worried about losing the compass. The horses began finally to relax and slow.

"Whoa! Horse!" called Tom as he again yanked back on the reins, at last bringing the team to a complete stop.

Almost in tears Billy whispered, "Tom. What are we gonna do? Do you know where the hell we are?"

"Not exactly," he answered. He wiped sweat from his brow with a dirty glove. "At least we didn't blow ourselves up," he said dismounting. He looked in all directions, completely disoriented from their original heading. "Let's look for the compass...hurry."

Both men walked the ground surrounding the wagons, watching intently for even a glint of glass or brass, to no avail. They searched a minute more, coming up with nothing. Tom walked to the lead wagon, lifted the canvas, and checked on the nitro. One jar had been jostled out of its nest of blankets and he carefully returned it to its place. "One more good bump..." thought Tom.

Tom rechecked the map while Billy continued his panicked searching. He leaned against a large boulder as tall as he was, part of a rock-strewn ridge, and noticed it sat at the edge of a subtle, yet definite elevation in the ground around it. Through the mist he saw another, equally large boulder 20 feet to the left and he looked closely at his map.

"Billy," he whispered, "I think we're here."

Chapter 10

July 6, 2013 9:10 a.m.
Gettysburg National Military Park

Tommy Fuller was street smart, but he was just as comfortable in the woods. Without looking back, he made good time and knew the general direction of the encampment. His knees ached from the accident and he noticed the cuts on his uniform pant legs. Both knees had smashed into the dashboard of the truck during the accident and he was lucky he hadn't crushed his kneecaps or broken a leg. His head began to pound, not at the site of his chin wound, but on top of his head where there was no blood but a giant goose egg.

As he hustled through the woods he couldn't stop to feel sorry for himself. The troopers had to be close behind and he feared that before too long the place would be swarming with more of them, and dogs, too. Why he was running at all he didn't really know. He did know he wasn't ready to be caught and thrown in the general prison population as the crazy redneck who killed a black kid. So running, he felt, was his only option.

He had hoped that the police hadn't done all their detective work yet and he'd be safe for a while among his own company of Confederates. Susan wouldn't tell them the name of his unit; she didn't know it. Blending in with 15,000 other re-enactors would be easy, he hoped, but he wasn't sure of anything. Even if he was able to hide among the thousands of Reb soldiers, what then? He couldn't hide forever. He'd have to face the authorities eventually; he knew that. Though Susan had threatened before to leave him, suggesting that they were growing apart, he couldn't, he wouldn't just take off. These thoughts and a hundred others raced through his mind as he made his way through the thick brush of the woods, toward the encampment.

•••••

"Where's Tommy Fuller?" Captain DiCarlo called out, looking over his unit, which had just returned from Morning Parade. "Anybody seen Fuller this morning?" he called again. The men looked around and murmured to one another about his whereabouts, but no one had seen him and that's just when he appeared.

"There he is." said DiCarlo. "Nice of you to make it." He looked closer at him and saw the large bandage on his chin.

"What the hell happened to you?" he asked. "Cut yourself shaving?"

"I ahh...had a little fender-bender this morning."

"Oh man, Tommy. I'm sorry. You all right?"

"Yeah, yeah.... I'll be fine. Anybody got any aspirin?"

DiCarlo disappeared into his tent to retrieve some pain-killers. A few of the men teased Tommy about his driving skills and patted him on the back, listening to a story he fabricated about an accident back in town.

Greg Jackson and Mike Phillips had been chatting before Fuller had arrived at their camp.

"Poor kid," said Phillips to Jackson, nodding in Fuller's direction.

"Yeah? Poor kid?" asked Jackson, still stinging from the comments Fuller had made at MacAuley's the night before.

"Couldn't have happened to a nicer guy."

"Oh, come on, Greg. He's alright. I know he's... a little red around the neck, but cut him some slack. He's been through a world of shit."

Jackson harrumphed and turned away. He stewed about Fuller's racial slur and was annoyed with his boss as well, but kept his thoughts to himself.

"Tell him to wash down those aspirin at a crackers-only drinking fountain," he said under his breath.

Members of the press were everywhere, and when a segment producer from *Discover History Channel* suggested they wire a few reenactors with cordless lapel mikes, Tommy Fuller, again, quietly disappeared out of camera range. He wandered toward an officers' meeting where Generals discussed the day's battle plans. Even away from the publics' prying eyes, these Confederate officer reenactors play-acted a scenario in which they might win a battle whose outcome had been pre-determined. But that didn't stop them from flights of fancy complete with military protocol and stern faces.

•••••

July 3, 1863 8:30 a.m.
Near Emmitsburg Road
Gettysburg, Pennsylvania

"This has got to be it," said Tom, looking at his map.

"Ain't we runnin' out of time here?" asked Billy.

"Well, yes…but the Yanks ain't likely to move just on account of us; they could take a pot shot at us, though…that'd be bad. Our men won't move until they see the flare, so we're probably okay for a bit, but we gotta find that cave. Heads or tails?" asked Tom, fishing for a coin from his pocket. That was how the brothers had been deciding things since they were boys, whether to fish or swim, go to school or play hooky, and now they were deciding with a coin which way to lead the "Yankee Surprise," as they'd been calling the massive bomb. "Heads is left, tails is right. Okay by you?" Billy nodded.

Tom tossed the coin into the temporarily visible morning sun, it disappeared for a moment and fell back to earth landing on heads and so the men turned their wagon train of destruction to the left and continued their search for the cave somewhere beside Emmitsburg Road.

•••••

At the encampment the bulk of Lee's troops were poised and waiting with the battle plan firmly in place. A series of flares, to be sent up by the Grissoms, would indicate the explosives were ready and to start the charge up either flank of the battlefield.

This charge of some 70-percent of the available Confederate troops would leave Lee's army dangerously thin, but it was the only way to insure Meade would send most of his Yankee troops to meet them, and force them to the middle of the battlefield.

The Grissoms would send up the first flare from the cave. That would indicate that they had positioned the wagons, lit the ten-minute fuse and were about to ride east toward the Yankee Army. Additional Rebel forward positions at the sides of the battlefield, half way between the Ridge and their army, were there to relay a second set of flares insuring that the Confederate Army knew it was time to start their charge. The five commanding Confederate Colonels synchronized their pocket watches and knew, from the sighting of the second set of flares, they had nine minutes, more or less, to lead a charge loud enough and fast enough to draw the bulk of the Yankee army out into the middle of the battlefield, up and over the slight ridge. It was hoped that the expected Yankee artillery barrage would be lessened when the Yanks themselves had taken to the center of the field.

At the fighting's fiercest point, the Rebs would then turn around in a surprise, illogical retreat, and get back far enough to avoid the devastating explosion that they hoped would destroy a large contingent of the Union Army of the Potomac.

While some of the men feigned optimism, all of them had serious reservations. But loyal soldiers do as commanded and none were more loyal to their beloved leader than those in the A.N.V. The five-man crew of the Confederate Balloon Corps was no exception. With giant bellows to speed the process, hot air was funneled from a coal fire into Captain Bryan's 25,000 cubic foot balloon, *The Carolina*, and it began to take shape. Bryan hopped into the small basket while he and members of the small unit began attaching leads to telegraph equipment and the cables that would send the information directly to Lee's Communication Corp.

The Carolina climbed silently toward the morning sun. The only sound it made came from the cables slowly rolling off their spools. Prussian born Ferdinand von Zeppelin was so impressed with the Balloon Corps that he visited the United States and worked for the Union as an advisor in 1863. Through the next half-century, Germany tried in vain, during two World Wars, to use the airships of von Zeppelin's, whose inspiration began in fields over Virginia, Washington D.C., and the Carolinas in the late 1860s.

Chapter 11

9:55 a.m. July 6, 2013
Gettysburg National Military Park

The toasty, Christmassy smell of burning firewood filled the air at Gettysburg National Park, though it was early July. A celebratory mood flowed through the crowd of thousands and little solemnity regarding the event being recreated was apparent. Too distant from the actual blood and battle, most of those watching were just spectators witnessing a curiosity, a grand play. Many brought picnic lunches and containers of coffee. Children played video games on smart phones, bored with the grown-up games now underway. When a shift in the wind and an unseasonably chilly updraft caused the fog and smoke to lift momentarily, and the expanse of the battlefield, between the two famous ridges could be seen, a subtle change came over the crowd.

Laughing and loud conversations were replaced by hushed tones and quieter observations. The accumulation of reenactors in their encampments was breathtaking. The carnival atmosphere waned slightly in favor of private contemplation. In spite of the noise of cars and trucks roaring in and out of service roads, and other modern additions to the soundtrack, including mood-breaking police sirens, it was not difficult for spectators and participants to cast their eyes forward into the reenactment, block out those distractions, and find themselves transported 150 years into the past.

This was precisely why reenactors and experienced viewers so loved these big battles. Something about the living history and the authentic reenactment was both exhilarating and sobering. The white-haired, bearded old men, along with young boys in uniform, told an old story of brother against brother, father against son, of widowed wives, orphaned children and of a terribly sad chapter in American history; the crowd couldn't get enough of it.

Tommy Fuller slid back up to his group as the men assembled for roll call and counting off. He'd bummed a cup of coffee from a local film crew, but he was asked by a pair of organizers to get rid of it. Styrofoam wasn't used in the 1860s, therefore not allowed in the encampment by reenactors. Spectators were allowed anything, but reenactors were held to a higher standard.

He still had his musket, the murder weapon, as law enforcement was already calling it, slung over his shoulder, and he thought it somewhat ironic that working guns were allowed at the reenactment, but not plastic cups. One event host threatened Tommy with expulsion because of the clean, bright white bandage on his chin. The "authenticity police," as they were sometimes called, asked him to allow a female spectator to use her make up to "dirty" it up a bit and make it more believable.

Mounted commanders began riding back and forth organizing the troops and answering last-minute questions. One-hundred-seventy-five Rebel cannons were already in place with crews preparing their black-powder cannon charges which, when fired, recreated the look and sound of actual artillery without the deadly consequences. The buglers were in place, the juvenile drummers readied, and just five minutes remained before the first charge, sending 6,000 Rebel reenactor soldiers straight ahead toward Cemetery Hill.

According to history, and the day's battle plan, Pickett's Charge, a double-quick advance straight into enemy hellfire, was responsible for a 50 percent casualty rate, and many felt that loss, combined with others, dealt the final blow to the Confederacy, which could never recover psychologically.

Longstreet is reported to have said: "General, it is my opinion that no fifteen thousand men ever arrayed for battle can take that position." Just before ordering Pickett to charge, Lee said: "The enemy is there, and I will strike him there."

Despite the devastation, the Civil War would drag on two additional years, the last shot fired on June 22, 1865, by a Confederate Navy ship, the *CSS Shenandoah*. The ship had been responsible for capturing nearly 40 Union vessels in just 12 months of service. Her final act of war came from shots she fired on a whaling ship off of the Aleutian Islands in the northern Pacific, many miles from the Virginia countryside for which she was named. The crew had sailed from England, around the Cape of Good Hope, up into the waters off Alaska, and had no idea Lee had surrendered on April 9.

This Gettysburg reenactment, possibly the largest in history, would become a living history lesson for all those attending, both spectator and participant, but something strange was afoot, threatening to spoil the event.

"I don't remember seeing so many cops at the last anniversary," remarked Philips to Jackson, as the men glanced around noticing dozens of Park Police, State Troopers, and local law enforcement. The police officers wandered through the ranks of reenactors, looking like extra-terrestrials with their out-of-place modern hats, shiny nickel-plated handcuffs, handguns, and squawking radios.

"Yeah, I know what you mean," Jackson remarked. Though this was his first reenactment he was a bit surprised, if not annoyed, at the police presence threatening to spoil their stage.

"They are definitely bursting our bubble here," he thought out loud. "Completely unnecessary."

Tommy Fuller noticed the authorities, too, though he alone among his unit knew why they were there. He took some solace as he realized the police still must not have specific information on his whereabouts. Although they were certainly looking for him, they didn't know exactly where to look among so many Rebel troops. He took this opportunity to blend in, fearing his anonymity couldn't last long.

"Hey guys," came his slow greeting to Jackson and Philips, forcing a smile and grimacing with pain when he did. "Ouch," he said to no one in particular.

"Be careful there, Tommy. Are you sure you shouldn't have that looked at?" Phillips asked, looking at his bandaged chin.

"Naw. It'll be all right until after the battle's over."

The order to "Fall in!" was made across the battlefield, repeated by individual unit's officers for nearly a mile.

As the men (and a few women disguised as men) were called into formation, and thousands advanced in neat rows at the edge of the Battlefield, Tommy's eyes darted left and right. He worried that though there may have been thousands of Rebel uniforms to hide among, how many other men had three-inch bandages on their chins. He felt sick again, turned quickly and walked to the farthest edge of the unit thinking about what to do. He saw two troopers closing in from the left. They were asking questions of the men in the next unit over. Two Park policeman and a local Gettysburg cop made their way toward him from the right and from behind, and just twenty yards away, more uniformed officers were unmistakably now headed in his direction. He began to shake and felt his heart pounding painfully in his chest for the third time that morning.

"Are you okay?" he heard someone ask as if from a hundred miles away.

"Tommy?"

He felt a hand on his shoulder and he jumped. It was Ben Holloway, the pharmacist from town. He'd hopped down off his horse to say 'Hi' to the group and noticed Fuller's distress.

"Kid, you don't look well. Are you sure you're up for this? I heard you had a little fender-bender in town. You could have a concussion, you know. I'm not so sure you should be out here, son," he said with some medical authority.

"No, no, I'm okay. It's just hot in this uniform, that's all." Fuller again forced a smile. Holloway heard his name being called to rejoin his mounted regiment, and so he mounted his horse and turned back to look at Fuller.

"Well, stay hydrated, and you take it very easy and slowly. I'm telling you this is not a good idea. Think about sitting this one out, will you?" With that he rode off into the haze, which had re-intensified.

Fuller was still worried about being identified too easily with a bandage on his chin and he thought about removing it altogether. His heart rate steadied and an unexplainable calm came over him.

"I wouldn't miss this battle for anything," he said aloud with a chilling detachment. As he was about to peel the bandage from his still fresh wound, a loud static squawk shook him and he jumped. He saw out of the corner of his eye two Pennsylvania State troopers talking to Captain DiCarlo, his unit commander.

"No way. Not possible," he could hear DiCarlo say as he snuck a glance in his direction. When the troopers made eye contact, they had little doubt they'd found their man. With their hands on their holstered side arms, they moved toward their suspect, now just twenty feet away.

"Tommy Fuller!" one trooper shouted and drew his gun. Fuller froze. A couple of other men from the unit standing between the troopers and their mark stepped backward.

"Tommy Fuller! Drop your weapon and lie face down on the ground!" shouted the second trooper.

Before anyone could take another breath, buglers from 100 yards away blasted their horns and Pickett's Charge of The Battle of Gettysburg, of 2013, was underway. Murder investigations not withstanding, nearly 7,000 Rebel soldiers, unaware of the real drama unfolding at the front line, let out war hoops and nearly trampled the police and the few stunned men of Tommy Fuller's unit. The crowd, filling two enormous grandstands, cheered, puzzled by the police presence, but fully engaged in the organized chaos before them in the fields of Gettysburg.

Also unaware of the ongoing police investigation were Jackson, Phillips and a few other reenactors, who let out battle cries and marched forward on the double-quick.

Fuller was not among the few who stayed behind. He let forth a blood-curdling Rebel yell as if it might be his last battle here on earth. He was going down fighting. The police gave chase, clicking their radios, screaming orders to halt, but were easily out-shouted by the thousands of Rebs, thundering horses, cannon fire from both sides and the cheering crowd of some 85,000 onlookers. Fuller, lost in the chaos, slipped into the fog and the fray.

Cannons thundered, sending out orange flame and black-powder smoke rings twenty feet from their muzzles. Some smoke rings would coil on unseen turbulence, stay perfectly formed and drift 100 yards or more. One hundred mounted officers led the charge with sabers slicing through the thinning mist and their horses kicking up clods of dirt as they pounded and shook the ground.

Greg Jackson was having the time of his life. Screaming like a schoolgirl, heart pounding, he now knew why these guys did this. It was more than just playing army, more than a glorified history lesson. He felt part of a brotherhood of men, all passionate about their cause. The cause itself was unimportant at that moment; it was the passion of the players and the group dynamic that took over.

As Jackson ran down the field toward Emmitsburg Road, he looked to his left and saw Mike Phillips next to him, no longer his boss, but now a comrade in arms. Philips nodded to him and managed a smile that said, "Told you so." Holes in the fog would suddenly open up offering several hundred yards or more of visibility out into the battlefield. It was then that his heart almost stopped at the realism of this reenactment: the horses, the cannons, the gunfire, the war cries, the dead and wounded men already piling up out in front of them. He looked to his right and saw Fuller, running, crying, and bleeding from the chin, his bandage gone. If ever there was a picture of a real Rebel soldier in a real Civil War battle, it was embodied in this crazy kid from Gettysburg. The passion, adrenaline, and endorphins overwhelmed Jackson; he was seeing the elephant. Completely caught up in the all too real play unfolding before his eyes, he surrendered to the moment and ran, through his own tears and the smoke of war, toward the road bisecting the battlefield.

Chapter 12

July 3, 1863   9:03 a.m.
Near Emmitsburg Road
Gettysburg, Pa.

The "Yankee Surprise" bumped along pitching precariously with enough explosives to vaporize all of Gettysburg in an instant.   It was deathly quiet with the exception of the plodding horses. No birds were singing, neither brother spoke, and the uncertainty of their immediate future made them both ill.

"I can't wait to get this done," said Billy.

His brother didn't have to agree; it was understood.   It was also understood that they might not survive the ordeal.

"Remember summertime back in Murfreesboro?" asked Tom of his younger brother. Again no answer was required. "Huntin', fishin,' 'n' swimmin' on the Stones River? Working for Pa at the paper?"

"The barn dances," added Billy with a grin.

"After the barn dances," countered Tom with an even bigger grin.

"And that heart-shaped birth mark right on Liz Robbins'..." This time Billy was interrupted, unable to finish his lovely thought.

"Billy...that's it!" Tom said in a husky whisper.

Less than twenty feet ahead a black expanse, like a great gaping mouth, peered out through the mist. A natural rock formation jutted out from the low rise, like the bill on a giant baseball cap. Under it they could just make out a black hole disappearing into the ridge. As they inched closer their plan began to take on new possibilities.

"I'll be damned," Tom said, finally getting a good look at his cave. "It'll be a tight fit, but it looks like we can get all three wagons most of the way in."

The earth around the cave entrance and inside was hard-packed and had been so heavily traveled by man, ancient and modern, that the two men could, by themselves, wrestle the heavy wagons, once unhitched, and roll them into place.

They unloaded the camouflage brush that had been strapped to the middle wagon and set it aside. The three bodies of the anonymous enemy would be part of a funeral pyre, the likes of which had never been seen. They very carefully unloaded the 15-foot anaconda-like fuse Sergeant Henderson had fashioned for them. This was their lifeline, their only hope of carrying out the mission and surviving it, as unlikely as that prospect seemed.

With some difficulty they rolled the two remaining wagons into the cave as close to one another as possible. Henderson had also given them a crude plastic explosive formed out of some mystery chemicals, gunpowder and clay, to be used as a detonator. The softball-sized ball of explosive putty was placed underneath the center wagon and the canvas-covered fuse was secured firmly to the center of the mix. Finally, Tom took one of the two flares from his pack and jammed the steel spike into the ground, aiming the two-foot tall rocket flare slightly back toward the Confederate front line. He hoped it would be easily seen against the morning sun.

"That's about it," said Tom, surveying the work, and placing the last of the brush to cover as much of the makeshift armament as possible.

"Well, let's see if these stinky Yank uniforms will work." They pulled the dark blue Yankee Cavalry officer's jackets from behind the wagon's seat and put them on, along with their leathers. "I got the flares ready," said Billy.

Their plan was to be as inconspicuous as possible among the hoped-for oncoming rush of Yankee soldiers. They would ride across the open field, through the Yankee charge and disappear off into town or the woods or somewhere, anywhere safe. First they needed to light the flare indicating the charge was in place, and then wait to see the second flare from the Confederate line, listen for the confederate bugle charge, listen for the Yankee charge, then light the timed fuse and move out. Simple enough. It could work. But would it?

"I love you brother," said Billy. The two men hugged.

"Ready?" asked Tom.

"As I'll ever be."

"Okay then. Here goes for Ma and Pa and the Ol' Man." He took a single, waterproof match from a tin case, struck it against his boot, and lit a small magnesium fuse on the end of the signal flare. They waited a few seconds and then with a whoosh that startled both them and their horses, a bright red-flamed rocket ascended 2,000 feet into the air, and lit the whole sky forming a giant, pink sheet with a glowing, red center. There was no way this wouldn't be seen by anybody within several miles. It was spectacular by anyone's standards.

•••••

The Confederate Army of Northern Virginia, along with a very believable General Lee, thrilled the crowds in attendance at the Gettysburg National Military Park, and the Yankee Army was equally striking on the far side of the battlefield. The Goodyear Blimp was grounded because of the unusual early July fog, but would have otherwise had a fantastic and dreamlike view of the battle unfolding beneath them.

Captain DiCarlo had not moved forward with his company when the bugle sounded. He was among the few reenactors still answering questions of the police back at staging area. A handful of additional law enforcement officers ran out amid the crowd, but were ineffective among all the screaming, gunfire and general mayhem of a fully engaged battle.

Without DiCarlo to lead them, the unit was a little unsure of exactly where they were to take up position. Though not the unit's next highest ranking officer, Mike Phillips took charge and thought he might fudge the rules a little bit and make it more fun for his closet pals. The original orders were to stop three quarters of the way to the road, wait for the Yankee onslaught, and fall over after some close-quarter combat and rifle fire.

"Aren't we supposed to stop and wait around here somewhere?" shouted Jackson, over the din of battle.

"Screw that!" yelled Philips, still running. "Follow me!" Phillips and his handful of insubordinate reenactors ran over the battlefield with a reckless abandon, wearing ear-to-ear grins. This type of renegade behavior was frowned upon, especially by so called "stitch counters," those who worried about every uniform "stitch" being in place and absolute authenticity and solemnity.

Philips was always one to bend the rules. As a litigator he'd been warned hundreds of times in court about inappropriate questioning of witnesses, improper procedure, and had even been held in contempt, spending an overnight in jail when he crossed the wrong judge one too many times. He wasn't careless or ignorant of the system; he just worked it to his advantage, always pushing it to the edge. He assumed, since DiCarlo was nowhere in sight, that he could claim confusion and that he was doing the best he could. His new plan was to take his men straight to the road so they could have the best vantage point possible, up onto a small rise, smack-dab in the middle of all the action.

Only four of the original 65 men in the unit were with him. The others were either back at the front line with the police, separated after the charge, or had stopped on the battlefield carrying out their orders to shoot a few times, and die like good soldiers. This made his plan revision that much easier to carry out, and so they ran with a half-mile still to go before they would reach the intended stopping point, a rock outcropping.

Phillips, Fuller, Jackson, and Lake now made up the renegade 3rd Virginia Militia Sight-Seeing unit, and they were beside themselves with their own naughty cleverness. They stopped occasionally to load and fire their weapons at anyone wearing a Yankee uniform. Shooting, after all, was most of the fun of the reenactments, which essentially was little more than a bunch of grown men playing army like 11-year-olds. But not everyone shared in the fun. Tommy Fuller couldn't bring himself to load his musket and just moved forward with the men. He saw the Yankees, but he was on the lookout for uniforms of a different type.

•••••

Billy and Tom Grissom watched in awe as the flare painted the early morning sky in otherworldly tones of red and pink. They had to remind themselves to move forward with the rest of the battle plan.

"Okay. So far so good," Tom said with a nervous smile. "You watch for the next flares, and keep your eyes and ears open for anything, from anywhere."

He double-checked the fuse and prepared a match for striking when the moment was right. He was to light the fuse, then they would mount their horses and go. They were to be as far away from the cave as possible for several reasons, the most important of which was not to expose to the enemy the bomb and the slow-burning fuse leading to it.

The camouflaged cave was convincing from a distance, but within 40 feet of the entrance it was obviously filled with things other than old Indian arrowheads. But they knew it was the best they could do and it was really too late to worry about it.

"There it is!" cried out Billy, losing control of the volume of his voice.

"Shhh!" reprimanded Tom. "Let's not invite the whole Yank army over for tea. Okay?"

The second flare was easily visible and within five seconds they heard the bugle sound the charge, and within seconds after that heard the distant thunder of running men and horses.

Tom was shaking so badly that he dropped the match he'd been holding and fumbled for another.

"Come on! Come on!" Billy moaned in frustration. The horses whinnied nervously.

With the next match lit, he had to steady his arm with his other hand as he moved toward the end of the fuse. He consciously controlled his breathing to calm himself.

"Easy, Tom," he said aloud and placed the burning match end to the magnesium starter on the end of the fuse. It sparked brightly, and then dimmed to a barely burning ember, and then went dead. The brothers looked at one another in utter abhorrence of this motley looking fuse that seemed to not be working.

"Henderson, you little bug-eyed...." Tom Grissom would have continued cursing Sergeant Henderson had the fuse not suddenly sparked to life again. This time it burned white-hot, slowly and steadily, sending up a thin trail of smoke as it coiled its way to the business end of the massive bomb.

Tom glanced down at his pocket watch. The timed fuse was to burn at the rate of around six inches per minute, which was frightfully slow for a fuse and had taken some experimentation back at the camp to get right. Henderson had combined gunpowder and magnesium, which was virtually waterproof, in a clay mixture that was designed to slow and steady the burn rate, and to the Grissoms' amazement, the fuse seemed to be doing just that.

With the fuse burning securely, they went to mount their horses when a loud whistling through the morning haze stopped them dead in their tracks. It was the unmistakable sound of a cannon ball flying through the air, and though it was very near to them, they couldn't see it. It landed with a loud thud and deafening explosion less than 50 feet away. The ground shook, the horses neighed wildly, bucking into the air, and they both lost their grips on the reins as their two steeds fled away from the misplaced friendly fire.

It's not known exactly how many men were killed by friendly fire during the Civil War, but estimates range from 100,000 - 200,000 from both sides, and the Grissoms feared they might be added to the list.

"Shit! Shit! Shit! Tom," cried Billy. "What are we gonna do?"

"High tail it out of here," he answered. "Them idiots! Artillery fire isn't supposed to be within a half-mile around us. They coulda destroyed the bomb."

"Or worse," remarked Billy. "They coulda set it off."

They were covered with specks of mud and dirt from the fallout of the near miss, but were otherwise unharmed except for an annoying ringing in their ears. They moved to the right, running along the Confederate side of the Emmitsburg Road. Escape would be tricky.

Chapter 13

July 6, 2013 9:57 a.m.
Emmitsburg Road
Gettysburg, Pennsylvania

Despite the honorable motivations behind reenactments, up-close they could be unintentionally comical. The men of DiCarlo's renegade unit, for instance, had each been shot dead, at near point-blank range, a dozen times, but ignored the fake gunfire and refused to fall over and play dead. They were impervious to fake Yankee bullets like some superheroes of the Confederacy. The way it was supposed to work was: a ranking field commander would tell them, 'Men, start taking some hits,' meaning the next time a volley of blanks is aimed and fired in your direction, fall over and play dead. At smaller reenactments, where every soldier was needed, this often didn't happen until late in the battle, much to the amusement of the crowds. Even then reenactors could suddenly resurrect from the dead, only to rejoin their comrades, which also became a comical high-point in an otherwise serious effort to portray something quite horrific.

At some larger reenactments a brightly colored, paper round, placed at random by an officer, in a soldier's cartridge box, signified, when retrieved, that it was the soldier's last shot. Larger reenactments were more organized. A soldier might be killed early and lie there until the all clear was sounded and everybody got up and went back to camp, or home. A few of the men from DiCarlo's unit were not playing by the rules. They had out-lived their "official" battlefield duties by 20 minutes or more and just ignored any Yankee that tried to engage them, yelling modern obscenities and laughing riotously.

Like a bunch of drunken frat boys, Phillips, Jackson, Fuller, and Brad Lake were the bullies of the battlefield, and all, but Fuller, seemed to enjoy every minute of it, infuriating the Yankee reenactors. Cries of "Oh, come on! I shot you twice! Fall over!" and "That's not fair..." could be heard over the cannon and gunfire. The irony was lost on those who took it all too seriously, but hysterical to the defiant men, who didn't care if they were later reprimanded. The story they'd have to tell was worth it.

Elsewhere on the battlefield similar scenes were unfolding with lone-rangers deputizing themselves and breaking from ranks. Everyone knew the Yanks were supposed to slaughter the Rebs, but the Rebs seemed to be dying harder and at a much slower pace than the event organizers had planned, and that history had reported.

Reenactors are not professional stunt men either, so the dying and limping often looked horribly suspect, even from a distance. The death and mayhem is accompanied by laughing, cursing, and accidental maiming, which leads to more cursing and laughing and so on. To help suspend disbelief, the best place to view a reenactment is from far away.

One member of the unit could not enjoy himself. Tommy Fuller couldn't share in the jesting of the other men and Greg Jackson took note of his sour, somber mood.

"What's his problem?" Jackson asked Mike Phillips, nodding in Fuller's direction.

"I don't know. He is certainly acting stranger than usual," said Phillips. "Maybe that car wreck this morning shook him up worse than we thought. I don't know, but don't give him any grief, okay?"

"Oh, not me, boss," replied Jackson, oozing sarcasm.

The remnant of the unit made it to the rise near Emmitsburg Road. The mist was lifting, but hadn't completely cleared. In the distance they could see State Troopers and Park Police walking through the staged battlefield. They were asking dead soldiers to sit up and identify themselves. Some spectators began booing, and between cannon and musket fire their protests were easily heard.

"That's really weird," remarked Phillips. "What the hell are those cops looking for?"

A peculiar wind blew thick patches of dense fog around them periodically, and the sky changed in rapid flashes that almost looked like lightning, but not quite. It was as if an entire overcast sky simply changed hues in an instant. The strangeness was unsettling, but it added to their enjoyment and helped with the overall experience.

They lay prone to survey the battlefield. Breaking ranks was taboo, and so they suspected they were in trouble with the event hosts. Not wishing to push it, they felt it was too disrespectful to blatantly stand among the bodies and carnage, so they lay on their bellies, watching the battle unfold. They'd found a perfect spot.

Most of the action would take place on the Confederate side of the ridge, so, lying flat, they pointed themselves in that direction. Tommy Fuller was nearby, surveying the battlefield for other things. Police.

A loud static squawk got their attention and they turned in the direction of the noise to see Tommy Fuller removing his portable scanner from his cartridge box.

"Fuller!" Phillips called out. "What's going on?" He didn't answer. "Fuller!" he called out again. Tommy Fuller stared glassy-eyed into the battlefield.

Phillips, Lake, and Jackson belly crawled over to him to find out just what was going on. When they arrived they could see Fuller was crying.

"Tommy." Phillips put a hand on his arm. "Are you all right? What's happened?"

"I killed a kid this morning." He looked helplessly at the other men. "I didn't mean to." He sobbed uncontrollably at his own confession. "I mean, I did mean to, but I was protecting myself. It was self-defense. I swear it. They were coming at me with baseball bats and knives. There were three of them. What was I supposed to do? I shot one of them and took off, and now the police are looking for me."

•••••

The sounds of the battle were growing closer and only three minutes into the Grissom brothers' escape, hand-to-hand clashes were already taking place along the outer flanks. They could see Yankee troops moving their way, less than a quarter mile from the ridge. Confederate troops were almost upon them. Several hundred Rebel infantrymen had actually already crossed over the ridge into Yankee musket and canister-shot fire. They were dropping like flies.

"Those are brave boys," Tom said respectfully of the troops ordered by General Pickett on what they all knew was a suicide mission.

They were quiet for a moment, and then Tom spoke.

"Well, 'cept for losin' our horses, this is goin' just about right. We actually got more to worry about from our own men than the Yankees. Let's move off this ridge and then toward the tree line. We only got a few minutes."

The two men kept a low profile stumbling their way through the thinning haze, away from the cave. Cannon balls flew overhead from both sides, crisscrossing in the sky. They really didn't want to meet up with anyone, Yank or Reb, but dressed as Yankee officers they stood a better chance of making it out on the Yankee side. In the confusion of the moment, Tom Grissom reached into his haversack and retrieved his Confederate cap, which he put on his head.

77

The Rebs were doing a good job of flanking Meade's Federals, and so Billy and Tom, to avoid the bulk of the Yank blitz, decided to increase their speed to the hard right. It would be dangerous going anywhere but they figured this was as good a bet as any.

Tom looked at his pocket watch.

"Six minutes or so to the "Yankee Surprise"." He looked back over his shoulder and was troubled by what he saw.

"They've got to draw the Yanks over the ridge faster."

During their strategy planning, they had estimated six to seven minutes to get the bulk of the Yankee army on the Rebel side of the ridge. Because the Rebs wouldn't give them any resistance up the middle, the Yanks would surely pursue and move forward in a hurry. Though the Yanks were moving toward the road as planned, they were not moving nearly fast enough. For some unknown reason, they were being cautious. At this rate the blast would kill more Rebs than Yanks and Tom was worried, really worried. He pulled his scope out and surveyed the battle trying to gain a feel for the numbers of Yanks in front of the cave. He was discouraged by what he saw.

"We've got to stop the fuse," he said. He wiped sweat and dirt from his forehead with the sleeve of his jacket.

"What?" asked Billy in disbelief, hoping he had heard his brother incorrectly.

"We're going to kill more of us than them if this thing goes off like it's supposed to in...," he looked again at his watch. "Five minutes! They need more time to draw the Yanks over the ridge."

"Tom, this is crazy. You know we can't do this. We're dressed like Yanks and the Rebs are already to the road. They'll never let us get close enough and even if we could stop it, we'll kill ourselves after we re-light. There'll only be one or two minutes left on that fuse. We don't have enough time."

"I'm sorry I got you into this, Billy. You go on. It won't take two of us...this is my move. Find Liz Robbins. Look for that heart shaped birthmark..."

A bullet whizzed through the air from an unseen gun and stopped Tom Grissom mid sentence. Billy ran to his brother's side. Catching him before he collapsed to the ground, he saw a trickle of blood running down his brother's cheek. A single small caliber bullet had found its way through the mist and struck Tom Grissom in the head. Aide-de-Camp for General Lee for less than 12 hours, 23-year-old Tom Grissom was dead, one more Confederate casualty among the mounting tens of thousands.

Billy pulled the gray cap from his brother's head and found it to have a single hole through its right side. Tom had been killed instantly, probably by friendly fire, a stray bullet among the millions flying in all directions.

Through unspeakable grief Billy screamed to the heavens.

"Nooooo!"

In an instant his mission became clear. He hoisted his brother's limp body on his back and ran back toward the burning fuse and certain death.

•••••

In stunned disbelief, the men lay silently for a moment. Tommy Fuller cried softly into his hands.

"Tommy," said Phillips. "It will be okay. I promise you. We'll help you through this. Look, you've got the best attorneys for a hundred miles around in your unit. This one's pro-bono." Fuller didn't understand.

"On us," Phillips explained. "We'll help you out, buddy. You are looking at your defense team right here."

He nodded toward Jackson, who, though less than enthusiastic, didn't show it. Jackson was not absolutely convinced of his new client's innocence.

"We've got to get back to the police at the parking lot," said Phillips. "You've got to turn yourself in, right away."

Whether fatigued or conceding to the inevitable, Tommy Fuller placed his future in the hands of a few men, brothers in arms, and they all stood together to walk through a hail of fake gunfire, back toward the waiting law enforcement authorities of Gettysburg.

As the battle raged on around them, the sky flashed with an electric sizzle, and the temperature dropped in an instant. What had been an exhilarating, historical exercise just moments earlier, had suddenly lost its appeal in light of Fuller's revelations.

"Where's a cop when you need one?" asked Phillips, scanning the battlefield and seeing only reenactors. Even the crowds seemed to have vanished, although a few civilian reenactors dotted the sidelines.

Brad Lake, silent to this point, spoke up.

"Tommy, I want you to know that I believe you completely and we'll do what we can at the paper to get the story right. I think it'll help you."

As Lake finished his sentence he spun like a marionette puppet. Crying out in pain, he grabbed his left shoulder. He pulled his hand back to reveal blood on his palm.

"I've been...shot...I think..." He collapsed to the ground.

"What the hell!?" cried out Phillips. "Are the cops shooting at us?" he asked aloud, spinning his head wildly looking for a rogue, trigger-happy cop. Jackson and Philips went to Lake's side and raised his head off the ground. He was nearly unconscious but coming around.

"Brad... Brad!.. BRAD!," yelled Phillips, gently shaking his friend.

"Come on buddy. Wake up! You'll be all right. I don't   know how it happened but you've been…I guess you've been shot."

Phillips pulled open Lake's outer jacket to reveal a bullet hole through his shirt and the soft tissue of his left shoulder. They sat Lake upright and saw that the bullet had exited his shoulder as well, but left a massive amount of tissue damage. He was bleeding from front and back. It was bad but it could have been worse.

"Okay. What do we do?" Jackson asked. "Pressure," said Phillips, "put pressure on both sides to slow the bleeding and let's get to some help!"

Lake yelled in pain as the big man squeezed the fresh wound.

The band of brothers worked their way down the ridge and watched for police. Trigger-happy or otherwise, they needed them. They knew the general direction to go and did their best to make haste. Yankee reenactors flew over the ridge from behind them in groups and clashed with Rebel troops. A big Yank came running down the hill toward them with his bayonet at chest level, intent on running one of them through. He looked at the men carrying their wounded comrade, and moved on, just as another came upon them. They all yelled, Jackson the loudest. They were particularly surprised because affixed bayonets were strictly prohibited in reenactment battles.

"Chill out, Yankee! Stow that damned bayonet. Are you friggin' crazy? We got a man wounded here. For real!"

The Yankee, not appearing to heed the truth of the situation continued his running approach, only to fall over and play dead six-feet away.

Jackson managed an impressed smile.

"Man, he looked good. Did you guys see that? That was Hollywood good. Real commitment. Put him in for MVP. They got a MVP for this thing, Mike?"

Lake was getting stronger, but was still using Jackson as a crutch. They heard a small explosion from off to their right and turned to look.

"What the…." began Phillips as a rain of mud and rock poured down upon them. Sometimes harmless air-charges are planted under loose soil and remotely detonated for special effect, but those are rare and always well planned. This had to be something else.

"Somebody's cannon explode?" asked Jackson. "This is really getting too weird. You didn't tell me about this shit, Phillips."

Mike Phillips didn't comment. He was helping the emotionally distraught and exhausted Tommy Fuller back toward Rebel lines while Jackson was doing the same for Brad Lake, the man with a bullet wound. This was all a little too real and all the men dreamed of a cold beer and a baseball game at MacAuley's. They'd had quite enough of playing army for the day.

The fighting seemed to intensify all around them, and Phillips, a veteran of dozens of reenactments, thought he'd never seen a more convincing battle. They were witnessing a perfect mix of action. It even smelled like war, with thick waves of smoke swirling around them. The battlefield was filled with the most realistic looking reenactors he'd ever seen. Many of them looked like zombies: rail thin, dirty, miserable, crazed.

"I can't believe that some psycho idiot out there is using real ammo," said Phillips. "I've read enough forensics reports and seen enough pictures to know that Brad's bullet hole was not caused by any police revolver. This had to be some nutcase shooting a Minié ball out of a Civil War musket." He paused.

"No offense, Tommy."

"None taken," Fuller offered.

"I think you may be right," managed Lake, who was coming around. "I never thought I'd become my own headline. You guys watch yoursel...."

Whiz! Crack!

The noise came from behind them and again Lake's sentence was cut short. He slipped through Jackson's grip like a sack of cement, and fell to the ground, a fatal gaping hole evident through the back of his head. The exit wound at his forehead was too gruesome to imagine. The entire front of his skull was missing, his face unidentifiable, a mass of blood, bone and brain tissue.

"My God!" Jackson screamed. "Holy shit! He's been shot again!" He looked down at the horrific sight of his comrade's mangled head and had to look away. His heart raced and he had to take a knee to keep from fainting.

"I can't believe this," he said. "Stop shooting at us you psycho mother..."

Another louder, whizzing noise came from the sky, this time whistling as it got closer, and then...blackness.

All was silent and peaceful for a moment. Jackson tasted cool, green grass in his mouth and then the ringing started. A high-pitched, painful ringing in his left ear brought him back from a semi-conscious daydream and he found himself facedown halfway back up the ridge, alone.

•••••

Not knowing what else to do, but to follow his brother's dying wish, and their shared dream of Confederate victory, Billy Grissom moved forward with new determination. He made his way back over Emmitsburg Road to the Rebel side and moved quickly in the direction of the ticking time bomb, the "Yankee Surprise."

By the time he reached the wagons he had managed to elude troops from both sides, the thickening smoke and general chaos helping in his task. At the cave's entrance, he could smell fresh gunpowder burning and knew that the fuse had to be somewhere close to finishing its work.

Frantically, he pulled brush away from the wagons and looked for the burning end of the time-fuse. When he found it, a mere two feet remained to be burned before detonation. He gently pried the still burning fuse from the detonator clay, and crushed the sizzling end under his boot heel until it was extinguished.

His brother had been right. Not nearly enough Yankees had made it into the trap yet, though just then they had started coming en masse and he hid himself in the cave with the explosives, pulling the brush in behind him, doing his best to cover up. He would wait for the right moment to replace the fuse, relight it, and finish the mission, whatever the consequences.

Billy was in shock at his beloved brother's death, but was so engrossed with the task at hand, that proper mourning lay somewhere still ahead. He checked his sidearm, an 1860 Colt Model .44 caliber revolver. It was fully loaded and ready to defend the cave.

The Yanks, sensing victory and certain Rebel defeat, were now pouring over the road, ignoring the cave completely. They had the Rebs on the run, just as the Confederates planned. The trap was working. Billy lost count of the horses and men that he could see. He could only imagine similar movement all across the half-mile expanse between Seminary
Ridge and Cemetery Ridge. He prayed that the Reb forces were pushing them to the middle. Killing a few hundred Yanks would not win this battle; massive casualties were needed in order for Lee's army to gain the upper hand.

A cannon ball landed and exploded near the cave; Billy cursed the close call. Having not seen any fellow Confederates in several minutes, he felt it was time. He couldn't risk waiting and only hoped he hadn't already waited too long. Pulling the last match from the tin in Tom's pack, he said a prayer for his brother, himself and for the cause he hoped wasn't lost. He then resumed the countdown. He'd already replaced what was left of the fuse into the clay detonator and had guessed maybe 90 seconds, or at the most, two to three minutes remained; it was hard to tell. He was ready to strike the match and run as fast as he could toward the oncoming Yanks, wearing a blue Federal cavalry jacket.

•••••

Tommy Fuller was lost to what he was sure was another psychotic break with reality, though this time, he was glad to have company. Men were being shot and killed all around him, cannon balls were exploding at his feet, and yet he was fairly sure he owned a small garage south of Gettysburg, and had an unhappy wife who worked at the local M-Mart.

"Are we in hell?" he asked Mike Phillips, in all seriousness. "Am I in hell because of what I've done? Have I dragged you guys down here with me?"

Phillips couldn't answer him. He wasn't sure. He knew something was terribly wrong, but couldn't make the pieces fit.

•••••

Billy Grissom struck the match on the steel of the wagon wheel, placed it to the remaining fuse, watched it catch and made his way a few yards from the cave, hunched over, nearly crawling. He heard men talking very near to him. A large black man in a Rebel uniform was holding his head and stumbling toward the cave. Two other Reb soldiers were close behind, one bleeding from the chin and the other stumbling behind him, shell-shocked. Two Yankee infantrymen flew over the ridge, stumbled upon the cave and investigated.

Phillips and Fuller made their way to Jackson, who was regaining his senses. Ten feet to their left, they saw the cave, which appeared to be hiding wagons. The horrific sounds of war surrounded them, as did the acrid smell of burning gunpowder and magnesium. It hung thick in the warm July air and was stifling.

"It's a bomb!" one of the Yanks yelled. "And a biggun by the looks of it. A damn Rebel trap. We've got to stop it! Put out that daggum fuse or we're all dead!"

"Hey! We need help here!" yelled Phillips. "We've got real injuries, and somebody's using us for target practice."

The two Yankees turned their attention away from the burning fuse toward the Rebs asking for their help. This distraction gave Billy Grissom just enough time to shoot them dead where they stood. Grissom looked at his injured Confederate comrades and yelled to them.

"You three! Come with me now if you want to live!"

Chapter 14

A Yankee soldier looked curiously at the three men and replaced a smoking sidearm in his holster. He peered inside the cave as if checking on something important, and then turned to his fellow Rebs.

"Are you comin'?!" he yelled.

With all they'd seen and heard in the previous twenty minutes, they didn't need to be asked twice. They stumbled past the cave entrance, to where the Yankee was standing.

"What in God's name is happening out here?" asked Phillips of the unknown Yank.

"The Ol' Man told you already," said Billy Grissom to three strangers. "Wasn't you listenin'? We're standin' on top of the world's biggest bomb. If we don't move now, and quick like, we're gonna be nothin' but ashes. Run as fast as you can, like your britches is on fire! Watch out for Yanks and don't look back."

As confused and shaken as the men were, they tended to believe this young man, who seemed to be very sure of this one thing, the need to move quickly. They followed, trying to figure out into what kind of strange dream they'd all landed. Though exhausted and injured they managed to keep up.

They had been running hard at an angle toward the woods near Cemetery Ridge for several minutes when they saw the sky light up with a blinding flash that came from behind them. A half-second later a shockwave, moving at twice the speed of sound, knocked them off their feet and before they hit the ground the deafening boom caused them to black-out.

On the ground, just less than a mile from ground zero, they were pelted by dirt embedded within an intense, but brief, windstorm traveling at several hundred miles per hour. When they dared to turn they saw a mushroom cloud and debris in the air reminding them of slow motion U.S. War Department films of nuclear tests.

The intense heat from the explosion vaporized the haze, allowing the sun to shine brightly behind the growing smoke and debris cloud, lighting up the battlefield. They had been witnesses to, and survived, the equivalent power of a 25 kilogram fission bomb, minus only the radiation.

Stumbling to their feet, they instinctively made their way to the woods fifty yards farther. Before they reached the tree-line, chunks of rock and dirt, some the size of cows, began falling all around them. Smaller projectiles of earth, a piece of a wagon wheel, even pieces of burning wood and smoking rocks assailed them, like the fire and brimstone Tommy Fuller was sure they were dodging. When an empty, smoldering wicker basket, made of what looked like part of an old-fashioned hot air balloon, crashed to the ground, the men were overcome with fear and confusion.

They had barely escaped the massive explosion, thanks to the strange reenactor. Phillips wondered if the explosion was the result of some twisted domestic terrorist? Maybe a Southern sympathizer with a screw loose. They all wondered how this could be happening? The answers, if they were ever to come, would have to wait. Survival came first.

•••••

They staggered, fell, and then crawled, on their hands and knees, through the hardwood forest, moving as far away as possible from the twisted events they knew should not be happening. This was supposed to be a battle fought with little puffs of harmless smoke, bad actors, and good-natured rivalry, between men taking a break from their everyday lives. Yet these men had witnessed, first-hand, a reality far from what their minds allowed them to believe was possible. One man was dead, a good friend, shot twice from unseen assailants. Live rounds of large caliber munitions had nearly taken off their heads, and an explosion of unimaginable power, even by modern standards, nearly blew their limbs from their bodies.

There was only one in the group who seemed to know what was going on: a reenactor, or so they thought, named Billy Grissom.

Mike Phillips caught his breath and spoke first.

"What in God's name is happening out there?"

Grissom stopped the forward movement of his rag-tag unit and looked quizzically at his charges.

"How is it you men missed the orders to retreat back after the second flare?"

"What flare? What orders? Who the hell are you?" answered Phillips, angry and frustrated.

Grissom's face flushed and he rushed to Phillips grabbing the man's uniform in a tight fist.

"I am William Grissom, Assistant to the Aide-de-camp Adjutant Tom Grissom, and, by the way, I'm the man who saved your sorry lives. Were you all sleepin' through Mornin' Parade? Who's your company commander?"

"Uhhh...Joseph DiCarlo?" answered Phillips honestly.

"Who? Look, I don't know this DiCarlo. But there's somethin' about y'all that don't add up."

Grissom stepped back, his face drawing new conclusions about the three strange Rebs he'd just led into the woods. He pulled his revolver from its holster and pointed it directly at Mike Phillips' head.

"Oh, I see now...y'all are Yankee spies...and now y'all are dead Yankee spies." He cocked back the hammer of his pistol and his eyes went cold.

"Whoa, whoa! Wait a minute," pleaded Phillips, not 100 percent sure that the Yankee was threatening with blanks, and still in role-playing mode.

"We just got separated from our company, and some nut-balls out there started using real ammo. They killed one of my best friends and almost killed us. This stupid game is over. I don't know whose idea it was to start blowing things up, but people got hurt out there. You know those two reenactors by the cave you pretended to shoot? Well, my guess is that they, and a thousand other men, got blown to bits when that bomb, or whatever it was, went off. I'm all for realism but...what the hell?"

The thick growth of the forest blocked some of the sound of the continuing battle, now just sputtering, a mile and half away. The clearest sound was that of Rebel whooping, which made its way through the thicket. An artillery barrage let loose from the Confederate line, with only a small number of Yankee guns answering. The stunned Federal forces had not been prepared, and the Rebels wasted no time taking advantage.

"You spy scum hear that out there?" asked Grissom, now smiling and waving his gun wildly. "I think we're finally winnin' this one."

"Of course you are," said Phillips, noting Grissom's Yankee uniform. "We all know the Yankees win. But they weren't supposed to win by actually killing the reenactors."

"Not the Yankees, you damn fool – The Ol' Man's Army, the ANV of the CSA. This is not my uniform. Me and my brother set this whole thing up. We were supposed to escape together through the Yankee lines," Grissom explained, still pointing his gun at Phillips.

"Look, Mr. Grissom, we just want to be left alone and get back to our cars. We have some serious problems to sort out, so let's quit the little charade and all get back to 2013, okay?"

Greg Jackson was missing nearly all of the conversation because of the ringing in his ears, but he knew it had turned bad when he saw the pistol drawn. Tommy Fuller collapsed in a heap and lay still on the forest floor. Jackson leaned over to see if Fuller was dead or dying and wasn't exactly certain. He leaned his back against a mammoth Oak. All of the men were fading under the physical and mental strain, and shock of this battle that had gone so wrong.

Billy Grissom was now as confused as his prisoners. These were strange words being spoken.

"What are you talkin' 'bout?" No one answered him.

"Re-actors? Ca..Cars? Real ammo? 2013? It don't make no sense. For starters it's 1863 and 'course they's usin' real ammo. Is there any other kind? Y'all may not be spies, but you're...I don't know what's wrong with ya."

Grissom replaced the gun to its holster, removed his cap and leaned against a tree.

Mike Phillips, the only one of the three hearing any of Grissom's words, was not about to believe the man who had been talking. He searched his mind for a rational explanation. The problem was, that in light of the last hour's occurrences, there was no rational explanation. His mind raced and he became dizzy. He frantically searched for proof of his sanity. Bits and pieces of recent memory flooded his consciousness all at once.

"I flew to New York last week," he mumbled. "I watched the ball game at MacAuley's on TV, listened to the radio this morning, spilled coffee on my laptop, drove my car here. Barack Obama is President. It is 2013. It has to be. It has to be...."

Phillips, a bit of a sci-fi fan, knew of the general concepts surrounding time warps. He knew about Ockham's Razor, the notion made popular by English philosopher and Franciscan friar, William of Ockham, that suggests that all things being equal, the simplest explanation is probably correct.

He walked a few steps toward Jackson, who was also leaning against a tree, covering his ears and working his jaw muscles in an attempt to alleviate the discomfort. Grissom took several steps nearer the men. Tommy Fuller, who struggled to his feet, backed away and stumbled on a tree root, falling and rolling down an embankment, sending leaves and debris flying through the air. In an instant Grissom pulled his revolver and fired, fearing an escape. The bullet whizzed by the standing men, and Phillips and Jackson took cover by following Fuller down the same embankment. All three rolled and landed hard with a thud. They looked up the hill, expecting to see the psychotic reenactor with his gun blazing, but saw no sign of him.

They took the opportunity to escape from, who or what, they couldn't imagine, by running deeper into the woods until they were exhausted and finally collapsed on the forest floor. With no sign of Grissom or the sounds of battle, they closed their eyes and drifted in and out of consciousness.

Chapter 15

Greg Jackson was the first to move. He spit leaves and dirt from his mouth as he came to, with no idea how long he'd been out. When he sat up, fresh blood pumped to his brain and the ringing in his ears and pain returned like a thousand, late-night Georgetown hangovers, and he cried out.

"Ahh. Shit! That hurts." He held his head in his hands.

Fuller, hearing the moaning, sat up and surveyed the scene. The sky was bright blue through the forest's canopy and the woods were still except for the rustling of his companions. All sounds of the battle had disappeared and he wondered how long they had been lying there. He remembered the Yankee reenactor they had followed out of the fog, who had shot at them. That's all he remembered. He stretched his sore muscles and started to yawn, then he, too, cried out in pain. Putting his hand to his chin, he felt dried blood and a wound caused by something he couldn't quite remember. As his memory of the day returned in bits and pieces, he started to feel dizzy again and lay back down.

Mike Phillips stirred next and opened his eyes. He, too, was not eager to start remembering the puzzling and horrifying events that had just transpired, but they came back to him, in spite of his efforts to lie peacefully. When he visualized the man with the gun pointed at his head, he sat up and looked around. There was no sign of him. He began mumbling to himself.

"What was it that crazy mother was talking about? 1863…?"

The rumbling buzz of an airplane motor drawing near was the first sound the men had heard, other than the slight breeze rustling through the trees. Soon the noise of the engine filled the air, and looking up they saw the large, gray, twin prop plane fly overhead. A sudden wave of relief filled Phillips. He had not gone crazy after all. Surely it was 2013.

"Let's get out of here, you guys. They gotta be looking for us," he said. "It will be better for you, Tommy, if we go straight to the police." He reached in his pocket and pulled out the wristwatch he'd stashed earlier and found it to be just about 11:00 a.m.

"They're probably not too far anyway. They must be searching the area."

Fuller didn't answer, but had heard Phillips, and he sat up.

"I don't think I can move," said Greg Jackson painfully. "My damn head hurts like you won't believe. When I find out who was lobbing cannon balls at us, there'll be an ass-kickin'. Brad Lake will have plenty to write about when we start litigating this mess."

Hearing Lake's name was like a slap in the face as they recalled watching their friend, Brad Lake, die after having been shot twice as they attempted to escape the mayhem. The memory was horrifying.

"Shit...Brad," Jackson said, speaking their fallen comrade's name.

"This is still so screwed up I can't think straight," complained Phillips. "But we won't get any answers out here in the woods. Let's head back."

With some difficulty the three men got to their feet and started walking back in the direction of the open field they'd just left. As they neared the edge of the forest, the clear day presented itself. Greg Jackson tripped on something and looked down to find half a wagon wheel covered in moss and leaves, barely visible.

"That's old." he thought to himself, and continued walking.

"Battle's over," said Fuller, the first words he'd spoken since before passing out by the tree.

"Tommy. You know they're going to arrest you, cuff you and take you away, right?" asked Phillips.

Tommy sighed. "Yeah."

"And you know we're with you the whole way. We'll try to get bail set immediately and have you out of jail as fast as possible. I also recommend that Susan leave the house, if she hasn't already. This thing could turn into a media circus, and neither of you want to be in that neighborhood. Does she have somewhere she can go?"

"No, not really. Well...yeah," he answered. "Her grandfather's got a little hunting cabin out in the country, but it ain't much."

They walked on for another half-mile and were standing at the battlefield's edge, wondering where everybody was. One hundred thousand people don't just disappear in 20 minutes, and this was an all-day anniversary event, scheduled to go well into the night. While the missing reenactors and spectators was puzzling, they weren't the only thing missing. They stared in disbelief at the landscape ahead of them.

Emmitsburg Road, a mile off in the distance, now had a giant piece of itself missing. The explosion they had witnessed had changed the topography of this historic Civil War site forever.

"Look at that..." Phillips exclaimed.

"I can't believe it," added Jackson. "Who's gonna pay for that?"

"Damn." Was all Tommy Fuller could muster.

"It must be later than 11," said Jackson. "There's not a soul around here. I wonder how long we lay in that forest. And what happened to that crazy Yank reenactor."

"We were only out there for twenty minutes. This whole damn thing only started an hour ago," said Phillips angrily. "And he wasn't a Yankee. He claimed to be a Reb on some special mission to...well, do that," he said, pointing to the half-mile wide gap in what was once Emmitsburg Road.

The men walked silently for 10 minutes toward the Park entrance and were now within a few hundred yards of the hole blown out of the earth.

"Where's all the...ground?" asked Jackson. "You know, all the dirt and rocks that were raining down on us?"

"Good question," said Phillips. "Maybe that's part of it," he added, pointing to a large boulder the size of a Volkswagen Bug sitting in the middle of the field.

They walked to the large stone and stood, baffled. Large tufts of long grass were growing from under it and the neatly manicured grass surrounding it had been recently mowed. They circled the boulder and were shocked at what they saw. Graffiti. Spray-painted slogans. 'Confederate States 4-ever!' Swastikas. 'United States Now!' Kaffirs back to Africa!' There were more slogans they couldn't read, obscured by time and weather. Some had been crossed through and replaced with other remarks, all of which were confusing.

"'Kaffir' is a South African word, roughly translated "Nigger," said Jackson. "Who would use 'Kaffir' here in Pennsylvania?"

"I don't know, Greg," said Phillips. "This is really starting to freak me out."

As they reached the edge of the crater left by the detonation, fear and confusion took a firm hold. Instead of freshly exposed earth and smoldering debris, they found lush grass and well-worn foot paths. The crater itself was oblong, about three quarters of a mile wide from end to end and a half-mile wide in the middle. But even stranger, the crater was filled with water. A mother duck and nine ducklings paddled lazily at its center, dunking for fish.

"Weren't we just...standing here?" asked Tommy Fuller.

"What the hell?" asked Phillips in disbelief, the panicky feeling he'd felt earlier, returning in earnest.

They circled around the rim of the crater toward a large stone monument, a historical marker. These were common at Gettysburg National Military Park. But this one they'd never seen before. Atop the base was a 30-foot bronze statue of a figure. Though frightened as to what it may reveal, they made their way to its front. Mike Phillips read aloud what they all could plainly see, but not believe.

ON THIS HALLOWED GROUND, ON THE DAY OF OUR LORD JULY 3rd, 1863, THE CONFEDERATE STATES OF AMERICA WON A DECISIVE VICTORY OVER THE FEDERAL TROOPS OF THE UNITED STATES OF AMERICA. THIS BATTLE OF GETTYSBURG TOOK THE LIVES OF 13,000 ENEMY U.S. FEDERAL TROOPS AND 2,305 CONFEDERATE SOLDIERS. FOUR MONTHS LATER, ON NOVEMBER 4TH, 1863, THE UNITED STATES OF AMERICA FORMALLY ENDED ITS TYRANNICAL ATTACK ON THE INDEPENDENT SOUTHERN STATES OF THE CONFEDERACY, TRANSFERRED DEED OF THE TOWN OF GETTYSBURG AND ITS SURROUNDING COUNTIES TO THE CONFEDERATE STATE OF MARYLAND, THUS ENDING THE WAR BETWEEN THE STATES, AND FIRMLY AND IRREVOCABLY ESTABLISHING THE CONFEDERATED STATES OF AMERICA. LONG LIVE FREEDOM FROM TYRANNY!

Next to these strange words another historical marker added a comment equally confusing.

"We thank God for our victory here and our victory against oppression. May all the fair people of the Confederate States Of America live in peace from this day forward." - Jefferson Davis, President, C.S.A. 1863-1875

The three men looked at one another in disbelief, and then at the towering figure of Davis. "This can't be happening," said Jackson. "Is this some sick joke?"

"I don't...know. I don't understand," said Phillips.

There was little to be done to stem the rising sense of fear and panic all three men were feeling, as they tried to make sense of the twisted reality that lay before them. Another airplane flew overhead. A few people and cars could now be seen in the distance, near the park entrance.

As the men stood dumbfounded, the sun shone on them, a light breeze blew in their faces, and yet, they were facing an impossibility that must be a dream, but clearly was not. The conclusions they were drawing were too bizarre to speak aloud, yet Mike Philips dared.

"If this were some elaborate terrorist plot or sick joke, as you said, Greg, that took place an hour ago, then where are the police and the FBI? And how do you explain this monument that looks to be 150 years old? I don't know what's happened here...but based on what we're all plainly seeing. I think....I think I'm gonna be sick." He couldn't finish his thought. Tommy Fuller attempted to put into words their worst fears.

"You think history's… been changed? And somehow we're not in the same place we were when we started this awful fucking day?"

No one answered. "This just isn't right," said Phillips, breaking the silence. He looked around, hoping to see anything that might give him reason to think he hadn't gone mad. "Where the hell are we?"

"Listen to what you're saying." Jackson said, agitated, refusing to even contemplate what was being suggested.

"Have you guys lost your minds? Some neo-Confederate, white supremacist, Civil War freaks used today to make some ridiculous point and killed who knows how many in the process. Let's just get back to our cars, and get the hell back to town. We'll find the police and find out what really happened out here."

"We are NOT goddamn *'time travelers'*."

•••••

Tommy Fuller didn't enjoy the prospect of finding the police he'd been running from all morning, but moving from that spot was the one thing the men could agree on. They continued forward toward the parking lot and answers they hoped they could grasp.

The sun was now high in the sky and they knew from Phillips' watch, that just about an hour had passed since the ill-fated, 10:00 a.m. reenactment had begun. They walked silently for the next mile, until they reached the edge of the park. They closed in on a group of people they hoped were reenactor civilians, or locals with the answers they so needed.

An elderly man was bouncing a baby girl on his knee and cooing to her, while a smiling woman in her thirties looked on. Philips walked closer to them and saw their countenance change, as his bloodied and battered troops followed close behind.

"Excuse me?" Phillips asked. "Were you here earlier for the reenactment?"

The civilians looked confused and didn't answer. "Please don't think I'm crazy," said Phillips, "but…what is today's date."

The old man cleared his throat. "July tenth," he answered in an unusually strong, southern drawl.

"Oh my Lord," said Phillips. "Pardon me. What year?"

"What year?" the old man asked, looking as bewildered as the man asking the question. The woman took three quick steps toward her child, and quickly, but calmly, took the girl into her arms and backed away.

"Twenty-thirteen," he answered, never removing his gaze from the three men. "Are you fellas all right? Look like y'all seen ghosts."

93

"Was there a Civil War reenactment here earlier today?" asked Phillips hopefully.

"Naw. They done away with them things years ago, illegal now, like all public gatherings. You best not get caught out here playing war with your colored boy. They'll have a fit. You know betteran 'at."

Jackson would have flushed with anger, except he was so dumbstruck at the old man's revelations that he was speechless. Phillips trembled and could only manage a nod. He motioned to his companions in this unfolding nightmare and they followed.

They walked toward the parking lot where two or three cars were all that were left from the thousands they had seen hours earlier. The gentle babbling of a fountain reminded them they had not had water for hours, and their thirst called.

It looked as if a small classic car club had been meeting as all they saw were vehicles that looked to be 1930s or 1940s models. The men looked toward the field where they expected their own cars to be, but found only green grass.

"Where's my car?" asked Jackson to the air. "Where's my frickin' Beemer? I'll be damned. Did they tow our cars? Those sonsofbitches."

"Don't you mean 'Where's the parking lot'? It was five times this size an hour ago," said Phillips. "You don't get it, do you Greg? We're not home. I don't know where we are, but this is not the same place we knew when we woke up this morning."

"No," said Jackson. "I don't believe it."

"Don't or won't believe?" asked Phillips. No answer came. "I don't know how or why…but face it, something happened to us, or to the world, or…who knows…?"

Jackson immediately thought of his family, his mother back in D.C. and sister in Oakland, California.

"I've got to get to a phone," Jackson yelled, panic-stricken. He began to run, until the pounding in his head slowed him.

"We've got to stick together," Phillips pleaded with his friend, running to catch him. "Let's get something to drink, clean up some, and try to get into town. There must still be a town. These people came from somewhere," he said glancing at the bewildered onlookers. "We'll find a phone there, maybe."

They re-grouped. Fuller and Jackson followed Phillips toward the public bathrooms across the parking lot. From a distance a young man and woman in their late teens or twenties, stood by a sedan, and looked curiously at the three men. The vehicle was as large as a tank, had the big rounded fenders, and the enormous, round headlights of cars from the '40s. The couple seemed dwarfed by its over-all size. They got in their car and watched the men as they approached the small brick building with a sign that simply read: *Public Facility*.

Two drinking fountains jutted out from the outside wall, and as the men approached to quench their parched throats they missed the smaller brass plaques above each fountain. While Fuller and Phillips simultaneously took long, satisfying drinks, Greg Jackson had the opportunity to see what the others had missed.

"Oh my God." He spoke aloud pointing to the signs. "This is a bigger nightmare than you realize." Above each of the fountains was a legal admonition "White Only" and "Colored Only."

Fuller and Phillips stopped their drinking long enough to look in the direction of Jackson's pointing finger.

"Oh shit," Phillips concurred, when he read the plaques. Tommy Fuller was silent.

They filled their bellies with much-needed water. Jackson made a special point to use the "Whites Only" fountain, before the three men cleaned up as best they could, and walked back toward the parking lot. All the cars were gone, except for that of the young couple. The teens, now sitting in their car, had taken notice of the three strangers and sat, carefully watching.

With few other options, Phillips approached the car and hoped he'd get more answers and some help for his beleaguered group. The men stayed back as Phillips drew nearer. The young man cautiously rolled up the window half way. Phillips spoke. "Hey folks." He forced a smile. "Any chance on catching a ride into town with you? Our cars seem to be... missing."

Tommy Fuller thought about the start of his day and suddenly remembered that his truck wasn't missing from the parking lot. He'd abandoned it earlier, down a twenty-foot embankment, while being chased by the Pennsylvania State Police.

Greg Jackson would have normally been outraged at the thought of someone stealing or towing his $60,000 BMW, but he had other concerns at the moment. If history had changed, what would he find in this new reality? His first tastes of this place gave him reason for real concern.

The teen in the old car turned toward the girl whose head was wrapped in a pretty, yellow scarf, worn the way women of the thirties might, tied under the chin, and while she looked nervous about the prospect of allowing these strange men into their vehicle, shook her head yes, giving permission.

Phillips motioned to the others and then attempted to open the back door of the enormous automobile. He lost his balance and almost fell, when to his surprise the door opened backward, a "suicide door." The three men sat comfortably, side by side, in the backseat, and could've fit another one or two, had it been necessary. The young man turned the key and the big car rumbled to life. As he wheeled the vehicle around and pointed it toward the Park gate, he asked carefully and suspiciously,

"Where y'all headed?"

The men looked at each other and Phillips spoke. "Ahh MacAuley's Tavern."

"I don't know that one," the young man said. "Where's it at?"

"Front Street at Armory Square."

"Well, I do know where that is. I live up the street from there." The men felt hopeful for the first time since the ordeal began, until the driver continued.

"But there ain't no MacAuley's there. It's a service station. Ahh….Fuller's Auto."

Tommy Fuller spoke nervously. "Who owns that, do you know?"

"Yeah, sure. We know 'em good. The twins. Bobby and Billy Fuller. Good mechanics. They keep this hunk a junk running. Real nice fellas."

"They're my uncles," said Tommy, to no one in particular. The driver looked at him through his rearview mirror. "…only my uncles can't own a garage," he said quietly. "They've been dead for 11 years."

No one spoke as the car wheeled out of the parking lot onto Rt. 97 and they picked up speed, heading toward downtown, an urban center they would barely recognize, filled with people who shouldn't be there, and missing many who should.

As the car left the parking lot, Tommy gazed out the window and saw a giant oak tree half a mile ahead. It stuck with him, a peculiar vision, coaxing a memory from the not too distant past. As they approached the tree, he yelled, breaking the silence and startling everyone in the car. "Stop! Wait a minute! Stop here, please…just for a second."

The driver applied the brakes hard and the big vehicle slowed, drifting just past the mighty oak.

Fuller looked at Jackson and Phillips. "This is where I had my…umm… accident this morning. My truck slid down the embankment, right here, just in front of this tree. I remember it clearly. Let me look."

"Oh, you poor man. You were in an automobile accident this morning?" the attractive girl in the front seat turned to ask Tommy, sounding sincere. These were her first words since meeting the strangers and she sprang to life on the news of Fuller's misfortune. Fuller couldn't answer her immediately, because with his first good look at the young woman, he gasped at her likeness to his wife, Susan. She looked at him, waiting for an answer. The driver turned to look at Tommy, and he was again startled at what he saw. The boy driving, who was also looking very familiar, had been a groomsman in his wedding, two years earlier. He was the clone of Susan's brother, Joseph.

Phillips and Jackson hadn't known Susan or Joseph and didn't make the same connection. They looked at each other, both sharing the unspoken concern about Fuller and another possible breakdown. But in the last hour, they couldn't be sure of anything. They felt as if they had all fallen from the sky and landed in this strange, new world together.

The car stopped. Tommy shook off the shock of seeing Susan's doppelganger and was the first to jump out. He ran up and over the small hill leading down to the embankment and as his companions followed they heard him cry out. "It's here! My truck is here!"

•••••

Jackson and Phillips jumped out after him and started toward the embankment when they heard car doors slam and the big vehicle spin its tires, leaving in a hurry. They turned to see their frightened driver, and the girl he was with, speed down the road.

"Well, there goes our ride," said Jackson. "I guess we were too much for them."

"Shit," said Phillips as he watched the car pull out of sight.

At the edge of the road, they looked down the embankment to find Tommy Fuller circling his 1995 Nissan pick up truck. It was banged up badly, but it was the first thing that looked normal in a sea of abnormal.

"Fuller," yelled Jackson down the hill, more annoyed at losing their ride than anything else. "Is this really your truck?"

"I can't explain it," he answered, "but somehow, yes. This is my truck."

•••••

Clouds had appeared and the July day was turning unseasonably cool, as light drizzle fell. Walking to town dressed like leftover Civil War lunatics was not a pleasant prospect, nor was death by hypothermia in the damp coldness. Another ride was not likely, as the young couple seemed to be the last to leave the park. The now soaked reenactors, dripping, circled the truck, their only link to the place they'd known hours earlier, which seemed to have vanished.

Beyond explanation in this time-warped world, Tommy Fuller's 1995 Nissan pick up truck sat silently. Obviously battered from multiple collisions, the truck, otherwise, was as Tommy had left it. The passenger door was crumpled and jammed closed, but after some doing, Jackson pulled the driver's door open with a loud, metallic clank. The dome light went on and the chime under the dash began ringing, signaling keys still left in the ignition.

"Maybe the radio works," said Phillips. "Let's get in."

In contrast to their last ride, the three men barely fit in the only seat of the little truck. Jackson and Phillips were wedged together uncomfortably on the passengers side, the cab made even smaller than usual, courtesy of

97

the Pennsylvania Highway Patrol's 60-mile- an-hour side impact. Fuller sat in the driver's seat. He turned the key and the vehicle sprang to life. They looked at each other, pleasantly surprised. Although they knew the truck was not drivable, they hoped to rest for a while and think through their predicament. Fuller adjusted the heater control and in seconds air was gushing out of the vents, drying them.

"I think the radiator's cracked, so it won't run for long like this. It'll overheat soon," he said.

Phillips reached for the control knob of the radio, turned it with a click and loud static filled the cab of the truck. He turned the volume down and began a slow manual search for a radio station. Fuller searched the floor behind the front seat and produced with great satisfaction a small bottle of *STOP THE LEAK- RADIATOR FIXATIVE*.

"A good mechanic, driving an old car, never travels without this stuff," he said, examining the bottle like it was a fine, vintage wine. He hopped out of the truck, pried open the hood, with some difficulty, fiddled with the radiator cap, and emptied the powdery, metallic contents of the bottle into the now steaming, green blood of the cooling system. Fuller re-sealed the radiator, returned to the cab of the truck. He looked at Phillips who had finally found an AM radio station and was listening keenly, open-mouthed.

"...now in international news...President Calvin Ramsbottom today announced that new talks would begin with the Federated States Of America, addressing the increasing violence along the borders of the two nations, in hopes of finding ways to quell the recent spate of terrorist attacks by rival factions. He decried the recent attacks, in both Richmond and Washington, that each killed close to 50 people."

The news anchor paused and the unrecognized voice of Ramsbottom rattled the speakers in the little truck.

"My fellow Confederates, we have known heartache and trouble since the founding of our nation 150 years ago, yet, have held strong in the face of these difficulties, repelling enemies from abroad and from within. It is only through the strengthening of our land and sea borders that we can be assured of our way of life. We will prevent those who would wish to re-ignite old grievances by building stronger and more secure walls between the continually aggressive North and our own Confederated States. We will work to uphold apartheid and our way of life, while assisting those members of our society who need our help. And we will work to prevent further erosion of our colored workforce, through the ending of all emigration from the Confederated States, except by special, governmental authorization."

With the pre-recorded speech over, the news anchor continued:

"Earlier today an explosion in the courtroom of the Confederate States Supreme Court in Richmond, left 40 dead, including fourteen troops of the Confederate Guard. Two Justices were wounded, but are said to be in stable condition. The Freedom Fighters, a reunification group, claimed responsibility for the suicide attack and said the action was 'in retaliation for the June 25th unanimous vote to uphold Indentured Servitude for all colored peoples working for the Agriculture Department.' The controversial vote took place after concessions had been made between President Ramsbottom and the Federated President, Donald Trump. President Trump has promised stepped up efforts to eradicate the Freedom Fighters if the Confederated States would move toward improving their human rights record."

The anchor paused again and President Trump spoke.

"With the abolition of slavery nearly 125 years ago, little additional progress has been made by the CSA in Human Rights. While we find violence an illegal, counterproductive, and reprehensible act, we understand the frustration of those who are committed to protecting the freedoms citizens of the Federated States of America enjoy and who are committed to exporting those ideals to Nations where freedoms are denied."

The news anchor moved on to other stories, including an ominous weather report, but the men had stopped listening.

The efficient heater of the Nissan could not dispel the unseasonable cold creeping into the souls of these reluctant warriors who were now faced with the absolute truth of their arrival in an alternate and altogether unpleasant reality.

Phillips spun the knob again and found music. A mournful song about "love and struggle" came from the sweet, sad voice of a woman accompanied by steel guitar and piano. The men sat silently and one by one nodded off.

•••••

Greg Jackson awoke with a start, sitting up and hitting his head on the roof of the truck.

"Ouch, shit!" he said, damning his big frame and the truck's tiny interior.

Phillips awoke quickly and noticed the clock on the radio read 8 p.m.; they had slept for hours. The engine was still running. Fuller was thankful they'd cracked open windows or they would have all probably been asphyxiated.

"I thought I heard something outside," said Jackson. "It woke me up, whatever it was."

Fuller, also now awake, reached to the ignition, turning the motor off. The radio went dead with the motor. They sat still in the silence and the darkness, with only the sounds of an approaching summer storm, and their breathing.

Outside a twig cracked and leaves rustled.

"Shhh," said Jackson, though no one was making any noise.

They heard voices. They estimated that maybe two or three people were no farther than 50 feet away, and seemed to be unaware of them hidden in the tall weeds.

"They disappeared over the hill and went this way," said one of the voices.

"Then we took off," the voice continued. "They scared the hell out of us."

"Speak for yourself," said an unseen girl. "I wanted to find out who they were."

The three men huddled in the truck and recognized the voices as having come from their reluctant, and short-lived, transport hosts from earlier that day.

Fuller whispered with concern. "They're back for us. They brought somebody with them and we're screwed."

"Shhh," said Phillips, still listening to the conversation, now a bit louder.

"Whacha pick 'em up for anyway?" asked a third, new voice with a Brooklyn, New York, accent and delivery as thick as any young mob boss.

"They looked wounded... and kinda confused," said the younger male voice.

"Helpless," said the girl. "They were draggin' themselves around, bloodied up, barely walking. Looked like they were wearing old Civil War uniforms. I guess they didn't look like they could hurt us. And then the colored guy....he drinks from the Whites Only fountain. So, we figured, you know, maybe they're FF."

"FF?" said the kid with the heavy accent. "They ain't no Freedom Fighters."

"Anyway, they sounded like Yankees," said the boy. "Especially the Negro guy, but they started talking some crazy shit about ghosts, and dead uncles, and car wrecks, and something called a Knee-sahn. The one guy made us stop the car, and they got out. Sis and I freaked out and...well, we just took off."

Still stuffed inside Fuller's truck, the men were hearing bits and pieces of the nearby conversation.

"I think they're all just kids," whispered Jackson. "But they might still be able to help us."

"Help us to do what?" whispered Phillips, his frustration growing. "We don't even know where, or when, we are."

The beam of a flashlight sliced through the growing darkness, momentarily illuminating the cab of the truck.

"What's that over there? I saw a flash, like glass," said the kid from Brooklyn. "Shine ya light over there again."

The beam was transfixed on the side window of the truck, shining directly into Greg Jackson's face. The three men inside froze as the teenagers moved closer. The kids rustled through the tall grass and saw the small, strange vehicle. When Jackson turned his head directly at the onlookers and smiled broadly, the kids screamed in unison, threw the flashlight in the air and knocked each other over trying to get away from this ghost in the truck.

Not wanting to lose them again, Jackson pulled on the door handle trying to get out of the crumpled vehicle with no success. He hip-checked the door, with all of his weight, and it gave. He yelled through the partially open door while squeezing his large frame through an opening two times too small.

"Wait! Help us! Please!" he pleaded to the darkness. He could hear them yelling and trying to get through the thicket back to the road and he ran in their direction. Phillips and Fuller were soon close behind and had picked up the dropped flashlight. Jackson was gaining ground on the teenagers and again begged for them to stop.

"You kids! Please stop." He could see in the fading twilight that they had just about made their way to the top of the embankment and were almost at their car.

With one last plea in a moment of inspiration and desperation Jackson yelled out.

"We're Freedom Fighters!"

•••••

With the distant thunder and dark clouds rolling closer, and a cool wind picking up, all the men could see was the blackened silhouettes of the teenagers, who, for the moment had stopped. Jackson could hear them talking quietly.

"That was risky," said Phillips, climbing the embankment with his comrades. "Clever, but risky."

"You got any better ideas, boss?"

"No, not really," said Phillips. "Let's go see if we've made any friends tonight. Hey, at least they speak English."

"What did you expect?" asked Jackson

"I don't know…maybe Martian?"

Almost to the top of the embankment, they could hear the kids talking in hushed tones as they stood by their car. They looked nervous, but they didn't seem to be going anywhere. When the men reached the top, they too, were out of breath, giving the youths a chance to speak first.

"Who are you guys?" asked the young driver from earlier in the day. Phillips held up his finger, asking for one more moment to breathe before talking. He put his hands on his knees and took two long, deep breaths.

"My brother thinks you guys really are Freedom Fighters," said the girl. Tommy Fuller was again astonished just looking at her. This young woman and his wife were more alike than twins; they were clones of one another.

"We're in big trouble," Phillips finally managed. He knew they wouldn't believe the truth. He didn't even believe the truth, so he tried a new tack.

"Like my friend said, we're Freedom Fighters. And we're stuck here....ahh....behind enemy lines." It sounded good to him, but the kids were less than convinced. Brooklyn spoke up.

"If you're FF, like you say. Prove it."

Phillips wasn't sure if he was supposed to know some secret handshake or password so he switched gears, again.

"Look, guys. We're...FF alright," the words were strange to him and he was faltering. "But we're kinda like *Lone Rangers* out here." They looked confused. They'd never heard of the Lone Ranger. "We're doing our own thing, apart from the "official" FF." He made air quotes with his two fingers around the word "official" and the kids looked even more suspiciously at the stranger making strange gestures. "We're all from up north. I'm from New York." Then he pointed to Jackson. "He's from D.C., and..." he pointed to Fuller and was stuck.

"I used to live here," Fuller added.

"Right," Phillips agreed. "He... used to live here, ahh, and we got, um.... diverted."

Jackson spoke and the kids looked surprised to hear him speak up. It was very unusual to hear conversation from such an unreserved and confident black man. The "coloreds" they knew always hung their heads and avoided conversations with white people. "We were on a mission to...," Jackson struggled for the right words.

"Undermine the government," added Phillips. It was a bad, vague lie that he didn't think sounded believable.

"We've got to get to D.C.," said Jackson. And that he said with sincerity, because he really meant it. He held on to a grain of hope. Maybe things were normal in the Nation's capitol. Maybe he could look up old friends, have dinner with his mother, call his sister. Maybe things were sane in D.C.

The two boys looked at each other and finally Brooklyn spoke up.

"Okay, come on. We work for a guy. We got a place."

The three teens piled in the front of the car, and the men in back. They drove silently for a mile or more, until Tommy Fuller's curiosity got the better of him.

"What year is this Ford? I don't remember them ever having suicide doors."

The kids gave each other that look that said, silently, "Where did these idiots come from?"

"This old thing?" asked Brooklyn, proudly. "It ain't a four...whatever you said...but she's a '91."

It was now the men's turn to share quizzical looks.

"A 1991?" asked Fuller. The girl giggled and put her hand to her mouth.

The driver glanced at Tommy through the rearview mirror. "Yeaaahhh," he said, drawing out the word. "A 1991. D'ja think it was an 1891?" The teens chuckled and the car went quiet.

"I bet your friends from New York and D.C. have some hot machines," said the younger boy.

"Those cars from Detroit...nice equipment. Too bad they're outlawed here."

The car went silent until the driver added; "If they ain't made in Nashville, we don't drive em."

Phillips worried about how they'd keep up the charade in this chaotic world of which they seemed to know less and less. They were better off keeping their mouths shut, and he shot Fuller a glance that made the point.

The girl spoke. "You know, we don't even know your names. "I'm Suzanne." She held her hand out over the back of the seat and hung it in the air in front of Tommy Fuller, who sat paralyzed.

"Ahh, this is Tommy Fuller," Phillips said, rescuing him. "I'm Mike Phillips and this is Greg Jackson."

The young Freedom Fighters in the front seat assumed these were aliases, but made no mention.

"Well, I'm Suzanne Roberts, this is my brother Joey, and this is...our friend...Anthony." The kid with the Brooklyn accent looked sharply at Suzanne and then back to the road, shaking his head.

Joey and Suzanne seemed the most affable of the three. The men were not surprised that when the youngest, Joey, spoke, Anthony seemed even more annoyed.

"We're kinda new at this, too," said Joey. "We've helped on a couple of raids and done some surveillance and stuff. You know the big hit down in Richmond today? We met the brother of the bomber. A real idiot if you ask me."

"Shut your pie hole, Joey!" said Anthony.

"Geeze...I was just tellin' em..."

"Too much. Too damn much!"

They drove on in silence for another few minutes. Out of the side window, the men could see houses that they recognized, and the old warehouse districts on the outskirts of town. And while most of the streets and houses looked pretty much as they should, the businesses were either not there or were all wrong. Where were all the convenience stores, factory outlets, and gas stations? The motels? The 16-screen Cineplex? The town looked both familiar and foreign, and they found it unsettling.

The driver turned left on Sullivan Ave., the street on which Greg Jackson lived, and it was now his turn to ask for the car to be stopped.

"Anthony. Pull over here. Right here!" he insisted. Anthony slowed the car to a stop.

"This is my place. Right here. 341 Sullivan Ave."

He started to get out of the car when Anthony reached over the back seat and took a firm hold of Jackson's forearm.

"Not a good idea," said Brooklyn, looking nervously in the rear view mirror.

"You grabbing my arm is what's not a good idea," seethed Jackson. He couldn't believe a kid half his age and half his size would grab him like that, and he shook his arm free of the boy's grip.

Brooklyn spoke again.

"I don't know what you guys are up to, who you are, or where you're from, but I am not gonna let you jeopardize our cell and blow our cover. We got important work to do, starting with finding out just who the hell you really are." He pulled a black .45 caliber revolver from a hidden holster and held the barrel three inches from Jackson's face.

"You're not getting out here. We're going to the safe house right now." At that moment, Anthony, the driver with the Brooklyn accent, was calling the shots, and Jackson settled back in his seat, watching his apartment disappear behind him as the car rumbled down Sullivan Avenue.

Flashes of distant lightening, illuminated the poorly lit streets, and a loud crack signified the storm was getting closer.

"So what's the real story here, gentlemen?" asked Anthony, acting tough and waving his gun in the general direction of all three men. "What's with the costumes? Where you been? Where you going? Hows 'bout some answers?"

Anthony was acting like a guy who'd seen too many movies, but he was unquestionably the group's leader. He'd taken a more intense interest in his guests, especially after Jackson's move to exit the car, a move that, had Jackson accomplished, would probably have gotten him shot by the police, or Anthony, or both.

"It's a long story," said Phillips rubbing his temples. "We can't tell you, yet. But we will. I promise. And we're on your team. Please believe that. Can you just get us to a safe place to sleep tonight and some food?

We haven't eaten all day."

"We have a safe place for you," said Brooklyn. In fact, we're almost there. You three get down on the floor of the car until I tell ya it's okay to get up."

The men reluctantly jostled into position, but found it relatively easy to accommodate the request in the roomy, oversized automobile. They felt the car take several turns. Lefts, rights, some sharp, some gradual, and they drove on for another five minutes, until the car stopped.

"Stay put," said Anthony, while he and Joey got out of the car. They heard a garage door open and Joey returned to the big car, easing it into the garage. Anthony holstered his pistol and opened the car door.

"We're home," he said with a fake smile.

"Bullshit," muttered Jackson. "My home is back at 341 Sullivan Avenue."

The men climbed over each other and made their way out of the car, to stand in a dimly lit two-car garage, with no windows.

"What is your deal with Sullivan Ave.?" asked Anthony. "Surely you know that's a whites-only neighborhood?"

"Of course, I do," said Jackson, incensed. "But that doesn't mean I don't live there."

"Trust me. You don't live there. They'd shoot you on sight for walking down the sidewalk without your Redcap."

"My what?"

"Your Redcap. You know…with your ID? The one you wear on your head so they don't hang you."

Jackson looked stunned. The three hosts looked even more stunned.

"Well, I know you're not Con-feds," said Anthony. "A loose Kaffir, like you, wouldn't last two minutes out there. So just who the hell are you guys? It's like you're from a different planet."

Joey and Suzanne walked to an interior door and Anthony motioned for the three men to follow while he brought up the rear. They walked through a small hallway, and down a flight of stairs to a furnished basement.

One large room was divided into different sections. In one corner sat a large table, sturdy-looking and well worn. Eight mismatched chairs were tucked neatly underneath. Next to it sat an old gas stove, with the white porcelain chipped off in so many places, it looked like a spotted Dalmatian. An old refrigerator stood to the right, three feet shorter than the one Tommy Fuller had pulled a Coke out of at his home earlier that day. A variety of dressers and chests filled up other wall space and in the middle of the room sat a large, not too attractive sofa, covered by a slipcover, probably not much better looking than that thing it was covering.

An enormous, antique radio stood against the wall in front of the sofa, in the spot where a TV might sit. The only door, other than at the top of the stairs, led to a small bathroom, which had a shower stall, toilet, and sink. In the darkest corner of the room, they noticed a large desk, with an old shortwave radio. Scattered across the surface of the desk were stacks of paper, a cup of pencils and pens, a desk lamp, world globe, coffee cup, and an old, rotary-styled telephone. While the room took on an air of 1940s poverty, it was what they saw tacked to the wall above the desk that took their breath away.

Anthony saw the men staring and he pulled a chain attached to an iron floor lamp, improving the room's light. There it stood, in full color. Eight feet wide, five feet tall, an almost perfect map of the North American continent, with what should have been the United States of America in its center, Mexico below it, and Canada above it.

The shape of the continent looked right, but upon closer examination, they found things that made their blood run cold. Where were Texas and New Mexico? The strange map said that particular real estate now belonged to the Mexican government. California, Nevada, Utah, everything west of the Rocky Mountains was labeled *New Spain.* Alaska apparently still belonged to the Russians, or Canada; it was unclear. The Hawaiian Islands were nowhere to be seen.

As disturbing as those revelations were, the other borders drawn in the map were even more disconcerting, borders that flew in the face of history.

The Missouri Compromise of 1836, that had established a boundary between the southern slave states and the free states of the North, seemed to have become a permanent, national border. The border was once erroneously referred to as the Mason-Dixon Line because it included surveyors' Mason and Dixon's short, 244-mile stretch along its eastern-most portion.

The men understood this history, but what they couldn't comprehend was the establishment of a new line that picked up at the Mississippi river and proceeded all the way to the Rocky Mountains. Pennsylvania had a notch cut out of its perfectly straight southern border surrounding Gettysburg. The borough, and the surrounding county, now appeared to be annexed by the State of Maryland, a Southern state, part of the C.S.A. A thick, black, international border bisected what should have been the lower 48 contiguous states.

The strange border seemed to be a permanent feature of this new North American map, the top half highlighted in bold, black letters *The Federated States Of America,* the bottom half, *The Confederate States Of America.* The three dazed men looked at one another and now knew for certain they were not in a place they'd ever before been.

Suzanne had been busying herself with food and had sausages grilling on the stove before the men remembered they were hungry. Bottles of Coca-Cola had been opened and offered, and the group was settling around the big dining room table. The Cokes were a bit different from the ones they were used to, but mostly had the same look and taste, except for an oval logo off to the side of the bottle that read "Extra C."

They were grateful for the drinks and looking forward to the food; as good smells now permeated the room. Tommy and Suzanne stole glances at one another, though they did not speak. As they sipped their Cokes quietly, the men were curious about their location; a place that had been referred to as a "safe house." As curious as they were, they didn't ask any questions for fear they would have to start answering their own impossible questions, yet, there was some comfort in the place, and they hoped some safety, too.

The filthy uniforms the men were wearing stunk of sulfur, saltpeter, smoke, and real war. Suzanne had taken notice and walked to a large cedar chest, opening it to rummage through stacks of men's clothing. She produced three pairs of jeans, Levis, holding them out and mentally sizing up the intended wearers. She went to a closet and did the same with three shirts. Joey and Anthony watched, but didn't comment. She went to the men with her arms loaded and distributed the bundles of folded clothing before returning to the stove.

"You can change into these," she said. "They're clean. You can wash up in there." With a pair of kitchen tongs, she pointed to the bathroom, and returned her attention to the stove.

Phillips thanked her. "This is fantastic. It's like the Salvation Army has come to rescue us," he said, trying to lighten the mood.

"The Salvation Army?" she asked. "Are they part of the FF?"

"No, no…never mind. Not important."

"We have lots of…. visitors," she said, hesitating, looking at Joey and Anthony, a bit nervously, as if she might be saying too much. "So we always have plenty of fresh clothes on hand."

The men didn't understand, but were delighted to get out of the all-too realistic costumes of the Confederacy and into clean clothes. Levi's jeans, long sleeve shirts, and Coke-a-Cola hadn't changed too much, and for that they were appreciative. One by one they entered the bathroom, stepped into a hot shower, and into clean clothing, feeling much better physically, even if they were losing ground mentally.

They sat back at the table refreshed, famished, and more confused than ever.

Tommy Fuller couldn't keep his eyes off of Suzanne and finally leaned over to Mike Phillips and whispered.

"Mike, she's the spittin' image of Susan. And her brother looks just like my brother-in-law, Joseph. I can't get over it. Plus her name is Suzanne and his is Joey. This is weird and really freaking me out."

"No weirder than anything else that's happened today," answered Phillips. "I don't know about you, but I really feel like I'm going to lose my mind. I keep hoping I'll fall asleep and wake up with the TV blaring some Civil War documentary. I would love to blame this nightmare on pizza and PBS."

Phillips spoke to his hosts.

"I don't suppose you guys have a TV down here?"

"A what?" asked Joey.

"TV. Television?"

"More code words?" piped in Anthony, annoyed with the gibberish he felt he was enduring.

"A box with pictures that move, and voices that come out of it," said Jackson, starting to lose his cool.

"Like a radio, you mean?" asked Suzanne, turning away from the stove to join the conversation.

"Well, like a radio except with moving pictures, images," continued Phillips in disbelief he'd landed in a world without TV.

"Like the movies, only shrunk down?" asked Joey.

"Exactly," said Phillips, turning hopefully to the boy.

"No such thing that I've ever heard of, so no, we don't got one," concluded Anthony. "But that would be somethin' else. I suppose they got those where you're from?" No one answered.

They silently sipped their Cokes, each lost in a world of private thought. Greg Jackson finished his drink and was kind of craving another. He lifted the bottle and asked "May I?"

"You sure?" responded Suzanne. "Two of these will either knock you out or make you bounce off the ceiling."

"Why's that? Because of the extra vitamin C?" he asked, pointing to the label.

She chuckled and retrieved a second bottle.

What Jackson and his friends didn't know was that each 10 oz bottle of "Extra C" Coke contained enough pure, uncut cocaine to have a 2013 street value of $15.00 each. Not enough to send you flying high, by modern recreational standards, but enough to alter your mood.

"How much does a six-pack cost... down here?" asked Phillips, struggling for the right words.

"You can only get twelves, and it's about five bucks," answered Joey, again the more friendly and helpful of the two young men.

The talk of money reminded Phillips of his billfold, and he instinctively patted his back pocket, but it wasn't there. The men had each left their wallets locked up in their cars, so they were without any I.D., not that it would do them much good in this foreign land.

Greg Jackson, a logical thinker, couldn't set aside the fact that all this was quite impossible. He was in this place; he knew that. He'd decided he was conscious, and while his ears still rang from the near miss of the exploding cannon shell, his hearing was improving. He thought the second Coke was helping. But he struggled, more and more, with what had happened to them and why, not to mention how? These were the questions that consumed all their private thoughts, creating, in the process, more impossible questions.

Tommy Fuller, more than his two companions, was closest to an all out psychotic episode. His shooting incident from the morning was still a part of his recent memory, but was competing for importance in light of the new nightmare they were all enduring. The stubble of a couple days growth of beard helped hide the wound on his chin, though it was a wound Suzanne had noticed.

Plates of sausages, along with biscuits warmed in the oven, and a pot of green beans, with chunks of pork fat, were delivered to the table, family style, as proficiently as if they had been served at the local diner. Etiquette and tradition were not foremost in the thoughts of the very hungry men. Ravished, they dug in, only pausing when they witnessed their three hosts holding hands and saying a silent grace for the meal.

After another heaping plateful of food was served to each man and another Coke delivered, the conversation picked up again. Anthony had mellowed some since their arrival, but still seemed more troubled about his guests than did Suzanne or her brother.

"Uh, Greg, right?" he asked nodding in Jackson's direction.

"Yeah," he answered through a mouthful.

"You say you used to live on Sullivan Ave?" continued Anthony.

"Yeah. 341 Sullivan."

Phillips went to kick him under the table, but missed and hit a table leg rattling the plates and the mood. The lights flickered with a loud crash of lightning. The rain was pouring down outside and a small drip had formed in the corner of the ceiling nearest the stairway. Suzanne got up to place a bucket under the leak.

"You look too young to have been property," said Anthony. "Were you a Redcap, working for someone?"

Jackson slammed his fork on the table. "I have never been anyone's property, I can assure you."

"Well, I believe that. You're Yankee through and through, no doubt, and educated, I can tell...but how was it you came to live on Sullivan Avenue in the CSA?"

Jackson thought for a minute. He understood the earlier attempt by Phillips to keep him quiet and he could not think of a logical way to get out of answering. More lies would just be harder to explain.

"I guess I was just confused. I never lived there." It was a weak lie, but it ended Anthony's inquiry.

The Brooklyn boy looked at Tommy Fuller, turning his interrogation to him.

"Now you *do* live here, right?" He gazed hard at Tommy. "You're not confused, right? Your last name is Fuller, and your uncles own Fuller's

Service on Armory Square?"

"No," Tommy answered.

"Oh, but I thought you told Joe and Suzanne earlier that Bill and Bobby were your uncles?"

"No. They're...they're not. I don't know them."

"Well I do," snapped Anthony, "and we're gonna pay em a little visit tomorrow."

Anthony got up from his chair and walked to the desk picking up the phone. He dialed a number and spoke quietly while Suzanne cleared the table. Tommy jumped up to help her and she looked startled.

"Finally, a true gentlemen," she said loudly enough for the rest to hear. Joey rolled his eyes, got up and walked to the large freestanding radio that sat on the floor near the sofa. He turned the appliance on with an audible click. A few seconds later Big-Band swing music played quietly from the large speaker.

While Tommy crossed the room with a stack of dirty plates, Suzanne got a closer look at the gash on his chin, which was still damp with blood, the hot shower having reinvigorated the wound. Standing just inches away from him, with a gentle hand she turned his head slightly.

"That looks nasty," she said. "You should've had stitches, but it's too late for that. You'll just have to keep it clean and bandaged. It will heal slower but should be all right. Probably leave a nasty little scar." Another crack of lightening shook the small house and the lights went out. Surprised, Suzanne let out a small yelp and instinctively reached out for Tommy and he held her. When the lights came back on a few seconds later, she looked embarrassed and backed away.

She went back to the sink, finished the dishes, rinsed her hands and went to the bathroom cupboard, returning with medical supplies. She sat Tommy down, applied an ointment to the raw wound and Tommy flinched.

"Sorry," she said, grimacing with him. "I know this stuff stings a bit."

She peeled open a small sterile gauze, applied it to his chin, and taped it in place with medical tape.

"You seem to know a lot about this kind of stuff. Are you a doctor?" he asked with an appreciative smile.

"Not quite," she laughed, "but I have had some experience with the wounded. I'm really more of a...nurse."

"Oh," he sighed, unable to help himself from looking directly into her eyes, seeing the eyes of his wife, Susan, and she looked back at him. He wanted to kiss her. He wanted to wrap his arms around her and tell her he was sorry for all the trouble he'd caused. He wanted things to be the way they once were, and tell her he'd be home soon....

"Tommy," Mike Phillips said a little too loudly, breaking the bittersweet spell.

"You might want to catch the news with us." He gestured toward the

110

big radio. The others were listening attentively. Joey turned up the volume and they all took seats within earshot.

The live report was coming from the Nation's Capitol, Richmond, Virginia. Through a slight, static fuzz the announcer delivered the latest:

"In another development in the ongoing investigation of the Supreme Court bombing earlier today, Attorney General Jason French told reporters just moments ago that they had, quote 'very strong leads in the case' and that there was 'no doubt the Freedom Fighters carried out the horrific act of terrorism against the Confederacy.' French promised swift and severe punishment for anyone involved with the organization or anyone withholding evidence pertaining to the case. More later as the story develops. We now return you to Songs of the South, live from the Jefferson Davis Center in Charlotte."

With the close of his announcements, music returned to the air. Anthony got up from his chair and returned to the phone, making another quiet call.

"Well," Suzanne said, drying the last dish and wiping down the stovetop. "Sorry we don't have more comfortable accommodations, but the sofa pulls out and is big enough for two of you and I've been known to catch some sleep in that recliner. It's not too bad. There are blankets in the chest."

Anthony finished his call, gathered some papers from the desktop and from a file drawer. He stood next to Joey and Suzanne with a hand nervously flipping at the leather strap on his holstered pistol. A slow drip echoed softly in the bucket in the corner of the room, but the rain had slowed, and only distant rumbles could be heard from outside.

Listening to the news on the radio wasn't so strange…learning that the Nation's capitol was in Richmond, Virginia, however, was incomprehensible. Everything the men had known to be true, everything every history teacher had ever taught, nearly every fiber of their very existence, had been overturned in a blinding flash of gunpowder and nitroglycerin. The not knowing, not understanding was physically painful. The only thing that could have made their pain worse would have been to have endured it alone. Each of the men was grateful for having comrades to share in the mass insanity.

Before the programming had turned to music, the men watched their young hosts intently. Based on their yawns and general disinterest, they came to the conclusion that the rest of the evening's news must have been mostly unremarkable. Little of what they heard made sense. The names were all wrong, the headlines unfamiliar. It was maddening. Where was the war in Afghanistan? Where were the political scandals of yesterday's news? Did they simply vanish? Had they ever existed? With no way to judge the merits of the events of the day on their own, they found themselves learning what they could, as much from body language and facial expressions, as from what anybody in this mad rabbit hole actually said.

"It's getting late," said Anthony, directing his comments to his friends. He turned to Mike Phillips. "You guys will bunk down here for the night. You'll be locked in, safe. Don't try to get out. You need to just stay out of sight, especially the colored guy." Phillips couldn't help but glance at Jackson, who gave Brooklyn an angry stare that turned into words.

"I'm in the room, you know. I can hear you," said Jackson.

"Hey, don't get mad at me," Anthony said, acknowledging Jackson's remark. "I'm just tryin to keep yas alive. You don't have the sense to act right. You may be a free black man from the Federated States, but you're in the South now. There's laws down here...and worse, there are people who don't need no laws, who'd shoot you on sight, on principle alone. Hell, ten of them live on this block. There was a lynching at the end of this street just three months ago. A black guy just looked the wrong way at a white girl, and that was that."

Brooklyn paused, looking at the men and thinking carefully about his next words.

"You know there's a lot about you guys that just don't add up. To be honest with yas, I wouldn't have had anything to do with you except Suzanne talked me into helping. You were wearing Civil War uniforms for God's sake and are all beat up and bloody. What the hell is that all about?"

The men did not, could not answer.

"It's obvious you're not from here, so I don't think you're G-men trying to infiltrate, you're not with the Richmond cell, I just checked... I just don't get it. But I'm gonna figure you out." He turned to his friends.

"Let's get out of here." With that the three young hosts, the junior Freedom Fighters, made their way up the stairs to the door. "We'll be back in the morning."

They disappeared into the night leaving Jackson, Phillips and Fuller even more baffled than when they had first awakened in the woods outside of town.

•••••

The men sat in silence for a few moments and then began to finally get a good look at each other. A loud crack of thunder shook the room, signaling a re-intensifying of the storm. The rain came back, blowing hard against the side of the house where the men sat trying to make sense of the strange new land. Even washed and in clean clothes, they were a mess.

Tommy Fuller looked the worst. He had been involved in a fatal shooting, had had a car wreck, had out-run 50 or so cops, and had been nearly blown to bits, all in just under 12 hours. Greg Jackson looked the most troubled of the three: worrying about all the things the other two had on their minds, putting up with horrible ringing and what he hoped was temporary deafness in his left ear, plus the added indignity of being a Black man where Black men were clearly treated as sub-human property. Phillips seemed to have escaped without physical malady, but was as exhausted, and as shaken up as the others. He yawned widely and stared straight ahead.

"What's happening?" asked Tommy. No one answered. "What the hell is happening?"

This time his urgent, pleading eyes darted back and forth between Phillips and Jackson. He needed an answer.

"I feel sick, like I'm gonna puke any minute. I feel like I've lost my mind or I'm having a nightmare...but then...so are you guys...right?" His voice trembled and he was on the verge of tears.

"Right?" he asked again. "We're in this together?"

"Yeah Tommy, we're here. We're in this together," consoled Phillips. "Whatever 'this' is."

"We are *not* dreaming," said Jackson. He slammed his open palm on the table. "Let's try to start making sense of this. Let's put together what little puzzle pieces we know for sure and can all agree on. We'll start there, and build, okay?" They nodded in response.

"First, like I said...we're not dreaming." No one answered. "Agreed?" he insisted. Jackson refused to continue until he received an affirmative from each man. The other men nodded and thought it bizarre to actually have to agree together that it was so. But in light of the circumstances a mutual dream was not out of the question, or any crazier than any other explanation, so it had to be ruled in or out, and they decided it was definitely, unfortunately, *not* a dream.

"So, if we're not dreaming, then this must be real. Right?"

"What must be real?" asked Phillips, coaxing the process.

"The fact that we woke up this morning in the United States of America with all that was good and bad in the world and good and bad in our lives...and now we're somewhere else and just about everything we know is different," concluded Jackson.

"Okay, I'll buy that," said Phillips. "But are we some*where* else, or some...*time* else? I mean, if we're...and I can't believe I'm even saying this...Time Travelers, how were we in 1863 one minute, and then back in 2013 the next? And if it is 2013, then why does it look like 1940?"

No one answered. No one could answer. They sat silently, the soft, flickering glow of the lamps crackling occasionally from dubious electrical circuits.

"1940? No, this is 2013," said Jackson. "The kids said it was. The news said it, too..."

"Okay, then we're some*place* else," said Phillips.

"Are we?" challenged Jackson. "The town is mostly the same: street names...the hills, the mountains, the creek we crossed getting here to this house...even my neighborhood...those kids knew the streets...they're all pretty much the same."

"But yet changed..." added Phillips.

"Yeah, okay," agreed Jackson. "Changed. But how? How did everything, or almost everything, change?"

"I think I might know," said Tommy Fuller, finally speaking. "I think this might be my fault."

The other two men sat in silence waiting for his explanation. As implausible as whatever Fuller might have to say, it couldn't be any less likely the truth than if he were to tell them that the Easter Bunny did it.

"Well...," he started slowly, as if not sure he believed or understood the things he was about to say.

"My truck is here with us, and that doesn't make any sense. Most everything else seems to be different, changed...but not my truck. None of your cars were where you thought you'd left them when we wandered out of the woods; the parking lot wasn't even paved. Did you notice that? Why do you suppose?" he asked rhetorically. After a long painful pause he continued:

"This morning, when I was on my way walking to my truck and those thugs on my street came up on me....I started to...like...flip back and forth...I don't know how else to explain it. I know I was scared, but I'm not insane. I've been scared before, but I never tripped-out like this morning. This was something different. I was standing on my street watching them come at me with a baseball bat and a knife and...I know you'll think I'm nuts, but that baseball bat turned into a rifle, and the knife turned into a loose bayonet."

"Those kids were wearing those track suits, you know, the baggy track suits they all wear?" Jackson ignored the stereotype. "...and their clothes turned into Federal Civil War uniforms, and I could hear their stereo blasting out some gangster rap crap. But then it turned into cannon fire in the distance. It don't make sense, I know, but somehow I'm involved in whatever caused this mess. And I'll tell you something else," he smiled in a way that gave his companions pause. "That girl, Suzanne...that's my wife, Susan. I don't mean they look alike. I mean that's her."

There were a thousand questions to ask, each leading to a thousand more, but the events of the day and the accompanying exhaustion took over and they surrendered to sleep, the chair reclining into a makeshift bed for Jackson and the sofa pulling out, accommodating Phillips and Fuller. Sweet sleep was welcome, but it would bring no relief from the realities of this place that seemed so un-real.

They darkened the room, but flashes of light peeked through a small, barred window near the basement ceiling as the storm continued. The sound of the rain was soothing, as was the distant thunder. They left the radio on, volume turned low, playing old-styled, Big-Band instrumentals, slow and sad.

•••••

Awakened by light streaming through small scrapes in the paint of the otherwise completely blackened window, Jackson was the first to rise the next morning. His first thoughts were to wonder where he had slept that night.

"Did I get drunk at MacAuley's and crash at Mike's house?" he thought.

He nearly asked it aloud. When he saw Tommy Fuller on a pull-out sofa bed with a bandage on his chin, it all came flooding back to him like an evil demon crushing his skull. Emotion swept over him and he held back tears. It was just too much to handle and he lay back down, trying to sleep. He hoped sleep would make it all go away, and he dozed, fitfully.

Twenty minutes later he was re-awakened, hearing the door at the top of the stairs rattle. Expecting the three young captors, as he was beginning to think of them, he was relieved to see that the noise was from Phillips checking the only door out. Phillips looked down into the room and saw that Jackson had awakened.

"Well, we're locked in, just like they said."

"What time is it?" asked Phillips.

Jackson looked at his wrist and thought his hi-tech Rolex was strangely out of place in this antiquated world.

"Nine," he said. He got up and turned up the volume on the radio and heard classic sounding country music, like Bluegrass, but more electrified, he thought. It was something almost familiar, but not quite. The voice of the announcer gave his 10 a.m. call and Jackson looked at his watch again.

"My watch is an hour slow or their clock is an hour fast." He looked up at Phillips. "But this thing is never off," he said, tapping on the glass face of the watch."

"Don't you remember?" asked Jackson. "At the Park? The Date? This ain't July 7th, brother. It's July 10th. We're way out of whack."

Phillips shrugged, one more mystery added to the already long and growing list.

Tommy Fuller sat up, stretching his arms over his head and yawned widely before yelling to no one in particular.

"Ouch, shit, that hurt!" He put his hands to his bandaged chin. The yawn had pulled at the two-inch gash on his chin causing shooting pains. "I've got to find some Advil or something." He walked to the bathroom and studied the old fixtures, peeling wallpaper, and an old medicine cabinet. He looked in the mirror and caught up with himself.

"You are a mess," he said, shaking his head at his own image. He opened the cabinet, finding the usual array of products, only with names he didn't recognize. He pulled a small glass bottle from the shelf and shook it, hearing the tablets rattle inside. He read the label: *Doctor William's Pain and Chronic Stiffness Tablets.*

"I wonder how old these things are," he said to himself. There was no expiration date, but the bottle, while it looked turn-of-the-century in design, was in brand new condition. He unscrewed the metal cap, removed the little piece of cotton and sniffed tentatively. He popped four tablets in his mouth and turned on the faucet.

Brown, rusty water gushed out as he unbuttoned and removed the shirt Suzanne had given him the night before. The water finally turned clear and he hesitantly filled the small glass and washed down the strange pills he hoped were aspirin.

He glanced at the other items in the cabinet and found *Doctor William's Tooth Powder, Dr. William's Tea Tree Oil, Dr. William's Blood Cleansing Elixir,* and a half-dozen additional items, most bearing the William's name and "Promise of Purity." He closed the door to use the toilet and to wash up. Removing the bandage, damp from the ointment and last traces of blood, he touched his wound with soapy fingertips, trying to assess the damage. He found a split in his chin that he agreed should have had stitches, but was already beginning to heal. He thought about Susan, where she was, how was she dealing with his absence, his status as felon on the loose. This, he thought, will be the final nail in the coffin that was their troubled marriage. Then he thought about how much he missed her, and about how much in love they had been in high school.

Their marriage had started out as pure heaven: puppy love mixed with youthful enthusiasm, hormones, and passionate hours every day behind closed doors. But soon after they'd married, the troubles started in their neighborhood, and it put a real strain on the relationship. Susan was supportive, faithful and empathetic, but she hadn't signed on for this kind of life, and after nearly two years it was wearing on her.

"Where is she now?" Tommy wondered. "Where are we?"

He slipped his shirt back on and thought about how nice it was of Suzanne to have provided them with the clothing; it was something Susan would have done. He replaced the bandage with fresh gauze and tape, again courtesy of *Dr. Williams.*

Fuller wandered from the bathroom feeling a little better due to the simple, restorative warmth of hot water and a washcloth. He walked to the phone and picked it up. A strange dial-tone prompted a long-shot attempt at making a call. He looked at the rotary dial, having never seen one, other than in the movies, and dialed Susan's cell-phone number. An erratic

116

beeping that almost hurt his ears caused him to hang up. He noticed at the bottom of the phone a small, typed message: 'Orchard 7-567'.

He put it out of his mind when hunger pangs stopped him, dead in his tracks, and turned him toward the kitchenette.

Opening the junior-sized refrigerator he found lots of vegetables, eggs, milk in glass containers, and a variety of packages, all with unknown names emblazoned on their labels. One product, however, looked exactly like it should, and he grabbed for it.

The bottle of Coke was perfect in every way, except he couldn't twist the cap off and had to use a bottle opener attached to the side of the cabinet. The drink fizzed to life and he guzzled it, enjoying the reassuring sweetness and comfort of his favorite beverage. The familiar kola-nut-derived flavor, the shot of caffeine, and the almost unnoticeable numbing tang of the infused cocaine, made the drink a comforting, truly medicinal elixir.

In the world Fuller and his companions knew, the final traces of cocaine had been removed from Coca Cola, under growing pressure and public concern by 1929, but the original medicinal formula, far stronger, and potentially highly addictive, was readily available in this place with the label "Extra C."

Soon all three men were hovering around the open refrigerator, realizing how famished they were. Not wanting to bother with cooking, they ate chunks of sharp cheese cut from a wheel, and they shared the bottle of whole milk, which tasted like heavy cream; skim milk did not exist. Temporarily sated they made their way back to the radio.

"Well," said Jackson with a frown. "I guess it wasn't a dream. I'm finally convinced that I'm awake and I've lost my mind and you're all in it with me. Where's my damn cell phone?"

The men smiled and even managed to share a chuckle; the first laughter they'd allowed themselves since this horrible ordeal had begun. Phillips and Jackson discussed the fun they had had during the first 20-minutes of the reenactment.

"You know this thing started out great," said Jackson to Phillips. "At first I was mad at you for getting me involved. I'm still mad, by the way, but really, I was just starting to get into it, you know? When we were up on that ridge watching the battle …it was incredible. And then it all went south…pardon the pun."

The men chuckled again, but their laughter was short-lived. They began to think about Brad Lake, who'd been shot to death on that ridge; a hole blown through his skull. It was a sobering memory. One minute they were play-acting like neighborhood kids using sticks for guns, refusing to fall over, pissing off the "enemy," and then in the next minute, embroiled in a hellish fire-fight with real rounds snuffing out the lives of their friends, and almost killing them, too. It was all too horrible to dwell on, though the memories were hard to escape.

"We've got to get to D.C.," said Jackson, who was worried about the fate of his family and of his friends, hoping the big city might have some answers.

"Who was that crazy Yankee reenactor that pulled us off the ridge before the explosion?" asked Phillips, of anyone who might remember.

"He said he was…," Jackson scratched his head. "Captain William Grisham, or Grissom, or something like that. He kept on about his brother Thomas. The two of them planted that bomb, I guess…"

"Well that's obviously where that explosion and crater came from," said Tommy Fuller, joining the conversation. "But the monument said that the crater was formed like 150 years ago during the battle."

"But it shouldn't have been," said Jackson. "Remember your history…Pickett's Charge, the slaughtered Rebs, no explosion. There was never any plan for a surprise explosion at The Battle of Gettysburg. That didn't happen until the Siege of Petersburg, and The Battle of the Crater. So…what the hell?"

Chapter 16

The unmistakable sound of an old car with a big engine rattled the floor joists of the old house, and the men knew that their hosts had returned. The noise from the unshackling of several locks reaffirmed their captivity. Though they hadn't been mistreated, or bound, or led to believe they were in imminent danger from their hosts, they sensed mistrust and well-reasoned suspicion.

Phillips, in particular, had been considering new ways to try to gain the confidence of their young captors, and convince them they were on their side. They needed friends in this place, but the truth certainly wouldn't work. Who would believe it? They, themselves, didn't believe it.

Brooklyn, as the men now referred to him, walked down the stairs first, followed by Suzanne, and then Joey. The men had feared the young Freedom Fighters might bring with them older, more seasoned members of their cause, and with them potentially unpleasant, interrogation methods, but fortunately, it was still just the three wet-behind-the-ears, kids.

"No offense," said Jackson. "But don't you guys have a boss or something?" Brooklyn looked insulted and annoyed at the question.

"It's just that we've never met...FF...that were so young."

"We can handle ourselves," retorted Brooklyn. "Don't you worry about that. And, yes, we have bosses that we're in touch with." Brooklyn frowned and looked away.

Suzanne walked to Tommy Fuller and put her hand on his shoulder.

"How are you feeling, Tommy?"

Stunned again by her likeness to his own Susan, and her kindness, he barely managed an answer.

"My chin is sore but Dr. William's seems to have helped me a bit." They smiled shyly at one another, and both sensed some strange chemistry at work.

The friendly chitchat halted when Brooklyn spoke up.

"We need to know a few things before we can help you anymore," demanded the dark-haired teen, crossing his arms in front of his chest.

Anthony seemed new to his skin, a duck out of water, something to which the three men could relate. This kid, who they'd later find out was a 19-year-old, was acting like a superspy. While he seemed to struggle with his task, and was grumpy all the time, he was the only one of the hosts who was really acting with any intelligence.

Joey, Suzanne's seemingly naïve, younger brother, had a sweet innocence only found in those hovering between childhood and maturity. He was along for the ride, and like the others, in way over his head. Phillips guessed that Joey, who shared his sister's good looks, was 18 or 19. Tommy, who'd known the kid in whatever former life had just unraveled, corrected him, confirming he was just 17. Tommy and his young brother-in-law had become friends even before he had started dating Susan. Here in this place Joey seemed to be essentially the same good kid that he remembered, and just like his sister, acted as if they'd never met.

There was a disconcerting notion felt by all the men, especially Tommy Fuller, that being in the room with these familiar, yet strange people, was like returning home from work one day to find your family all there sitting around the table, yet none of them knew you. There was no shared history of family vacations, favorite pets, funerals, and in Tommy's case...weddings. He found it frustrating, confusing, frightening, and terribly sad.

"Okay," said Phillips, taking the floor and holding court. "We will tell you as much as we possibly can without jeopardizing our...mission."

"Let's start with your mission," said Brooklyn.

"Can't do that, classified."

"Where are you from?"

"New York"

"How'd you get here?"

"Uh...his truck," Phillips answered, looking at Tommy, immediately wishing he hadn't said it.

"Yeah...about that truck...we checked it out. Seems it was made in Japan. How do you explain that?"

"Japan makes lots of trucks," Fuller interjected.

"The hell they do...they live in caves, the ones who aren't crippled from the radiation," said Anthony.

"Well, yes that's true," said Phillips slowly, trying not to reveal his ignorance of some unknown and horrible history. "But we dropped the bomb a long time ago and they're...they're recovering."

"We didn't drop the bomb," corrected Anthony. "Hitler did."

"Hitler?" Jackson asked, unable to help himself.

"Ahh, yeah..hello...duh..," said Joey, proud to contribute. "Adolph

Hitler? The evil King of Europe? Until 1962...or was it '52...I can't ever remember that."

"It was 1962," added Suzanne, like the smart schoolgirl called on in class, who always knew the answer. "And he wasn't a king, Joey. When he died, William Patrick Hitler, his nephew, took power, and then in 1975 William Patrick's son, Werner Hitler, took power, and he's still ruler today."

"Yeah, yeah, okay...but what about a Japanese truck?" asked Anthony, tired of the history lesson.

"The truck...," said Phillips, rolling his eyes trying desperately to improvise some reasonable answer. "The truck came from a group of Japanese inventors who work with some...machinists...and they... slipped it into this country...to...."

He was cut short, mercifully.

"I call bullshit on that," said Anthony, easily seeing through the poorly disguised adlib. He crossed the room and directed his comments at Fuller.

"Well, you might like to know that we slipped your truck into Fuller's Auto late last night. We towed it out of the ditch to the shop and the Twins have a few questions for you. Want to go see it?"

With no other plan and no other options, they agreed. Tommy grabbed his Rebel cap from the top of the dresser and stuffed it into his back pocket. They all walked up the stairs into the blackened garage, and piled back into the big car.

The Marathon was a sturdy car, a model made in Nashville, Tennessee, since 1906. While the first models were open-aired ramblers, this model looked like a big Checker Cab. It was huge and roomy enough for a herd of elephants. It had real wood panels and leather seats, stained and worn from age and countless passengers. Its motor rumbled and roared to life echoing loudly in the closed up garage. Not shy about its power under the hood, the Marathon stood in stark contrast, Tommy thought, to his own 4-cylinder Nissan. Fuel efficiency was apparently not an issue in this place.

Jackson was handed a red, knit cap with a cloth I.D. sewn to the front of it. It was called a "Redcap" and was required headwear for most all minorities venturing into public places. It displayed a series of numbers and letters, like a hunting license, and a license was precisely what it was. To be legal within the borders of the Confederate States of America, all dark-skinned people of African, Caribbean or Hispanic descent had to be licensed. The law, adopted in 1998, under pressure from reformers, replaced the permanent forehead tattoo that had been the norm since the '20s. A non-white minority adult, over the age of 16, caught without a

121

Redcap, would go straight to jail and maybe worse. Jackson reluctantly put the cap on, seething, but realizing it was safest for his friends if he complied.

As they made the drive across town they marveled at how things could look so different and so familiar all at the same time. Their little tourist town had been knocked back 65 years. They half expected to see Poodle Skirts on the girls and slicked-back, Greaser hair cuts on the guys. From the cars, to the streetlights, to the little stores on the corner, it looked remarkably like a Norman Rockwell *Saturday Evening Post* magazine cover.

The downtown was especially Rockwellian: with a Five and Dime, a Movie House, Men's and Boy's store, Ice Cream shop, barber shop, several diners, banks, two dress shops, and a real energy that had been missing from most small towns for decades. Also in this downtown was an automotive service center that shouldn't have been there, Fuller's Auto, run by Tommy Fuller's uncles, 45-year-old twins, Bobby and Billy Fuller.

Joey wheeled the big Marathon in front of the full service pumps, crossing a black air hose on the ground, which rang the bell inside the shop, another vestige of a by-gone era. They pulled around to the back and looked nervously out the windows before exiting the car. Greg Jackson adjusted his new red cap and threw Phillips an annoyed look.

"It itches," Jackson said, and Phillips suppressed a smile.

They walked through the back door of the shop just in time to see two plump men maneuvering a giant pry bar in an attempt to pull the front grill of the little Nissan away from the radiator. They had already managed to straighten the fenders, and had pulled most of the weeds from around the mirrors. With a great heave, they yanked and grunted until the front grill resembled something close to normal and then they rested, satisfied. The burly mechanics smiled at the kids and greeted them warmly. When they saw the strange men with them, their smiles faded. Tommy Fuller stood frozen in disbelief when he saw, clear as day, his two uncles, both of whom had died 10 years earlier in a tow truck accident.

The twins sized up the strangers, but they weren't the only ones with an interest in the newcomers.

•••••

Within a small, nondescript house in a residential neighborhood across town, two men talked and stirred their coffee while standing in the kitchen. Both in their 30s, the men appeared average in every way. One on the tall side was lean and strong. The other was short, liked to eat. They were not too handsome or too plain. Just average Joes in black suits, and this made them perfect spies. They had been sent across the border by the security forces of the Federated States of America, or Fed-Stat as it had come to be known, with the full cooperation of the C.S.A. They were there on a covert mission to assess the strength of the Southern insurgency, Freedom Fighters, most of whom lived and worked south of the border. Some worked from inside Fed-Stat as well, and their numbers were growing.

The "official" line was that both governments were working together to eradicate the insurgents in their respective home countries. There were those on both sides of the border wishing to re-unite the two small nations, and though most outspoken public leaders of the movement condemned violence, they felt forced to recognize the efforts in which the radical elements were involved. These activists and politicians walked a treacherous tightrope between backroom politics and all out terrorism. These two men, currently working in Gettysburg, had carte blanche to work both sides for information. They were super cops, a North American version of Interpol's secret police. Some might call them double-agents.

As far as Anthony, Suzanne, and Joey knew, the agents, who'd been supporting them with a little money and minor surveillance missions, were sympathetic to the cause of reunification and were there to help the FF. What they couldn't know, and something only a few, high-level Cabinet Officers knew, was that the agents' employers, the National Security Agency of the F.S.A., secretly supported the Southern Insurgency, while publicly denouncing all such activities, terrorist or otherwise. Keeping the South in chaos, but not too much chaos, was to Fed-Stat's advantage, according to the current administration under President Trump.

The C.S.A had plenty to be nervous about. Just as was true 150 years earlier, the North was the better bet for victory if it should ever again come to war. But not everyone agreed that the states belonged together. Conservative factions on both sides liked the status quo and the geopolitical arrangement just as it was.

The South had faced horribly crippling embargoes for the first four decades of its existence as a nation and had no love for their former countrymen of the North. The South hadn't *won* the War of Secession as much as the North had *lost* its will to hemorrhage any more blood. Before the War ended the North had suffered casualties nearing 300,000 men, between the ages of 15 and 40, and the South nearly twice that number. When Lincoln and Davis signed the first truce and cease-fire agreements it had essentially ended the War and set the stage for the recognition of a Confederated States of America, known by most people as "Con-Fed," or sometimes, derogatorily, as "Corn Fed."

Just after the peace treaty was signed by Jefferson Davis and Abraham Lincoln, ending hostilities, the Northern states were uneasy calling themselves "United." After 15-years of wrangling, the frazzled government, by constitutional decree, changed the name of their homeland to the Federated States of America (F.S.A.), with a lasting nickname "Fed-Stat." Both countries adopted new constitutions and had formed new governments that resembled their former in many ways. From Dog Catcher, to City Councilmen, to President, elected officials still called most of the shots in a representative form of government that supposedly reflected the will of the people...as long as they were white, male and of European, but not Spanish, descent. This was mostly true on both sides of the border.

The South's post-war military was small. There were only 50 million people in Con-Fed to begin with, and while their military consisted of the usual branches: Army, Navy, Air Force and Marines; there were just 300,000 servicemen in all the branches combined. Women were not allowed to serve, nor were Black men. Blacks and other minorities were not allowed to own or even handle guns.

Mandatory military service had ended in the '50s, with the election of a populist President who ran on ending conscription, which he did, with some difficulty. The military in the North had become much larger and more powerful. With its bigger cities, better rail lines, more varied shipping routes, rivers, canals, better supplies of fresh water and stronger ties to Europe, the North moved on more efficiently just after the war. Its population of 80 million and armed forces of 600 thousand were of growing concern to Con-Fed and also to Germanic powers across the Atlantic, whose leaders had begun to take notice.

While the North and South had lived in relative peace with one another, many on both sides of the line never felt very comfortable with the way the conflict had ended. Originally, the War was seen, only by some, as inevitable. It was a minority that wanted to split the young nation, and it would have been to the majority's preference to have had a compromised solution without bloodshed.

The South screamed for States' Rights as the only way to protect their agrarian society, but the North favored a strong Federal form of government, which superseded States' Rights in favor of a stronger national union. In the middle were the three million enslaved blacks, and millions of Native Americans, who became the focal point in a conflict that had no choice but to boil over. Politicians jockeyed for power, insults were hurled, and finally shots fired at the Federal Fort Sumter in Charleston, South Carolina. Memories are long, and 150 years later, attitudes had changed little.

Though Jackson, Phillips, and Fuller didn't yet know it for sure, in this new world, history books would fail to match their own understanding of the world they thought they knew. From the Battle of Gettysburg, forward, little would make sense to these three strangers in a strange land.

The Fed-Stat agents, sipping their coffee, were on a covert mission to assess the strength of the Freedom Fighters and assist only to the point that would allow for intelligence gathering. They were primarily on a fact-finding mission. Today's job was to listen to six hours of tapes recorded at the Gettysburg safe house the previous evening. When one of their young operatives phoned in about three men acting very oddly, who had arrived in Civil War uniforms, it piqued their curiosity and they'd started the overnight monitoring.

"You know our junior spy squad has captured three rogue FF," joked the taller of the two men.

"Yeah, they seemed pretty excited about it," said the other. Neither man seemed too interested in the task ahead.

"Let's just get it over with," said the taller man.

The agents moved into what was once the home's master bedroom and found their places at two large desks. They sat amidst electronics that looked as if they'd been scavenged from the sets of old sci-fi movies. Enormous reel-to-reel tape recorders and giant gray boxes with antennas and flashing lights filled the room. Without a Silicon Valley to invent miniaturized microprocessors and lead the world toward the digital domain, this place was stuck with analog technology, more in tune with the 1950s, than a decade into the new millennium.

There was not a TV screen anywhere in sight. Television had not been invented. There had been crude attempts as far back as 1888, but television, as it is known to the modern world, with its electron beams and vacuum tubes, would have been invented by Philo T. Farnsworth, of San Francisco, in 1927. But Philo's father was executed as a "subversive" in 1911 by a New Spain military tribunal. Therefore Philo's father was never able to marry, and thus Philo was never born, nor was the television, to which he would have given birth.

The Fed-Stat spies set their big machines humming, produced two yellow pads and a handful of pencils, and adjusted the over-sized headphones. They sat expressionless for the first several minutes and then began to write. They were both listening to the same recording and would write a sentence or two, breaking pencil points in their rush, and then glance at each other quizzically. This went on for 30 minutes until both men looked at one another and the taller man stopped the tape player, pulling the headphones from his ears.

"Did you hear what I just heard?" asked the taller man.

"I think so, but I don't believe it," said the other agent.

He read a transcribed, slightly paraphrased version of Fuller, Phillips, and Jackson's private conversations.

The smaller man lit a cigarette while his partner read through their notes out loud.

"One guy says... 'Are we dreaming? I feel sick," blah, blah, blah,' and then another guy says... 'We woke up this morning in the United States of America...and now we're here?'"

125

He scanned the notes again. "They're talking about an explosion and a battle.... You think they were in on the Richmond job? One guy says

'We've got to get to D.C.' What are these guys up to? Who are they?" The men slid their headphones back on and resumed listening and writing, this time with renewed interest.

•••••

Across town at Fuller's Auto, the twin mechanics, not entirely unlike Humpty and Dumpty, made their way cautiously toward the three strangers in their shop. Tommy Fuller was glassy-eyed and suddenly spoke, surprising all who heard, including himself.

"Hi, Uncle Bill. Hey, Uncle Bob."

The two men looked at one another and approached Fuller. "Do we know you?" they asked.

"I'm Earl's son, Tommy."

Jackson and Phillips were watching, horrified, unable to imagine where this might lead.

"I doubt that very much," said Uncle Bobby.

"Earl died when he was six."

"Not where I came from," said Fuller, without any outward emotion on hearing of his father's death. He had broken the unspoken, but well understood, rule against saying anything that could jeopardize their ability to function in this place. Fuller had finally lost any remaining internal filter, saying whatever was on his mind. He was tired of it all, and didn't care that he was acting recklessly. With nothing to lose, he was ready to involve anyone who would listen.

"We don't know who you think you are, but this ain't cute anymore," said Uncle Bob. "We know you're a 'Fuller' because we saw your papers in the glove box. But you ain't no kin to us and those papers ain't right anyhow..."

"We're sorry...Bob," offered Phillips, taking two steps closer to the twins. "He was in a car wreck yesterday and had a severe concussion..."

Tommy Fuller smiled slightly and shook his head, lost in thought, far away.

"We'd like to ask you about your truck and your so-called registration papers. We've never seen anything like them before," said the other uncle, Bill. "Plus, this motor has something called 'fuel injection' and "electronic ignition,' not to mention it only seems to have four cylinders."

"And that ain't the least of it. It was made in Japan in 1990. It just ain't possible," said Uncle Bob.

126

"Well, how does it feel to be confused?" asked Fuller, rhetorically. "Welcome to my world." He opened his arms wide in an uncharacteristic, dramatic, sweeping motion.

"I know it's complicated," said Phillips, stepping in. "Even we don't know all the details. But... can you get it running?" he asked, trying to change the subject.

"Oh, it runs fine," said Uncle Bill, wiping his hands on an orange shop rag. "Once we got fuel inside of it. Our gas nozzles wouldn't fit in that small hole.

"That's because it takes unleaded," said Fuller, knowing this, too, would throw the mechanics.

"Well, whatever that is, we got a funnel and made it work. We also popped the fenders out of the tires and the grill out of the radiator. We welded a little spot where it was leaking." Even after having the vehicle for most of the day, it still amazed and confounded the mechanics. This truck was a mystery, a modern marvel, though just an old junker to its owner. From the radial tires to the lack of a carburetor, it may as well have been a UFO. They were stunned and in awe of a machine full of technology they couldn't begin to comprehend.

"You got a nice shop here," said Fuller, truly envious. It was exactly what he had once hoped to open himself, before his troubles began. "Three bays, two lifts, gas pumps...man, this is nice."

The twins ignored the compliment and looked suspiciously at their strange guests, one of whom had just recently claimed to be their nephew.

•••••

At the makeshift communications house the taller man picked up the phone receiver and frantically dialed on a rotary phone. The pair were sure the three new men in town were up to no good. They had concluded that they were working for some radical political element that their agency had no knowledge of, and that they must be speaking in codes, and it didn't sound good. They knew where to find them though, as their young assistants had told them right where they were headed, Fuller's Auto.

The phone rang in the shop's office, and Uncle Bob went to retrieve the call.

"If you're getting these kids messed up in something..." Uncle Billy chided, with a glance toward Joey, Anthony and Suzanne.

"No, no, no. We're just a little behind in our...mission," said Phillips, whispering the word, as if it somehow made it more believable. He'd assumed the mechanics were at least friendly to the cause.

127

Bob Fuller spoke on the phone in low tones, and spun on his heel. Everyone saw the worried look in his eye.

Tommy Fuller was close enough to see the keys in the ignition of the Nissan and began rubbing his fingers nervously inside his pants pockets. Uncle Bob hung up the phone and moved just out of sight in the office. He appeared a moment later, obviously hiding something under his coveralls, stealth not being his strong suit.

Tommy Fuller lunged for the door of the truck, which opened with a loud clunk and a clang, and jumped behind the wheel.

"Get in the back...now!" he shouted to his friends and fired up the engine. Phillips and Jackson stood for a moment, stunned. When they saw Uncle Bob produce a revolver from his work clothes, they ran and jumped for the bed of the truck.

A Nashville Marathon rounded the corner two blocks from Fuller's Auto, squealing its tires and moving faster than cars normally move in downtown Gettysburg. Uncle Bob, clearly not comfortable with a gun, but determined to stop the strangers, yelled, panting as he jogged toward the idling Nissan.

"Stop, dang it. I'll shoot!" he yelled.

Joey, Anthony, and Suzanne stood in shock, unable to move. The bay doors were closed, but that didn't stop Tommy Fuller. "Lay down!" he yelled out the window to the back of the truck and Phillips and Jackson knew what was coming.

"Oh shit...,"said Jackson as Tommy Fuller threw the shifter into reverse, popped the clutch, squealing the tires and creating a choking, black cloud of smoke. He piloted the little Nissan, tailgate first, into the garage door, easily ripping it from its tracks. The truck screamed out of the garage accompanied by a symphony of twisting sheet metal, screaming tires, and shouting. The service bay door lay neatly situated in an A-frame across the back of the truck, making the rig look like a tin-roofed, redneck camper.

Shots were fired, three rounds, in the general direction of the Nissan, which was weaving in and out of gas pumps. Uncle Bill wrestled the revolver from his less-intelligent twin, saving them all from a fireball and gasoline-fueled explosion. Fuller deftly wheeled the Nissan toward the road, and just before entering Main Street, had to slam on his brakes to avoid hitting a blue Nashville Marathon motorcar, sending Jackson and Phillips crashing into one another in the back of the truck bed.

The two agents inside the Marathon and Tommy Fuller locked eyes for a moment. Each knew the score and Fuller threw his truck into reverse, turning sharply. In the process the garage door flew off the truck bed, exposing the stowaways, who were rolling around like rag dolls in the back. In the half-second that Fuller stopped to put the truck into first gear, another stowaway jumped aboard, Suzanne. Before anyone could protest the new passenger's arrival, Fuller flew out of the lot and down the road with the Marathon in pursuit.

Chapter 17

Fuller had made a bold move and no one could yet say whether it was right or wrong. He slid open the small glass window behind his seat and glanced back seeing Phillips and Jackson and, for the first time, Suzanne.

"What are you doing?" he yelled, slowing the vehicle to extract her before she got hurt.

"Go, go!" she yelled, ignoring him and waving her arms in a forward motion. "You need me. I can get us out of here."

In the cracked rearview mirror, still stained with his blood from the accident the day before, Tommy Fuller could see the Marathon moving in, its big V-8 engine roaring and pushing the car to close the gap. Suzanne wiggled and writhed her small frame through the sliding window in the back of the truck cab, headfirst, accidentally elbowing Fuller in the chin on her way through.

"Ouch! What are you doing?" he screamed, one hand on the wheel and the other patting his still bandaged and now throbbing chin.

"Sorry, sorry," she apologized, working her way into a sitting position in the passenger's seat. "Turn left here," she ordered, and Fuller obeyed. In the mirror he could see Jackson and Phillips holding on for dear life, squinting, eyes nearly shut in the whirling dervish of dust and debris.

"Take your next two rights. Pick it up or they're gonna be on us," said Suzanne.

The Marathon clearly had much more power and would win in a drag race, hands down, but its 4000 lb. bulk couldn't handle the turns as well as the little truck, with its lighter weight and road-hugging, modern tires. Tommy seized on an opportunity and yelled to the men in the truck bed.

"Mike! Greg! Use that tire-iron back there and split open those four bags of sand and dump them out near the tailgate."

"Why?" yelled Jackson, screaming to be heard over the road noise and squealing tires.

"Just do it! Fast!" They did as told and soon had 200 pounds of sand emptied from the four bags.

"When I yell, open the tailgate up, hold on, and kick the sand out as fast as you can!"

They made the first of the two right-hand turns and were approaching the second. Tommy briefly slowed the vehicle and yelled back into the truck bed.

"Now! And hold on!" He punched the gas as his companions did as told.

Phillips opened the tailgate and half of the sand instantly poured out onto the road covering the surface for ten square feet. They wasted no time frantically pushing the bulk of the remainder out with their feet. Fuller hit the gas again, forcing most of the rest of the sand out of his truck, almost losing Phillips and Jackson in the process. Sand scattered across the roadbed in the middle of the turn, just as he had hoped. The little Nissan, now lighter by 200 lbs., squealed around the corner and when the Marathon attempted the same high-speed turn, the big car spun 180 degrees in the freshly laid sand, its back wheels landing in a ditch. The Nissan pulled away, out of sight, as the agents sat helplessly hung up, outsmarted by the three men and the girl they thought was a trusted aide.

•••••

"Where are we going?" asked Fuller. A fair question he thought, since Suzanne was navigating.

"I know a spot down Old Route 116. My daddy's hunting cabin is there."

This was sounding familiar to Fuller. "Next to the Manning Farm?" he asked.

"You are just full of surprises," Suzanne said, almost smiling, puzzled at his knowledge of rural Gettysburg.

With no sign of the Marathon behind them, Tommy relaxed and slowed the truck to a manageable, safer speed. The whirlwind of sand and debris settled down in the truck bed, allowing Jackson and Phillips to open their eyes for the first time in several minutes. Jackson thrust his head through the window.

"You could have gotten us killed at that garage," he fumed.

"Look, things were turning bad quick, and I had to get out of there. You didn't have to come. I just didn't want to stay anywhere where my dead uncles shoot at me. That was just a little too weird."

131

He had a point. Jackson mumbled something and sat back in the truck bed.

Phillips took his turn through the window. "Where are we going?"

"My daddy's hunting cabin," said Suzanne.

"You don't think whoever's chasing us will look there?"

She thought for a moment and then shook off her doubts.

"Joey won't say anything, and Anthony doesn't know about it. We'll be all right. The guys won't tell 'em where we're going."

No one commented, and she sensed the need for an explanation regarding the agents and of Brooklyn's behavior.

"I know my boyfriend can be a hard-ass sometimes, but he's just trying to keep us all out of jail, or from being hung. Con-Fed doesn't look kindly on FF. Those guys we left in the ditch were supposed to be on our side..."

All Tommy Fuller heard was the word "boyfriend" and he automatically recoiled at the sound of it. This was the first revelation of a romantic link between Suzanne and Anthony and it made him uneasy. He ignored the comments about Con-Fed hanging him. In his mind he was hung already. He had shot a black kid at point blank range while wearing a Confederate Civil War uniform. He was already dead, so what was the point in worrying about it too much.

A sign reading "Manning Farm" hung from a cross bar on rusty chains at the side of a dirt road. The Nissan pickup, carrying the motley crew turned down the road, full of potholes, bumping the riders in the truck bed, eliciting complaints. The road turned sharply left and Suzanne said:

"Turn right, here."

"Where?" asked Fuller, pretending not to know. There was no obvious road to turn on. A faint path with two worn tire tracks in the tall grass was barely visible and Suzanne pointed to it. Fuller gingerly let the Nissan creep forward, like testing ice on a frozen lake.

They wound their way through a countryside befitting a Thomas Kinkade calendar, complete with meadows, meandering creeks, high hills, and virtually untouched, lush green and mid-summer beauty. It made them all feel a little better and they would have reveled in the land's bucolic healing power, if they weren't facing such desperate circumstances. Within minutes the old path led to a small cabin that was in obvious disrepair, but looked no worse than many of the houses they had seen in town.

"This is it," Suzanne said, nodding toward the one story dwelling. "There's not much here. It hasn't been used since winter, I think, but there might be some leftover provisions stocked up. Let's hope there's enough to feed you boys."

Tommy Fuller opened the door of his truck, which clunked loudly and felt like it might fall off its hinges. The two men in back jumped out and rubbed their sore parts. They followed Suzanne to the front door, which had a combination lock securing a rusty latch. She moved the dial on the lock back and forth a few turns and it popped open. Within seconds they were inside.

The early afternoon sun was sliding behind a large hill. The interior of the cabin already darkening, Suzanne hauled down three kerosene lamps, stored on a cabinet top. The men considered their new refuge. It was essentially a small, wood-frame house with one large room that served as kitchen, living room and bedroom, not unlike the safe house from the night before, though much more rustic and remote. A back door led to the bathroom–an outhouse.

"Good feng shui in here," remarked Jackson to Phillips, sizing up the place. Suzanne had overheard him and wondered what code he might have been using, but said nothing.

A permanent ladder, reaching from the floor to six feet above, led to the loft, a cozy, small, open-air bedroom under the rafters. There were no electric lights or electric appliances of any kind. A cast iron wood stove and an icebox were it for modern luxuries. Cabinets lined the walls and Suzanne opened one to reveal stocks of canned food and a box of matches. She filled the small hopper of the stove with hunks of oak and hickory that had been piled in a bucket on the floor. She lit the kindling and fanned the small flame with her hand before closing the door with a squeak and metallic ring. She was clearly at home as a frontierswoman and was again proving her resourcefulness. She moved with speed, skill, and grace, as if she had been doing these things all her life; and she had. She took a seat and the others followed suit.

"Okay, now what?" asked Phillips. No one answered. No one ever answered any time anyone asked a question in this place, a place full of contradictions and upside-down realities.

"This old cabin has been in my family as long as I can remember," said Suzanne, breaking the silence. "My grandfather built it. In fact, he and my grandmother lived here when they were first married."

"Would that be Popo and Maw-Maw?" asked Fuller. Suzanne's face went white. She slid her chair back, startled.

"How do you know these things?" she asked, shaking her head, eyes flashing. Fuller's knowledge of her family was frightening. "And WHY? Why would spies care about my dead grandparents? Anthony is right. This is way too creepy. When are you going to tell us who you all really are and just what the hell is going on?"

Fuller sighed, sorry he'd upset the girl. "As soon as we know ourselves."

•••••

133

After a late lunch, the group moved to the threadbare furniture set in front of the fireplace, though it was too warm for a fire.

Before Tommy sat down, he produced his cherished Confederate cap, from his rear pocket. He had folded it, in haste, before leaving the safe house earlier that day, and the leather bill now showed a crease in the center. He reverently straightened the cap and let his fingers examine the small hole in its left side.

"I wonder what happened to this poor guy?" he asked, still gazing at the cap. "Looks like a bullet hole, don't it?" he asked, showing the cap to Jackson, in an unusually comfortable, conversational tone. Fuller hadn't said more than two words to Jackson in his life; one of which was unrepeatable. Jackson seized the friendly moment and managed a smile.

"Yeah, afraid so," he answered, taking and examining the historic relic. "Bad spot for a bullet hole." He turned the cap upside down and his eyes caught the inside, back panel.

"Where'd you get this, Fuller?" asked Jackson.

"An antique store about 10 miles out of town, on old Highway 97. I bought it when I was about 15 and first getting into the reenacting stuff."

"Do you know anything about where it came from?" asked Jackson. "I mean before the antique store got it?"

"Nope. Nothing, only that it's the real deal and that the hole in the side was, more than likely, from a small caliber weapon and that it probably killed whoever was wearing it at the time."

Jackson felt the stitching in the back and looked closer, flipping up the interior hatband.

"Whoever it was…his initials were 'T.G.'"

The wheels of their collective memories turned slowly at first, chewing up the new information, daring not to swallow. The three men each began to feel a tightening in their chests. Waves of unease and revelation washed through each of them from head to toe.

"Thomas Grissom?" Phillips asked and then answered himself. "I'll be damned. T. G. - Thomas Grissom. It could be, but what are the odds that Tommy would own this Grissom guy's cap?"

The stunned men almost didn't hear Suzanne, who had been listening while cleaning up from the meal.

"You're not talking about Thomas Grissom, the War hero?" she asked innocently.

"Maybe," said Phillips. "I think he's the Confederate soldier that owned this cap. His brother may have saved our lives," he continued, realizing, too late, how odd that would sound to the young woman, and how implausible it sounded to them.

"What do you remember about him, Suzanne?" asked Phillips.

"Well, we have Grissom Day every year, on his birthday, June 9th, and

134

in school we learned that he and his brother placed a lot of explosives near Emmitsburg Road, blew up the Yankee army, and they won the Battle of Gettysburg. By the fifth day of the battle, it was all over. The Grissoms, Pickett, and General Robert E. Lee became heroes."

"Fifth day?" asked Jackson, protesting her facts. "Pickett? A hero?"

"Yep," said Phillips. "That's what we remember too…" He kicked Jackson at the ankle. She couldn't know that in their understanding The Battle of Gettysburg was only three days long, there was no explosion, or even a plan for one. She knew nothing about how Pickett's Charge was a disaster with a 50-percent casualty rate, and that the Rebs never recovered from the losses. But this Suzanne, a smart girl, knew her history, just a very different version.

If Suzanne had a million questions for them, she held her tongue. And since the men had a million more for her, it was easier just to make small talk.

"I don't suppose you have any more of those Cokes in the fridge?" asked Tommy.

"No, sorry. No fridge here, just water," she said, pumping a handle near the sink and filling three glasses with ice-cold well water.

"Those Cokes were good. Better 'n' ours at home," said Tommy, thinking about how good another would be.

"They were good," said Jackson. "Something different about them, for sure." His mind drifted back to his studies and a history that seemed to be changing every minute.

After Jackson had first accepted the invitation to join the reenacting group, with its first big reenactment looming around the corner, he approached the opportunity with an almost obsessive need to know everything he could about The Battle of Gettysburg. The same compulsive work ethic that had made him a great prosecutor and lawyer had helped make him a quick and thorough study in this venture as well. He spent most of his free time at the local library and on the Internet poring over documents surrounding the Civil War, American history, and this battle in particular. The fresh insight, they would soon find, would prove invaluable. But he needed more information.

"We need to find a library," Jackson said. "Somehow, I don't think I can Google too much around here."

There were details about the battle he wanted to review and knew were important. Going on-line for research would not be an option. "Is the Gettysburg Public Library still on Washington Avenue?" he asked Suzanne.

"No, it's never been on Washington Ave.," Suzanne answered. "It's on Jeff."

"Jeff?" he asked.

"Jefferson Davis Boulevard."

None of the men had ever heard of a street named for the Confederacy's First President, but here, in this place, it made sense and they trusted her information.

"We might find some answers there," Jackson added. "If we can start to sort out when and how things changed…" Suzanne looked at him, puzzled by the strange comment. It was too early to hope that they might find a way out of this mess, but for their own sanity they had to at least try to find out *what* had happened and *why*. That, they hoped, might be possible.

"Tomorrow we should go," said Jackson, resolute.

"Umm…you can't go into the library," said Suzanne. "It's Whites only. But it's real small anyway. No one hardly uses it."

"What about a bookstore?" he asked with a sigh.

Suzanne looked even more puzzled. "Books aren't for sale, only for loan. You know that. You can't own any books here. It's illegal."

Jackson, though shocked, was too tired to rant and realized it wouldn't do any good anyway, so he slumped back in his chair. Suzanne sensed his disappointment.

"But if we cross the border," she said, "Blacks are allowed just about everywhere, including the library. D.C. is your best bet," she offered.

She *was* a smart girl. This was good news to Jackson and he sat up. A chance to go home and hopefully find his family, his mother and two aunts, and to go to one of the finest reference libraries in the world: The Library of Congress on Independence Avenue, in the heart of D.C.

"How will we get there?" asked Phillips. "We can't be seen in that truck of Tommy's"

"I'll borrow Anthony's Marathon," said Suzanne.

"I don't like that idea," said Fuller. "First, I don't think he likes us, especially me, and second, I think we need to keep this trip on the D.L." Again Suzanne twisted her face in puzzlement.

"Oh, sorry," he explained. "That's the "down-low." You know, keep things quiet."

"We don't really have any other options," said Jackson. "I trust Suzanne and if she says we can trust Anthony and use his car, then I think we should. We will learn more in three hours at that library than in three months skulking around Gettysburg. And I really want to get to D.C. and outta this place, no offense, young lady."

"No offense taken. We've got problems here, I'll admit it. I think I can borrow the car without him knowing," she said. "That should help keep it on the…L.D.?"

Tommy smiled broadly at the incredibly cute girl sitting across from him.

"D.L.!" he laughed. "Get it right!"

"We're agreed, we've got to go," said Jackson, "and I vote we go in Anthony's wheels." The men nodded, Fuller was unable to refuse the woman's encouragement.

"Okay then," said Suzanne. "Tomorrow I'll hike into town, should take me a few hours, get Anthony's car, and come back for you."

"It's too far to hike in," said Fuller. "We could drive in before daybreak, ditch the truck, pick up the car, and come back for you guys. This cabin is sort of on our way out of town… anyway, it will be a lot less suspicious, if we're seen without you two riding in the truck bed."

"Who says it wouldn't be you in the truck bed?" asked Jackson, almost smiling.

"Well, it's my truck," he answered, almost smiling back. "And we're not letting this pretty girl in the back of it ever again." They all nodded, recalling Suzanne's spontaneous move to join their team at the gas station, with a daring leap into the back of a moving vehicle under gunfire. This was one tough, committed young woman. They were glad she was on their side, for whatever unknown reasons.

"Okay," she agreed. "We'll go in before sunup."

"Thank you, Suzanne," said Fuller, becoming emotional. "You are the only one helping us at all." Tommy was unusually talkative. "You've put us up twice, nursed my wounds, fed us, helped us escape, and now you're putting yourself back on the line. We can't thank you enough. I can't thank you enough."

They spent an uneventful afternoon napping, taking short walks outside the cabin, and enjoying a picnic dinner outside. They watched the sun set, and the sky turn shades of vivid orange and finally, deep indigo blue. After cleaning up the dishes and preparing makeshift beds in the loft and on the couch near the fireplace, Tommy and Suzanne slipped out the front door. The moonless night was cool and clear. Tommy couldn't remember ever seeing so many stars. "It's beautiful out here," he said.

"Yes, it sure is. I've been coming to this cabin since I was a little girl. I used to love to play out here. I dreamed of living here for a while. Can you imagine?" He could imagine. It would be easy with a girl as beautiful as Suzanne, leading a simple life, away from repair shops, the inner city, gangs, courtrooms, and bill collectors. He could easily imagine.

"You seem so familiar to me," Suzanne said to him softly. "I know we've never met, and yet you somehow know things about me, so I can't help but think that maybe we have met before, but I don't know where. Have we?"

"I think so," said Tommy. "I think we're," he hesitated, "joined together in ways we can't understand."

This made Suzanne a bit uneasy and she shivered, partly from the cool night air, and partly because of this strange, young man she was so attracted to and the things he was saying. Tommy moved close to her, warming her arms with his hands and daring to pull her to his side. They stood together, saying nothing, gazing up at the sky.

Chapter 18

Suzanne and Tommy shared the loft and managed to get a few hours of fitful sleep. The task at hand kept them from really relaxing and they finally just gave up trying, rising from the cozy bed when Suzanne told him it was 4:30. Phillips and Jackson, on the other hand, were snoring away enjoying a sound sleep on the lower level.

"Very romantic," whispered Suzanne, and at first Tommy was taken back by the bold comment. He agreed, but it seemed a forward thing for her to say. Then, following her gaze, he looked down from the loft and she nodded at the two men sharing a foldout bed, nearly spooning one another. Mike Phillip's arm was thrown over the hulking body of Greg Jackson and it did paint a comical picture.

"If I had a smartphone, I'd get a shot of that," said Tommy.

"I wish I understood half of what you guys say," she added. Together they made their way, still dressed from the day before, down the sturdy ladder to the middle of the room. They left the cabin quietly, Tommy with keys in hand.

"Don't you think the cops will be after us?" asked Tommy.

"Are you kidding? No," Suzanne answered, "they're so corrupt that nobody trusts them... even the agents. Nobody tells them anything. Besides this truck is pretty quiet, no one will hear us coming."

"Who are these agents, anyway?"

"Yesterday, I would have told you they were working for the FF, but now I'm not so sure."

The driver's door clunked so loudly upon opening that it echoed across the valley like a shotgun blast. They both shared a hearty laugh at the truck's so-called quietness. He liked laughing with her. He and Susan rarely laughed anymore. Financial pressures, legal troubles, and the difficult circumstances of their plight in that neighborhood weighed heavily upon them both. There hadn't been much lately to laugh about. In the midst of all the horror, this was a nice change.

Hearing the loud clunking outside, Jackson peeled Phillips' arm from around his waist, got up, and drew back the thin window curtain just in time to see taillights disappearing around the corner.

"What was that?" asked Phillips, stirring, still in bed.

"Fuller and the girl leaving. I guess they felt like they didn't need us."

"Are you beginning to feel like we're intruding on a little chemistry here, or is it just me?" asked Phillips through a wide yawn.

"Oh yeah, definitely some sparks flying between those two," said Jackson. "Horny little shit, isn't he? He's wanted for murder, and we're in the middle of some mind-blowing weirdness, and he's all working his little lost boy routine."

"Jealous?"

"Hell, yes, I'm jealous. Did you see her?" Phillips laughed again at his always-agitated friend. "He says she's his wife," continued Jackson. "That really complicates things."

"I'm not so sure she isn't," said Phillips. "I only met his wife once last year, and I don't remember her that well, but I think this girl seems familiar to me, too. I mean those two mechanics were definitely his uncles, even if they didn't know it. There are so many things that are the same here. Why couldn't some of the people be the same, too? It's no crazier than anything else about this place."

Jackson sighed, too tired to think about it. "I just hope they hurry back with that car, so we can get to D.C. I know we can start sorting some of this out."

"You realize your family may not be in D.C. when we get there, Greg. Prepare yourself for that. Even if they are, I don't think they'll be the same. They probably won't recognize you. That could be hard to take."

"Yeah, I've been thinking about that. I know you're right, but we've got to go look. I have to know. So, what about your family?"

"Well, we were never that close. My dad lives in New York...I think, and my brother was out West, last I heard. At least he was day before yesterday, but now...? Who the hell knows? By the way, you snore like a raspy hyena."

"You too, buddy. You too." The men folded up the bed, washed up a bit and opened a mason jar of some mystery meat and gravy. They finally decided it was venison. They stoked the small fire under the stove and were cooking and eating within minutes.

"You know with all the advancements we think we have in our..." Phillips couldn't think of the right word, "world," he continued. "They've got things worked out pretty well here. This food didn't take much longer

140

to cook than in a microwave, and it's a hell of a lot better. Plus, did you see how nice the outskirts of town looked? It's like *Mayberry*."

Jackson shot an angry look at his friend.

"Don't get too comfortable here, Mike. This place ain't all that. You don't see it the way I do. You don't have to be licensed to walk down the street. You can go to any library in any town without people looking sideways at you. We are going to figure out how we got into this hellhole and how to get back to the good ole U.S. of A., that I know. Fuck Mayberry! I'll spend the rest of my days figuring out how to get the hell out of here. I will not live in this racist, twisted place one second longer than I have to."

Phillips was silent for a moment, absorbing the scolding, and the truth of what his friend was saying.

"You're right. I'm sorry. I wasn't thinking how that sounded. This has got to be a bigger shock for you than the rest of us. I'm with you. I really am. I know we have got to get black...back, I mean 'back'." They laughed at the slip.

"I know we do, too," said Jackson. "Besides, I miss my cell phone and my Beemer."

•••••

The Nissan moved along smoothly in the pre-dawn of day three in their new world, new to Tommy Fuller anyway. For Suzanne, all was status quo, except for the visitors, and especially on one of whom she was developing a serious crush.

"So tell me about Anthony," asked Fuller. Suzanne smiled. "I wondered when you'd ask." She looked out the window at the eastern sky, which was showing hues of beautiful blue as the daylight slowly encroached on the waning black of night.

"We've been friends for years, since high school really. He likes me more than I like him. He's very jealous and very possessive. I finally gave in about three months ago and he's told the whole world that we're in love and going to get married," she paused, "but I just don't feel that way about him. I don't want to hurt him, with his family situation the way it is. He doesn't need any more sadness and pain in his life."

"What do you mean? What happened to him?"

"Well, he's from Little Italy, that's where the accent comes from."

"Little Italy?" Tommy interrupted. "I thought he was from Brooklyn, the way he talks."

"You don't know much for a spy," Suzanne teased. "He's from New Brooklyn in Little Italy, in Virginia. You know, where, like five million Italians landed after they immigrated during the War For Europe?"

"Oh, yeah, yeah...right," said Tommy. She was not convinced that he had any idea what she was talking about.

"Anyway. His whole family died from the Yellow Fever epidemic of 2006. His aunt arranged for him to come live here, when he was 13. He got into the usual trouble, typical of kids like him. There were so many orphans. He started hanging with a bad crowd and they beat up a shopkeeper in town, almost killed him, and he went to reform school for a year."

Tommy's blood ran cold at the thought of gangs roaming the streets and beating up shopkeepers, but he said nothing to her of his own troubles.

"I met him when he came back from reform school, when he was 15. He had changed. He was actually one of the few that *were* reformed. Tony and my little brother Joey got to be friends, and now, the three of us share an apartment. Tony had, basically, just kind of grown up and started to get his life together. He was approached by the Resistance last year and he got pretty gung-ho into reunification and we just kind of followed along. Nothing else to do and it seemed like a good idea."

"What about work?" asked Tommy.

"They pay us," she said. "Not much, but it covers basic expenses. We help with the effort in small ways. We do believe in reunification. I mean, not all the violence, but it just seems we should be one nation again."

She stopped herself. She was pouring out personal details of their lives that could potentially get them all hanged. In Con-Fed even discussing reunification was treason. But she trusted Tommy Fuller and it angered her, because she couldn't figure out why.

"We're almost to the turn," she said. "Left, here." Tommy made the turn, off the main road into town, passing a few small houses and then up to a three-story, wood-frame building that had ten small apartments within. Tommy saw Anthony's big Marathon in the parking lot and Suzanne instructed him to park next to it. He turned the motor off and looked at her nervously.

"I'll go in, Tommy. You, please wait. I'm going to sneak his keys away, so I don't have to get into it with him. We just don't have the time and it will be easier that way. He sleeps like a rock, so I think I'll be in and out before he knows what's happened."

"Won't he think his car's been stolen when he gets up?"

"Well, he'll eventually see his keys missing and probably figure out it was me. I'm the only one who knows where he keeps them. But, even if he did report it stolen, the cops won't do anything. They're involved in half of the car thefts, themselves."

"Okay, but hurry. I'll worry if you're not right back out."

"I will, but one more thing, pull your truck around back and drive it down that dirt path. No one ever goes there. Hide it the best you can. People used to dump leaves and tree limbs back there, so it should be easy to cover it up some. And don't get out of the driver's side."

Suzanne exited the truck and walked briskly to the front of the complex. Tommy could see her walking up the first flight of stairs on the outside of the building and stopping in front of apartment B-3. Then he made his move. He did as she told him and found that the dirt road in back was, indeed, the perfect place to hide his truck. He did a pretty thorough job covering the Nissan and felt confident it wouldn't be found, unless someone were really looking hard for it. He slipped out the passenger side door and quietly walked around front to wait by the Marathon.

Entering the apartment, which was barely illuminated by bits of morning light peeking through the windows, Suzanne crept quietly to her bedroom and saw the form of Anthony under the covers. On the dresser, behind a change jar and Anthony's wallet, she saw what she was looking for. She lifted some cash from inside the wallet and the keys from the dresser top. She turned, stepping quietly toward the door.

"So now ya stealin' from me?" came the clear, cold voice of her boyfriend. Surprised to hear his voice, she took a quick breath, and turned to see him as he sat up in bed.

"Tony, you scared me."

"I don't know what's happened to you, Suzanne. Are they blackmailing you? That Tommy guy got your head messed up?" He was hurt and upset and it showed, almost on the verge of tears. It was exactly what Suzanne had wanted to avoid. She walked to the bed and sat on the edge. She put the back of her hand on his cheek.

"Tony...I...I'm sorry. I just didn't want to try to explain everything right now. I was going to call you when I got to a phone. I'm not sure exactly what's happening with these guys, but I trust them. Especially Tommy. He knows things about me. Please let me help them get their job done."

"What job, Suzanne? What do you know about them?" He was getting agitated and raised his voice. "They talk in codes, even when they're alone. That Tommy Fuller guy called you his wife. One of the agents told me so!" He was shouting now. "What's that supposed to mean?" Suzanne was baffled by this new piece of information.

"What do you mean? When did he do that?" she asked.

"The first night, at the safe house, after we left. They got it on tape. Tommy told those other guys that you were his wife. Maybe you're all in on it together and have been playin' me and Joey for fools?" He pushed her hand away and stood up, grabbing the cash and the car keys away from her. Joey appeared in his boxers at the bedroom door, rubbing sleep from his eyes, focusing on his sister.

"Sissy...where you been?" he asked. "We were crazy worried about you. What's all the yelling about?"

"She's stealing money and cars now, Joey," answered Anthony. He jumped out of bed, grabbing both of her wrists.

"Ouch, Tony. You're hurting me." She struggled to get free from his strong grip.

"Okay, okay, everybody calm down," said Joey, stepping in to defend his sister. He was met with a hard backhand to the face, which knocked him to the floor.

"Joey!" Suzanne screamed, still locked in her boyfriend's grip. "Tony, what are you doing? Let me go!" she demanded.

"I can't let you go, Suzanne. We're going to be married and you're going to be *my* wife. You're not thinking straight. This is for your own good."

He grabbed both of her wrists in one powerful hand, reached into the closet and produced a belt. Whether he was planning to tie her down, or beat her, she couldn't be sure. Before he got too far, he found himself on the receiving end of a punch, very much like the one he had just delivered. He fell backwards and a glass on the bureau was knocked to the floor, shattering. Joey was strong, and Anthony had not seen the punch coming. Before he could rise, Joey kicked Anthony in the jaw with his bare foot, rendering him nearly unconscious.

"Ahhh! Damn! My foot!" Joey screamed through clenched teeth, both jaw and foot throbbing.

In the living room the locked front door was rattled by an unseen hand, then blasted open by Tommy Fuller's booted foot coming through first, followed quickly by the rest of him. He followed the commotion to the bedroom, and was there in two running strides ready to knock someone down. Joey was closest. He cocked his arm back when Suzanne cried out.

"Stop! Will you ridiculous men stop hitting each other? What is it with guys?" she was furious and crying. Tommy glanced around at each, trying to figure out what was going on. Anthony lay on the floor, coming to. Joey was hopping on one foot, trying to get his balance, leaning on the doorframe.

"Are you all right, Suzanne?" asked Fuller of the crying girl.

"No, I'm not all right. This is horrible. Why is it that fighting and shooting and kicking are the first things you men do?" No one answered.

"Tony, listen to me, "she said through sobs. "We're friends. We're only friends. I am not your possession. I'm sorry I let it go this far. I never meant to hurt you. You know I believe in the Resistance and want to work with you, but we are not together like boyfriend and girlfriend anymore. You've got to let it go. I need to help these men, to help Tommy and his friends fix whatever problem they're having. They're good people and they need our help."

She rubbed her wrists, which were red and puffy from her brief detention. Anthony averted his gaze, ashamed at the brutal physicality of

144

his treatment of the girl he loved, and embarrassed by having been beaten down by her younger brother.

"Please...let me borrow your car and $20. I'll pay you back, and I'll bring your car back, too. We need to go to D.C. and we need to go now."

"Go," was all he said with a dismissive wave, and she picked up the keys and two $10 bills from the floor.

"Please, you two...," she pointed at Anthony and her brother, before leaving the bedroom, "kiss and make up. I mean it. We're family, all we have is each other, and we've got to keep it together."

Tommy and Suzanne quickly exited the small apartment and made their way, running down the stairs, to Tony's Marathon. She would drive this time. They pulled quietly away, heading back toward the cabin where Phillips and Jackson anxiously awaited their return. Anthony and Joey watched out the window as the Marathon rounded the corner out onto the main road. There were others watching the Marathon as well.

•••••

A smoke spiral drifted from the partially open window of a black sedan parked at the far end of the apartments' parking lot. A cigarette butt dropped to the ground, creating a shower of red sparks, as the car's engine came to life.

"That's them. Let's go," said the taller man. "The little dago was right. He said she'd be back. Now she's leaving again."

The agent's sedan pulled slowly out on to the road and they could just see Anthony's car barreling down the two-lane. They were trained in tailing people and knew to stay back, especially on a mostly deserted road.

Tommy and Suzanne sped back toward the cabin and were on the road for a few minutes before either of them spoke.

"You've got a bit of a lead foot, don't you?" asked Tommy. She didn't answer.

"Thanks for...worrying about me," said Suzanne, glancing in his direction. "I think he was getting ready to hog-tie me to the bed or something." She sighed heavily. "He's really not a bad guy...he's just...obsessed. He's obsessed with me, obsessed with the FF, with reunification, and he's only 19, that has something to do with it, too."

Tommy thought about Anthony's age and about how fast he'd had to grow up. Though he, himself, was just 23, in the four years since his 19th birthday, he had endured things most people never deal with in a lifetime. He felt decades older than any 19-year-old. Still a young man by anyone's definition, Tommy Fuller was already longing for the innocence and carefree days of his of lost youth.

"How old are you, Suzanne?" he asked, already knowing the answer.

"I'm 20. You?"

"Twenty three"

"Bull," she said with a little too much enthusiasm.

"No, really I'm 23. I'll be 24 in two months."

"No offense, but I thought you had to be at least 30." She grinned.

He feigned incredulity. "Gee thanks."

"Don't worry, you're still kind of cute. You just look, well, kind of, worried." He furrowed his brow, creating his best, exaggerated, worried look.

"Like this?"

"Yes. Exactly. That's how you look all the time."

He smiled at her and caressed her shoulder. This was how he and Susan used to flirt before all the troubles. He missed their carefree silliness, terribly and with Suzanne it was like their first year together, all over again.

Their car turned down the dirt road at the Manning Farm and they eased their way to the little cabin. The dark sedan following them slowed, pulled past the farm road and backed in behind two large trees, providing both a vantage point and cover.

"Now, we wait," said the driver. The shorter agent fired up a cigarette and rolled the window all the way open.

Jackson and Phillips walked outside to meet the arriving car, having heard it coming. Tommy and Suzanne got out and met them half way to the door.

"Any trouble?" asked Phillips.

"Nothing we couldn't handle," answered Suzanne, a little quickly, preempting any possible rehashing of a fight she clearly didn't want to discuss.

"You guys ready?" asked Fuller. They nodded in the affirmative. "Greg, um…your…hat."

Jackson rolled his eyes and walked back into the cabin. Tommy's own hat was folded, partially exposed, hanging out of his back pocket. For the past year, he'd gone everywhere with it. He found himself unconsciously feeling the scratchy, wool fiber with his fingers and poking through the bullet hole. Jackson emerged from the cabin, Redcap in hand, and they got in the car. With Suzanne again behind the wheel, they were off, headed toward Washington D.C., 80-miles away, hoping to find at least a few of the answers they so desperately needed. They never saw the black Marathon pull out behind them.

Chapter 19

"You're going to take 97, Baltimore Pike, right?" asked Phillips. Suzanne shot him a look he couldn't quite identify.

"It's safer to stay to the back roads," said Suzanne. They were on a path that would take them on secondary roads, southeast, through Maryland. It was odd to be headed south in order to go toward the North. As a part of a permanent re-drawing of State borders after the War, the eastern half of Maryland, including Baltimore and the counties surrounding D.C., would remain part of the Federated States, but the western half of the State was now Con-Fed territory.

The first 45 minutes of the trip was uneventful and the men were amazed at the scenic beauty along the way. Many of rolling hills that were once obscured by shopping malls and car dealerships, were now plainly visible and they marveled at the countryside.

"The border is closed, unless you have credentials, or know the other way through," said Suzanne. She smirked slightly, pleased at knowing things these super spies didn't.

They switched roads and headed southwest, on a two-lane toward Frederick, Maryland. What the men had no way of knowing was that along the border there were sympathizers who had bribed local officials, built secret roads, and a few tunnels, that could generally get people and goods back and forth with a minimum of risk, though in recent years it had been getting trickier. Suzanne knew exactly where to go. The Cross Continental Border Fence, this close to the Fed-Stat's Capitol, was as solid as a rock and well guarded. She explained the Border Fence and the tight security to her passengers.

"Then how do we get through?" asked Fuller.

"We go under," she said.

One of only six carefully hidden and maintained tunnels along the entire 1500-mile border, was well known to Suzanne. They were fortunate it had been so near. The tunnel was what was left of the rail system in the region from long before the War started. After the War, all of the north-south rail lines were dismantled and all of the tunnels bisecting the border, some 300 of them, were filled-in or otherwise destroyed with explosives.
In the hilly countryside, near Gettysburg, and farther west toward more mountainous regions, some five tunnels had been destroyed, all but one.

No one really knew how it escaped unnoticed by either side. The tunnel had been part of a little-used rail line that had fallen into disrepair and had been unused since the late 1850s. A century-and-a-half of thick vegetation hid the entrances so well, that when the trillion-dollar Border Fence was erected, the engineers went right over the top of the mountain, never even seeing the three-mile tunnel beneath. Patrols from both sides drove the roads along the border in routine inspections, but still never noticed the entrances and exits on either side.

The Freedom Fighters, and a few crafty smugglers, were given this prize 10 years earlier by the grandson of an old railroad man. He was in his 70s and kept the tunnel secret until he figured the information might be safe. The FF purchased as much land surrounding the tunnel entrance as they could and built small, unassuming, working farms on both sides of the border. Their goal was to blend in, and that they did well.

When Suzanne turned the big car into the driveway of a house that looked like it had been there for 100 years, the men in the car with her were surprised. A screen door slammed as three stone-faced men immediately appeared from the house and stopped the car from moving any further. For a moment Phillips and Jackson had thought Suzanne might have sold them out. Tommy Fuller knew better.

They all got out and stood in the driveway, eyeing each other.

"Hello sweetie," said the oldest of the three to Suzanne. They greeted one another with a big hug.

"Hey Unka," she said with a broad smile. "These are my friends. We're going to D.C." She said it as matter-of-factly as if she were announcing a trip to the mall.

"Pleasure to meet you, boys," said the old man, shaking each of their hands. "I'm George Dietz."

As a family friend since long-before Suzanne's father had died, he had become a surrogate father to the girl and their affection for one another was obvious. She'd called him 'Unka' since she was three and not quite able to say 'Uncle.' Dietz looked at Tommy Fuller noticing the small bandage on his chin.

"Cut yourself shaving?" he asked with a friendly, but protective smile.
"Something like that," Tommy answered shyly.

"Well, any friend of Suzanne's... you know the rest. We'll get your car tags switched out right away and you should have clear sailing. I just happened to be talking to the North end and everything's clear there, too. Quiet day, just how I like 'em."

"Unka, can you change these bills for us?" she asked sweetly, handing him the two $10 bills she'd stolen, then borrowed from Anthony.

"Sure darlin', but that won't get you too far. You know about them Yanks and their crazy, runaway inflation. Let me get you a little more."

He stepped lively to the house and returned with a fist full of money, $300 in counterfeit, Fed-Stat currency.

"You all be careful," he said eyeballing the men, who were now getting back into the car. "That's my sweetie you got there with you."

The other two men with Dietz disappeared into the barn and swung open the wide doors from inside, leaving an entrance big enough for a tank. They all piled back into Anthony's car and drove forward through the barn doors. When inside, the farmhands closed the doors behind them and set to work replacing Anthony's Con-Fed Maryland car tags with Fed-Stat D.C. tags. It took their practiced hands less than 90 seconds. In front of them were workbenches, farm implements, and miscellaneous Confederate memorabilia nailed to the wall, all for show. The men easily slid two large benches, on rollers, out of the way, and then grabbed onto two handles in the wall, hidden by old hubcaps.

When they pulled open the camouflaged doors, lights went on automatically, revealing the entrance to the tunnel. Like a gaping hole in the side of a mountain, which is exactly what it was, the hand-hewn rock of the 200-year-old tunnel entrance offered a glimpse into the past. The B&O sign above the entrance was clearly visible, displaying a big number 21, signifying the Baltimore & Ohio Tunnel, # 21. They eased the car forward. The railroad ties had been long since replaced with hard-packed gravel, and the going was slow, but smooth. Behind them they saw the doors slide shut and that was that. They were on their way.

"Holy crap! That was cool," said Tommy, like a kid.

"Got to agree with you there," echoed Jackson, "this is some real James Bond action you've got here, Suzanne," he added.

"James who?" she asked.

"Ahh, never mind," said Jackson. "You wouldn't know him. This is quite impressive, that's all."

She wondered how a simple hidden tunnel would elicit such a reaction from supposed Freedom Fighters engaged in cross-border espionage. There was much more going on with her new friends than she could imagine, and it troubled her. She was patient, but only to a point.

A car moved slowly past the farm some 500-feet before stopping to do a k-turn in the road. It pulled back within a hundred feet of the only driveway and parked.

"This is it," said the driver. "They're crossing over." The two agents were well aware of the tunnel, though they had never used it before. It had been to both governments' advantage to leave the tunnels operational. It was much easier to track illicit activities knowing exactly where and how your enemies and contraband might move.

"You think we should follow?" asked the passenger, lighting a smoke.

"Yeah, I think we should. I don't like this one bit."

•••••

The lighting along the tunnel's roof stopped abruptly and Suzanne flicked on the headlights, by pulling a large knob on the dashboard.

"This is the halfway point. Just about another half-mile to go," she said, and the men swallowed hard, nervous about what would greet them on the other side. This would be their first visit to the F.S.A., the Federated States of America, and they were eager to see this new country, irrationally hopeful for a return to some kind of normalcy.

A moment later the lights returned to the tunnel's roof and Suzanne spoke:

"We're just about there, they should be ready for us."

She slowed the car as they neared a large wooden wall, hanging on rollers like an airplane hangar's bay doors. They waited.

"It should just open," she said. "They know we're coming."

They waited another minute and still no movement. She honked the horn, which echoed wildly in the tunnel. A red light flashed on the wall and illuminated a phone receiver, mounted to a wooden stand.

"That's not good," Suzanne, said, as she exited the car and hurried to the phone. She picked up the receiver and put it to her ear. The connection was bad, full of static.

"Susie, this is Unk...are you in... kind of trouble, honey? Two Fed-Stat guys...ago. They told me your friends...wanted for questioning and that...escaped once already in Gettys... local police want...bad. They tore up a garage in town. Honey, they said you've been harboring fugitives...now you're wanted, too."

"Unka, no! I'm not in any trouble," she yelled into the receiver. "Yes, I'm helping these guys, They're on our side. They're just getting their...their plan together. Where are the agents?"

"Look, I...no choice. They have credentials, they knew about the...Honey, they have guns and...on their way through to meet you. Don't get back in...car. Stay low and wait...the phone... they should be...any..."

She dropped the phone and ran to the car jumping in and slamming the big door hard and fast. "They're after us. They've been following us," she said, throwing the car into reverse, spinning a cloud of gravel and dust into the air, while backing the tank-of-a-car up 30 feet.

"We're not getting caught," she said. "Remember your little stunt at the garage, Tommy? Well, here's part two."

She threw the shifter into drive and barreled toward the wooden doors, gaining speed and gritting her teeth. Her death grip on the wheel and the resolve on her face were proof enough to the men that she planned to blast through the big doors, using the Marathon as a battering ram.

An "Oh shit," came in unison from the back seat. In her rear-view mirror she saw the approaching headlights of the two agents. She was gaining speed, and through the noise of the engine and gravel roadbed, they all heard the gunshots coming from behind them. Just 20 feet from the tunnel's end, like a crazed, blonde Kamikaze, Suzanne pressed the accelerator to the floor, laid on the horn, tightened her grip on the wheel and yelled "Hold on!" just before piloting the large car into the heavy wooden doors with a deafening crash.

The agents chasing them were blinded by the cloud of dust and had to slow their car. When they heard the crash, they slammed on their brakes, skidding to the edge of a pile of rubble. Thin beams of light from outside shown through the debris, and as the dust settled, they realized they were alone in the tunnel. The four fugitives had made it through and they were stuck 20-feet from the tunnel's exit with no way to continue the chase.

•••••

The north end of the tunnel was a carbon copy of the south end; a modest farm with a barn built to conceal the tunnel's opening. The view from the driveway, leading to the barn on the north end, had been as quiet and peaceful as a summer's day. Birds chirped in the trees and lazy, puffy clouds floated in an azure sky. The peace surrounding the phony farm was shattered in an instant when Anthony's two-ton Marathon blasted out through the barn doors, sending a dozen geese squawking and flying in all directions. They spun 180 degrees in the driveway in front of the barn and the car jerked to a full stop. Three chrome teeth, now missing from the car's expansive grill, gave it a toothy smile, like a proud seven-year-old dreaming how to spend the Tooth Fairy's money.

After they all caught their breath, Tommy looked at Suzanne, and spoke softly:

"You are crazy...but you did it."

They were all in shock as they watched tiny chips of wood and dust fall from the sky and settle on the car hood. They had a clear view of the damage they had just inflicted on two sets of barn doors and the pile of rubble left in their wake. Three men, who had heard the car horn and the unmistakable high-speed approach, emerged from the barn, thankfully unharmed. No Marathon followed. Suzanne and her passengers felt confident no one would be chasing them in their immediate future, but they wasted no time leaving the scene of the highly illegal border crossing.

"Let's get out of here," she said, wheeling the virtually undamaged car out to the road, heading east. "Too bad about their doors. I'm gonna get it from Unka."

•••••

Though they were racing to put distance between themselves and the tunnel doors they'd just crashed through and demolished, the men had time to notice a few subtle changes in their surroundings—the differences between North and South. The farm country they were traveling through at first looked pretty much like that back in Con-Fed, but as they got closer to D.C., they saw, for the first time, the advantaged North showing more prosperity.

A wider variety of cars and trucks shared the road, as opposed to the three or four models of Con-Fed's nationalized Marathon brand. The cars in Fed-Stat also looked as if they belonged in a gangster flick, but these Northern vehicles had more modern styling; they were smaller, sleeker, had sharper corners, and tailored fins, as opposed to the bulky roundness of the mighty Marathons. The Yankee cars looked more 1960, while the Con-Fed cars looked like 1940.

They also witnessed more commerce, not just because they were near a larger town, but rather because the economy, though bad, was better than its southern neighbor's. Fed-Stat hadn't had to endure decades of embargoes, and on-again off-again blockades, and had simply moved forward faster into a modern world of sorts. Though progress had slowed for two decades during the War for Europe, the mass European immigration and refugee traffic caused by the World War, at first caused great hardship, but within a decade spurred new economic growth.

The political machine of Fed-Stat didn't take to losing the Civil War very well. In 1862 Abraham Lincoln told his bodyguard: *"...do you know I believe there are men who want to take my life? ... If it is to be done, it is impossible to prevent it."* Though he did escape the fate of assassination, he was not so fortunate in his political life. He was impeached, and thrown from office in 1865, having fallen victim to the "What have you done for me lately?" syndrome, and "How could you have lost our war?" sentiments. Vice President Hannibal Hamlin became the 17th President of the now fractured Union, while a disgraced Abraham Lincoln and wife Mary Todd moved to Rolla, Missouri. Lincoln practiced law for a few years, retired, and died at 96, in 1905.

After reorganizing the new North, Stephen A. Douglas, a one-time bitter rival of Lincoln's, became the 1st President of the new Federated States of America. Douglas had defeated Hamlin for the Republican Party's nomination, and he immediately set about making life in the South as difficult and miserable as possible, for as long as possible.

Con-Fed eventually rallied their own trade partners, fended off blockades, and made progress, but it was well into the 1920s and 1930s before they ever fully moved out of the Post-War period. Fed-Stat, on the other hand, raced into the 20th century, unwilling to share anything with the rest of the world, let alone their enemies in the South.

All this history was lost on these three Travelers, who struggled, every minute, trying to reconcile what they thought they knew, with what was coming into focus.

"We're a little less than an hour out of D.C.," said Suzanne.

"Not too bad," said Jackson, realizing it took him nearly that long to make the trip in his BMW.

"I'm really confused about the men in the Marathon," said Phillips to Suzanne. "I thought you said they were Fed-Stat guys, helping the reunification underground?"

"They are, they are," she said emphatically. "Or at least I thought they were. They set us up in that apartment, got us fake jobs in town...they even got Joey's history teacher to change a grade from an F to a B+. They're underground themselves, they said, but it seems almost like they're working for...both sides? I don't get any of this. It also doesn't help that you guys keep busting loose every time they get close. I'm sure at first they just wanted to talk to you. Now, they're totally convinced you're up to no good. And I'm not helping much."

"Suzanne, thank you," said Tommy. "No one else would believe in us with so little to go on. I'm sorry that we haven't told you more. It's just so...complicated."

She heard the sincerity in his voice and saw it in his eyes. She knew, beyond a doubt, that she was doing the right thing. He would tell her what he could, when he could, she was sure of that. They drove on in silence for the next 30-minutes, the only sounds coming from the car's radio and Suzanne's quiet singing in accompaniment. The station was playing songs the men had never heard before until one tune, in particular, caught their ears: *Sweet Home Alabama*. Suzanne knew every word. The men looked at one another and Phillips spoke.

"How is that possible?" he asked.

"What? The song? It's new," said Suzanne. "It's a big hit. Everybody loves it on both sides of the border. We request it all the time."

"New?" asked Tommy, a longtime Lynyrd Skynyrd fan. "That song is from the mid 70s, it's like, almost 40 years old."

"Well, they just started playing it on the wireless a month or so ago…that's all I know."

"I hate to mention this," said Phillips "But I need a pit stop … and something to eat. Maybe we could blow a little of that Fed-Stat green your uncle gave you?"

"You guys sure talk funny," she said. "I don't know what a 'pit stop' is, or anything about Fed–Stat green, but if you mean you've got to pee and want to spend some money on food, I'm in."

"You catch on quick," said Tommy, patting her playfully on the head. They sang the final refrain of the song together and hearing it, somehow, comforted them all. *"Sweet home Alabama, where the skies are so blue. Sweet home Alabama, Lord I'm comin' home to you…"*

•••••

The "All-American Diner" had found its way to this new world and the four fugitives were about to pull into an establishment straight out of *American Graffiti*. The restaurant gleamed in shiny, stainless steel and had real neon lights, something they hadn't seen anywhere in Gettysburg. A sign reading "Hungry Boy's" beckoned them to choose one of two options: "Drive-In" or "Sit-A-Spell."

"I guess we're safer in the car," said Jackson, sounding a little afraid to test the racial tolerance of this unknown country.

"Yeah, let's do the drive-in and grab a quick burger," said Phillips. "Order me a cheeseburger and a Coke. I've got to hit the head."

Phillips ran from the car, even before it stopped rolling, and made it through the front door finding three restrooms. The signs read "Men," "Women," and "Colored."

"Greg isn't going to like this," he muttered to himself.

Outside, a busty, extremely top-heavy girl on roller skates, wearing an exceptionally low-cut sweater, power-slid to the window and smacked her gum while reaching for a pad and pencil from her apron. Her hair was piled high on top of her head. From the bottom of her roller skates to the top of her beehive, she was nearly 6 and ½ feet tall.

"How are you folks, today?" she asked with a nasally, high-pitched squeak.

"We're good," said Suzanne, faking a smile, clearly not approving of the cleavage thrust in her face. "Four cheeseburgers, four 'NC' cokes, and four fried potato cakes. That'll do it."

"Okay, guys. Be right back." She took off in a whirl, using the pole near the front door to fling herself into the building, like a mad stripper on wheels. When she did, she flew chest-first into Mike Philips, knocking them both to the ground. He sputtered at the collision, then laughed, got up

154

and helped the young woman to her wobbly, roller-skate-clad feet.

"Abby!" shouted the manager, who'd seen the whole thing. "I've told you a hundred times not to swing on those poles. What am I going to do with you?"

"No harm done," said Philips. "I'm not litigating much these days."

"I'm so sorry," said the balding, 40-something manager, as he brushed dirt off of Phillips' back.

"Have you ordered yet, sir?" asked the still apologetic manager.

"Yeah, I think so. I'm with them out in that... Marathon," he answered, pointing to the car, which was bouncing slightly from the laughter of those inside who'd seen the spectacle.

"A Marathon...," said the manager, his eyes widening. "I haven't seen one of those in years. What a great car! They make the best hot-rods I've ever seen. Hard to get those Nashville V-8's in any car up here. They're unbeatable!"

"Well, you're right," Phillips agreed, pretending he knew. "It's a fine automobile."

"Yeah, for a crappy Corn-Fed city like Nashville, they did all right in the car department. They should be thankful Detroit left them alone. Sorry, again for Miss Abby's carelessness. Your food order is on me."

"That's not necessary, but thanks," Phillips offered. He smiled at Abby, silently mouthing the words "Don't worry." She did the same back to him, saying, "I'm soooo sorry."

"Where' you folks headed anyway?" asked the manager. "D.C.," Phillips shouted, walking toward the car. Jackson was the first to crack wise. "Did she distract you with something, Mike? You get a lap-dance in there? That was a bad spill."

"No, no," he answered. "I'm just clumsy, I guess. Though I saved us a few bucks; the Manager's paying for this one."

"Your skills are as sharp as ever, Counselor," said Jackson.

"Hey, when you're good, you're good," Phillips agreed.

"Life goes on," thought Tommy Fuller to himself, as they laughed and cajoled with one another. Here in this unknown world, in unimaginable trouble, no closer to finding a way back home, they still had it within them to laugh and enjoy each other's company. The four were becoming fast friends in the midst of terrible circumstances and it made Fuller smile. He needed some friends.

"By the way," asked Jackson, tapping Suzanne on the shoulder. "What's an 'NC' Coke? Is that a diet thing?"

"You don't know?" she asked, turning to look at him in the back seat. He shook his head. "None of you know what an 'NC' Coke is?" she asked of the car's occupants, in disbelief. The men had a feeling this was basic stuff and they were about to look foolish.

"No Cocaine," she said. "The 'NC' stands for 'No Cocaine'. It's been out on both sides of the border for 30 years. Regular Cokes have a little cocaine, 'Extra C' has a little more, and 'NC' Cokes don't have any. What is with you guys? Are you all from a different planet?"

The food came with more apologies from the girl, and they tipped her $10, which she hadn't expected. It wasn't haute cuisine, but the ravished fugitives wolfed down the burgers and potatoes in minutes. The food tasted fresh and unprocessed, quite different from their last fast-food experience.

"Okay, let's move on," said Philips, wiping the last crumb from his mouth.

"I guess I need to hit the head myself," said Jackson. He started for the door handle when Mike Philips touched his forearm.

"Greg," he said, looking him straight in the eyes. "Don't lose it...but there's a 'Colored' bathroom inside."

"What?" Jackson yelled as if Phillips was the perpetrator of the indignity. "Even up North? Even here?"

"I wanted you to be prepared. That's all. At least you don't need your hat. I saw another black guy in there and he wasn't wearing one."

"What the hell?" Jackson spoke into his hands, slumping back in his seat. "One hundred fifty goddamn years of Civil Rights washed down the drain?" He opened the car door and walked to the entrance of the diner, head hung low, and disappeared inside.

No one spoke for a moment and then, Suzanne, unable to hold back, almost shouted her question to the two still in the car.

"Who are you people?" The men looked nervously at one another, surprised at her sudden agitation, not knowing how to answer. "Really...are y'all from another country?"

"Yeah," said Tommy Fuller. "We sure are."

Chapter 20

Within 20-minutes of hitting the road, the urban sprawl of D.C. became apparent, but it was a different kind of development from the world they'd left behind. Farms went right to the city's edge, and the roads were not lined with strip-malls and strip clubs, or cookie-cutter housing developments. Instead, Brownstones, teeming with life, like beehives, filled every block. They would learn, later, that population centers were within the cities, not the suburbs; there were no suburbs in the late 20th century sense. Barbershops, mom & pop hardware stores, restaurants, markets, and theaters were everywhere. Policemen with whistles worked the busiest street corners, and the City was absolutely alive, packed with pedestrians and commerce. The men smiled and drew a deep breath at what they saw when they crossed the Potomac River and turned down Pennsylvania Avenue.

"Awesome," said Jackson. In the distance, past tree-filled parks and neatly manicured lawns, stood the Washington Monument. It, unlike nearly everything else, was exactly how they remembered it.

The construction of the Washington Monument had started in 1838 and at its finished height of 555 feet, would be the tallest structure on earth, a full 100 feet taller than the Great Pyramid in Giza. It held that record until the French built the Eiffel Tower in 1889. After Hitler destroyed France's beloved icon during the War for Europe, the Washington Monument took the "tallest" prize once again and held the spot until 1960 when the skyscrapers of Manhattan came into vogue. Hitler, not to be outdone, commissioned a monument to the Third Reich, which would capture the world's attention.

Hitler's architects, under penalty of death if they failed, were to design a memorial to Deutschland that had to be no shorter than *twice the height of the tallest structure on earth and wider than the Palace of Bucharest in Romania,"* which was the worlds largest building. The winning design was that of an eagle, looking to the sky, with outstretched wings carrying a flagpole in its beak, waving a movie-screen-sized Nazi flag. From the base of the monument to the tip of the flagpole, it rose a staggering 2,120-feet, and was 1,700-feet wide. Hitler didn't live to see its completion in 1970, but his son, Rudolf, told the world via short-wave radio that the "Third Reich would outlast all time and eternity" and that its monument, Der Grosse Adler des Drittle Reich (The Great Eagle of the Third Reich) would "outlast any inferior temples built by Jew gods and other lesser races."

The men knew nothing of this history, and at that particular moment, they didn't care. They were so happy to see their beloved American icons and were so immersed in the familiar, that for a brief moment they felt hopeful. They passed the Capitol building, the White House and the Jefferson Memorial. Mysteriously absent was the Lincoln Memorial. Apparently, the government of the F.S.A. had never forgiven Lincoln for allowing the South to secede and weren't eager to build memorials to a President who had lost a war and had been impeached. The men did find Trump Tower in its place. The comb-over tycoon, who became the 49th President, built a memorial to himself, thus ensuring his place in history.

Their innocence and ignorance of a world, that for a brief moment looked vaguely familiar, was about to be turned upside down. Among the countless volumes stored in the Library of Congress, a select few would enlighten them in ways that they couldn't begin to imagine.

•••••

"Well, I see parking hasn't improved any in D.C.," said Jackson as they circled the Library, no less than three times, waiting for a parking space to open up. Suzanne expertly navigated a maze of one-way streets until they parked and exited the car, locking the doors. Excitement was building as they considered the opportunity before them. The greatest reference library in the world would have to, they hoped, help shed light on the events of July 3, 1863 and just maybe, if they were lucky, might help them figure a way out of this version of 2013, and a way back home.

"We in D.C..., right?" asked Jackson, using his best urban affectation.

"Oh yeah, buddy," said Phillips, excitement growing with each step toward the Library entrance.

"Then where the Brothers at? This is D.C., man. It's supposed to be like 80-percent black and 20-percent politician. Where all the Brothers at?"

He had a point. While they'd seen a few blacks here and there, he had noticed that the demographics of this D.C., in no-way resembled anything close to the town he knew and loved.

"Looks like any other day to me," said Suzanne.

She knew the City well. She'd been traveling back and forth between Gettysburg and D.C. for as long as she could remember. Her dad had once been a small-time border runner, a smuggler of whatever one side or the other wanted, but couldn't legally obtain. He quit at the urging of Suzanne's mother. He'd tried to go legit, but found the allure of flying under the radar, literally, too hard to ignore. The safer job of 'tunnel keeper' was a compromise yet still allowed him occasional forays into the North on various courier assignments. Suzanne begged to tag along every time he went, and she usually got her way. After her father's death from a ruptured appendix with no hospital near enough to treat him, her beloved Unka took over the job as both tunnel keeper and surrogate father.

She loved D.C., and the vibrancy of the City was one of the most compelling reasons she fought for reunification. She saw something in D.C. and the old "American" system, good and bad, that legitimized the FF movement. The Con-Fed capitol, in Richmond, Va., was impressive, but it in no way came close to the 300-year-old architectural magnificence of Washington, D.C. She didn't have to be talked into reunification. This was a movement grounded in the hearts of a growing majority of the people living on both sides of the border. The popular movement adopted the slogan "UBD", meaning, "United is better than divided."

The Library of Congress had been a home away from home for many students and attorneys practicing in the D.C. area. Jackson and Phillips knew it well, though Tommy Fuller had never been. It was the world's largest repository of information, with more than 30 million books on 800 miles of bookshelves, and a staff of several thousand. With its gilded rotundas, museum quality art and artifacts, marble floors and great massive columns, it truly was a wonder of architecture and of modern civilization and intellectualism. In a land without the Internet, this library, and a few others like it around the world, were mankind's best hope to learn from its past mistakes.

Upon entering the Library, they noticed the layout was essentially the same as they had remembered but gone were the rows and rows of access computers that helped visitors narrow their searches and plot a course around the massive building. In their place they found a large, five-sided counter, teeming with librarians dispensing information to dozens of patrons, coming and going. They walked up to the counter and waited for an available librarian and were finally greeted by a friendly, older woman they guessed to be in her 70s. Her nametag read simply "Margaret– Librarian."

"Hello," she said, a bit louder than you'd think a Librarian might normally speak. Her snow-white hair, worn in a small bun in back, framed a narrow, friendly face. While she looked sociable enough, she was all business and efficiency.

"Hi," said Phillips with a smile. "American History? Civil War, The Battle of Gettysburg, specifically."

She gave him a quick glance over her glasses and straightened the stack of books she had been checking in. She let herself out from behind the desk and turned to attend to the visitors.

"Come with me," she said and scurried along, her heels clicking on the hard, marble floors. They struggled to keep up and looked like baby ducks scampering along behind their mother.

They walked up two flights of stairs, down three corridors, around half-a-dozen corners and were led to the Reference Desk of a room containing 500,000 books on American History. She positioned herself behind the massive reference desk and spoke.

"I happen to be a Reference Librarian, so you're in luck." She snapped her fingers *Mary Poppins'* style, and managed a satisfied, but brief, smile.

"That *is* lucky," said Phillips, smiling, engaging. He had worked the system a thousand times before. Part of being a good attorney was in knowing how to get people to help you, and in that he was an expert.

"Anything in particular about Gettysburg in which you're interested?" Margaret asked, probing slightly. Phillips thought he saw her wink at him and he was unsure if she was taken by his charm or letting him know she had his number.

"Actually, The Civil War and Reconstruction, and most anything 1860 - 1865" said Philips.

"Ahhh," she said, taking a sudden new interest in the group. Her tone changed and her entire demeanor shifted.

"That's easy. Civil War volumes make up the largest collection within the American History section, even bigger than the American Revolution." She paused, thinking how to ask her next question.

"But what's this... 'Reconstruction?' I'm not familiar with the term." In this place there was no 'Reconstruction' because the North never offered their help to the devastated South. Phillips figured it out on the fly.

"That's okay, just the Civil War section," he said.

"It's along that back wall," answered Margaret, pointing to the other side of the large room. "You'll find card files and subject descriptions over by the window and that should help you narrow things down a bit."

"No computers, so it's the good old Dewey Decimal System," said Phillips to his friends, turning to look toward the card files across the room.

"Pardon?" asked Margaret the Librarian.

"Umm..the Dewey Decimal System?" repeated Phillips.

"No. Never heard of that," said Margaret, winking. "We use L.C.C. - our own Library of Congress Classification system. L.C.C. is fairly straight forward, but can be a little confusing so...just come back if you need help."

They thanked her and turned in the direction she was pointing. Margaret busied herself with stacks of books but never took her eyes off the strange troop of people in her library.

"I wonder what happened to Dewey," whispered Jackson as they walked.

What they couldn't know for sure, but were slowly beginning to comprehend, was that so much of what they thought they knew, either never happened, or was changed so significantly that they felt like foreigners in their own land. They couldn't know that Melvil Dewey, born in 1851 in Adams Center, New York, credited as the genius behind the system that would bear his name, would never leave college, and never invent the Dewey Decimal System.

The 'back wall' was easily the length of a football field and was filled with books from floor to ceiling. Twenty-foot, oak ladders hung from rails mounted to the tops of the walls. Large tables, big enough for banquets for all the past and present Kings of Europe, separated more rows of shelves and books. This room was much quieter than the hallways and the large visitor desk on the first floor. Carpeting softened their steps as they walked toward what they hoped was the information that might help them begin to understand what had happened and why they were in the middle of the unexplainable.

"What exactly are we looking for?" asked Suzanne, still unsure of what to make of this peculiar mission to the library.

"Civil War History, for starters," said Phillips. "Mostly we want to see specific accounts of the Battle of Gettysburg, day three."

Tommy roamed the volumes randomly, still in awe of the sheer number of books, just in this one room. Not much of a reader or an academic, he'd never seen anything like it. Suzanne followed slowly behind him, clearly with a lot on her mind. Phillips and Jackson walked to the card files and tried to make heads or tails of the L.C.C. system. They found a section entitled Civil War, then Civil War History, and then thousands of sub-sections from 'Armament' to 'Ziegler's Grove.' Under the 'Battles' section, there were hundreds of listings, major battles and minor skirmishes, all lumped together and it was there, under the "G," that they found 'Gettysburg, Battle of.' The card instructed them to look in Section five, Row fourteen, Shelf three. All the books, some 150 volumes focusing on that battle, were there, together.

Suzanne caught up to Tommy who had wandered away from the books and the card files and was gazing outside. The irregular window glass stretched from a cozy bench all the way to the crown molding of the Reference Room's ceiling. The window's bubbles and warping cast the outside world in an abstract half-truth, which was exactly how he pictured himself at that moment.

"When are you going to tell me what's going on, Tommy?" she asked. They sat on the window seat and he took her hand in his. The intimate act felt natural and right somehow, even though they'd just met.

"I've been trying to figure you guys out," she said. "But I keep running into dead-ends. "You're all good men, I know that, don't ask me how, I just know. I trust you completely – all of you guys - and I have no idea why. But I am confused. You all act as if you dropped in from another planet... and yet you seem to know me. Are you foreign spies? Is that why Greg doesn't know about Colored bathrooms, and Redcaps? Or NC Cokes? Everybody knows about NC Cokes. Everybody." She sighed, head cast down. "You just don't make any sense, any of you."

"It's so complicated," he said, catching her blue eyes, as she looked up at him. "If I told you, you wouldn't believe me. And I couldn't bear that."

"Try me. What have you got to lose?"

With that simple encouragement, Tommy Fuller began to tell Suzanne the entire story, the best he could. He felt energized, saying it aloud. He told her about the United States of America, as one nation, not two, and about the modern world, its troubles and its achievements: man landing on the moon, probes landing on Mars. He told her about modern airplanes, and cars, and GPS navigation systems. He told her about television, cell-phones, the Civil-Rights movement, the Kennedy's, Vietnam, World War-II, the Middle East, Bill Clinton, 9/11, Osama Bin Laden, and Barack Obama. She listened quietly, in rapt attention, as he told her of Lincoln's assassination and a hundred other details about life in his world.

He told her about the reenactors, the battle, the explosion, his Nissan truck, and that they didn't know how they had gotten to this 'other' place and that that's the main reason they were at the library–to try, just like her, to understand.

She hadn't said a word through his entire monolog. She hadn't raised an eyebrow, or made a move that indicated one way or another if she believed any single bit of his fantastic story. After a long pause, she finally spoke.

"Cell Phones? You mean people walk around talking on cordless telephones ...constantly?"

"Constantly," he laughed. "It's like they're glued to our ears. We can't live without 'em. And when we're not talking, we're texting, or tweeting, or Facebooking."

She looked at him deeply, her smile fading slightly. "What else?" she asked.

"What do you mean 'what else'?"

"I mean...what else? There's something you're not telling me. Don't think I didn't notice the mark on your finger where a wedding band used to be. Women notice these things." Instinctively he rubbed his hand and looked at the pale line where the gold band had kept the skin white. "And you, more than the other guys, are hiding something or ...you're in some kind of trouble."

Here in this vast library she read him like a book, just like his wife could. He told her about Susan, how they'd grown apart, their troubles with the gangs, the violence, his nearly being beaten to death, money problems, and about the shooting two days earlier and his running from the law. Then he told her the one thing that finally got a reaction:

"Suzanne. I don't know how...but you are my wife, Susan."

Her eyes fluttered and she almost fainted. The color drained from her face. The rest of the information could be processed as having come from a lunatic, but this revelation was almost too much to handle, because she sensed he was right. The simple statement made everything else he had just told her, ring true. She knew then that he was not lying. That one simple comment, amid a hundred tall-tales, was, for her, the glue that pulled his story together. It explained why he knew who her grandparents were, why the men knew their way around town. It explained a dozen other things that hadn't added-up a moment before: why she loved him, and why he seemed to love her, and why they felt so connected. Against all odds she believed him. She loved him, as she dreamed as a girl she might hope to love a man.

But this was a man she'd just met.

•••••

The two government agents had been forced to drive nearly a mile, slowly in reverse, because of the inability to turn their big car around in the narrow tunnel. When they arrived back at the barn Suzanne's uncle and the two assistants met them. The agents questioned them and decided they were inculpable in the foolish, but successful, escape. They wasted no time in starting the 40-minute drive east to an official border crossing, where their credentials would get them through without delay.

Embarrassed at their lack of success in detaining the men, and their having been given the slip by their femme-fatale, they decided not to issue an All Points Bulletin, but would try to catch up with the fugitives and make the collar themselves. This had become personal.

"How hard can it be to find a 1991, Nashville Marathon in D.C.?" asked the taller agent. "Besides this one we're driving, there can't be but a dozen in the entire city.

"Yeah," answered his partner, "and theirs is missing part of its grill." They'd contacted the guards at the north end of the tunnel and had gotten a description of the scene, including the condition of the car, and the fugitives' direction.

After crossing the border they sped through town, heading west, re-tracing the only main road from the Northern tunnel entrance, hoping to see them coming at them from the opposite direction. They made it to the destroyed tunnel entrance without any luck, so they turned around and headed back toward D.C., deciding to stop for a quick bite. They wheeled their own Marathon into Hungry Boys' Diner and pulled up into the drive-in. The manager, having noticed their arrival, jogged over to greet the men himself.

"Boy, two in one day!" said the restaurant manager, as the agents rolled down their windows. "I just can't believe it," he said, nearly jumping up and down. "You must be with those other folks."

"What other folks would those be?" inquired the driver.

"The other guys and that girl driving another Marathon."

The agents looked at each other. "Yeah, yeah...they're... friends of ours...but we lost them. Did they say where they were going?"

"I think one of them said they were headed to D.C."

"How long ago did they leave?"

"About half an hour ago," said the manager.

Fearing the worst, that Confederate terrorists were on their way to the Nation's capitol with a car full of explosives, the agents, without a word to the bewildered manager, tore back out on the two-lane and headed east, back toward Washington, D.C., the Fed-Stat Capitol.

"It's time to call this in," said the taller agent. The other nodded in agreement and radioed in an APB for the greater Washington, D.C., area, for the apprehension of three males, two in their 30s or 40s, one in his 20s and a female, late teens or early 20s, driving a 1991 black Nashville Marathon.

•••••

Jackson and Phillips made their way to Section 5, Row 14, and found countless volumes, all with 'The Battle of Gettysburg' in their title. The four that intrigued them the most were titled: *'The Battle Of Gettysburg–The Battle that was Almost Won,'* *'The Battle Of Gettysburg–An Eyewitness Account',* *'The Battle of Gettysburg: What Went Wrong'* and, most intriguing, the one that caused a lump to form in Mike Phillips' throat–*The Battle of Gettysburg: The Strangers at Emmitsburg Road.'* From the dusty shelves, they removed those four books and another volume that contained Civil War-era maps. They called

Tommy Fuller to come join them at a quiet table in the corner of the Reference Room. Fuller walked toward the table with Suzanne, hand in hand. Greg Jackson was the first to notice the intimacy, and he whispered to Philips.

"Check those two out. Young Love in bloom, I guess." Phillips acknowledged his comment but didn't look too happy about what he was seeing. They all sat at the big table, Tommy and Suzanne across from Jackson and Phillips. Tommy took a deep breath and spoke as he exhaled.

"I told her everything."

Phillips and Jackson looked at one another, slightly startled.

"Oh, I'd have loved to have heard that story," said Jackson with a quiet chuckle. "How 'bout telling *me* everything?"

"Everything?" asked Phillips, looking at Fuller.

"Yes, everything," said Suzanne. "Don't ask me why, but I believe him. I believe you guys."

"Wow," said Phillips dealing with his own disbelief at her easy acceptance of a story they didn't themselves understand, let alone believe. "You don't seem to be in as much shock as I'd have expected."

"In light of all the other possibilities, it's the most believable explanation I can think of," said Suzanne. "But it's more than that.' It's something...I feel inside. I can't really explain it. I want to help you. Besides," she hesitated. "Tommy is my husband."

With that improbable and awkward remark out on the table there was not much left to say. They began leafing through the volumes, skimming the pages for clues that might help them confirm what they were already beginning to suspect, but dared not articulate.

Always the organizer, Greg Jackson cleared his throat and focused the team on their mission.

"Okay, we know from our history that the explosion should never have happened," he said. "Let's try to start there."

"You mean the Confederate detonation at Emmitsburg Road?" said Suzanne, high school history still fresh in her young head. "What do you mean 'should never have happened'?"

She was trying to process that which Tommy had told her and the reality of what it all meant. The story of that explosion was part of her earliest, childhood memories. They had gone to the Park a thousand times to play, swim, and fish in Crater Lake, the town's centerpiece. Now she was being told that the explosion that created it never happened. Like the three men at the table with her, Suzanne, too, was facing the fear of looking at her world and history through another set of uncomfortable lenses.

"Well, Suzanne," said Phillips, taking his turn. "Where we came from...," he stopped to take another tack. "Tommy told you about the United States of America, right?"

"Yes," she said.

"Well, the reason the U.S.A. exists for us is because the Confederacy lost the Civil War."

"Okay," she said, humoring him. "Tommy mentioned that."

"And they lost the Civil War, mainly because they lost at Gettysburg. The explosion that you know from your history never happened in our history. The Federal forces defeated Lee's army at Gettysburg and sent the Confederacy running; they struggled on for a while, but never really bounced back. Lee surrendered at Appomattox less than two years later and...that was that. But even weirder is that there had never been a plan for a bomb to begin with."

Suzanne listened with very little comment, but her gears were turning. Finally, she spoke her mind and asked a difficult question, one that Tommy Fuller was asking himself as well.

"Let's suppose that what your suggesting is true. Are you also saying that your world is better than my world? Sounds like you've got bigger problems in your world than we have here in this one." She was almost defensive in her tone. Though she didn't yet realize it, she and her entire existence had just been insulted. She'd just been told that everything she knew in her reality was just a big mistake made 150 years earlier.

"Why is your world better than mine?" she insisted.

"Oh, I can give you at least 50 reasons," said Jackson, jumping in. "The National abolition of slavery in 1862, the Civil Rights movement of the 1950s and 1960s, our involvement in World War II, which eventually stopped Hitler in his tracks, ahh...human rights, democracies, television, cell phones, computers...digital cameras...How's that for starters?"

He was making his point, but had one more to throw in. "I'm going to go out on a limb here, but I have a hunch...when was the last time you voted in an election?"

"Women can't vote, Greg."

"They can in my world, little darlin'," said Jackson with a smug expression. "And nobody but a family member would dare call a grown woman 'little darlin,' and hope to go unscathed. In our world women lead nations. There's Margaret Thatcher, Golda Mier, Hillary Clinton, plus women are doctors, lawyers, engineers, jet pilots, surgeons, Senators, Congresswomen...they even run for President."

Suzanne was legitimately shocked. She had heard about Suffragettes, but their movement was stopped in its tracks. Several of its leaders had been assassinated or had mysteriously disappeared.

"Okay," interjected Tommy Fuller, playing Devil's advocate, "but what about poverty, pollution, global warming, terrorism...inner-city crime?"

"So, what are you saying, Fuller...you like it here better?" Jackson was getting heated.

"I'm just saying that here everybody seems to…know their place." He immediately regretted his choice of words.

"Oh, you did *not* just go there…" said Jackson, fire in his eyes.

Fuller tried to regroup, but it only got worse. "What I mean is there ain't any, you know, gangs roaming the streets, selling meth, and beating up anybody gets in their way."

"You mean *Black* gangs?" Jackson asked, incensed. Fuller didn't answer. "How about Latino, Chinese and Russian gangs?" Again, no comment. "You know, you're right," continued Jackson, oozing sarcasm. "It *is* better here. I haven't seen a single redneck shooting any unarmed kids today, so I guess I like this place better, too."

"All right," said Phillips, "look you guys… everybody cool it. This doesn't help any of us. 'Better or worse' isn't the point. History and the future are both messed up. We all know it." He glanced at the young woman, still digesting the conversation. "Except maybe for you, Suzanne. I wouldn't expect you to fully understand…but we've got lives, careers, and families back there, wherever *there* is. Even you're leading a different life. We've got to get back if we can. We all know it. It's not just a matter of better or worse…it's… it's the way it's supposed to be." He made a reasonable argument. Good enough that everybody calmed down, but Suzanne was not completely convinced.

Neither was Tommy Fuller.

Phillips slid a book to each of them and they began silently leafing through the pages, Jackson, still steaming over the racist undertones in Fuller's comments. He was looking through the book 'The Battle of Gettysburg–The Strangers at Emmitsburg Road.' A historian who compiled first-hand accounts of the events during the battle had written it and Jackson found one particular diary entry interesting.

"Hey check this out," said Jackson. "This came from the diary of Lucas Campbell." He read aloud.

July 3, 1863. We won! The biggest bang the world has ever known has crushed the Yank army and we've beaten the bastards. I was at Emmitsburg Road no less than four or five minutes before the explosion, and I owe my life to William Grissom, God rest his soul.

"That's our boy," said Phillips, shifting in his seat, taking a keen interest. "What else?"

He was wearing a Yankee uniform, but I recognized him right away. He and his brother were scouts, somebody called Spies. I figure he was dressed that way to make a clean escape into Yank territory. Shells were exploding all around me, and bullets whizzed by my ears more than a few times. I heard men yelling from every direction, but I couldn't see them on account of the smoke. I did see three confused Reb soldiers who looked out of place. Hell, we were all confused.

Jackson stopped reading for a moment and looked around the table. All wide eyes were on him. He had been reading passages from a diary that was 150 years old, yet here were current events from three days earlier. Jackson swallowed hard and continued.

"One of them was hurt and was bleeding from the chin."

He stopped reading again and they all looked at Fuller, who put a hand to his bandaged jaw.

"We hit the jackpot with this one," said Jackson. He scanned the next few lines. "Uh oh, here I am," he continued.

And another of the men, a Negro, confused the hell out of me because we didn't have any Negroes serving in our battalion, but here he was none the less and he was awfully brazen and chummy with the other soldiers. Grissom shot two Yankee soldiers who were trying to put out the bomb fuse and then he called out to the men and I heard him say 'If you want to live, come on!' They followed him and so I did. I was 50 feet behind them the whole time and we ran and we ran until the explosion knocked me to the ground. When I came to, I couldn't hear a thing but the ringing in my ears. The smoke cleared and I stumbled around. I didn't know which way was Richmond. Couldn't see a thing. I ended up in the woods and then I just about tripped over the body of Grissom. I figured him for dead. He was holding a Kepi in his hands and I knew it was special to him – so I stuffed it in my haversack and made my way back to our line. There was no sign of the three Reb soldiers. Guess they were blown to bits. I never knew.

"That's where the entry ends," said Jackson.

Tommy Fuller reached around to his belt and retrieved the very cap they had just read about. He looked carefully at it, as did the others. The Rebel cap with a hole in the side and the embroidered initials "T.G." seemed to take on mystic qualities, and it made them all uneasy.

"I think that's what we were looking for," said Phillips, shaking his head. "I can hardly believe it— just don't know how…"

"So this is all because of us?" asked Jackson, spreading his arms in a wide gesture.

"How so?" asked Phillips.

"Well, if I were a gambling man," said Jackson, "which I am, I bet those two Yanks did put out the fuse, originally, and with us there, we distracted them, I guess, and Grissom had the few seconds he needed to put a couple bullets in them. And because they never put out the fuse, the big bang went off like they expected it to. Only one problem..."

"Just one?" asked Phillips.

"Yeah. A big one. We talked about this; there never was any plan to detonate a bomb in Gettysburg."

"This is interesting and all," added Tommy Fuller, still stunned at the revelations. "But you're ignoring the bigger question. How did we get there in the first place? And then how'd we get here?"

Greg Jackson stared hard at Fuller. "Where is 'here,' and more important, how we do get back home?"

·····

In a small apartment situated on the outskirts of Gettysburg, Anthony nursed his wounds, physical and emotional. He and Joey had mended their temporarily broken friendship. Anthony had even told the younger boy that he was proud of him for defending his sister and told him "You did the right thing." But he worried about Suzanne, and despite her pleading, he didn't trust the guys she had so completely befriended. He became especially worried when Suzanne's Uncle George called and told him about the incident at the tunnel. They hadn't heard from the agents in more than a day, so he and Joey hitched into town, borrowed a Marathon from Fuller's Auto and started to launch their own investigation.

The boys went to the cabin first, and while they could see someone had been there, there were no useful clues, or anything leading them to an understanding of just who the strangers might be, or what they were up to. In a good bit of sleuthing, Anthony noticed narrow, fresh tire tracks in the dirt outside.

"Wait a minute, Joey." He bent down and looked at the tire tracks that had to have been made by something other than a Con-Fed vehicle, all of which would have had tires twice as wide.

"That Tommy guy's truck is around here somewhere."

They searched the grounds around the cabin for a few minutes when Joey stated the obvious. "They probably drove it to the apartment and ditched it there when they picked up your car."

"'Course. You're right." The two boys hurried back to their apartment. Knowing what they were looking for and where it might be found, they quickly uncovered Tommy's hiding place. The small road behind the apartment was where Anthony and Suzanne had shared their first kiss. It infuriated him that she would bring this guy back to their spot.

He shook it off as they cleared the brush away from the poorly hidden truck. This was their first good look at the Nissan, other than the brief encounter at the Fuller's Auto, and to them it was certainly a strange machine. They examined the truck from the inside. Unusual gadgets and instruments lined the dashboard and they touched everything, like doctors examining a body.

They looked over the visors and under the front seat, where, in an attempt to feel for any unseen objects, Anthony inadvertently pressed the power button on the side of Tommy Fuller's cell phone. A faint beeping caught their attention. It was a sound they had never heard before, like an insect or a tiny child calling out "beep-beep." There was a long pause and then again "beep-beep." They followed the sound to a spot under the driver's seat, where, wedged beside the seat's springs, they discovered and retrieved a device strange to them. The battery icon was flashing indicating an imminent loss of power with the accompanying "beep-beep" to confirm it. They, of course knew nothing about these devices, other than it looked like a miniature radio.

Anthony started randomly pushing buttons including one that said 'PWR'. When the device began to play music they nearly jumped out of their skins, and, startled, Anthony threw the phone against the roof of the truck cab. It landed in his lap still playing the first two bars of "*Dixie.*" The boys looked at one another and then back at the device. It read: "Low Power 14 missed calls 5 New Messages." The device beeped a few more times, and then went dead.

"That was queer," said Anthony, still mesmerized by the encounter with the strange little contraption.

"Yeah, queer," agreed Joey.

"What do you suppose it is? "

"I don't know. It's weird." They pressed all the buttons they could, trying in vain to bring the small device back to life but had no luck.

"The Twins," they said in unison, tripping over one another, heading for the Marathon with plans to drive straight to Fuller's Auto.

•••••

The reference librarian, Margaret, appeared from around the nearest freestanding bookshelf. She bent down close to the table and addressed the group, using her best librarian voice.

"Have you found what you're looking for?"

Phillips sat up and tried to put on a normal face.

"Yeah, I think so. Thank you," he said.

She surveyed the expressions of the group sitting at the table and smiled, shaking her head slightly.

"I can always spot new Travelers," she said. "I spotted you three right away." She looked at Fuller, Jackson and Phillips. "I'm not sure about the young lady, though." She smiled at Suzanne. "You're a pretty thing."

"I don't understand?" asked Phillips, his interest piqued.

"Oh, you don't think you're the first, do you?" she laughed quietly. "True, I haven't seen your kind in quite a while, but you all think you're the only ones. It's so funny to me. You newbies, the smart ones anyway, usually end up in the Reference Department, looking for answers." She glanced around the room, as if checking to see who might be nearby, and she leaned in to speak. The others leaned in to hear what this strange woman might say next.

"It makes sense, really," she continued. "...coming to the Reference Department. If you can't find the quantum physics information you're looking for here, it probably can't be found." She was immensely proud of her library.

"Please," asked Phillips, "explain to us who you are and what, exactly, you're telling us. We don't understand."

"Who am I?" she asked, again amused. "I am a librarian. I've been working here for 53 years, and I've learned to spot newbies, like you."

"You keep saying that," said Fuller "What do you mean, 'newbies?'"

"You're from the other place, right? After 53 years I can usually tell right away." The four stared, dumfounded.

"What other place?" asked Jackson.

"May I?" she asked pulling a free chair out to sit with them. "Some of you think it's time travel, like Jules Verne's, but that's only part of it," she answered. "It's much more complicated than that. You've gone...sideways, and done a bit of skipping around, I'm afraid." Suzanne shifted nervously in her seat.

"Sideways? Where are we?" asked Fuller.

"It depends on who's asking the question. It's all about perspective. For your girlfriend...she is your girlfriend, isn't she?" Fuller blushed. "I suspect, for her, this is Washington D.C., in the Federated States of America. For her, this is where she's supposed to be, as natural and normal as everything else in her life. But for you...I'll bet you came from the United States of America."

Greg Jackson slid back from the table and stood up beaming, so happy to have heard from someone who finally made sense. He approached the woman to give her a hug and she backed away.

"I'm sorry," she whispered. "Too many eyes. They really frown on that kind of thing. Nothing personal." He sat back down, still excited to hear from this marvelous woman who knew about their home.

"How did you know about us?" asked Phillips.

"You asked about Reconstruction, for starters. No such thing in this world. It never happened. You mentioned the Dewey Decimal System.

Doesn't exist, nor computers." Margaret smoothed the front of her smock.

"Are there more...Travelers... here?" asked Phillips.

"Oh my, yes. In the past 53 years I've spoken to nearly a dozen of you. I believe some have made it back home, a very small percentage even come and go as they please, and still others won't ever be able to get back, I'm afraid. Sadly, some of you Travelers are institutionalized as lunatics and that's very distressing to me because I know you're not crazy." She patted Greg Jackson's hand. "The smart newbies, like you, always come to the Reference Department asking about American History." They sat speechless and she reached into a pocket in her smock and pulled out a small pad of paper and a pencil.

"First, this book may help." She wrote down a shelf location in the Science / Metaphysics section of the Reference Department. "And second, call this number and tell the man 'Margaret sent you.' He's from your side. He may be of some help. Good luck children. I hope you find happiness, wherever you may land."

With that she stood up from her chair and straightened her dress. "Oh, and if I were you, I'd keep a low-profile. Chances are you've already caused a fuss somewhere." She hurried away, disappearing behind the bookshelf, like Alice's rabbit, down a hole.

They sat in stunned silence trying to absorb what had just transpired. Jackson spoke. "I'm not sure if I feel better or worse. But I think better."

"I know what you mean," said Phillips. "It's nice to know we're not alone, but what the hell was that?"

Tommy Fuller sat looking at the table with his head in his hands. Suzanne softly stroked his back with one hand and clutched his arm with the other.

•••••

The taller of the two agents sat behind the wheel and drove the big Marathon toward Washington, D.C. and within 20 minutes they were approaching downtown. They listened to their police radio, hopeful of hearing a report on the whereabouts of their fugitives from Gettysburg, but none came. They cruised through the City relying on instinct and blind luck.

"Maybe we should call the kids back in Gettysburg, to see if they've heard anything," said the shorter man, lighting a cigarette and flicking the match out of the open window.

"Yeah, good idea. There's a pay phone." He maneuvered the big car into a space and they walked a half-block to the phone booth. The taller man placed a third-person, long distance call to the apartment but got no answer. They tried the safe house and got no answer there either. They finally tried Fuller's Auto and found the boys. Anthony was summoned to the phone.

"Is that you, Mr. Tate?" asked Anthony, excited to tell him about their find.

"Do not use my name over the phone. Remember? We talked about that."

"Sorry...did you find Suzanne?"

"No names!"

"Geeze...sorry. Do you know where my girlfriend is?"

"She's not your girlfriend, Anthony," yelled Joey, who was listening in on an extension.

"Who's that?" asked the taller man. "Who else is on the phone?"

"It's just me," said Joey, ... "the brother."

"Have you boys heard from the girl or any of the others?"

"No," answered Anthony "But someone is trying to leave messages for...you know...the guy." He was afraid to use Tommy Fuller's name for fear of the agent's wrath.

"What guy?" the agent asked.

"You know, the younger guy. The one in the little truck."

"Who did you hear from? Who was asking for him?"

"Dunno. We found a little radio thingy in his truck, but it went dead. We're trying to power it back up."

"Okay, listen, keep up the good work, fellas, and we'll call you later tonight. If you figure out the messages, don't tell anyone, and be ready to read them to us when we call you back. Don't tell the men or Suzanne." The boys didn't like that part of the instruction.

"Got it, Chief," said Anthony, who saluted the phone to entertain his friend, and then heard the dial tone, after the agents abruptly hung up on them.

The two men in black suits made their way from the phone booth, back toward their car. The shorter man pulled a pack of cigarettes and a lighter from his shirt pocket and ducked behind a marble obelisk to light up another smoke, away from the wind. The brass nameplate attached to the massive hunk of chiseled stone read "Library of Congress."

•••••

Mike Phillips checked the piece of paper Margaret had left with them and spoke quietly to his companions. "I'll be right back. Don't go anywhere."

"Where would we go?" asked Jackson, always ready to point out the absurd. He drummed his fingers on the table and then broke the silence. "So we're not alone in this. That's kind of interesting." Tommy was so

173

deep in his own thoughts and Suzanne so busy consoling him that they didn't respond.

"Hellooo?" said Jackson. No response. "Come on Fuller, snap out of it. We're all just as freaked out as you are. I admit it. It's freaky, *Twilight Zone* stuff, I know. But come on…"

Phillips returned to the table placing a large volume down with a quiet thud.

"This is really getting weirder by the minute," he said. They gathered around the dusty tome and he cracked open the cover exposing the title page: The Multiverse and Our Place In It – by Dr. Benjamin Radcliff.

"This is the book she wants us to read," said Phillips, who flipped to the Table Of Contents. "Look," he said, "there are pencil marks, arrows pointing to specific chapters." They turned to the first chapter indicated by the scribble – "Chapter 4, An Argument for the Existence of the Multiverse." Two paragraphs were circled with pencil. Mike Phillips read aloud.

> *Philosophers and thinkers throughout the ages have contemplated time and space. It's an often-cited quandary that, given enough time, could a monkey placed in front of a typewriter recreate the complete works of William Shakespeare? How long would it take? Who knows? Maybe ten thousand years, maybe a hundred thousand or a million, but if one were patient enough it could, nay, statistically it must happen eventually. There are only 26 letters in the alphabet and mathematics supports the postulation. A monkey, given enough time, will complete the works.*

"Okay, great. That's a lot of help," said Jackson "We're looking for typing monkeys?

"Wait. It gets better," said Phillips. He continued to read.

> *"If we live in infinite space and time, which current theories hold to be true, then matter, also infinite, with which all things are made, will recreate itself many times over somewhere in the vastness of space-time. Like the works of our prolific monkey, our world and all that is in it could eventually come to exist in an exact likeness to that with which we know. Again, given enough time, say 'eternity,' mathematics supports the hypothesis of the Multiverse."*

"So this book is suggesting that we're in a…Multiverse? What's that, like an alternate universe? Like our own but not our own?" asked Jackson.

"I think so," said Phillips. "Remember, Margaret said that we haven't time-traveled."

"She said it's *more* than just time travel," corrected Fuller, finally checking in.

"I'm going to go find that woman," said Suzanne and she hurried off in the general direction of the Reference Desk.

"There's more," said Phillips.

"We are more than the sum of our parts. We exist in multiple universes throughout the cosmos. Perhaps there are billions or trillions of us each making the same moves, thinking the same thoughts. But we are finite beings and we can only comprehend one universe at a time, and we run the risk of catastrophe should our universes mix."

"That sounds bad," said Fuller.

"Well, it's only a theory. Don't panic yet," said Jackson

"Here. This chapter has an arrow, too," said Phillips "Chapter 6 - Quantum Theory and the State of Being."

In our singular universe, every action has a reaction. A match is struck and it lights. Or, a match is struck and it does not light. Or, a match is struck and the match-head flies off   starting a fire. Or a match is struck and the match-head flies off and does not start a fire. For every possible outcome of every possible action - past, present and future, there is a universe created. They all co-exist on dimensional planes that take up no more relative space, as we might understand it, than would just one dimension. After all, ten trillion to the ten trillionth power, which is virtually incomprehensible, is just a drop in the bucket in light of the infinite.

Each of us has the power to create and see the infinite anytime we want. One particular exercise can be helpful: Take a small hand mirror and hold it up to another mirror and look at the image. Most of us have done this at one time or another. But do you remember the first time you did it, probably as a child, and the wonder you felt seeing the infinite images recreate themselves again and again? The naked eye can maybe make out 20 or 30 increasingly smaller images of the hand mirror, before they disappear into a single point. But with enough light, and a powerful enough telescope, you could count millions of images and only be limited in the number of countable reproductions by

175

the loss of light and the power of the telescope's optic capabilities, and the mirror's imperfections. It's a simple, childish trick, but it displays the infinite in ways we can begin to grasp.

"So whoever marked up this book, wants us to know that we are in some kind of parallel or alternate universe? One of many?" asked Phillips.
"Yeah, sure why not? Sounds as logical to me as anything else we might come up with," said Jackson.
"Okay, well, not to beat a dead horse, but how did we get here?" asked Fuller.
"*That* is an excellent question," said Jackson.
"This might help," said Phillips, smiling slightly.
He spun the book around to show them.

"Chapter 17 – Traveling through the Multiverse."

"Time runs in a never ending stream, never beginning and never ending. But it's not a nice, neat, even line. The time-stream bifurcates, that is splits, creating branches, like forks in a never-ending river, or tree branches that go off in their own direction. When a human spirit, the miraculous God-like sentience that can even begin to imagine these things, moves from one branch to another, a new, or parallel universe is created. It is theoretically possible to move in and out, back and forth between these bifurcations through wormholes."

"You, know I've never liked science fiction," said Jackson.
"But, this almost makes sense," said Phillips. He continued.

"A wormhole is not only a shortcut through space but also may jump forward or backward in time. Wormholes are not just the stuff of popular television science fiction programs where dashing heroes, piloting their spacecrafts, jump back and forth between galaxies at will. Wormholes may also be microscopic and connect parallel universes one atom at a time, or they can be the size of an entire universe and send a cosmos reeling through space and time."

"Wait a minute... there's no TV in this place," said Jackson, ignoring the bigger implications.
"Or spacecrafts," added Fuller.
"So?" asked Phillips

"So how's this dude writing about television and space travel?" asked Fuller.

"Another good question," said Phillips, sliding his chair out from the table.

He walked a few steps to the card file and looked up Science, then Metaphysics. There were a handful of books on the subject, but not the one Margaret had sent him to. It didn't exist in the card file. He looked to the copyright information inside the book. It read: "William Harris Publishers, San Francisco, California, 2006." He turned back to the table.

"This book is from our world," said Phillips. "California doesn't exist over here, remember? It's called New Spain. Remember that wall map? That means this book did not come from this place. It also means, if you believe any of this, that *things* can travel from one universe to the next. That explains Tommy's Nissan."

"Uh, hey, Einstein...it explains *us* traveling here, too," said Jackson. "If a book and a truck can make the trip, why can't a couple of hack attorneys and an auto mechanic?"

"Someone from our side planted that book and left it here for us, and anyone else who might need it," said Phillips.

"Maybe Margaret?" added Fuller.

Suzanne arrived back at the table, out of breath.

"Guess what, guys," she said through quiet gasps for air.

"She's gone. I asked a Negro cleaning woman if she'd seen her, but she hadn't."

"Hey, ahh, Suzanne, sweetie," said Jackson. "We prefer 'black' or 'African American,' or better yet, how about just 'cleaning woman?'"

"Why," she answered innocently. "Negro' means 'black' and what if you're black and not from Africa? Or what if you're a cleaning person, and not a woman? Men do occasionally clean."

Jackson smiled and shook his head. "Never mind, sweetie. It's not important."

"I prefer 'Suzanne,'" she said, with a wink.

Chapter 21

The District-wide All Points Bulletin issued for the four fugitives from Gettysburg mobilized the D.C. police force and Federal authorities, which were all on a high priority search for a 1991 Nashville Marathon, with a damaged front grill. The car was somewhat rare in the North, their import being technically illegal (except for licensed collectors) and many considered, incorrectly, that the automobile was sub-standard to Detroit's automobiles. Though the car was unique to the C.S.A., it did share some general characteristics of cars of that age and looked similar to many Detroit models, making its detection challenging.

The agents had passed by the Marathon of interest three times without noticing, and countless patrol cars, and cops walking the beat missed it, as well. The fugitives had no idea how widespread the search was but they knew the agents would be on their trail, so they were cautious when leaving the Library. The counterfeit cash Suzanne's uncle had given them was about to come in handy.

"We need a safe place to sort this stuff out and call Margaret's friend," said Phillips, "but I just don't trust driving around in that car. Too many people know about it and probably have the tag numbers."

"You're right," said Jackson, "and the fact that the four of us are standing around on the street isn't too smart, either. We need to find a couple of rooms in a hurry."

"There are a lot of hotels around here," said Suzanne, "but I think the cheaper ones are only a few blocks away. Let's just drive there and get out of downtown."

"I'm not sure driving is a good idea," said Phillips. "Those agents will, by now, have figured out where we were headed, and they know what we're driving."

"Okay. I left my sweatshirt in the backseat," said Suzanne. "Let me go get that and we'll grab a cab or the Underground."

They could see the Marathon half a block away. Jackson and Phillips waited while Suzanne and Tommy went to retrieve her sweatshirt. They had just crossed the street and when traffic began to move again, they spotted the D.C. Police, who were pulling up to double-park just to the rear of their car. The cops were circling their Marathon and looking up and down the streets. One of them reached through the window of their patrol car and grabbed the microphone attached to the police radio. Tommy and Suzanne froze.

"Turn around slowly," said Tommy, "and walk back to the guys." She started to pick up the pace, almost jogging. "No, Suzanne. Don't run. Everything's casual, we're just crossing the street. Don't look back."

They rejoined the group and motioned for them to walk away from the front of the Library and away from the direction of the car.

"What's going on? Where's your jacket?" asked Phillips,

"They're on to us," said Fuller. "They just made our car."

A city bus whizzed by, belching black fumes, as it downshifted and slowed for the next pick up, a block away.

"Go for the bus, now!" said Phillips and they all speed-walked toward the bus just loading its last passengers. The driver shut the door as they were approaching and Greg Jackson banged his enormous flat palm against the side of the moving bus and it stopped with a lurch. The door opened and a man in a D.C. Metro Bus uniform, two sizes too small, stepped out of the door as the four approached.

"What do you think you're doing, boy…hittin' my bus?" his angry comments were directed at Jackson. Before he could speak, Mike Philips stepped in.

"I'm sorry Sir. I asked him to do that. He works for me and doesn't know his own strength. I do apologize." He smiled at the driver, hoping to appease him. They needed to get on that bus without incident as four D.C. Police cars and two unmarked vehicles screamed around the corner, and several patrolmen on foot were closing in behind them. The driver reluctantly accepted the explanation and apology, even if Greg Jackson didn't.

He waived them up the bus's steps and Suzanne pulled four counterfeit $1 bills from her wallet, paying the fare for each of them. They walked toward the back and were relieved when the bus started moving. They took seats, Jackson sat next to Phillips. The driver again slammed his brakes on, nearly crippling the busload of passengers in the process. He stood and looked back at the four of them.

"Hey, colored boy!" he yelled. Jackson felt the blood rush to his face but he didn't budge. "What…you can't hear good, boy? I'm talkin' to you." No one spoke as all eyes turned to Jackson. Mike Phillips feared the worst.

Jackson looked up at the driver.

"Yassir! I'ze can hear yas jus fine, Sir!" He said it with a broad, fake smile that bordered on maniacal.

The driver eyed him suspiciously and then spoke. "Get to the back of the bus then. You know better'n that."

Not able to leave it alone, Jackson quipped. "I'ze sorry Mr. Boss man, I'ze gwonna shuffle my feets right back there, right away Boss. Right away!" And he did just that. Like a madman possessed with the spirit of Al Jolson in blackface, and Stepin Fetchit, mixed with Uncles Tom and Remus, he shuffled, skipped, and tap-danced to the back of the bus. His companions felt badly for him, but still had to suppress laughter at the Oscar-worthy performance. Jackson sat in an empty seat and didn't speak to six other black riders banished to the back with him. Phillips turned to look and caught Jackson's eye. He wasn't smiling any more. Defeated for the moment, Jackson shook his head, utterly disappointed in his hometown, the Nation's capitol.

They had ridden for 15-minutes, watching carefully for trouble, and they had seen no sign of the police. Suzanne spotted the small, out-of-the-way hotel she'd been looking for and pointed through the window, down a side street to a flashing, bright red neon "Vacancy" sign.

"Here," she said, standing and waving to Jackson to come forward. "I know this place." She pulled the call bell cable and they all walked toward the front of the bus as it slowed. Fuller, Suzanne and Phillips stepped off first and Jackson would have followed, but he stopped at the top step of the bus and turned toward the seated driver just as the door closed. While the other three couldn't hear what Jackson was saying, they saw his finger wagging in the driver's stunned face. It went on for at least a minute and then the six black riders from the back of the bus, stood and cheered just before he walked down the three steps to join his friends. They stared at the smiling Jackson, trying to figure out what had just transpired.

"What was that all about?" asked Phillips, with some concern.

"I 'splained it to him, that's all," said Jackson with a self-satisfied grin.

"We had a little church in there." Phillips didn't dare ask for details. What they didn't hear was Greg Jackson's calm, perfectly executed two-minute monolog filled with Civil Rights legalese and ending with liberally borrowed passages from Martin Luther King Jr.'s "I Have a Dream" speech. He had used the same monologue in a college Speech Communications class and it had earned him an 'A'. They didn't see the bewildered driver actually apologize to him. Jackson was particularly pleased with himself and his big grin lasted for 20 minutes.

Twilight was setting in and the four made their way down the darkening street toward the *Washington Inn*, a small boarding house / hotel combo that Suzanne, her father, and uncle had stayed at, during several overnight trips to D.C.

"It's nothing special, but the rooms are clean and cheap, at least they were last year, and I think Unka and my father were quite friendly with the front desk guy."

The four made their way to the unadorned, wooden counter and rang the bell. A small, thin man with wispy, gray hair and wire rim glasses shuffled to the desk and didn't look up until Suzanne spoke.

"Hi. Remember me?" she asked, hopefully.

He pushed his glasses up the bridge of his nose and gazed at the girl for a moment before speaking. "Well, sure I do. Aren't you Eddy's daughter?"

"Yes, Sir, I am." They were all very pleased that he remembered her.

"He was quite a guy," said the Clerk.

"Yeah, we miss him a lot."

"How's his crazy brother? Ol' Georgey Dietz?"

"Unka? Oh, he's fine. I just saw him this morning." She didn't elaborate on the chaos from earlier in the day and was still feeling guilty for having involved her uncle.

"Well, tell him I said 'Hello.' Are you folks in need of a room?"

"We are," said Suzanne. "Two, actually." Fuller blushed a little.

"Yeah," piped in Jackson, still high from his encounter with the bus driver. "Mike and I need to be alone." He pressed close in behind the embarrassed Mike Phillips and put his arms around his neck, playfully flicking his shirt collar. The clerk was not amused, or didn't show it, though Jackson certainly was.

"He's just kidding," said the annoyed Phillips, shrugging off the lecherous advance of the large man. "What has gotten into you, Jackson?"

The clerk pulled down his glasses to peer over top of the rims. "Good thing for you he's only kidding, 'cause we've only got one room left. But it's a suite with a kitchenette, king bed and pullout king sleeper sofa."

"We'll take it," said Suzanne before anyone might complain. She filled out the small registration card the clerk had slipped her.

"Okay, $147 little lady. I'm Mr. Myers, in case you forgot me." He looked up and smiled. "Just ring if you need any help."

"Well, we might actually," said Suzanne, handing him $150.

"Yes?" asked Myers.

"It's very important that we…" She struggled for the best way to ask. Phillips came to her rescue.

"…that we remain anonymous," he said. "It's possible we're being…looked for."

"I understand," said the clerk, as he ripped up the registration card with her name on it and handed her back the money. Suzanne protested, but he insisted.

"Any daughter of Eddy Shepherd is my guest, and, anyway, if I know Eddy, this money isn't worth the paper it's printed on. You folks be careful and 'mum's the word.'" He winked, zipped his fingers across his lips and handed Suzanne the room key.

"Up the stairs, 2nd floor, down three doors on the right, room 13. It's not marked on the door."

As they headed toward the stairway, he called after them. "I'm sorry the Honeymoon Suite isn't available. You two fellas would have liked that. Has a heart-shaped tub."

"He's a funny guy," said Phillips. "And what's up with you, Eddie Murphy?" He elbowed Jackson playfully in the ribs.

"I'll tell you 'what's up?' I'm getting hungry." The old Greg Jackson was slowly returning, as the afterglow of his successful Civil Rights lesson with the bus driver waned.

•••••

The Twins, Bob and Bill Fuller, had just finished replacing the mangled garage door Tommy Fuller had destroyed a day earlier. They were none too pleased with the fugitive, and happy to help Anthony and Joey get the goods on the strange men, who had turned their town upside down.

The Twins had carefully disassembled the cell phone and quickly determined that it ran on batteries, not ordinary batteries, but batteries nonetheless. The few details printed on the circuit boards, and even the dead cell phone battery, were a complete mystery, leaving them to guess at the right amount of power. Too much and they'd fry the device, not enough and it wouldn't work. The cigarette lighter battery charger in Fuller's glove compartment would have made the job much easier for them, but having never seen one before they dismissed it as unimportant, and it sat there coiled, as just another piece of mysterious gadgetry.

As carefully as any bomb-squad working on a sensitive explosive, the Twins worked on the small device. They attached two tiny alligator clip leads to the battery terminals inside the phone's battery compartment and the other end of the leads to a car battery they had sitting on the work bench. They pressed the power button and the little phone lit up and beeped its way back from the dead. They congratulated one another, beaming at their own cleverness.

"What do we do now?" asked Bill.

"I guess wait for it to…ring?" said Bob.

With the phone powered up, it cycled through its usual start-up procedures, and re-discovering stored messages, it did ring, startling the men. Once again the first few bars of "Dixie" played through the tiny speaker.

"Well push a button! Answer it!" yelled Joey.

"Okay, okay," said Anthony, a little nervously. He carefully picked up the phone, still tethered by wires to the car battery, and pushed the "TLK" button.

"Hello?" he asked the phone, as if unsure what to say.

A small robotic voice answered: "You have five new messages. Press one to hear your messages now."

"It said it had five messages and to press one to hear 'em." Anthony looked for direction from those waiting eagerly to hear what the little voice in the black box was saying.

"Maybe we should wait for Mr. Tate," offered Bob Fuller. "I'm sure they would want to be here for this."

"Okay," agreed Anthony. "But I don't know how to reach them. They said they'd call us later today, at the safe house."

"Well, leave this durn thing here," said Bob, "and you two skedaddle over there and wait for their call. But then call us at home and ask 'em what they want us to do with this gizmo."

The boys left Fuller's Auto, excited at the prospect of a real spy-game unfolding in their usually sleepy border town. This was exactly the kind of adventure they'd been waiting for. Just one thing worried them, Suzanne's safety.

•••••

At the Washington Inn the four fugitives settled into their room, and, famished, ordered Chinese food for delivery. They turned on the radio and again heard unfamiliar songs by unfamiliar artists. Greg Jackson dozed in the easy chair and Suzanne and Tommy napped on the large bed. Mike Phillips sat at the desk and retrieved the name and number given to him by Margaret, the librarian. He unfolded the note and picked up the phone and then replaced the receiver, deciding to wait until the others were awake before calling.

While he sat at the desk, daydreaming, almost asleep, something on the radio caught his attention. Electric guitars and unmistakable vocals gushed out of the big wooden box. The singers harmonized: *"Sweet home Alabama, Where skies are so blue, Sweet home Alabama, Lord I'm comin' home to you."* The guitars launched into screaming solos and Phillips raced over to the radio and cranked up the volume, waking the others.

"Feel like partying?" asked Jackson. "Isn't that a little loud?"

"Don't you recognize this?" asked Phillips

"Sure," said Tommy, propping himself up on his elbows "It's Skynyrd again. '*Sweet Home Alabama.*'"

"Don't you find that a little odd? I mean, this is the first song we all recognize and it's exactly like the one we know."

"Yeah, unfortunately," quipped Jackson, clearly not a fan of that song, or of Southern Rock, in general.

The song faded and the announcer came on the air.

"Oh yeah, new music by D.C.'s own Alabama Rum Runners. This is Billy The Kay, and we'll be back after these important messages, so stay tuned to D.C.'s new music leader, DC-1560."

"That's not the Alabama Rum Runners," said Tommy Fuller, offended at the blatant lie about his favorite band. "It's Skynyrd. Everybody knows that."

"I don't know that," said Suzanne. "Up until a month ago, I'd never heard that song before. And it's pretty unusual for a Fed-Stat radio station to be playing songs about the Confederacy. I always thought it was against the law."

"It's Skynyrd, I'm tellin' ya'," Fuller repeated emphatically, "and that song has been around for a long time."

"You're out of your nuts, Fuller," teased Suzanne. They all laughed at her mixed metaphor.

"I am not out of my nuts," he scolded.

"He's right, Suzanne," said Phillips. "I'm calling that radio station. I want to find out where this "Billy the Kay" guy got that music."

He opened the desk drawer and retrieved a phone directory and found "DC-1560" in the Pink Pages. It was not a particularly busy time for the station. At 6:25 p.m. drive-time was nearly over and the call was answered before finishing the first ring.

"DC-1560, Billy Kay here, what's your name and what's your request?"

Phillips hesitated, not expecting those questions.

"Ahh...John Doe. And I'd like to hear some more Lynyrd Skynyrd." He wondered how the radio jock would handle that request. There was no response, but he could tell Billy Kay was still on the phone.

"Who is this?" asked Kay, no longer sounding so chipper.

"This is John Doe," repeated Phillips, loving the fact that Caller I.D. had not yet been invented and his anonymity would stay intact for as long as he wanted.

"Well, Mr. Doe," Kay spoke slowly and softly, a complete reversal from his on-air style. "We don't play any Leonard Skinner."

"Oh, but you surely do. "Sweet Home Alabama" is one of my favorite Skynyrd tunes. You must have more. Maybe "Freebird?" or, "Gimme Back My Bullets?"

"Well, funny you should mention them. We plan to play those songs, too, Mr. Doe, but they were written by yours truly, Billy Kay, and performed by the band I manage, the Alabama Rum Runners." He was silent for a moment. "Let's quit playing games. Who is this? Really?"

"Maybe we could meet to discuss the legal ramifications of plagiarism, copyright infringement, fraud, and pirating," said Phillips, as sweetly as he could manage.

"Okay, Mr. Doe. I'd like to meet you. My shift is over at nine. How about coffee at the West Wing Diner on M Street?"

"Perfect, we'll see you there," said Phillips.

"We? Who's we?"

"Just a couple of friends of mine. No trouble, I assure you. We just want to talk. I may have some additional songs for your band." He threw in a little bait, already suspecting that this guy was somehow profiting from songs that were not his own.

Mike Phillips hung up the phone and looked at his sleeping friends.

"This should be interesting," he said to himself. A loud knock came at the door, which startled all of them. Jackson shot out of his chair and blocked the door, as if expecting someone might try to knock it down. He looked through the peephole and saw just an empty hallway. When a second set of knocks came, he jumped back from the door, looking at it strangely. Small voices yelled from the hallway.

"Foo' deriverey – fry rice, here!" They all exhaled, relieved, having almost forgotten their dinner order. Jackson opened the door and found two small boys, eight or nine years old, carrying sacks almost as large as they were. They stood no more than four-feet tall, which explained their mysterious absence in the peephole. Suzanne walked to the door, smiling at the boys, and reached for her wallet. She waved them in and bent down to their level, pinching their little round cheeks.

"Hi, cuties." The boys giggled, shyly and looked down, avoiding eye contact. "How much do we owe you?" The slightly shorter boy put his bag of steaming food down on the bureau and ripped the ticket off handing it to Suzanne without answering her.

"Seventeen dollars and thirteen cents," she said aloud. She handed him a $20 bill and told them to keep the change. They smiled, bowing slightly while backing out of the room.

"Let's eat!" said Jackson.

They pulled large cartons of food from the two bags and distributed heaping mounds of beef fried rice, paper cups of egg drop soup, chicken lo mein, and egg rolls. Phillips scanned radio frequencies, stopping at a game show based on answering trivia questions, where contestants risked their cash if they answered incorrectly.

"This stone monument is the world's tallest obelisk at 555 feet 5 and 1/8 inches," said the host.

"The Washington Monument," answered Jackson, even before a radio contestant could buzz in.

"Wrong!" said Phillips. "*What is* The Washington Monument?"

Suzanne had been quiet while they all ate and listened to the show called "Risk It." Something was obviously on her mind and she finally spoke.

"I'm worried about Anthony and Joey, and I know they're worried about me. They must have heard about our little maneuver back at the tunnel. And Mr. Tate usually keeps us on a short leash."

"Who's Mr. Tate?" asked Phillips.

"One of the agents that's been following us."

"And shooting at us, lets not forget," said Tommy.

"I know they were shooting at our tires. They wouldn't hurt us...I don't think. They wouldn't hurt me, anyway. I wish I could just explain it to them."

"These phones can't be traced, right?" asked Phillips.

"I don't know what that means," replied Suzanne.

"It means they can't figure out a location by where a call originates."

"No, I don't think so."

"Well, why don't you call Anthony and Joey to tell them you're okay? I don't see the harm in that. Just don't tell them where we are, or any details about the...you know...about where we, ahh... came from."

"Good idea. I will." She picked up the phone and dialed "0." She asked to place a long distance, collect call to Con-Fed, Gettysburg, Maryland, and she gave the operator the number. She held the receiver end of the phone slightly away from her ear so the rest in the room could easily make out both ends of the conversation. Within a few seconds the phone was ringing at Suzanne's apartment, but no one answered. When the operator came back on the line, she asked her to dial the safe house number and Joey picked up right away. After accepting the charges, he spoke excitedly to his sister.

"Where are you? Are you alright?"

"Yeah, I'm fine, Joey. Are you and Anthony okay?"

"Yeah, we're okay. Anthony went out to grab us something to eat. We're worried as hell and we miss you. It's not the same around here."

"I miss you guys, too, but we're doing something important. I can't tell you what."

"Suzanne, I think you're in some kind of trouble. Unka called and told us about your little stunt at the tunnel."

"I'm fine, really, Joey. I'm fine. Tate and his pal just got a little carried away."

"Hey, Suzanne! We found Tommy's truck and a little radio-telephone thing inside it. It says it has messages."

Tommy sat up alert, and choked on a spoonful of rice while trying to assemble Joey's words in his head.

"My scanner?" he asked aloud. Phillips shrugged, not knowing.

"These are the best friggin' egg rolls I've ever had," said Greg Jackson, easily eating one in two bites. Soy sauce dripped from the corner of his mouth.

"It's kind of like a phone, I guess," said Joey, "except it plays songs instead of ringing. It played "Dixie" with little beeps and   bells."

"That's my cell phone!" said Tommy. "Dixie" is my messages ring."

"It says there are five new messages and 14 missed calls," said Joey. "We're waiting for Mr. Tate to try to retrieve the messages." Anthony had just come down the steps and saw Joey on the phone.

"Who's that?" asked Anthony.

"Suzanne," said Joey, matter-of-factly.

Tommy stared straight ahead and spoke softly. "My God. The messages must be from Susan."

"You didn't hear any of the messages?" asked Suzanne, a tear forming in her right eye, overcome by the possibility that Tommy's wife, some version of herself, was trying to reach him.

"Nah, the thing went dead in like a minute," said Joey, "but we brought it back to life over at Fuller's Auto and we're waiting for Mr. Ta..." Joey was cut short, just as Anthony grabbed the phone away from his friend.

"Suzanne! Suzanne!" shouted Anthony into the phone. She didn't answer him. "I know you're there. Are you okay?"

"Put Joey back on, Tony," said Suzanne.

Furious, Anthony threw the handset on the floor and ran up the stairs, and out the door.

"Hello?" said Joey.

Tommy grabbed the phone from Suzanne's hand. "Joey. This is Tommy Fuller. Do exactly as I say... and no one will get hurt. Do you understand me?" Suzanne buried her face in a pillow. "Do you understand me?!" he repeated, yelling.

"Tommy, no," Suzanne pleaded, gripping the pillow, almost ripping it in two. "Don't do this to him."

He put his hand over the mouthpiece, and turned his head, speaking quietly.

"I'm sorry, Suzanne. This is the only way. My phone is our only link to the other side, and if the agents get hold of it, we may never get back..." He almost couldn't bear to say it. "And if they figure out how to retrieve those messages...it just can't happen. It could be very bad. Joey can help us, but only if he thinks he absolutely has to. You know I'd never, ever lay a finger on you or let anyone else. But Joey doesn't know that." Suzanne ran to the bathroom, slamming the door behind her.

"Joey, stay on the line," Tommy commanded.

"This is not a good idea," said Phillips. "You're way out of line here."

"I agree," said Jackson. "You'll get that kid in trouble or way worse. Do you want another dead kid on your conscience?"

Fuller ignored them. "We can do this," he pleaded. "Aren't you at all interested in hearing from back home? Look, guys, we're running out of options. This could be important. Who knows what those messages are? Susan may have information about the…about my shooting, and our disappearance."

"Yes. But to threaten Joey, and imply kidnapping," said Phillips. "Not smart."

"We're already wanted men. Every law enforcement officer and government agent on both sides of the border, not to mention back home, is already looking for us. How could this make it any worse?"

"He's right," said Suzanne, who had emerged from the bathroom, dabbing her eyes with a tissue. "I'll go along with it. We'll get your message machine back."

•••••

Mr. Tate, the taller of the two agents, was contacted by radio shortly after the group had slipped away by bus. The police had found the car and Suzanne's jacket, its pockets empty, and no sign of their fugitives. Most downtown businesses had closed before they had a chance to canvas the area looking for any witnesses. The agents decided to make a call to the safe house in Gettysburg.

"Hello." Anthony answered the phone and tucked it under his chin, as his arms were full of groceries.

"Hello," said Agent Tate. "Have you heard from your friends yet?"

"No, they haven't called." He lied for them, and looked over at Joey, sitting on the couch.

"Alright," said Tate. "We'll check in again later tonight or first thing in the morning." Then he abruptly hung up.

Tommy Fuller had told Joey to make an excuse to leave Anthony and the apartment later that night and to call the Washington Inn at exactly 11:00 pm. He could call collect and tell the desk clerk he was calling on behalf of Unka for Suzanne. Before making the call he was to steal the phone out of Fuller's Auto, take a car, drive to Hagerstown, Maryland, and make plans to meet them near the North/South border. A tall order, but Fuller knew he was a clever and competent kid, and would do anything for his sister.

"You alright, Joey?" Anthony asked. "You look like something's going on."

"No, I'm fine. Just…tired, I guess."

"I really don't like those guys," said Anthony. "They've got Suzanne up to her eyeballs in trouble. I don't like it."

Joey was silent. Anthony didn't press the issue, and went to the kitchen to dig through the groceries, purchased with money given them by the agents. He fixed them both something to eat.

•••••

A light drizzle created a mirror-like sheen on the streets of downtown Washington, D.C., as the two agents began to check the area immediately around Anthony's Marathon. They came up empty. A guard unlocked the doors to the Library of Congress to let out a librarian just leaving for the night.

"Let's go talk to her," said Tate.

They walked toward the steps leading up to the main door and caught the librarian just as she was about to hail a cab.

"Good evening, Ma'am," said Tate. "We're Fed-Stat Marshals, and we have a couple of questions."

"Certainly," she answered, with a confident smile. "How may I help?"

"You haven't by any chance seen two white men, a Negro man, and a young girl today, have you? We believe they're traveling together and they're wanted for questioning."

"Why, no. I haven't seen anyone like that today. I helped a number of people, but no one fitting that description."

"You're sure, Ma'am? This is important. Our national security may be at stake."

"No, Gentlemen. I wish I could help, but I've not seen them."

Agent Tate looked at the woman's nametag. "Okay, well, thank you, Margaret. Let us know if you do." He handed her his card and they tipped their hats as they walked back to their car. Margaret disappeared around a corner.

"They can't be far from here," said the shorter man, pulling out a cigarette, "unless they stole another car."

"Nope. They're probably on foot," answered Tate. "Maybe they saw us. They could have taken a cab, or the underground."

A D.C. Metro Bus whizzed by them. "Or a bus," said the shorter man, taking a long drag.

"Let's get a bus schedule," said Tate, heading for the stopped bus. They got on board, flashed their credentials, and asked the driver if he'd seen their fugitives. He shook his head, but went on to say, that there were five additional drivers that all covered the same route about the time they would have been in the area. The agents retrieved the drivers' names and the phone number to Metro Dispatch. They walked a few blocks to M Street to stop in at their favorite 24-hour donut shop, The West Wing Diner. They ordered coffee and the shorter agent ordered two jelly-filled, powdered donuts. Tate sipped his coffee, while his partner devoured both confections. They ate and sipped in silence, looking out the window at the rain, which had just started to come down hard.

•••••

Still digesting both the Chinese food and the fact that his cell phone had waiting messages, Tommy Fuller was not feeling well. He apologized to Suzanne over and over for involving her and her brother in this mad scheme. She said she understood, but he still felt ashamed. They stopped talking about it and finally dozed together on the bed, holding hands.

Mike Philips unfolded the piece of paper he had been guarding and dialed the number to a Dr. Henry Rollins. The phone rang twice and Rollins answered.

"Hello, Henry Rollins here." The voice was old and crackled, but contained a youthful effervescence.

"Hello, Dr. Rollins," said Phillips. "I'm calling from downtown D.C. Margaret, at the Library of Congress, gave me your number and said you might be of some help."

"Oh. I see. So you've met Margaret," Rollins said, sounding delighted to have heard her name.

"Yes. She was very helpful, but we're still in desperate need of answers. We're still very confused."

"Yes, yes, these things do usually come as a shock, the first few times."

"What things? What do you mean by the 'first few times?'"

"Crossing over, of course. You're MTs, Multiverse Travelers, aren't you?"

Phillips sat stunned for a moment, the reality of what was being asked was unsettling.

"Well, we're not sure... but right now it seems like the best possible answer."

"Ahhh. A newbie. Margaret always sends the newbies to me. She knows I'm a sucker to educate brand new MTs; it's the teacher in me. Let me guess, she recommended you read a book: '*The Multiverse and Our Place In It.*'"

"Yes, that's right."

"And you'd like me to fill in the blanks?"

"At the very least. What we really want is to get home, so please, educate away. Dr. Rollins, this situation is getting stranger and more dangerous by the minute. It's almost too much to handle."

"I know it can be very disconcerting," said Rollins, "and if you get stuck here, it can take a while to adjust. Margaret comes and goes as she pleases, as do a few others, that I know."

"Margaret is a...what did you call them, a 'Traveler?'"

"Quite a good one, indeed. She's been at it for some fifty years, flipping in and out of dimensions, as easily as if through a revolving door." Phillips felt his spirits lift. Maybe there was a way home. If she could do it, then maybe they could, as well.

"Are you a Traveler?" asked Phillips.

"I was once, long ago, but my portal has closed and won't allow me back over. I've been trying for 63 years... not to discourage you, too much. Maybe you'd like to meet and I can tell you more."

"Absolutely, please."

"Tonight?" asked the eager doctor.

"Tomorrow would be better," said Phillips. "This evening I'm meeting with a Radio DJ I suspect is from back home, maybe he's a Traveler, too. And then later this evening, we're meeting a friend from the C.S.A."

"Please tell me you're not meeting with Billy Kay," said Rollins.

"You've heard of him?"

"Oh yes. I know him well, and you should know he's a scoundrel, liar, thief, and general all around bad guy. Don't trust him. We were friends for a while when he first got here. I heard him on the radio and knew he was from back home. He used to crack Bill Clinton jokes on the air all the time, just for his own amusement. He fancies himself a bit of a ...oh, what did Margaret call him? A 'shock-jock.'"

"So, I sought him out, in hopes we could share our common heritage, so to speak. We spent months and months discussing my specialty, Quantum Mechanics and Metaphysics, and he used me for all the knowledge I had, and then came to realize how much he could profit from being able to cross over at will. Too late, I realized that he was only motivated by greed. He brought a music machine of some sort and thousands of recordings with him. He's created and managed three rock 'n' roll bands in four years. His first two recreated bands–you won't believe this–The Beatles, and the Rolling Stones, both lost all hands in two, separate plane crashes. Band members, wives, children, crew...everyone dead. And it happened just after their songs hit the top of the charts and created quite a media frenzy and sold a lot of records. I think he's behind their deaths, but it was never proven, though the insurance companies who paid out plenty to him sure tried."

"My God," said Phillips. "That's incredible. I think he's working a new band, too, another stolen from home, from our universe." The words were still strange to Phillips, but he was beginning to understand Rollins' teachings, at least in a rudimentary way.

"I'll be very careful. Thanks again for your willingness to help. This is really very good news. Maybe we could meet tomorrow?"

"Sure. You know where the Hungry Boy Drive In is, as you're heading west, out of town?"

"Well, actually I do. I was there for lunch today."

"Fine, then. It's not too far from me. How about I plan to meet you there at 10:00 am?"

"Perfect."

"Then, I'll see you tomorrow."

"Goodnight, Dr. Rollins."

"Goodnight, Mr. Phillips, and please be very careful. Oh, and Mr. Phillips, it's too much to get into, right now, but I believe you're being sought after by the authorities. Best keep a low profile."

Phillips thanked the Doctor and hung up the phone, puzzling over the call. "I never told him my name," he said aloud, but no one heard. Jackson was napping in the big chair, while Tommy and Suzanne were still out cold.

As 8:30 approached, Phillips realized it was time to meet Billy Kay, and in spite of the words of warning from Dr. Rollins, he decided to keep his appointment. It would be safer to travel with a partner, but he was afraid Greg Jackson might draw too much attention, and Tommy and Suzanne were still sleeping, and were so wrapped up in each other and their own unfolding drama, that he decided he'd risk it on his own. When he reached the first floor, the desk clerk, Mr. Myers, was immersed in a pile of papers, but he called to Phillips anyway.

"Where you off to?" he said with a smile. "I thought you were all laying low."

Phillips turned from the door and walked back a few feet to the desk. "Well, we really are keeping a low profile but there're a couple of...missions, we're still committed to. By the way, what's the quickest way to M Street from here? I can never remember."

"Looking for the West Wing Diner?"

"Yeah," Phillips smiled, wondering just how popular this place was. "I've got a nine o'clock meeting."

"It's only about 10-15 minutes walking distance, maybe 20. Go left out the front door, back out to Pennsylvania Avenue, and then right on Penn for six blocks, and then left on M Street for another six blocks, more or less."

"Thanks for the directions. And thanks for everything else. You can't know how much we appreciate it."

"Happy to help. No thanks needed as long as you take care of that little girl. I've been knowing her since she was knee high to a grasshopper."

"She's a great kid," Phillips agreed. "We'll all watch out for her. I should be back by 9:45 or 10:00. Ahh… just in case I'm much later than that, please tell my friends where I've gone, will you?"

"Sure," said the clerk. "Good luck."

Phillips walked outside and found much cooler and wetter weather than they'd had for a few days, though the hard rain had stopped. He wished he had a jacket. It seemed unseasonably cool for July. He wished he had anything. He was not used to traveling without I.D., his cell phone and a car. He remembered, too late, that he didn't even have a dollar in his pocket. The six-figure attorney, with the big expense accounts, had been stripped to his bare essentials. It was an adjustment he didn't altogether hate. Other than at his beloved reenactments, it was the first time in a long time, he felt alive. He ducked his head into the wind and started his brisk walk to the West Wing Diner.

•••••

Joey was unusually quiet and Anthony sensed something was wrong. He'd brought home some Extra 'C' Cokes from the grocery store along with a six-pack of beer. When 10 o'clock rolled around, Anthony had already consumed two Cokes and four beers, still grumbling about Suzanne. He dozed on the couch, listening to the radio, waiting for the phone to ring. He snored softly and Joey made his move.

For the second time, in as many days, Anthony's car keys were stolen from under his nose, though this Marathon was technically a Fuller's Auto loaner. Joey wrote a fake note, hoping it might buy him some additional time should Anthony wake soon. It read: "T – needed some air, out driving around for a bit. Back soon." He quietly made his way up the stairs and out the door of the safe house. Leaving in the big noisy automobile without waking his friend would be tricky, but he managed. Anthony stirred at the sudden rumbling of the V-8 engine in the garage overhead, but didn't fully awaken, and Joey was off.

Joey had never so much as stolen a stick of gum and the thought of breaking and entering scared the hell out him. Especially since the Twins were like fathers to him and his friends. He was furious at Fuller for putting him through this, and cursed him under his breath as he drove to the station.

When he reached Fuller's Auto, he turned off the lights and parked in back. Being young and thin worked to his advantage. He easily shimmied his way up a utility conduit to the roof of the garage. A 3' X 3' skylight would be his entry point. He had no choice but to make the next few moves as quickly as possible, hope for the best, and high-tail it back out. He kicked in the glass skylight, sending pieces of it crashing to the floor below. He cleaned off the edge of the frame with his booted foot so he could lower himself by hand, and though he was careful, he still managed to cut the palm of his right hand in the process. He dropped about 10 feet to the hard concrete floor and, luckily, didn't break or sprain anything.

The illuminated exit sign over the door gave just enough dim light for him to see the cell phone and car battery on the workbench. He stopped at the sink to wash his bleeding hand with soap and water, and to get a better look at the fresh wound. It was a pretty good gash but nothing he couldn't endure. He snatched three or four paper towels from the dispenser and wrapped his cleaned hand with the folded towels, using electrical tape. He found a small box and placed the battery and phone inside and then moved to the rear door to let himself out, the door not closing completely.

With the stolen property in the back of the Marathon, he thought it might look suspicious, with only the device missing, so against every grain in his being he went back inside and did a little light vandalism. He generally made a mess of the tidy shop, and grabbed what he hoped were a few, unimportant tools, the poorly staged crime scene now set.

"I did it...," he said to himself quietly, with some satisfaction. "Dad would have killed me if he'd ever found out, but I did it." He piloted the Marathon out of town with its load of contraband. Within minutes the reluctant conspirator was barreling down the two-lane that would lead him to Hagerstown, Maryland, and, he hoped, his sister.

Chapter 22

The streets of D.C. were nearly deserted, except for the few business people making the last dash for home. A handful of Metro Police patrolled the streets, but none of them looked too interested in Mike Phillips, who made it to the West Wing Diner with 10-minutes to spare. He sat at the most inconspicuous booth he could find and tried to straighten himself up the best he could. He was cold, damp, and had a three-day beard; not exactly the image a senior law partner usually presents. The waitress came by and looked at him suspiciously. "What'll it be?" she asked.

"Just coffee, please," he answered.

She was tall and thin and her uniform accentuated all the right curves, and she knew it. She looked to be in her 30s but could have been 50, it was hard to tell. She had bright red hair, a color not found in nature, and it was pulled tightly and adorned by two yellow pencils.

"And how you gonna pay for it?" Phillips looked like a homeless vagrant and the savvy waitress was used to his type.

"I'm meeting a friend here in about five minutes. He said he'd pick up the tab."

She rolled her eyes, popped her chewing gum and sighed. "Well, I suppose. But if your friend doesn't show in 10 minutes, you and your freeloading coffee-hole are out the door."

"Certainly," said Phillips, looking at her name tag, "Wanda. I understand. No problems, I assure you." She came back to the table with a china cup and saucer balanced on top of the coffee pot. In the other hand she held a wax tissue holding a jelly donut.

"Here. Don't say nobody never did nothin' for ya."

"Well, thank you," he said, warmed by her kindness and change of heart.

She walked back behind a long counter and Phillips chuckled to himself at managing to obtain his sixth free meal since the nightmare began. He calculated in his head the amount of money he'd saved. If he'd been home in Gettysburg, the "real" Gettysburg, as he'd started to call it, he would have dropped at least $20 on each breakfast and lunch, plus $50 on dinner, and more if he bought a couple of nice bottles of wine. He was pleasantly surprised at the good nature of most of the people they'd recently met. They stood in stark contrast to his hardened business associates from home, and the often suspicious and surly public that normally walked the streets.

He surveyed the diner and noticed it was in keeping with the rest of this world, seemingly stuck in the late 1940s. There were framed, celebrity headshots adorning one wall and not a single actor or actress was recognizable, except Nicholas Cage. Phillips laughed out loud and didn't even bother to attempt to put that puzzle into play. Portraits of Presidents hung on every wall. Characterizations of elephants, donkeys, and the symbol of an unfamiliar, third party, a beaver, were given equal time positioned in true, tri-partisan spirit. He was the only one in the diner besides two men at the end of the counter, near the cash register.

As if appearing out of a pulp fiction Mickey Spillane novel, the men wore matching, dark trench coats, with matching, dark Fedora hats. They took no notice of him. He was taking his second sip of coffee, when a man entered the diner with a self-assured swagger. It had to be radio DJ Billy the Kay. He looked to be about 40 years old, and had a long, graying ponytail that hung out the back of a New York Yankees ball cap. He wore bell-bottom jeans and leather sandals, and had a denim jacket with the "Alabama Rum Runners" embroidered on the back. Phillips tentatively waved to him and he nodded. He sat down across from Phillips and smiled.

"You look like shit," he said. "Let me guess, by the looks of your beard, you crossed over about three days ago."

Phillips smiled.

"And you're losing your mind because none of this seems real? You've already gotten in to some kind of trouble and are avoiding the police, and you desperately want to get back home."

"Very good," said Philips, sarcastically. Though he was indeed impressed, he wasn't about to let this pompous, big shot stroke his own ego. "You look like shit, too," said Phillips, smiling, "only I think you don't know any better."

Kay laughed, appreciating his new friend's spunky attitude. He waved Wanda over to the booth.

"Hey, sweetheart," he said just a little too loudly. The woman rolled her eyes and the men at the end of the counter looked up.

"Hey Billy."

"My usual, sweety." He slapped her on the behind as she turned to

196

walk away. She threw him a dirty look, but seemed otherwise unshaken by his crudeness.

"So, Billy Kay. You think you've got me figured out? Did you know that I just came here from 1863 and the Battle of Gettysburg?"

Kay, raised an eyebrow. "Oh really? That's a new twist." He thought for a moment and his eyes opened wide. "Wait a minute...are you telling me...you're the guy?"

"What guy?"

Kay raised his hands in disbelief. He was talking to someone who clearly didn't have a clue.

"Nah...no way!" shouted Kay, answering his own question. Phillips didn't respond. "The mystery man? The Rebel soldier who changed the course of history?"

"Oh," said Phillips, getting his point. "That guy. Afraid so. Well not me really, there were four of us." He paused. "One died and three of us crossed over."

"The old sonofabitch was right," said Kay, recalling hours of debate he and Rollins had trying to determine the origin of the split in time and space. Kay quietly marveled at meeting the man, or one of the men, responsible, but he was unmoved by the revelation of death. "But how do you explain being in 1863? You're obviously a man of our time."

"Not sure, to tell you the truth. We're Civil War reenactors. One minute my friends and I were part of a fake battle, and the next minute, one of us is shot dead and we're smack dab in the middle of the real deal...it was Hell."

"Holy crap," said Kay, slumping back in the booth as the truth of the revelation finally sank in. "That's what I figured," he said, trying to recover his cool. Kay's countenance shifted as he pretended to be unimpressed with the fantastic nature of multi-dimensional time travel, but he was already scheming and thinking of the untold profits of such a feat.

"Oh, you'd already figured that out?" asked Phillips.

Billy smiled. "This stuff is cake. I had you figured out on the phone."

"Let me try to see if I got you figured Mr. Kay," said Phillips. "First of all, that's not your name. You're from New York, maybe New Jersey. You used to work in radio when you were younger and you idolize Howard Stern, but secretly you hate him because you think you're every bit as good, or better, but you could never convince any station managers of that and then one day you found yourself out of work and miserable."

He took a breath, and a sip of coffee, before continuing.

"Your life changed when Fate decided to ship you over here, and with your understanding of radio, demographics, play lists, the musical tastes of the average teenager, you talked your way onto a station here in D.C. You found a way back through...what's it called?...your portal, brought a CD player and as many songs as you could with you. You claimed the songs as your own, found some young musicians to learn to copy the songs and then cut a deal with a record company or two to put these guys on the road." Kay smiled and motioned for him to continue.

"You play their music on the radio, ignoring those other artists who won't pay or play your little game. You've reinvented payola, illegal back home, and you've imported pirated music to a waiting and vulnerable universe. Your artists became big hits because you stole only the best; Beatles, Stones, Skynyrd, probably the Eagles, for starters." Phillips didn't comment on the demise and fiery deaths of two of Kay's bands.

Kay sat smirking at Phillips' cross-examination and accusations.

"Well smart guy, you think you're pretty clever, but you're wrong. There were never any CDs. I have an iPod with 10,000 songs on it and Hootie, Fleetwood Mac, and Phil Collins are next. I'm saving Grunge and Hip-Hop for next year. Wait until they hear Rap and Hip-Hop. They'll lose their minds!" He smiled, pulling the gleaming MP3 player from his inside jacket pocket, waving it in Phillips' face.

"Just what do you want from me, anyway?" Kay's smile faded.

"Mostly, I want to know how to get home," said Phillips. "I don't really ever want to come back here. I just want to get home. My friends and I all want to go home. We couldn't care less what you do here."

Kay looked at Phillips for a moment and considered all he'd said.

"Multiple crossings are rare," said Kay, revisiting his professorial air. "But it does happen. The Bermuda Triangle is a huge, but very unstable, portal. I'm sure you know the stories. In 1945, five Navy bombers, Flight 19, disappeared in clear skies and over calm seas. Well, guess what. They arrived here unharmed, all 10 crewmen. Two of them are still alive and live in D.C. Six of them went crazy. The smart ones just learned to live with it. Those guys were dumb though. The commander ordered the destruction of the planes. I guess they were worried about the technology falling into the wrong hands, reverse engineering, and all that."

"How do you know all this?"

"Because I'm smart and I study these things. That, and I ran into one of the old farts, a pilot, and he told me. What do you think? I'm just gonna bop over to a new universe and act like I walked in on somebody sitting on the can? I was just like you. Full of questions."

"What other multiple crossings can you tell me about?" asked Phillips.

"In 1915 an entire battalion of soldiers disappeared in Sulva, Turkey. Three eye-witnesses watched 25 English soldiers march up a hillside into the fog, never to be seen again. And I know it sounds like so much Hollywood hype, but for some reason fog is usually involved, not always though. Those are just two of hundreds of the most well-known accounts. Then there's the Philadelphia Experiment, but that's another story for another time." He took a breath and looked hard at Phillips.

"It's far more common to hear about individuals vanishing rather than groups. Obviously, sometimes people disappear at the hands of the bad guys or from accidents...but sometimes they haven't vanished at all, Mr. Doe, they've just crossed over to this universe or another. This one seems to be very popular, though. I think it's because it's on a Timeline very close to our own. Basically it's just easier for the Cosmos to send us here. The first stop, so to speak."

"Timeline?"

"It's complicated."

"How do we get back over?"

"The trick is to find out exactly *where* you crossed over, because that's where you'll cross back, assuming you even can. You should know that most Travelers can't ever get back, especially Multiples."

"Multiples?"

"It's complicated, Mr. Doe."

"How does it happen?" asked a completely exasperated Phillips. "I'm 46 years old and I've never vanished or crossed over anywhere before or known anyone who has."

"You haven't?" asked Kay "Are you sure? Have you ever had Deja vu?"

"Yes, of course."

"Or a premonition?"

"No, not really."

"Well, a lot of people do. Those are "near crossings," as close to crossing over as is possible without actually doing so. "Déjà vu" in particular, we believe is more or less a wobble in space-time." Kay was speaking with a knowledge and authority that didn't fit him. Phillips was sure he had gotten his information from the Doctor; and then Kay all but confirmed it in a rare show of humility.

"If you want to know more, you really need to talk to an expert." He stopped short of telling him about Dr. Rollins. "I'm afraid I only know enough to keep my sanity and to get myself back and forth. And my portal won't work for you, and vice versa. That's why millions of people travel through the Bermuda Triangle and never experience anything at all, and then, all of a sudden the next guy fishing or flying his two-seater prop-job to Miami, disappears into thin air. It's about personal space and alignment. You really need someone more knowledgeable than I to help you figure this out."

"Like Dr. Rollins?" asked Phillips. Kay's face soured.

"That old shit hole? Don't believe a word that bastard says. He's in too deep with that Library chick, Martha or Maggie or whatever her name is. They're meddlers."

"Oh, and I suppose you're not?" said Phillips. "'The Alabama Rum Runners'? Why not just call 'em Lynyrd Skynyrd?"

"I always hated that name, so I came up with a new one. And so what?" he said, feeling the jab. "I make a few bucks on some songs that this world would have never heard without me. What's the harm?"

"How are those bands doing? The ones you gave the songs to."

Kay leaned in close and grabbed Phillips by the shirt collar pulling him within an inch of his own face. "I had nothing to do with that. Did Rollins tell you that? Look, airplanes crash, that's all." He let Phillips go with a shove that pushed him back into his seat. "Hell, I'd never set foot on a plane here. There's no FAA in this place, no mandatory maintenance, no records. These things have barely evolved beyond what the Wright Brothers flew. And the pilots are all cowboys. It was a mistake on my part ever flying those boys to gigs. It was a tragedy and a coincidence that they were on top at the time, nothing more."

After 20-years of trial law, Phillips had become an excellent judge of those who were fabricating stories and Kay had none of the tell-tale earmarks of lying. Wanda came back to the table and leaned her hip against Billy Kay's shoulder.

"Ya need anything else, Sugar?" she said seductively. "More coffee? A piece of pie?"

"I just need a piece of you, darlin'," said Kay. He playfully bit her on the arm, and she squealed and pulled back, slapping the top of his head.

"Well, I'm getting off at 9:30, so could you two pay up, please?" she said, still flirting with the Kay.

"Baby, if you're getting off at 9:30, then Billy The Kay is getting off at 9:32." He laughed at his own crude cleverness.

"You're a pig," she said, and ripped the top check out of her book and threw it on the table. She walked to the counter shaking her head and smiling, just a little.

"I got you covered, Mr. Doe," said Kay, grabbing the check. "And I wish you a lot of luck getting home. It's either gonna be tricky as hell, probably impossible, or a walk in the park. Either way, nice meeting you and keep it tuned to DC-1560." He snapped his finger and made a gun out of his hand in one smooth, Vegas-style move.

They got up from the table and met Wanda at the register. The taller man sitting at the counter, slipped off his jacket, exposing his holstered weapon and government I.D. badge. Phillips' blood ran cold. The shorter man, face covered with powdered sugar, recognized Billy Kay and spoke to him through a broad smile and little puffs of white powder.

"Love your show, Billy. I listen every day."

"Thanks, man." Kay beamed, loving it anytime anyone recognized him. "Have you heard the new 'Alabama Rum Runner's' cut?"

"Yeah, that Sweet Home...ahh, Mississippi?"

"Close enough." Kay laughed and he handed Wanda $20 and told her to keep the change. She curtsied at the generous $14 tip on a $6 check.

Mr. Tate looked at the two and was not nearly as chatty as his chain-smoking partner. Mike Phillips avoided direct eye contact.

"Who's your friend here, Kay?" asked Tate, nodding in Phillips' direction.

He answered without hesitation. "Oh, just an old friend from back home."

"Oh yeah? Just visiting our fair city, Mister….."

"Doe," said Phillips, smiling, on auto pilot. "John Doe."

"Where's home, Mr. Doe?" he asked.

"New York City," said Phillips, saying the first thing that came to mind.

Agent Tate looked at Kay. "You're from New York, Kay? I always heard you were from the midwest, St. Louis?"

"Originally, New York," said Kay pointing to his Yankees cap, his smile fading slightly.

"Enjoying your vacation, Mr. Doe?" Tate was putting on a tough-cop show, mostly out of boredom and frustration, not because he sensed anything suspicious. He just enjoyed harassing people to see how thoroughly he could shake them up, but Phillips and Kay were both cool customers. This only made Tate pissier.

"It's always a vacation visiting my old friend, Billy Kay," said Phillips smiling, wrapping his arm around Kay's shoulder.

"Did you fly in from New York?" asked Tate.

"Hell no," said Phillips, laughing nervously. "Not with Kay's track record. I travel by bus or train whenever I'm coming to see this guy." The shorter agent chuckled. The stories of the plane wrecks had been well publicized, as was Kay's Grand Jury hearing that hadn't found enough evidence to warrant a trial, but raised plenty of suspicions. Tate stared at his coffee cup. He reached into his pocket and Phillips was sure this was it. He'd been made. Tate produced a business card with his name and office number on it.

"You see anything unusual out there, let me know. We're looking for some…out-of-towners. A colored guy, two white guys, one of them younger and the other about your age, Doe, and a hot little blond. We'd really like to talk to them but they keep disappearing." Tate managed a fake smile.

"We will definitely keep an eye out for them," said Kay. Phillips nodded without making eye contact.

"All right gentleman," said Kay, clapping his hands together. "It's time for Billy The Kay to get his beauty sleep. I've got the Morning Drive Show tomorrow. Got to be up at four."

They said their goodbyes and just before Phillips and Kay walked out the door, Tate tapped Phillips on the shoulder. "Your voice sounds familiar. Have we met?"

"Not that I can recall," said Phillips, a slight tremor forming on his upper lip. Tate saw the nervousness Phillips was trying so desperately to hide, but didn't say any more. Kay and Phillips made their way out of the West Wing Diner and stood for a moment on the sidewalk. It had stopped raining hard but was still drizzling and chilly. From inside, Tate watched the men out of the corner of his eye.

"Billy, can I hitch I ride with you? I'm only about a mile away."

"Sure, why not. Any Skynyrd fan is a friend of mine."

They crossed the street and got into a sports car–a very rare, very expensive and very fast sports car. The 1959 Canadian-made Austin-Healy Kay owned should have been made in England, but just prior to the fall of the U.K. in the War for Europe, the automakers moved to Canada with 10 million or so other English, Welsh, Irish and Scottish citizens. When Leonard, Lord of Austin, and Donald Healey, formerly of Cornwall, England, met in Montreal, they formed a car company. The two auto enthusiasts created an automobile sought the world over. Bifurcated timelines and alternate universes could not stop these creators of a magnificent car from fulfilling their destiny. Hitler or not, the Austin-Healey, it seemed, was destined by the master of many universes to become a great automobile, and Billy-the-Kay owned one. As they were pulling out, Phillips noticed the two agents getting into a car that had been parked directly in front of the diner.

"Can you lose them?" asked Phillips.

"Lose who?"

"Good cop, bad cop."

"Those guys? Probably. Why?"

"I'm not sure, but I think they may suspect I'm one of their fugitives."

"Fugitives?" asked Kay.

"Long story. Maybe they haven't made me, but I'd rather not take the chance. Can you lose them?"

"Oh crap. What kind of trouble are you in?"

"I really shouldn't be in any trouble at all. We just keep ditching these guys and they're getting mad, that's all. Now can we go?"

Clearly annoyed, Kay checked his rear view mirror. "Of all the…shit."

"It looks like they're waiting for us to pull out," said Phillips. "Let's do this. Please?" he asked again, with growing urgency.

"Are you kidding me? This is a '59 Austin-Healey. It'll out run, out maneuver anything on the road. This is my fun car. I keep my jalopy at the public parking garage. I can lose anybody anytime I want."

"Okay then, prove it."

Kay wiggled the little car out of its slot and he punched it, squawking the tires. He was down M Street and had circled around three blocks before the agents ever even made it out of their parking space. In a matter of a few minutes they were at the Washington Inn with no signs of Tate and his flunky.

"Okay, Mr. Doe, and by the way I know that's not your name, we share some of each other's secrets now. I know where you're staying and that you're a wanted man. And you know about my little songwriting business, though no one would ever believe you if you tried to rat me out. But anyway, I'd say we're even. You keep your mouth shut and I'll do the same. I'm sure I'll probably see Tate and his little buddy again…probably before the night is out. I'll tell them that we started drinking and got into a fight, and that I dropped you off at the other end of Pennsylvania Avenue, and that I didn't know where you were staying. Don't even worry about them."

"Thanks," said Phillips. "I have one more little favor." He hesitated, building the courage to ask. "May I borrow your 'jalopy?"

"Wow," said Kay, "you're sure not a shy fella. That's more than a 'little' favor."

"My name is Mike Phillips. I think I can trust you and you can trust me. We've got to meet a friend later tonight and we had to ditch our car. It's a slightly stolen Marathon."

"Oh, so you're a car thief? Three days in and you're a wanted car thief, and you're going to pass judgment on me?" He laughed and thought for a moment. "I guess us Travelers need to stick together. Yeah, I'll loan you my little junker. It's a Ford Atlantic, four-door. Here's the key." He pulled one shiny metal key from a large key ring and handed it to Phillips. "I keep it at the Capitol Parking Garage at 1202 J Street. I'm on the fourth floor, far back, right corner. My pass will get you in and out. Here it is." He reached into his wallet to pull out the red, white and blue parking pass.

"Don't get caught. I don't need any complications. When you're done with it, just put it back in the space at the garage. Look, I better get out of here, Phillips. I need a plausible excuse when they come to question me, and I figure they might. They won't know I've loaned you a car. Try to keep it in one piece, if you can. Oh hell, I don't really care, I've got enough money to buy 100 more. Ditch it for all I care. I can tell people you stole it."

"Thanks, Kay. You don't know how helpful this is. I owe you."

"Yeah, you do," he answered with a half-smile and drove off.

Downtown was mostly deserted, but Phillips hurried to the Hotel entrance. With Mr. Myers not at his post, he walked straight up to the room. His companions were up and about, waiting for his return.

"Mr. Myers let us know you were out making new friends," said Jackson. "How'd it go?"

"You mean besides having coffee with the two Dirty Harrys that have been following us?"

"You're kidding?" asked Fuller.

"I wish I was. I nearly crapped my pants. We lost them though. That Radio DJ, Billy the Kay isn't such a bad guy after all. He gave them the slip and loaned me his car. He's a Traveler, like us. He knew an awful lot about it."

"A *Traveler?*" asked Fuller.

"Yeah, I guess that's what we're called."

"Billy the Kay is a Traveler?" asked Suzanne.

"Yes, but that's on the DL," said Phillips.

"The down low," said Suzanne, self satisfied in picking up on some of her new friends' codes, though she'd ponder the possible meaning of a "Dirty Harry" for some time. "Did Tate recognize you?"

Phillips sighed. "I'm not sure, but I think they might suspect. Tate said he thought he recognized my voice, but I don't know how. He's never met us."

"The safe house is bugged," said Suzanne. "I guess they heard your conversations. Sorry."

"Well, we wouldn't have made any sense to them. We were delirious and clueless," said Phillips. "Anyway, it's in the past. More importantly I know we lost them. I think we're safe here for the time being." He flopped down in the easy chair, rubbing his forehead, clearly stressed by his close encounter. "Are we still going through with this plan to get your phone?" Tommy nodded in the affirmative and Suzanne looked away.

"We might as well get out of here," said Jackson. "While you were away I called every Jackson in the phone book. My family's not here in D.C. Not even the cousins or anyone I knew."

"I'm sorry, Greg," said Phillips, understanding how difficult it must have been to wonder what became of his family. Even a first cousin, one universe removed, is still blood, he thought.

"Well, I've got a car for us. It's on J Street at a parking garage," continued Phillips. He held the key up and showed them. "What's our next move?"

"It's 10:15," said Fuller, looking at the clock on the nightstand. "We wait for Joey's call. He'll let us know that he has the phone and is near the border crossing."

Suzanne stood at the window, watching the drizzle fall to the quiet street below. A D.C. Metro Police car pulled up to the front of the building and she stepped from the window, almost falling backward. She peeked out through the curtain and called the men toward her.

"We have company," she said, grabbing Tommy's arm nervously. "Are you sure you weren't followed, Mike?"

"Positive," answered Phillips, adding "at least I don't think so."

•••••

Two D.C. Metro Policemen entered the Hotel and rang the bell at the front desk. The clerk came out from behind a wall rubbing his eyes.

"Good evening, officers, how may I help you?"

"We're looking for four individuals that we believe are staying somewhere in this area. We're checking all the hotels. Did you check in a party of four today?" asked the Patrolman.

"I surely did not," he answered.

"Your 'No Vacancy' sign is lit up."

"Because I'm out of rooms."

"Mind if we look at your guest registry?"

"Be my guest," he said, the pun lost on the cops. He spun the registry around and the officers matched room numbers and registered guests against names from their notes. "Where's Room 13 on this registry?"

"Don't have a room 13. Bad luck, you know."

"Yeah, bad luck, I guess," said the cop, agreeing. "Well, let us know if anybody shows up, especially two white guys, a colored and a young woman."

"I will keep my eyes open for them. What did they do, anyway?"

"They're just wanted for questioning, at the moment."

"I'll let you know if I see 'em."

"Thanks." The cops walked out the door satisfied the hotel was clean.

Two floors up the guests in the unmarked room 13 breathed a collective sigh of relief when they saw the police cruiser pull away. The phone rang, startling them. Suzanne picked up the receiver.

"Hello," she said tentatively.

"Hey, little girl. This is Mr. Myers at the front desk. They're gone. I don't think we'll see any more police for a while. Just thought you'd like to know."

"Thank you, thank you. We did see them and were getting nervous."

"Okay, well relax. I got rid of 'em for you. Goodnight, now."

"Actually, we'll see you in 20 minutes or so, Mr. Myers. We're leaving for a meeting soon."

"You're busy kids, all these late-night meetings. The police are looking for you and they're in the area. It would not be smart to go wandering down the street together. But you know best. You'll need a cab, right?"

"Yes, please. We're expecting a call from my brother any minute. Could you call the cab for us when my brother calls in? And Mr. Myers, I'm sorry about the cops. Thanks, again, for your help. We'll find a way to make it up to you."

"Just don't get caught and be safe. That's all the thanks I need. I'll forward the call when it comes in." He hung up and Suzanne placed the receiver on the hook.

At 10:55 p.m. the phone rang and Tommy Fuller answered. "Yes?"

"It's me," said Joey, sounding tired, nervous, and younger than normal. "Is Suzanne okay? Please let me talk to her."

"Do you have my cell phone?" Fuller asked.

"You're what?"

"My radio phone," Fuller said, agitated.

"Yeah, yeah, I've got it."

"Okay, Good. You're doing good, Joey. Suzanne's fine and...I'm sorry about this."

"Let me talk to her." He was not moved by Fuller's apology. Tommy handed the phone to the visibly upset girl sitting on the bed next to him.

"Joey?" she asked

"Hey, Sis. You alright?"

"Yes, I'm fine. Are you alright?"

"Yeah, I guess. I had to steal a car, break into Fuller's, and sneak out of town. So, all things considered, I'm just great. What's going on, anyway?"

"We'll tell you more when we see you. Where are you?"

"I'm about five miles from Tunnel 2 on 37a headed toward Hagerstown. I'm at an all-night truck stop." He looked around for a sign. "Ahhh...It's called the "Fuel and Drool." I'm using the phone at one of the tables, it's really cool. All of the booths have their own pay phone." Tommy overheard him explain his whereabouts, and he motioned to Suzanne for the phone.

"Stay there," said Fuller sternly. "We'll bring your sister and we'll trade her for the device." They were all horrified at how cold and criminal it had sounded, but he was obsessed with getting his cell phone. "Stay there. We'll be about an hour." Fuller hung up the phone and looked at his companions. "I guess we better get going."

With no bags to pack, in just a few minutes, they were out of the room, down the stairs, where they met the clerk who was standing behind the front desk.

"Your cab will be here shortly," said Myers. "You kids aren't going out without coats are you?"

"Afraid so," said Phillips. "We didn't exactly pack correctly for this trip. And it's July? What's with the weather?"

"I guess our 40-year cold-snap isn't ending any time soon," said Myers. "Anyway, I've got a lost and found that dates back that far. You can't even believe what people leave behind in their rooms. Let me see what I can dig up."

He disappeared around the corner and within minutes came back with an armload of outerwear. "May not be the prettiest but you won't freeze to death, anyway." He flopped the pile of clothing onto the counter and they managed to each find a garment that would do the trick. Phillips found an interesting black nylon jacket with a short, ringed collar. Above the pocket it read "Member's Only." He pointed this out to Fuller and Jackson.

"Looks like we're not the first Travelers to stay here. This is from home, circa 1985."

"No, no," said Myers, not understanding exactly what Phillips had meant. "That ol' thing has been here as long as I have, at least since 1960." The men looked at each other trying to understand how a 1985 jacket arrived in the 1960s. This was a most unusual and complicated place.

A tired sounding auto horn tooted twice outside the Washington Inn and the four made their way to the waiting cab. Across town the two agents had temporarily given up on Billy the Kay and sat at their desks in Federal Tower One. Tate retrieved his pad and looked at his notes. It read: "5 D.C. Metro Bus Drivers."

"We've got to find out if any of these drivers picked up the four," said Tate aloud, "and if so, where they got off the bus?" It was their only lead, and not much of one.

The smoking agent nodded as Tate placed a call to the Metro Bus Line dispatch desk. After identifying himself, Tate asked the dispatcher for his help.

"We're looking to confirm the names and phone numbers of the drivers that ran the Pennsylvania Avenue bus route near the Library of Congress between, say, five and eight p.m., today." The dispatcher, at first, denied the request. Tate managed to talk him into cooperating, or run the risk of being charged with obstruction of justice and interfering with a Federated States National Security investigation. The reluctant dispatcher shuffled through some logbooks, confirmed the names, and gave him the drivers' home phone numbers.

"Well, here we go," said Tate to his partner. He went to the first name and number and dialed.

•••••

Mike Phillips gave the address of the parking garage to the cabby and they were off. No one spoke on the five-minute ride to Capitol Parking and Suzanne handed the driver a $50 bill for a $9 fare.

"Keep the change and you never saw us, okay?"

"You got it, Sister," said the appreciative cabby, smiling at the bill he didn't recognize as counterfeit.

The security guard came to greet them shortly after the cabby pulled off. Phillips showed him the car key, the pass, and told him he was a friend of Mr. Kay, and they were let in. The Ford Atlantic, a mid-sized four-door sedan, sat exactly where Kay had told him it would be.

"Let me drive," said Suzanne. "I know this town better than you guys."

"Why don't I drive?" asked Greg Jackson. "I'm from D.C. This is my town. I know it better than all y'all." Phillips handed him the key and Jackson slid behind the wheel, unlocking the other doors. Tommy and Suzanne got in back and Phillips took the front passenger's seat. As they circled their way down from the fourth floor toward the road, Suzanne snuggled in close to Tommy, sensing things were changing quickly and dramatically. She could tell that he was having an especially hard time. He closed his eyes and tried to rest. After showing the parking pass, the guard let them through without incident. Within minutes of arriving at the garage they were back out into the night and on the streets of the small Nation's Capitol.

Chapter 23

The first and second bus drivers Tate reached by phone, were of no help and reported nothing out of the ordinary. The phone of the third driver on the list, Paul Williams, rang and awakened Williams and his wife from a sound sleep. On the third ring she smacked him on the back of the head.

"Answer the damn phone, Paul."

"It's just those kids calling again," he said. "I will not answer and give them the satisfaction. Not after the day I had. No sir, I will not give in to those hoodlums." The phone rang four more times and finally went silent.

"Not answering," said Tate.

This was unusual. At 11:15 p.m. most everybody could be reached by phone. With no caller I.D. and no answering machines, people simply answered their phones, all the time. It was especially unusual, at an hour at which most people were home, to have not gotten an answer. Tate circled the name and moved on to drivers four and five, receiving the same reports as before. These drivers hadn't seen anyone matching the description and they hadn't seen anything unusual, but the fifth driver on the list did give Tate something useful.

"Have you spoken to Paul Williams yet?" the driver asked. Tate replied that he had not been able to reach him.

"Well, he would have passed by the Library of Congress right around 6:05 and I saw him briefly in the locker room back at the station. He was carrying on and ranting and raving about "civilian's rights" or some such nonsense and how maybe Coloreds didn't need to ride in the back of the bus all the time. Crazy talk is all it was and I wasn't really listening to him. We all bitch about our jobs when we get back to the station, but talk to Williams. He was acting queer. He might have seen something."

Tate hung up without thanking the driver, and immediately redialed Williams' number. Still no answer. He called the dispatcher and demanded Williams' home address, which he was given: 422 Douglas Avenue.

"Come on," Tate said to his partner, slapping the shorter man's feet off his desk.

Stubbing out his cigarette, and grabbing his hat, he chased after Tate, and they left their office, back into the rainy night. They were off to pay a visit to a bus driver on the outskirts of town.

•••••

Jackson piloted the sedan carefully through the drizzle and on to the main road out of town. Still 40-minutes from a second smugglers' tunnel entrance, and on their way toward a rendezvous with Joey, Mike Phillips clicked on the radio, which was still tuned to 1560 AM. There were no FM settings in this universe, FM had not yet been invented. All the stations were AM and produced the characteristic, thin, occasionally static-laden music that those in their world back home would have endured only until the early 1970s, when bigger speakers, high fidelity sound, and FM stereo would change the way people listened to the radio at home and in their cars.

A pleasant, but mournful voice of a woman sang about love and loss. The windshield wipers, on slow, kept perfect time with the tune, a song the announcer identified as "Shades of Blue and Gray." As the tune faded they listened to the sound of a newsroom full of typewriters accompanied by frantic, Morse-code styled staccato music. It signaled the start of the hourly news report.

"Good evening Washington. The time is 11:30. You're tuned to 1560 where all the news is updated hourly. I'm Ron Hanlon. A three-alarm fire on the City's west side took the lives of an elderly couple this evening and destroyed two city blocks. The cause of the blaze is unknown and under investigation."

"Federal agencies have alerted news media to an upgrade in the terror alert level to number two, just one away from the highest level, TA-1. The upgrade appears to be in response to a breach in the North-South border earlier today, just 35 miles west of D.C. Reports indicate four possible terrorist suspects successfully crossed over from Confederate Maryland into the F.S.A. Capitol. The whereabouts of the suspects are unknown but local and Federal agencies have stepped up the manhunt. Possible links to the outlawed North-South Unification Militia, also known as the Freedom Fighters, are suspected. This is Ron Hanlon. Your news and music source, DC-1560, will keep you updated."

The newsman went on to other stories but those riding in the borrowed Ford Atlantic had stopped listening.

"This is falling apart fast," said Jackson. "They're looking hard for us."

"No shit," said Phillips, agreeing, still in shock at what they had just heard.

"That tunnel entrance won't work now at all," said Suzanne.

"No matter," said Fuller. "We're still going forward with this plan. My phone is operational and it's our only link to home. We'll find a way over to the truck stop. Just don't do anything to get us pulled over."

Jackson glanced down at the speedometer to verify he was going exactly 30 miles an hour in a 30 MPH zone. They jumped when a State Trooper flew past them traveling at least three times their speed. Jackson began to sweat. They all began to sweat.

"We are not going to make it," said Phillips. "After what happened today at the first tunnel, you know that other tunnel will be guarded, along with every inch of every road within 200-miles of here. This place will be crawling with cops."

"Just keep driving," said Fuller, clearly in charge of this stage of the operation.

•••••

When the agents arrived at 422 Douglas Avenue no lights were on inside the house. They knocked on the door, waited a few seconds and knocked again. A light in an upstairs window flicked on and they could hear footsteps coming down the inside stairs. The peephole momentarily went dark as the bus driver, Williams, checked to see who was at the door. Chains rattled, several latches were pulled back, and Williams opened the door to the two agents.

"Paul Williams?" asked Tate

"Yes," he answered, groggily.

"We're with National Security, Mr. Williams. May we come in?"

They showed their badges and he opened the door for them to enter. In the hallway of the small house, Tate questioned the bewildered bus driver.

"Mr. Williams, any reason you're not answering your phone this evening?"

"It's those damned kids down the street making crank calls at all hours of the day and night. Third time this week. Is that what this is about?"

Tate ignored the question. "Mr. Williams, did you drive your normal route today?"

211

"Yes," he said, clearly confused.

"Anything unusual happen?"

Williams' eyes darted from left to right searching his memory for anything drastic enough to warrant National Security questioning. "No," he said, shaking his head, still thinking.

"Did you have any run-ins with a Negro, two white men and a young woman?"

Williams' eyes grew wide. "Yes. Well, yes, I did actually."

"Can you tell us about it?"

The driver described in detail the encounter he had had just a block from the steps of the Library of Congress, and how the black man had banged on the side of his bus and how he wouldn't sit in back.

"Do you remember exactly where you let them off?" asked Tate.

"Yes, I'll never forget," said Williams. "They signaled their stop and the other three got off first and then the colored guy talked to me like no Colored has ever spoken to me before. He said a bunch of stuff I really didn't understand, sounded like a politician, or a preacher, maybe... or a poet. He sounded very educated, like a college guy, and then he started yelling, preaching like, about all kinds of things mostly, about the equality of the races. Really kind of got me thinking a little bit, you know? He started talking about a dream he had. 'I have a dream' he kept saying..."

Tate interrupted him.

"Where, exactly, did they get off the bus, Mr. Williams?"

"I'll never forget it. On E street. Corner of Pennsylvania and E."

"Thank you." They turned, leaving the stunned man standing in his bathrobe, and they walked briskly to their car.

"What about those damned kids down the street?" Williams yelled at the retreating Federal agents, who never answered.

Tate and his partner were no longer driving their Con-Fed Marathon, but had switched to their regular transport, an unmarked black Chevrolet four-door. They radioed D.C. Metro Police and spoke to the Chief.

"Did your guys sweep the hotels around the Library of Congress?" asked Tate.

"Yeah, they did. I had 10 officers on it. Came up with nothin'," answered the Chief. "In fact, the last patrol just reported back. They're still here. Want to talk to 'em?"

"Yeah," said Tate. "We'll hold."

Tate floored the Chevy, weaving in and out of the suburban neighborhoods on his way back to downtown D.C. One of the patrolman got on the radio.

"This is Officer Johnson."

"Johnson, this is National Security Agent Tate. Did you check any hotels near E and Penn?"

"Yeah. We did, there's only one, the Washington Inn. Nothing unusual there, just a sleepy old man who let us look at the books and seemed very normal. No sign of 'em."

"Did you sweep through each room?"

The officer hesitated. "Each room? No. Didn't see a need to disturb everybody in the hotel. It was full. It was late and there are 20 some odd rooms in that place. The clerk seemed like a stand-up guy...very calm, helpful and routine."

"Okay, Johnson, that's all." They signed off and Tate hit the gas.

•••••

The mood in the borrowed Ford was failing. The retrieval of Fuller's cell phone, if they could pull it off, just didn't seem to be the entire answer to their predicament. But not trying didn't seem right either. The men in that car all shared an unspoken concern; eventually they were going to have to face the realities of spending the rest of their years living in this place. With every passing moment they feared prison, or execution, might be a part of that unpleasant future. But Mike Phillips wasn't ready to throw in the towel just yet.

"Pull over at the next gas station or restaurant that looks like it might have a phone," said a resolute Phillips.

"No!" Tommy yelled from the back seat, leaning his head forward to protest. "We've got to get to Joey. Do not pull over."

"Look, Fuller," said Phillips, "you know we'll never get across the border. You'll get us all thrown in jail. How will we explain ourselves to the Feds, huh? You heard the news report. We've got to come up with a new plan. This one isn't flying any longer."

Tommy slumped back in the seat, conceding, knowing Phillips was right. They were silent for only a moment before Phillips spoke again. "I have an idea. I'm hoping Dr. Rollins might help us. Get us to a phone, Greg."

They drove on for a few minutes then saw a restaurant, Paco O'Malley's Mexican-Irish Cuisine, looming in the distance.

"Here?" asked Jackson.

"I don't know. It's pretty busy. We've got to stay under the radar if we can. Okay, hell, just pull in. But you all stay low. Pull to the back of the parking lot. We don't want to be seen, especially you, Greg."

They parked the car in a darkened corner and turned off the lights. Phillips turned to look at his companions.

"Okay, it's a long shot, but I'm going to try to reach Rollins. He lives about 30 or 40 minutes from here and, besides being the guy who explained 'crossing over' to us, he knows this area and the people around here. He's a friend of Margaret's. We were supposed to meet with him tomorrow, but I'm going to see if we can move our appointment up a bit. I'm also going to try to reach Joey, at the truck stop, and tell him to hold tight; to tell him we'll be late."

Fuller nodded. This new tack was beginning to make sense.

"So, Suzanne, may I have some cash?" asked Phillips. "I'm going to have to make a few long distance calls. You guys stay put. Stay out of sight. I'll bring us back some coffee." Suzanne handed him a $10 bill and he trotted in the rain toward the front door of Paco O'Malley's, "Home of the Corned Beef and Cabbage Taco Special," according to the sign out front.

•••••

Agent Tate and his partner pulled in front of the Washington Inn and parked their car in the street. Inside, Tate rang the bell, none too gently, and the clerk appeared. The agents flashed their badges and Tate decided to play hard-ball right out of the gate, his patience wearing thin.

"So, Mr. Myers," he said, reading his name badge. "You decided to lie to the Metro Police earlier today?"

"I did no such thing, gentleman." Myers looked offended at the accusation. He was a good actor. He had been a friend of smugglers and insurgents for decades and he was not easily shaken.

"Then you won't mind if we look around?"

"Not at all. Let me get my keys." He disappeared into the back and returned dangling a large set of master keys. "We have 21 rooms on three floors. No elevator, I'm afraid. How would you like to proceed?"

Tate was annoyed with the friendly compliance. He had really hoped for more of a fight and he was certain the old man was hiding something.

"We have one vacancy and the other 20 rooms have guests registered. I'm assuming you'll want to wake all of them and question each of them thoroughly." Myers was really getting under Tate's skin. "We'll start with room '1' and work our way up?"

"No," said Tate. "I have a better idea." He reared his arm back, clenched his fist like he was going to punch the old man, but instead violently pounded the fire alarm six inches from Myers' head, glass shattering. The piercing bell began ringing immediately. "How many exits are there, Mr. Myers?!" Tate yelled over the noise reverberating in the lobby, and from all floors.

"Just this front entrance, one down that back hall and two fire escapes in back!" Myers yelled in response, still recovering from the near miss of Tate's ample fist.

Tate drew his revolver. "I'll take the back," he said to the shorter agent. "You watch the front."

As soon as Tate dashed out the front door to the alley leading to the back of the building, nervous hotel guests began descending the stairs in all manner of dress and undress. Most were businessmen, but a few young and middle-aged tourist couples, some with children, were in the mix. None of them looked pleased when they were greeted by Myers and the shorter agent at the foot of the stairs.

"What's going on here?" demanded a rotund, middle-aged man dressed only in his t-shirt, boxer shorts, and slippers.

"Sorry Mr. Patterson," said the clerk, who had a nearly photographic memory for names and faces. "A small electrical fire in my office set the alarm off. It's out and it'll be just a minute before you can go back to your rooms." He addressed the assembling crowd, yelling over the bell. "The fire is out, folks, but it's still raining outside, so please just wait in the lobby for the all clear and then you can go back to bed."

Thirty men, women, and children squeezed into the small lobby designed for half that number and the agent surveyed their distressed faces. No black men, young girls, or anyone else fitting the bill appeared. The bell stopped ringing and echoed in the hall for a few seconds. Tate assessed the back and saw no way for anyone to have escaped. He was in a blind alley with only one way in and out. Anyone who might try to leave would have had to run past him and the front of the hotel. He waited a moment longer, and seeing no activity on the fire escape, returned to the lobby, satisfied that all the guests had chosen the easier, interior stairwell.

He looked carefully at the group huddled together. The black man would be the easiest to spot, he thought, in the sea of white faces, and though he didn't seem to be there, Tate wasn't satisfied. They had to be here, or have been here recently, he thought.

"You have 21 rooms numbered 1 through 21, is that correct?" Myers nodded yes.

"Okay, quiet down!" Tate yelled, getting the crowd's attention. "Please raise your hands when I call out your room numbers. Return to your room only after I say so."

As each room number was called out, the guests dutifully raised their hands, allowing the agents to give them the once over and dismiss them. Guests in rooms one to twelve were all accounted for, but no one responded when he called out room 13. He called the number again, still no response. He picked up the count with room 14, and made it through to 21. Finally, he dismissed all the confused and somewhat angry guests, who grumbled and murmured their way up the stairs. Two fire trucks and a D.C. Metro police cruiser screamed up to the hotel, sirens wailing. When the Fire Captain ran inside, Tate flashed his badge.

"False alarm. We've got it covered."

215

"The hell you do," said the Captain. "I make that call."

"I slipped and hit the fire alarm," said Tate pointing to the shattered glass on the floor below the small alarm. The Fire Captain looked at him suspiciously.

"We're all set here," said Tate. "Thanks for coming so quickly." He showed his badge once again, but the Fire Captain wasn't ready to back down. "I'm Federal Agent Tate, with National Security, here on official business. There's no fire. Go back to your little spotted dog and your nice warm cots." The fire crew left the hotel lobby without any comment.

National Security had carte blanche, especially in D.C., and they knew not to mess with the Feds.

"Shall we pay a little visit to room 13?" asked Tate, knowing that most hotels had one, unnumbered room, for special guests. He was sure he would find the fugitives hiding under a bed.

"Certainly," said Myers. "Let's go." He led them up the stairs and opened the door to the room, the only room in the hallway without a number, and flicked on the light switch. Tate and the shorter agent squeezed by him, guns pulled. They found the small suite to be in perfect order. Unused towels hung in the bathroom. Linens were crisp and pulled taut on the bed. Everything appeared to be neat, tidy, and ready for guests. The agents didn't know that Myers reset the room just minutes after his guests had gotten in their cab. Tate and his partner checked under the bed and in the closet and found nothing. "Your 'No Vacancy' sign is lit. How do you explain that?" Tate asked.

"Oh," he started with a smile. "This is a special suite that I never rent out, except to very important guests."

"I see. And have you had any 'very important guests' here recently, Mr. Myers?"

"No. No. Not in weeks. I had the Spanish Ambassador's cousin here about a month ago." Tate paced the room, looking in at the spotless bathroom and touching things as he went. He leaned against the big wooden console radio and looked hard at the clerk.

"A month ago? Really?" he asked with a snarl forming on his upper lip. "Do you have a leak in your bathroom sink faucet? That's not too impressive when you're entertaining dignitaries, is it?" A few drops of water remained in the basin, Myers having missed drying it when he had cleaned up just before the agents arrived.

"And the radio is still warm," said Tate. "Better check that out. Could be a fire hazard. You certainly don't want anymore trouble with fires."

Myers was finally unable to provide a reliable explanation, and he stood, awkwardly silent. He felt some comfort knowing the agents could prove nothing. This was a world without video surveillance, without computer generated phone logs, without all the things modern law enforcement take for granted. But here, in this strange place, old-fashioned snooping, intuition and intimidation were all detectives had to use in many cases, and this was one of them. Tate flipped on the radio just in time to hear the 1560 radio I.D.

"Bet someone's been listening to Billy The Kay. Do you like Billy The Kay, Mr. Myers?" He walked slowly toward the old man and was just inches from his face. "I don't like Billy The Kay. I think he's a loudmouth, and I think he knows your friends. "Where'd they go, Myers?" he asked, almost too quietly for the older man to hear.

"To whom are you referring?" asked Myers, backing up against the wall. Tate finally reached his breaking point and grabbed the clerk by the shirt collar and pushed him out through the open door, slamming his body against the far wall in the hallway.

"You know damn well 'who'!" said Tate, pulling his revolver from his holster, about to pistol whip the uncooperative clerk.

Myers closed his eyes in preparation for the imminent blow. "One last time. Where are they?"

"I don't know what you're talking about." Myers was a good soldier, ready to take his licks. Tate raised the butt of his pistol, while at the same time the door to room 14 opened. A large man in bathrobe came into the hall, standing just feet from the agents and the trembling clerk.

"What's going on out here?" asked the man, having caught Tate with his pistol in the air.

"Get back in your room. This is no concern of yours," said Tate.

"It most certainly is. You will not lay a hand on Mr. Myers while I'm around. He's a 68 year-old-man. Go bully somebody else." Tate released the clerk's collar and started toward the big man in the bathrobe when two other doors opened and heads peered out, curious about all the commotion. Tate reluctantly backed down and shook himself, like a dog getting out of the water. He straightened his trench coat and smoothed the ruffles. After placing his revolver back in its holster, he wagged his finger in Myers' face, whispering in his ear.

"Better get that fire alarm fixed. You never know when you might need it again." He walked down the hall passing the annoyed but curious guests, while the shorter agent followed, adding his two cents.

"Go back to bed."

In the lobby, on the counter near the guest register, a slip of paper with 'Capitol Parking Garage – 12-A' scribbled hastily, sat folded and unread. Neither agent saw it as they stormed out into the night.

"We're going to pay Billy The Kay a little visit," said Tate half to himself. "I knew something was up at the West Wing. I should have trusted my instincts. I let 'em slip through my hands, damn it. But we're closing in on them. We're closing in."

Chapter 24

Phillips ordered coffee at the counter and asked for coins in the change. The heavy coins felt familiar, but different, too. He looked closely, for the first time, at the coinage Fed-Stat was using. While the denominations were right: pennies, nickels, dimes, and quarters, and the sizes were similar; the faces were all wrong. With the exception of Washington, on the quarter, all the rest of the faces were unknown to him, but this mystery would have to wait.

He took the steaming coffee with him to the phone booth and closed the door. Two glaring bulbs hanging in the roof of the phone booth shown down on him like a spotlight, which made him uneasy. He unscrewed the bulbs and used the ambient light of the diner to read the phone number he needed. With the small slip of paper retrieved from his pocket he dialed the number and deposited the coins required, $3.75. It was 11:45 p.m., much too late to call, but he and his panicky foursome were desperate. The phone rang six times before the operator came on and said there appeared to be no one at home.

"Please let it ring a little longer," Phillips asked and after four more rings a groggy voice picked up. "Hello?"

"Oh, thank God," said Phillips. "Dr. Rollins?"

"Who is this? It's nearly midnight," said the agitated and tired voice.

"This is Mike Phillips. Hi, Dr. Rollins...I'm very sorry to bother you. We have a little problem."

"Oh, Phillips. Yes, you do have a problem." Rollins waited to hear the operator's click, letting him know they had some semblance of privacy. "You've raised the terror alert level, you know?" he asked with a tired chuckle. "You Travelers can indeed cause a mess of trouble, usually by accident."

"I know," sighed Phillips. "Tell me about it. I think we're pretty close to your home and have not been followed. I'm in a borrowed, legal car. May we please come to talk with you for a moment? We desperately need your help."

The line was silent for a moment and then Rollins agreed.

"Yes, come on Mr. Phillips." He gave him directions and an admonition not to get caught. Phillips thanked him and hung up. He called the operator again and obtained the international long distance operator handling Hagerstown, Maryland. He deposited $4.75 and had his call put through to the truck stop where Joey was waiting.

"Fuel and Drool," came the not too friendly voice of a woman who must have gargled with whiskey and chased it with a cigarette.

"Hi," said Phillips "Is there a young man, sitting alone at a booth in your rest stop?"

"What are you? Some kind of creep?" asked the skeptical woman, too busy cleaning to be bothered by late night freaks.

"No. No. He's my friend's little brother and..."

"Look, we're not running a daycare here. Hundreds of young men come in and out of here 24-hours a day, non stop."

"Please, this is kind of an emergency. His name is Joey."

"Hold on," said the woman. She slammed the receiver down on the hard counter and it popped in Phillips' ear. He could hear the woman yell out across the dining room. "Joey! Is there a Joey here?" She picked up the phone. "You're lucky, not too many people here right now. He's comin'. Make it quick, this is a business line."

"Hello?" said Joey, not at all comfortable with having been paged.

"Joey, listen this is Mike Phillips. Everyone's okay, but we're having some trouble on our end and I need you to stay put and keep your head down. In fact, it's better if you wait in your car. What are you driving?"

"A Marathon, of course. Green."

"Do you have any money?"

"Like ten bucks."

"Get yourself something to eat and wait for us in the car. This may take us a while, a few hours, even. I don't know. Park the car out back, out of the way if you can, get some sleep, and we'll come find you as soon as we can."

"Okay. Is my sister okay?"

"Yeah, Joey she's fine, and look, I'm sorry my friend got carried away talking to you. She was really never in any danger. He just wanted to make sure that you'd deliver our....device. He thought the threats were the only way to get you out here."

"Yeah," he said relieved and annoyed at the same time. "I thought that might be it."

"Just stay put and stay hidden as best you can. But don't act suspicious."

"What the hell is going on? I think I have a right to know."

"I promise we'll explain it to you when we see you. I promise, Joey."

The boy believed him. These men had a knack for gaining the trust of complete strangers, and it was confusing to Phillips, especially. He and Jackson were used to living in a world where distrust and suspicion ruled the day. It was an endearing quality from the people they'd met in this place. They seemed far less cynical and suspicious, except, of course, for the agents, who were growing angrier, more suspicious and more determined by the minute.

Phillips walked back inside Paco O'Malley's and ordered four individual Corned Beef and Cabbage Tacos. He thought it sounded odd, but the menu was full of odd combinations of Irish and Mexican food. He walked back to the Ford with the take-out order. Though they had eaten Chinese food earlier in the evening, they were famished, and ate the surprisingly tasty food like hungry wolves, while Phillips explained his two successful phone calls.

Tommy Fuller never thanked Phillips out loud for keeping a cool head, but he was able to catch his eye and nodded slightly. That was all that was required. They were in this together and no one blamed anyone for the insanity that was unfolding around them. They hated the fact that Suzanne, an innocent, was now fully immersed in the chaos.

Phillips and Fuller had both been thinking the same thing independently. It was time to separate their group from Suzanne, for her own safety. They were becoming too much of a danger to her, and the added stress was weighing heavily on their shoulders. There was little conversation while they ate. After finishing their quick late-night snack, they hit the road, Phillips having taken the wheel.

"I've got the directions in my head," said Phillips. "Maybe I should drive." He was covering for the fact that having a black man behind the wheel, with two white guys and a girl, would be too suspicious. He told Fuller he needed him upfront and for the two in back to slump down out of sight. Greg Jackson knew exactly what was going on but appreciated the effort on his boss's part to spare him the embarrassment. They drove on, listening to the radio, trying to process all that had happened in less than three days.

•••••

When the agents arrived at Billy Kay's mansion in Bethesda, Maryland, at 11:55, they were unable to drive up to the house, their way blocked by an electric gate. Tate pushed the call button and received no response. He pushed it again and waited a few seconds. Not a man of great patience, and with no apparent answer coming anytime soon, Tate nudged the gate with the front of his car until it sprung the mechanism, swinging open and allowing them in. When they arrived at the circle near the front door, four dogs came barreling around the corner of the house and barked and growled non-stop until a light came on and Kay opened the door. He yelled and motioned with his arm, and the well-trained dogs took off as quickly as they came. Tate and his partner got out of the car and had no need to show their credentials. Kay knew who they were and was not completely surprised to see them.

"Good evening Mr. Kay," said Tate. Kay looked suspiciously at the car in his driveway, knowing he had not released the gate.

"Oh, ahh, your gate was...open, so we just pulled up. Hope that was okay with you."

Kay figured they had crashed the gate, but said nothing. "Yeah fine, whatever. How can I help you?"

"May we come in?"

"No. I don't think so," answered Kay, defiantly. "What do you want?"

"Well, that's not very friendly Mr. Kay," said Tate.

"You sure seem nicer on the radio," commented his partner.

"Get a warrant or tell me what the hell you want," said Kay.

"A warrant?" Tate looked at his partner and they shared a chuckle. "My, my, that seems drastic. Are you hiding something? Or...someone?"

"No. Tell me what this is all about."

"You were in a hurry leaving the West Wing Diner today. Nice little car, by the way."

"I was just showing my friend what she could do. Am I in trouble for speeding?"

"No, Mr. Kay. You're in trouble for harboring international terrorists. And guess what? We don't need a warrant. We're National Security." The agents pulled out their guns and Kay instinctively backed up as the agents pushed their way past him and into his home.

"Okay, Okay...I don't know who that guy was," said Kay, crumbling at the sight of the guns. "He called into my radio show and said he knew something about the bands I manage. That's all. So I met him for coffee."

"Oh sure," said Tate, surveying the entry way to Kay's impressive home.

"I thought he was a friend of yours from New York?"

"I know. I know I said that. I didn't think there was any harm."

"No harm? Lying to Federal agents in the midst of an ongoing National Security investigation?"

"Lighten up Dick Tracy," said Kay growing bolder. He never saw the punch coming. Tate hit him hard in the stomach, sending him to the floor.

"Billy, who is that?" came a young woman's voice from the top of the stair.

"No one, Bernadette, go back to bed," Kay managed to say from a fetal position.

"What's going on?" she asked taking a few tentative steps down the long staircase. Tate looked up to get a good look at the woman, thinking at first she might be one of his suspected terrorists, a young woman named Suzanne. It wasn't, but she was definitely young. Maybe too young, he thought.

"Young lady," said the agent. "This is Federal Agent Tate. Please come down here now." She took a few more steps and they confirmed that she was not their mark. To the agents, she looked to be between 15 and 20-years-old, it was impossible to tell, but she was likely, at least, less than half of Billy the Kay's 45 years.

"She doesn't know anything," said Kay, standing, holding his gut.

"Did Billy arrive home alone this evening, miss?" asked Tate.

"Yes," she answered, in a quiet, scared voice, terrified of what was unfolding in front of her at the bottom of the stairs.

"Did he tell you anything about who he was with tonight?"

"No. He didn't say anything. Billy, what is going on?" She was on the verge of hysterics.

"No need for alarm, miss, we just have a few more questions for Billy and then we'll leave. You can go back to bed now."

She ran up the stairs slamming an unseen door.

"Don't make this any uglier than it has to be, Kay. We could take you in right now for at least a dozen charges including…endangering the welfare of a minor. How old is she?" He didn't answer. "As I suspected," Tate continued. "What's it gonna be?"

"Okay, okay," said Kay, getting up off the floor. "He said his name was John Doe, and he knew something about my bands. He asked for a ride, so I gave him one."

"Do you expect us to believe that line of bull? I am insulted. You're Billy The Kay. You just don't meet strangers for coffee and give them rides. Do you think we're stupid?" He sucker punched Kay again in the same tender spot. He doubled over and fell with a grunt. Tate kicked him hard in the kidneys.

"You better call in sick, Kay. I don't think you're going to be joining your Zoo Crew tomorrow morning." Tate raised the butt of his pistol and Kay screamed out.

"All right, all right. I'll tell you! I'll tell you everything I know! Please, just give me a second." He staggered to his feet and sat on the bottom stair while Tate and his partner stood waiting. "He did call the station. I never met him before, I promise. He said he had some dirt on me about my bands and that we needed to meet. He had enough details that I knew he wasn't bullshitting me. He told me his real name - Mike Phillips."

That detail caught Tate's attention, as 'Mike' was the name thrown around in the safe house conversation they had transcribed two days earlier.

"Yeah? Go on," said Tate, momentarily appeased.

"He and his friends were staying at the Washington Inn."

"We know that. What did he have on you, Kay? Has he blackmailed you?"

For a millisecond Kay hesitated, sensing an opportunity.

"Yes," he said with a sigh, lying. "He told me that if I didn't give him $25,000 he would leak my little secrets to the press. So I met him and gave him what he wanted."

"What little secrets, Mr. Kay."

"The song."

"What song?"

"*Sweet Home Alabama.*" It's not mine. I stole it and he found out."

"Whose song is it?"

"It's...his," said Kay, flying by the seat of his pants. "He's a Con-Fed sympathizer, who wrote a catchy tune about Alabama. This Mike Phillips guy wrote it, and now it's a hit on both sides of the border and he needs the money for his cause."

"You had $25,000 in cash available?" asked Tate.

"I've ten times that much cash available," said Kay, rubbing his lower back. "Phillips told me to 'keep up the good work,' and that I was obviously about to make good money with his song, and that he'd be back to collect more. He also stole my car."

"Your cute little sports car?"

"No, I have a junker that I keep in the Capitol Parking Garage downtown. I gave him my key and the parking pass. It's a green '97 Ford Atlantic, 4-door sedan, Maryland tag 552-SWA. Now that's the whole deal."

Tate looked at his partner who had been scribbling in a notepad, then he turned back to Kay. They doubted some of Kay's story. Underground insurgent fighters rarely sue for plagiarism, but parts of the tale rang true. "If this doesn't check out, we're back for blood and you won't see the light of day for a long, long time. By the way, how old is she, Kay?"

"She's 17, okay?" There were no official 'age of consent' laws, but at 17, the girl squeaked by Fed-Stat mores.

"She'd better be, for your sake." They turned and walked out the still wide-open front door. As their car sped down the driveway, Tate's partner radioed in a new APB for Kay's Ford.

Chapter 25

As the four fugitives approached the turn-off for Rollins' home, they spotted an increase in police, military, and what they suspected was unmarked, government vehicle traffic.

"Stay down," yelled Phillips as he spotted the flashing lights of two State Troopers coming up fast behind them. A sense of dread filled him as he watched helplessly. The trooper was coming on fast. Phillips hit the steering wheel with his palms. "Shit. Shit." The siren's wail grew louder, filling their ears with its horrible cry.

"What's the point?" asked Phillips, rhetorically, as the police car was almost upon them. "I'm afraid this is it guys. They're pulling us over."

There was no place left to go and trying to out run the police, while tempting, was not seriously considered. After all the close calls, their number was up. He turned his signal on and eased on to the shoulder. They all sat stunned watching the flashing lights close in behind them. When the two law enforcement vehicles sped by, not even slowing, they started to breathe again and Phillips looked up and watched as the lights disappeared over a hill.

"Whoa," Phillips laughed. "That was too close."

"I can't take much more of this," said Suzanne, as she and Jackson slowly raised their heads to peer over the back seat.

"I know sweetie, I'm so sorry," said Phillips "It will all be over soon if we have any more luck left with us."

No one knew exactly what he meant or how it might 'all be over soon' but they were all too tired to think about it. Phillips eased the car back out on the road and saw the sign for the turn off towards Rollins' home.

"At least we can get off this road for a minute. Here's our turn," said Phillips.

He spun the wheel, piloting the car onto a little two-lane road that seemed to disappear ahead of them into the blackness of night. He made the next three turns, and now, just after midnight, he stopped in front of the house he thought was Rollins'.

"This is it, I'm pretty sure," said Phillips, turning into the driveway. They parked at the top of the gravel road and were greeted by a large, black Labrador retriever, who sheepishly wagged his whole body while his tail stood nearly motionless. Dr. Rollins appeared out of the front door and stood on the porch, waving them in.

Rollin's called out to his dog.

"Maverick, leave them alone. He'll love you to death if you're not careful," he said, greeting the motley crew piling out of the Ford. "Why don't you park that in the barn, for now, out of the way, if you know what I mean."

Phillips nodded, moving the car 50-feet further, disappearing into a darkened, ramshackle building. He walked to meet the others gathering on Rollin's porch.

Jackson was the first to speak "Dr. Rollins, I presume?" Jackson extended his hand and smiled.

"Splendid, splendid!" said Rollins, smiling back, shaking Jackson's hand. "In this timeline I'm afraid Henry Stanley never knew Dr. Livingstone, so only true Earthmen, as I call Travelers, would know that phrase. Splendid!"

His smile was genuine and warm. "And you must be Mike Phillips," he said, sliding his eyeglasses down over his nose to look over the new arrival. "And these two young people are…"

"This is Tommy Fuller, and this is our resident guide and heroine, Suzanne Michaels, and this explorer is Greg Jackson," said Phillips, acknowledging each in order.

"Pleasure to meet you although I can't say I like the hour too well. But it's quite all right. My wife isn't home yet, so I was up. Come in, come in," said Rollins, looking over his shoulder for signs of unwanted visitors. Maverick desperately wanted to follow the crowd inside, but Rollins shooed him away with a pointed finger. "Mav, stay." The dog whimpered. "Good boy. Go catch the bad guys for us." Maverick sat back on the porch and snapped at a low flying moth.

"First of all, a drink? Coffee, Tea, Coke?" offered Rollins.

"No thanks. We've been to Paco O'Malley's," said Phillips.

"I never quite understood that place," mused Rollins. "Corned beef and guacamole?"

"Actually, I'd love an Extra 'C' Coke, if you've got one," said Fuller.

"Don't tell me you're hooked? You know they're 100 times more addictive than cigarettes?" said Rollins.

"Cigarettes are addictive?" asked Suzanne.

"Oh my, now I know for sure from where *you* come, young lady." He smiled at her in the same way her Unka did.

Rollins appeared younger than his 83 years. He had a round, cherubic face adorned by bifocals, and a mop of gray-silver hair, neatly parted to the side. He wore slightly rumpled khaki pants, and a white dress shirt under a brown tweed jacket. He was the quintessential college Prof and would have only been more so, had he been smoking a pipe, which he did on occasion.

Dr. Henry Rollins had retired from teaching and spent a good deal of his time in research with the help of Margaret, who volunteered at the Library. He had retired as a Professor of Metaphysics and of Geology, but was still called on, occasionally, to consult. He had an uncanny knack for finding important minerals and precious metals.

"I'll get you a Coke, m'boy. Anyone else?" They all shook their heads 'no'. "Please, take a seat in the living room and I'll be back to hear about your troubles. Please, sit." He scurried out of the room, down a short hallway, while his guests went into a well-manicured and well-appointed sitting room with large comfortable chairs and antiques throughout. A gun case held several antique rifles, and handguns. Though he was a hobbyist, Rollins was an excellent marksman, and spent a good bit of free time target shooting along the tree line at the back of his property.

They each took a seat, Tommy and Suzanne together on a small couch. Rollins returned with a beverage for Fuller. He handed it to him and sat down.

"Tell me the latest. For starters, where'd you get that car?"

Phillips had hoped to ease into the whole Billy The Kay issue, knowing of Rollins distaste for the man, but decided to just dive in.

"Billy Kay loaned it to me."

Rollins scowled. "Dreadful, dreadful man. I'm sorry you ever met him. But still it seems like he might have been of some use, remarkably."

"He was actually very helpful and I didn't expect him to be, after what you'd told me about him."

"He's a fellow Traveler, you know, but his motivation is all dollars and no sense." As Rollins spoke he took turns engaging each of his guests with his warm eyes, a perfect host, a perfect gentlemen. Then he seemed to stare into space.

"Kay and I were friendly once," he said. "It was good to meet another Traveler. But when he discovered he could travel back and forth at will, he began to exploit the system, and called me a fool for not doing the same. 'Just go with the flow,' he'd say and 'make some money. Invent something that hasn't been invented yet like Velcro or Ziplock bags.' We had a bit of a falling out and when I threatened to expose him, he murdered those poor kids in his first two bands and profited enormously. He had insurance policies on just about all of them. It was big news for a while and then their fame, posthumously, grew ten-fold. What a mess. I just stay clear."

"For what it's worth," said Phillips. "He bailed me out of a really bad situation and he said those plane crashes were just terrible tragedies and coincidences."

Rollins harrumphed and leaned back in his chair. "That's what he claimed in court, too. I suppose it's possible. But I still don't like him or trust him one bit. He's working on some hi-tech rip-off that will 'revolutionize communications,' he says, and he takes tremendous pride in these things." He stared at Phillips. "Like he did anything other than import someone else's hard work? He's probably going to invent the Internets, or something." He smiled. "I'm sorry to jabber on about him. You didn't come here to listen to that."

"Dr. Rollins…," began Jackson.

"Please, just call me Henry."

"Okay…Henry," continued Jackson, "we came here because…we have a few simple goals. We want to understand what's happened, fix whatever mess we made, if possible, get home, get Suzanne home safely and never, ever come back here again. If Kay wants to travel back and forth, let him. We have no interest in him or what he does. I want to get home to my globally warmed, terrorist-filled world with my gas-guzzling car, my flat-screen TV, my friends, my job and my cell phone, which I miss most of all."

He took a breath. "Henry, how the hell did we get here? And where is *here*?"

Rollins sat up, interest piqued. "Hmm. I think I must start at the beginning, but I'll keep it brief. This is just a theory, mind you, but what I'm about to suggest is something I firmly believe, and Margaret, and even Kay, we all agree upon this basic premise. I trust you read the chapters highlighted for you in my book?"

"Not all of them," said Phillips, suddenly remembering something. "*Your* book? It was published back in our world and by an author of a different name."

"A pen-name, that's all. Margaret handled the publishing deal for me."

Rollins sat back in his chair.

"You see, I cannot cross back over. I've only managed the one accidental crossing, to where we are now, and have been trying to get back ever since, for 53 years, to be exact."

Rollins looked sad, like he was remembering things from his distant past. He shook himself out of the trance.

"But it hasn't been all bad. I've completed most of my life's work here. I developed my theories here and sent them home with Margaret, hoping to create a little friendly, metaphysical competition, in absentia, among my colleagues, to stimulate interest. But mostly they criticized my theories, the books and the absentee author. They never trusted my methods, or me, because they never met me. I could only correspond by letter, I could never attend symposia, or give lectures, so they never took me too seriously. In our world, your world, back home, I'm just another missing person. I'm a nobody, a footnote. And my alter-ego is a semi-crackpot author who believes in multiple universes."

He searched his mind for an old memory. "In your world I'm a 30-year old, missing college professor that has long since been forgotten. And here? Well, here I'm just an old man with a good nose for minerals. That's my profession. I'm a mineralogist. Nobody thinks in Metaphysical terms here. It's too far removed for them. There's no space program, no well-known physics minds, and so I wrote the book, not for this world, but to entice the thinkers in our world, back home. I hoped *they* might help me find a way back. So far, no luck. I've been trying to figure out why people like Kay and Margaret can cross over at will, and others like me cannot. It's really quite an obsession."

"Explain how it happens, please," asked Phillips.

"Well, my boy, if you had done your homework and gone back to the Library to study the chapters, you'd have a better idea," he admonished Phillips with a professorial air. "But under these circumstances, I'll let you slide." He winked and continued. "Here are the basics. Time flows like a river, a river that has branches, hundreds, thousands or perhaps millions, or perhaps an infinite number of branches. These branches all flow in the same general direction; that is to say, forward, as we might explain it. Time, itself, cannot move backward. And here's where it gets really interesting."

Maverick barked on the porch, momentarily diverting their attention, and Rollins continued.

"Each branch of this river of time, represents an entire universe and the branches that are closest together will share the most common characteristics of its nearest neighbor. And when I say universe, I mean *the* universe, all of it, infinite, ever expanding, all that modern man knows and dreams about...times infinity. That's a universe. Now each branch will lose a certain amount of similarity from its predecessor because change is inevitable, and so a branch, of a branch, of a branch, might be a significantly different place. We don't know because the Travelers that you and I know are only able to travel back and forth from this Near Earth to their Birth World, as I like to think of it."

"How do they, hopefully, we, travel?" asked Jackson.

"Good question. You know what black holes are?" asked Rollins, looking at each of them.

"In the simplest forms of science fiction drama, I think," said Phillips.

"No science fiction about them, lad. Black holes are hard science. They were first suggested way back in the late 1700's. Now they're almost universally accepted as fact. While we're not sure what causes or caused them, some say collapsing super-nova, we assume with relative certainty that they are generally objects with such a large gravitational pull that light and even spacetime, itself, cannot escape. When any matter gets close enough it's sucked in and adds to the relative size of the black hole, which endlessly enlarges itself. They are so massively dense at the center that they cease to exist, compressed into nothingness. When matter collapses in on itself, and is compressed to the point of 'Singularity,' as we like to call it, it has no weight, no height, no width and no depth. But that doesn't mean it's not there. It is an anomaly of spacetime that we really don't understand, only that it happens. How's that grab ya?"

No one spoke and they all looked confused. "It all relates to astrophysics, quantum physics, quantum mechanics and the sub-atomic," said Rollins, "but don't get hung up on Singularity." He took a breath and continued.

"Black holes can be relatively small, say the size of a small star, like our Sun, or they may be many million or billion times that size. The physics of the interior of a black hole are too much to get into right now, and are unimportant, but trust me, black holes do exist and they are no place you want to visit. But more importantly, and this is why I told you all about them, black holes have a much friendlier cousin, the wormhole." He shifted again in his chair and watched the blank expressions on the faces of his students.

"Are you with me?"

"Oh yeah, of course," said Jackson and they all laughed.

"I'm really stripping this down for you the best I can," said Rollins. "Wormholes are a bit more hypothetical but are allowed for in the theory of General Relativity, thanks to my former boss, the great Einstein."

"*The* Albert Einstein?" asked Phillips.

"Yes," said Rollins, gazing down. "The one and only. Sadly, in this world, the Socialists of Germany never let him leave Europe and he disappeared, vanished. I fear the worst befell him. The Third Reich was not kind to the Jewish elite, to put it delicately, in either world. But I knew him back home in our Birth World and worked with him for a very short time."

"Hold on, I want to understand," said Phillips. "You're confirming that our doubles, or clones, or whatever, exist in…multiple worlds?"

"Yes! Quite possibly, but you're getting ahead of yourself. I'll get there. Anyway, we think a wormhole is a conduit between space and time, which allows matter to travel through spacetime, a shortcut of sorts. Think of our universe as an apple, a sphere, more or less, hanging deliciously on a tree. A worm wishing to travel to the other side of this apple, the universe, is crawling along on the outside when it dawns on him that there is a shorter way to the other side. Not around, but *through* the apple. And so he eats his way through, making a tunnel in the process. When he completes the journey, the tunnel remains, allowing other worms to travel through as well: thus the wormhole."

"So we're worms on an apple?" asked Jackson.

"Kind of, my friend. But this is where I am alone in my research and my theories. I believe wormholes can be small or enormous, but unlike black holes they don't destroy the matter that passes through them. I am one of a handful of believers in a specific type of wormhole, the 'Schwarzschild Wormhole.' This little beauty not only connects two distant points in space, but it may *also* connect parallel universes."

"What parallel universes?" asked Phillips.

"Why, the one like you're in right now, and the one to which you'd like to return," answered Rollins. "Remember the branches? They are the parallel universes of which I'm speaking. Wormholes may also transcend time. You could leave your branch, your timeline at 3:30 p.m. and arrive in a parallel timeline ten minutes earlier - or later, relatively speaking."

"How about 150 year difference?" asked Jackson.

Rollins smiled. Jackson was getting it. "Possibly," he said," and with your little stunt, I would say probably. Remember, time is always flowing..."

"Like a river," said Fuller.

"Yes! Precisely! You're all catching on. Imagine time as a river and two timelines as two rivers flowing side by side. Picture a bridge, or a wormhole, connecting these rivers. When you cross you might move forward or backward in time depending on the angle of the wormhole. Or you might crossover and find you're at exactly the same relative time as when you left."

"What allows, or causes these jumps?" asked Phillips.

"Oh, now you're really getting it," said Rollins, gleefully. "I believe that certain artifacts or environmental triggers tie into the crossing."

"Artifacts?" asked Jackson.

"You know the strange feeling you get when you walk into an antique store or an old house or a museum? I believe those places, and the old items in them, literally call out to the past, their origins. And where these things are gathered, there is such a high saturation of this energy, the feeling is palpable. A locket owned by an Egyptian Queen resonates with the time in which it was created and it is forever connected to that period."

"Or a Confederate Civil War cap?" asked Fuller, producing an artifact that was never too far removed from his head.

"Yes," answered Rollins, smiling.

"But it's just one part of the puzzle. Time and quantum mechanics begin to fill in the spaces, though not completely."

No one commented. Rollins drew another deep breath and continued.

"Okay, think of it in these terms," he said. "You take off at 3:00 p.m. from an airport in New Spain...er, sorry, that's California to you, and let's say you're flying at 600 miles per hour and you land in Honolulu, Hawaii at 2:00 p.m. You've spent six hours on a plane, yet you arrive before you left. While that's not really a perfect model, it's just a trick of the spinning Earth and our feeble attempt to rein in time, it should begin to open your eyes to the relativity of time and travel."

"Think of that on a universal scale and you begin to understand the possibilities. You must look at these things through the eyes of a child: where anything and everything is possible. So, back to our time-rivers and their branches…what if the wormhole, for some reason, attached itself to an adjacent timeline, but way back along the river, say 150 years back? You've not only jumped universes, but to your perspective you've time traveled. Because adjacent parallel universes are the same in almost every detail, you might conclude you had simply gone back in time, and missed the part about crossing over. So, Tommy, Mike, Greg…your universe back home is the way you left it. There's no Confederated States of America, or Third Reich. In your Birth World, you all are missing persons."

"I think I know what you're trying to say," said Tommy. It was the most he'd spoken since Rollins began the impromptu lecture. He was thinking about Susan, while holding the hand of Suzanne.

"I remember as a child," continued Rollins, gazing into his unseen past, "playing in my room, looking at a large mirror that hung on the wall. I would gaze into that mirror for hours, thinking that if only I could get through it, not unlike young Alice and her looking glass, that I would have entered into some strange new world, similar to my own, only with slight variances. And think about it for a moment. Looking into a mirror you see a reflection, but it's more than just a reflection. It's an accurate, detailed, three-dimensional copy of the universe you're standing in. Just because the image is in a mirror doesn't mean it's not there. The mirror hangs on a wall, but also punches through that wall showing the entire universe in it, only limited by the size of the mirror. I say it's more than just reflected light and images. I say it *is* there. It's real; it changes what it shows you as things change in your own universe. The simple mirror provides the most compelling example of a parallel universe that I can imagine."

This was a revelation that finally sank in. Theirs was a home left unchanged, while this world, this version, had skewed off its timeline. But how? And Why? They had an idea, but wanted to hear the Doctor, in his own words, confirm it.

Okay, Henry, but you don't know the whole story," said Phillips. "We were in a Civil War reenactment that turned into the real battle, and we are pretty sure we accidentally changed the course of history."

"Yes, but only in this timeline, in this universe. Not in your own. You have not changed your own history, you've changed *our* history, *here*, and you did it 150 years ago. Then you managed to spin around spacetime again, stayed in this universe, and arrived here in 2013 to see your handy work just a few days ago. You not only crossed over, you swung backward 150 years, then swung forward 150 years to arrive in this new place, that had been changed by your actions 150 years earlier. While it's new to you, it's not to me or Suzanne."

"So that mean wormholes also allow for time travel within a universe?" asked Phillips.

"Yes! And to my knowledge, you're the only ones to have ever achieved it on such a grand scale. Like you've skipped a stone across a great pond. It's really remarkable and completely unique, to my limited knowledge of these things, anyway."

"Well, we screwed up this place pretty badly," said Jackson. "Had we not accidentally allowed that detonation, by distracting those Yanks who would have disabled the bomb, the South wouldn't have won The Battle of Gettysburg, and this universe would be like the one we know back home?"

"Very likely," said Rollins. "In fact it may have evolved in exactly the same ways as our Birth World and universe." The Doctor paused, and looked thoughtful. "For my money, this place is unhallowed ground."

"What do you mean?" asked Jackson.

"Even though I haven't personally seen home in half a century, I know what it's like. Margaret keeps me up to date. There's no question that the world is a better place with America as it should be, one whole, not these two anemic halves. I'm afraid the detonation that you all allowed is the one, greatest infraction your visit caused. One from which the North could not recover."

"Here's another issue," said Phillips. "The main reason the explosion never happened in our world is because there was never any attempt or plan for it."

"That's right m'boy," said Rollins. "It didn't happen in your universe. It happened here, in this one, or was supposed to, until you all showed up."

"How on earth, pardon the pun," said Phillips, "did you ever figure all that out?"

"How'd I figure it out? Margaret. She brought me something the day before yesterday that tied it all up in a neat little bow. She knows I'm a bit of a Civil War buff, so when she came across this item she knew I'd be interested."

Rollins got up from his chair and walked to a bookshelf containing stacks of newspapers. He singled out one paper in particular, and brought it to the center of the waiting group. It was a *USA Today*, dated July 6, 2013. He turned to Section D and there it was–the headline.

Gettysburg's Civil War Reenactment Turns Deadly

The story went on to detail the highly publicized reenactment and how newspaper editor, Brad Lake, and three others went missing, including a reenactor who was wanted in connection with a fatal, and possibly racially motivated shooting. The story included all their names, their personal histories, MacAuley's Pub, and the whole nightmare right up to the point of their disappearance.

"There it is," said Tommy, taking a keen interest. "Right there for the whole world to see. Reason number one why I can't go home."

"Now, now. All is not lost my young friends. I think I can help you," said Rollins. "It's a chance, the longest of long shots."

"How? What? I'm lost," asked Jackson.

"When Margaret travels she loses about 10 minutes. If she leaves here at 11:00 p.m. she arrives in our Birth World, what you're calling "home," at 10:56 p.m., but if she turns right around and comes right back immediately she arrives back here at 11:10 p.m. So, by her account she's only gone for a few seconds, but 10 minutes have disappeared for ever. It shouldn't happen, but it does. Time is a constant, but we've planted watches, and clocks, and even used sun dials and it's always the same, a miracle of quantum mechanics."

"And it drives him crazy," said Margaret, appearing behind them from the darkened den.

"Oh hello, my darling," said Rollins, rising to greet her. "You look 10 minutes younger every time I see you."

"He always says that to ease his guilt," said Margaret, smiling at the guests. "We figure I've lost a good 10 or 20 full days over the past… how many years? I should make him start smoking, to even things out."

Rollins kissed her and they shared a warm embrace.

"I'm sorry for the dramatic entrance," she said. "I didn't realize you'd be here. We weren't expecting you until tomorrow."

The group was stunned, unable to speak. Suddenly the things Rollins was trying to explain became a combination of exciting, unbelievable, and on some primitive level, clearer.

"She sometimes travels at this time of night," said Rollins. "Less likely to be seen disappearing and reappearing by the mailman or the paperboy. Crossing over can be quite disturbing to the uninitiated."

"I'm so sorry you children are having a time with this travel business," said Margaret. "Yours has been one of the most distressing cases I've ever witnessed."

"Please join us dear," said Rollins, pulling up a chair. "I haven't yet told you my most important theory of all. The how and why." They all sat up, listening more intently.

"It's all well and good to know that wormholes connect the universes," Rollins said, "but how do you get through one? Though I've never been able to find my own way to travel home, I did figure it out for Kay and for Margaret. These parallel universes are right here under our noses. They're not trillions of light years away, beyond the farthest galaxy–they're right here," he said pointing and jabbing at the air. "Right here, right there, sharing this space." He spread his arms wide. "Only in a different dimension. One I admit I don't understand very well. But getting in and out of these other dimensions is the real trick, and I believe that certain people are better suited, predisposed to the travel. They have an X factor that I can't explain."

"That's what he calls it now," added Margaret. "He told me at first it was a mutant gene, and as his book publisher, and editor, I asked him to find a sexier name for it."

"Yes dear, sexier. May I continue?" Margaret nodded and smiled.

"The X-factor, sexy or not, is simply just an individual's predisposition to traveling. Like being born more right-brained or left-brained, or musical, or a Savant, whatever. Some people have it, others don't. Something within these special people triggers wormholes to open. That's why I told you that multiple crossings are rare. So it starts with that rare, special individual, the one with the X-Factor, and there's more. I believe that to access the portal, we must be so closely aligned with the universe we're jumping to, that the timelines get confused for a moment. For example, Margaret cannot crossover, unless she is facing exactly due east…"

"That's why I have a compass around my neck," she said holding it up to show the group.

"And she must be wearing that dress, and only that dress."

"I lost 40 minutes of my life proving to that stubborn old coot that it had nothing to do with my shoes."

"It's true," agreed Rollins. "Don't ask me why the shoes don't matter, but they don't, at least for her. But change her dress and she can't jump an inch. And this irks me to no end; Maverick can cross with Margaret, as long as Margaret goes first. We adopted him here on this side and he isn't fazed in the least, travels like a pro. And they can only crossover from our den, Margaret's portal. By the way, this is our home, and I guess we hadn't told you…Margaret is my wife."

"You hadn't told them?" asked Margaret feigning shock at her husband's lack of manners. "I am so sorry he's playing his little games with you young people. Shame on you." She swatted him on the arm.

"I was getting there before you popped in," said Rollins.

"There is another house exactly like this one, in Maryland," he said, "in our Birth World. We spend a good deal of our time making sure it doesn't burn down or get bulldozed, because if it did, it would close that portal, and that wormhole Margaret uses would be gone forever. And the same is true for this house here. We have to keep the den exactly the same. One piece of furniture out of place and forget it."

"Oh my, that was a fiasco," said Margaret. "Ten years ago I was on the other side and Henry decided to do a little spring cleaning while I was gone, quite sweet actually, but after he vacuumed, and dusted, and slid chairs around, and moved the desk, I was stuck; couldn't get back for 10 days until he figured out what had happened and got things put back the way they were supposed to be. He had to grovel to that Billy The Kay character to communicate with me and we eventually figured it out. But that's another story for another time. Anyway, I clean the den, now, and do it very carefully."

"So if a person with the X-Factor is in the vicinity of a sympathetic wormhole," continued Rollins, "and the space is lined up just right, then they can jump back and forth." He paused, a mischievous grin developing on his wrinkled face. "Would you kids like to see?"

They looked at one another unsure of what he was asking. Rollins looked as though he had suggested doing something naughty.

"Oh Henry, don't bore them with that old trick," said Margaret.

"It'll bring it all full circle," he tempted, trying to coax the group into watching a show he never tired of.

"Hell, yes," said Phillips. "This I've got to see."

They stood up and walked toward the den. "You're sure?" asked Margaret. It costs me ten minutes of my life," she teased.

Suzanne, who hadn't said a word, finally spoke.

"No. I don't want to see this."

They looked at her, surprised at her first words since arriving at the Rollins' home. She grew more insistent and more upset. "We've left my little brother hiding in a parking lot and we're about to all go to jail and you want to see magic tricks? This is wrong. There's something very wrong about all of this!" She stood up and walked to the center of the room.

"What kind of twisted game are you people playing? It's just not right."

She ran from the house and fell down the front porch steps, landing on the cold, grass. A light rain was falling. Maverick ran to her side and sniffed her, gently, before lying down beside her. Misty raindrops formed on the dog's eyelashes, like individual tears. Tommy arrived seconds later, and lay on the ground hugging her, encouraging her to sit up. They sat together in the drizzle, while she sobbed and Maverick licked the water and real tears from their faces. The others watched from the porch.

"Oh look, Henry. Are you satisfied? Look what you've done to the poor thing?" Margaret walked from the porch holding an umbrella, and tried to comfort them. "Please, children. Come back inside. I know how hard this is." Suzanne looked at Maverick who nuzzled under her hand, looking for a pat on the head, which she offered, much to the dog's satisfaction.

Tommy helped Suzanne to her feet. The pair walked back into the house where Dr. Rollins handed them both large towels. What was really bothering her was almost too horrible to even be contemplated, let alone actually be spoken aloud, but she gathered her strength, looked into the eyes of the only man who seemed to know the consequences of all this metaphysical muddling.

"What happens if you're successful?" she asked. "What happens if you help them return to their home and they "fix" this timeline in the process? Tell us what happens, Dr. Rollins?" Suzanne had already figured it out, far ahead of the rest of them, who hadn't followed the progression of the logic, as closely as she.

"You're a smart girl, Suzanne," said Rollins. He sighed.

"There are two possibilities as I see it. If the boys go back and change our history, our timeline here in this world will resemble their world in almost every single detail. Con-Fed will have never existed. Life in Gettysburg will have taken its normal course..."

"My uncles will both be dead," said Tommy, "their garage will have never been opened. Joey will be a high school senior with C's and have a girlfriend named Becca. You will have never known Anthony because there is no Little Italy, or New Brooklyn, in Virginia Beach, because Hitler loses World War II, and Europe is saved. You'll have no recollection of this place or the life you've known. Your father will have been dead and buried for five years, but your mother will still be alive and living in the house you grew up in, and you will be a wife on the verge of divorce from a man very much like me, who's probably wanted for murder."

Suzanne looked into Tommy's eyes, longing to find some hope for a different way. "But you will always be Susan or Suzanne, the girl I met in ninth grade and fell in love with."

Dr. Rollins did not refute a single word of Tommy Fuller's assessment.

"What's the other possibility, Dr. Rollins?" asked Suzanne. "You said one of two things might happen."

"The other possibility, my child, is that they might get stuck in 1863, and who knows what that would do to the timeline? To have three men with a full knowledge of the next 150 years of history and of War, politics, inventions...who knows what it might do?" Rollins shifted in his chair. "It could be catastrophic, but it wouldn't be the first time. I believe Travelers have been influencing universes, ours and others, since the dawn of mankind."

It was not easy for them to digest what was being said.

"To me, it explains how Nostradamus, Da Vinci and other ancients could have known so much," said Rollins. "Take Jules Verne, for example. Do you realize, that in his book, *From the Earth to the Moon*, which was published in 1865, the year the Civil War ended, by the way, his astronauts

236

sat in a bullet shaped capsule, about the size of the Apollo 11 command module? The spacecraft, named the *Columbiad* was launched from Florida, and his crew, just as with Apollo moon missions, consisted of three persons. In Verne's story, after the projectile orbits the moon, it returns to earth and falls into the sea, and a U.S. Naval vessel retrieves the astronauts, who live to tell their tale. All of this written prior to 1865 and 100 years prior to NASA's moon program. Quite remarkable, don't you think?"

Most of this went over Suzanne's head, as she had never known about NASA or the moon missions, though she had read Jules Verne. She began to wonder about a third, unspoken possibility that seemed too horrific to contemplate. If the men were successful in traveling back to Gettysburg, and they corrected the "mistakes," might the very universe in which they were sitting disappear? Rollins contemplated the same unspoken third option, though made no mention of it.

For Suzanne, especially, the sobering reality of several unpleasant possibilities, did take the fun out of watching Margaret do a vanishing act.

Chapter 26

Sixty miles away, in Washington, D.C., two men sat troubled by a case taking on new and evermore confusing qualities. Agent Tate and his partner had checked out parts of Billy the Kay's story and found them to be true, although they still didn't fully trust him. The only information they really trusted was that their fugitives were driving a Ford Atlantic; they'd confirmed that much with the parking garage attendant. Where these strangers had gone was a mystery, as were a hundred other details. The Civil War outfits, the strange code in which they spoke, none of that made any sense, and wouldn't anytime soon. They decided to call it a night, with a plan to drive to Gettysburg the next morning. They hoped to pick up the trail in the historic town, whose ghosts and battle plans permeated the air, though they were reluctant to reveal themselves.

•••••

"Suzanne is right about one important thing," said Fuller as they settled back into the living room. "We cannot leave Joey hanging out to dry at that truck stop. What can we do?"

"We could call him again and tell him to go home," said Suzanne. "Is that phone-thing really that important?"

"It may be," said Rollins. "If it traveled over with you it could be an artifact needed to travel back."

"Plus, he's outside sleeping in his car," said Phillips. "We couldn't reach him anyway. I know that miserable woman at the Fuel and Drool wouldn't do us any favors."

"We can risk a tunnel crossing," said Suzanne. "There are other tunnels farther west that aren't watched as closely."

"That's risky," said Rollins, "that could take half-a-day to drive that far, and they'll be expecting that." Suzanne wondered how he knew about the tunnels. "Or we can cross the border with my credentials," he said.

"Really? How?" asked Suzanne, brightening.

"You have no idea how important I pretend to be," said Rollins. "I'm really kind of a big deal. Kay's not the only one working the system. Margaret and I, out of necessity, have pulled a few fast ones over the years. I have iron-clad travel papers because I'm supposedly quite a mineralogist, and have provided both North and South with the locations of gold reserves, silver, oil, natural gas. It's uncanny how I know where these reserves are. I just don't know how I do it."

"Oh, you old braggart," teased Margaret. "I know how you do it. I do all your research, that's how. It's easy to find gold when you already have a GPS map coordinate, and a list of gold mines from back home."

"Once again, my wife speaks the cold, hard truth," said Rollins. "And if you must know, that's the issue that separated Kay and me years ago. He wanted to exploit the knowledge and amass the wealth of a thousand kings in a matter of two or three years and I told him flat out, 'No,' and that we should use that kind of knowledge only as our ace-in-the-hole when, and only if, we ever needed it. He said he'd do it himself and that he didn't need us."

Rollins got the same mischievous twinkle in his eye they'd seen earlier. "One day I waited until he was out of his office at the radio studio, that's where his portal is, and I screwed it up so badly that he couldn't jump."

"Yes, you're good at that," added Margaret.

"So we talked him into finding another way to get rich that didn't involve me or mining. He came up with the music scam, and so I fixed his portal and told him we'd leave his music alone if he left our minerals and precious metals alone, and it's worked out so far, but I still don't trust him. I know one day I'll read in the paper how some music mogul named Kay has just found natural gas on land he just purchased. I just know it. He still doesn't know where Margaret's portal is, and I hope to God he never finds out."

"What about Joey?" Suzanne's concern was growing with the passing of each minute.

"Yes, well, I'll cross the border, meet him, and come back with the cell phone and that will be that."

"Sound's almost too easy to actually work," said Phillips.

"What could go wrong?" asked Rollins. "My papers were updated by both sides just three weeks ago and they're good for another month."

"Let me go with you, as your assistant," said Suzanne. "Surely you must travel with an assistant? And I know where the truck stop is."

"Yes, in fact, I occasionally do," he said, looking at Margaret. "I suppose it could work. My papers do allow for it."

"I don't like it, Suzanne," said Tommy. "You're the only one the agents have ever I.D.'d. What if your picture has been circulated at the border crossings?"

"It won't be. I'll wear a disguise."

"What about a Passport and an I.D.?" Tommy asked.

"How are you going to pull that off?" asked Jackson

"That's my department," said Margaret. "I'll go get the Poloroid and we'll print one up in no-time." She rose from her chair and headed toward their office before turning to her husband. "Henry, I've left the camera at the other house. I guess I'll go get it. Be right back."

"Wait," said Phillips. "Are you going to...do you mind very much if I...if we..."

"Watch?" she asked bemused. "Of course, I don't mind. You stand by the doorway and don't come into the den until I get back. Henry and I have about knocked each other's teeth out when he was standing too close on one of my return trips. I'm getting too old for that nonsense."

They stood by the doorway leading to the den and watched as Margaret looked at her compass, twisted slightly to the left, straightened her dress and walked two steps into the den before vanishing into thin air. No sound, no flashing lights, no strange machinery, no ancient Egyptian hieroglyphs or chevrons to align, just a simple disappearing act. Only it wasn't an act. It became apparent to the men, then and there, beyond question, that all things, everything, even this thing called "traveling," might be possible.

"Oh my God..." said Jackson, knees buckling. Phillips let out a nervous laugh and put his hand to his mouth to muffle a whispered, "Shit." Tommy Fuller even managed a rare smile at the astonishing disappearance, while Dr. Rollins shook his head and chuckled. "It's something else, boys, isn't it?" Suzanne had not watched but she turned to stare sadly into the empty room, fearing an uncertain future that was linked to a volatile past.

Rollins invited his guests into their kitchen where he prepared a pot of tea. Theirs was a simple home. Large, but plain and traditional in its layout. The kitchen had been remodeled, but still retained its Victorian charm. Hardwood floors creaked gently when walked upon, four comfortable stools surrounded a big island with an oak chopping block in its center. Glass fronted cupboards displayed pantry items and dishes, and a large window over the sink looked out into their backyard and over countless acres of rolling, Maryland farmland. Suzanne walked to the window and gazed outside.

"The rain's let up," she said. "It really cleared up quite a bit." A nine-tenths moon hung low on the horizon and was bright enough to light up the countryside. "It's really beautiful here, Dr. Rollins."

"Yes, it is. Truth be told, besides missing the excitement of a real research university and colleagues who know what the hell I'm talking about, in some ways I think I probably prefer it here." Jackson bristled at the comment, but stayed quiet. The kettle whistled and drops of water sputtered and spit from its spout until Rollins removed it from the gas flame. He poured the boiling water into a waiting teapot.

"Margaret brings me videos from home and I can't say I'm too happy about all that's been happening there," he said. "Some of it is glorious and wonderful, of course, but much of it is sad and rather discouraging."

"Not unlike this world, Dr. Rollins?" Jackson asked.

"Good point, and very true, very true, son," he conceded. "They're making terribly slow progress here, and in Europe. Well, Europe was lost many years ago, I don't think she'll ever recover." Rollins stared off into the distance, again lost in thought.

"That view you're admiring...back home it's now a Super Wal-Mart, Home Depot, and Best Buy shopping center. And the road you traveled in on is an eight lane 70-miles-an-hour highway, instead of two lanes at 40-miles-an-hour. But still our home stands strong and the portal remains open. For Margaret, anyway."

"I have a question, Henry," said Mike Phillips. He accepted a cup of tea from the doctor and stirred the spoon in the steaming liquid. "Where are the Margaret and Henry Rollins from this world? If so many things are the same, including people," he nodded at Suzanne who was still gazing out the window, "then how is it that you were able to move into a house that should have been occupied by...well...some version of you?"

"Oh my, this is yet another fascinating, and sad part of the Multiverse, Mike. You'll notice that you didn't run into yourselves in Gettysburg?"

"Yes, that's true but we did run into Suzanne, and we met Tommy's uncles."

"Sure," said Rollins, excited again at the opportunity to explain his life's work. "So with all that's the same, why can't you find yourselves here?"

"I don't know," said Phillips. "Is it because we never looked?"

"Even if you had looked, you wouldn't find yourselves. Not to chase this rabbit too far down its hole, but we, Margaret and I, believe in the individual soul, for lack of a better term, and that only one soul can occupy one universe at a time."

"The soul? As in...the spirit, like in the Bible? I really don't understand," said Phillips.

"Join the crowd," said Rollins. He thought carefully how he might make it clearer. "You have to understand why things are the same, first. This timeline changed from ours back home in 1863 and you know that prior to 1863 our histories are identical in every, single way. That begins to explain why certain things are so similar, Washington, D.C., for example. Much of it was built prior to 1863, and the same can be said for most major cities and even most small towns. The end of the Civil War, after all, was only about 150 years ago."

"Tommy and Suzanne's great grandparents were, like many, probably self-sufficient rural farm folk, independent business people who lived just outside of town. Life for them might not have been that different regardless of the outcome of the Civil War. Their great grandparents met each other long before 1863 and sired offspring who managed to meet one another, who in turn sired more offspring, who also became parents, and so on, and so on."

"You, Mr. Phillips, on the other hand, are not from rural Virginia but are from New York and only moved to Gettysburg 10 years ago. I know that because I read earlier today in your *USA Today* story…but for you and your family's set of circumstances to have repeated itself in this timeline is statistically so improbable that, well, you can see how it just couldn't happen. Too many things would be too different."

"Yes," said Jackson, "but here we are in your house, a house identical to the one back home that Margaret bounces back and forth between. But there's one thing really confusing me - the explosion in 1863. There's no mention of it in our history. There was never any plan for it, and it didn't succeed or fail, because it didn't exist in our world, at all, ever."

Rollins looked puzzled, squeezing his bushy eyebrows close together. "What do you mean, Greg?" said Rollins. "The failed detonation at Gettysburg is taught in every American History class back home. Ken Burns' documentary dedicates an entire episode to it. It's right here, on my bookshelf." He pointed to the living room. "Margaret bought us a DVD player and the box set for Christmas. I even studied the Grissom Plan in college."

"Doc," said Jackson slowly. "There is no Grissom Plan." He looked at Phillips, who nodded in agreement.

"My, my," said Rollins, slumping back against the counter, as if he were getting dizzy. "You're sure?"

"Yeah, Doc. We're sure," said Jackson. "So what does that tell you?"

"For starters, it tells me you and I are…are not from the same place. We do not share the same Birth World."

Dr. Rollins set his cup of tea on the island and gazed for a moment at the steam. The expression on his face turned from shock to acceptance.

"Well, that's a new twist, but I don't know that it changes how I suggest we proceed. Apparently the portal you traveled through skipped, and bounced around a bit."

"Skipped and bounced? Where?" asked Jackson.

"Right over top of my home universe, if I'm not mistaken. You all are distant Travelers from a place I do not know. But, if your sympathetic portal is like Margaret's and Kay's, it could, it should take you back to your Birth World. But that does complicate things."

"How?" asked Phillips.

242

"Well, I was hoping to travel back home with you boys, if that's what your plan is. But if what you're saying is true, then your home is not my home."

Jackson seized the moment. "Are you saying you think we can get home?"

"Yes," said Rollins. "I think it's possible. I'm just not sure where I might land, so to speak." He finished his tea and wiped his mouth with a linen napkin. "Well, I'll make it a matter of prayer, and put it in God's hands." He excused himself, lost in thought, and began washing the dishes.

Greg Jackson sipped the still steaming tea and placed the cup thoughtfully on the counter.

"About prayer," he started, slowly, "and forgive me if this is too personal, but where's God in all this? I mean, in light of all that you're suggesting...it sounds like you still believe in a God?"

"Absolutely." Rollins didn't hesitate. "Margaret and I both believe. We go to church twice a week and thank God every day for our lives together and we're strong believers in prayer." The others were quiet. "Does that surprise you kids? I know it's not popular to believe; especially for academics and scientists."

"Somehow people have gotten the notion that Science and the Bible are mutually exclusive. I find that they support one another in wonderful, remarkable, glorious ways. Not necessarily all the creationist rhetoric, but much of the Bible stands as an ancient, elementary science textbook. The long-suffering Job talks about the *'Lord stretching out the North over empty space and hanging the Earth on nothing.'* This was written in a time that even pre-dated the earliest notions of space. From Isaiah: *'It is He who sits above the circle of the earth and its inhabitants are like grasshoppers.'* When that was written men of the day had no concept that the Earth was anything but flat. *'It is He, who stretches out the heavens like a curtain, and spreads them out like a tent to dwell in.'* Those passages were written nearly 3,000 years ago and a full 300 years before Aristotle suggested in his writings that the Earth might be a sphere, or that the heavens might be vast. Scientists thought the Earth was flat and that it was the center of a very small, visible universe, well into the 1400's."

"The Bible put in plain language, truths about the Earth, its weather, its geology, the universe and, even more important than that, it's filled with accounts of ordinary men and women who were placed in extraordinary circumstances, and who used their heads and prayer and their moral compasses to do what they knew was the right thing. Much like we're trying to do."

"I never thought about it that way," said Jackson.

"This is from Hamlet," continued Rollins, "which, by the way, I think should be canonized: *'There are more things in heaven and earth, Horatio, than are dreamt of in your Philosophy.'* Shakespeare and I both apparently believe good scientists everywhere need to have a humility that allows for things outside the laboratory. I believe it's a part of the God Spark theory, that in all these many, perhaps infinite, dimensions and universes, and of all the potential Maggies and Hanks out there, each of us shares a soul with our counterparts, our soul siblings. This is why Travelers never see themselves. I don't believe it's possible. One soul per person, an infinite number of persons per soul. I believe we're all working out God's cosmic plan in ways we could never comprehend this side of heaven."

They sat in rapt attention as Rollins filled the very air with wild, new philosophies, new possibilities, and new ways to look at the astounding, unfathomable mysteries laid before them. He managed to meld Eastern and Western religion, along with his own brand of Christianity, into one plausible explanation.

"Where are our counterparts," asked Mike Phillips, "mine, Tommy's, Greg's?"

"It's possible they never existed here. But if they did, they've been... moved out. Just like mine and Margaret's others, Hank and Maggie," answered Rollins.

"Hank and Maggie?" asked Jackson.

"Our counterparts here. We're standing in their kitchen. We've taken over their lives, but only because we had to. It was the best option of several bad options."

"Were Hank and Maggie in love, Dr. Rollins?" asked Suzanne.

"Oh yes, my child. They were as madly in love with each other as my Margaret and I are and they deserve to be together and as happy as we are." Rollins dried his hands and sat on a stool. "I believe we share in each other's happiness and sadness through the vastness of time and space. I believe we're connected, Margaret and I, to Hank and Maggie."

He turned to look at Suzanne, who couldn't help but wonder what Susan was like and if all the things Rollins was saying could be true.

"Have you ever felt melancholy for no reason in particular?" asked Rollins. "Or wake up in a great mood? Or have unexplainable bad dreams out of nowhere? Those irrational ups and downs in our mood, even our health...I believe we're all eternally enmeshed with our others."

"The Hindus and Buddhists, I believe, were close with their beliefs. They sensed that there was much more to who we are in the present than just our life's experience. They knew innately of the connections. They teach that our current situations are influenced by past lives, to which I don't subscribe, rather, I think these connections, these feelings, come from many lives lived in the Multiverse, in the relative present."

He scratched his head, and looked thoughtful, as if he were still working on his own personal theology.

"All in all, I believe in Karmic implications. Hank number 15 or number 15,000 has a good day in some other dimension, then I wake up feeling slightly better than usual. If he kicks the dog and feels guilty about it, then I feel some of that same remorse, even though I can't put my finger on why. Don't get me wrong, we are each responsible for our own happiness, but we are connected, I believe, to the lives of our soul siblings."

He wiped his eyes with a tissue, a sudden sadness apparent.

"We really feel like we've pushed Hank and Maggie out and taken over their lives. It's still very upsetting, but we trust God has His Hand on them and it's out of our control anyway. Thank goodness they didn't have children or it would have been much harder for them and us. We did our best to assume their daily activities here, and assimilate their friends, relatives and their jobs. We tried to become like them, more for the people that knew them, than for us. It was wildly strange and traumatic at first, and sometimes even hilarious. We managed to share a lot of laughs. It's the only thing that's kept us sane."

He smiled, searching his memory for a 60 year-old story that always made him chuckle.

"Some of the family here thought we'd eaten bad cheese and had both gone nuts with a brain disease, really. Maggie's mother, my mother-in-law in this world, asked us in all seriousness, if we'd eaten any bad cheese. She never forgave us for laughing so hard while she was so upset at our behavior." Rollins' eyes twinkled. "To this day we can't eat a piece of cheese without making faces at each other. People here seem to love us, but they are quite convinced we are mad. Who knows, maybe we are?"

"The jobs were especially difficult, but we had to try, everyone expected us to, and there were bills to pay. Margaret was a teacher by trade. She'd never taught under this strange Public School system. When she tried to return to the classroom, her efforts failed and she had to quit. I was supposed to have been the part-time postmaster of this little 'Burg. Imagine how badly that went? She retired at 24 years of age, here, that is. She taught back home until she was 70. I became a full-time Metaphysics hobbyist, who's dabbled as a mineralogist and government consultant, to help pay the bills. Here we both receive small government pensions, but the mineral rights' royalties bring in more money than we know what to do with. We donate much of it to a few worthy causes, and institutions, including the Library of Congress. Margaret is a volunteer there and we are anonymous benefactors. They are forbidden from ever releasing our names. I think we've given $4 million and some change. I'm not bragging, mind you. We didn't earn a penny of it through hard work. But we like to keep a low profile, especially there at the Library."

"That explains why I couldn't find anyone who knew of her," said Suzanne, reentering the conversation.

"Yes, yes. It's all very cloak and dagger, my dear," said Rollins, with a saying whose meaning was lost on the young woman.

"Where and when did you jump, Henry?" asked Jackson.

"Save that old story for another visit," said Margaret, walking into the kitchen. "Joey is waiting and we've got work to do."

Chapter 27

At 2:00 a.m. young Joey Michaels was bored, tired, miserable and angry. He had found a spot for his car in the back corner of the Fuel and Drool parking lot. Local and State police, along with Con-Fed military, were in and out of the truck stop with increasing frequency and it made him uneasy. He started the car and switched on the radio. He twisted the dial until he heard music. He sunk back in his seat, closed his eyes and moaned.

"Not this song, again...it's all they play." Reluctantly, he listened to, for the fourth or fifth time that day, "*Sweet Home Alabama*," cursing Tommy Fuller, and wishing he were in his own sweet Gettysburg home.

•••••

In the Rollins' office, the group gathered to watch Margaret go into action. Within a large armoire, hidden from view behind two great doors, sat a computer, high-def flat screen monitor, scanner and printer. It was the first modern machinery they had seen in this world and the Rollins' kept it carefully hidden.

She sat in front of the monitor and flipped switches like she was launching the Space Shuttle. The machines hummed and whirred to life and Dr. Rollins was ecstatic. "I love to watch her work her magic on that stuff. I've tried, but I just can't get the hang of it. I'm told computers are starting to get very popular back home."

Margaret was proficient and the men smiled at the sight of the grandmotherly woman handling the high-tech machines like a nerdy teenager.

"There we go," she said and the system booted and was ready to begin. She opened a file that contained a high-resolution scan of Dr. Rollins' Border Pass, the equivalent of a passport. Before them on the monitor was the image of a simple, but official looking document that essentially granted Rollins access to border crossings and access into the department of the interior in Washington and in Con-Fed's Richmond. Rollins was one of no more than a dozen civilians with this type of multi-nation, high-level clearance. Two federal agents, one of them named Tate, shared the same privileges.

Suzanne finally looked appropriately shocked. She had never seen a television, let alone a computer, and this image, so easily manipulated by a wireless mouse, was to her, absolutely mind-blowing. To the rest of the men it was a reminder of the life they'd left three days earlier.

"Okay, Suzanne, stand against that wall and look straight ahead." She looked frightened and needed to be reassured that they weren't about to zap her off into some distant universe, and were only taking a photograph. Margaret readied her old Poloroid, and Suzanne, still in awe, stood dutifully against the pale yellow wall of the office. The flash clicked and the girl let out a startled 'Wow.' When the 3 x 4 piece of white cardboard whirred out the bottom of the camera and they began to see her black & white image appear within seconds, she smiled, amazed at the ghostly face, coming to life.

"Oh, this impresses her," said Jackson. "We travel from another dimension, apparently skipping over one on the way, and it's all 'ho-hum', but an instant picture knocks her socks off?"

"Wait until she sees a smart phone," added Phillips.

Margaret scanned, cropped, cut and pasted the photo and replaced Dr. Rollins information with that of Suzanne's. They opted for an alias in light of her 'Wanted' status. Within two minutes the printer had produced a better than reasonable facsimile of an 'Assistant Status,' full access 'Border Pass.' "We'll laminate it like Henry's," said Margaret with a smile, "and you'll be good to go."

Having 2013 hi-tech knowledge and machinery in a place still stuck in the Golden Age of Radio had its advantages.

"We'll take my car," said Rollins. "Shall we go? Are you ready?"

Suzanne helped Margaret remove the dishes to the kitchen and Tommy Fuller took the opportunity to pull Dr. Rollins to the side. They spoke in hushed tones and Rollins nodded in agreement to some whispered plan, finishing their conversation just as Suzanne returned to the room.

They all discussed the border-crossing strategy and were ready to go. Henry kissed Margaret on the cheek, they said their goodbyes, and they were soon out the door, on the way to the Fuel and Drool just outside of Hagerstown, Maryland, an hour-and-a-half drive and an international border away.

"You kids need to get some rest," said Margaret. "We have two guest rooms with double beds."

"I snore," said Jackson proudly, who was offered his own room. Hot showers, warm, soft beds, no noise and fewer worries helped the men settle in for some much needed sleep. The ringing in Jackson's ears was finally subsiding and he was looking forward to a long snooze.

•••••

Rollins' big car crunched quietly out of the gravel driveway onto the road. Within minutes they were on the main highway that followed the border between North and South. They passed the farmhouse that had acted as the secret Northern tunnel terminus and noticed a shiny new wooden door, still unpainted, hanging from the barn, hiding the entry point.

"That's from my handiwork, I'm afraid," said Suzanne. "I kind of drove through their old door."

"What you have been through, sweet girl, I can't imagine," said Rollins.

They were quiet for a moment, Suzanne lost in her own thoughts. Finally she spoke. "Dr. Rollins, Tommy says that I am his wife back in his world and he knows quite a bit about my family and things here, but how come I don't know him?"

"There might be several explanations," answered Rollins. "It could be that Tommy was never born in this timeline, or his family may have moved before you would know him. Or he might have grown up on the other side of town and you wouldn't have known him. Sadly, if another Tommy did exist in this timeline, he would have been displaced when he made the jump."

"Displaced?" she asked.

"Yes, like Maggie and Hank. Remember, the same two people cannot co-exist in the same timeline, there's only room for one, don't ask me why. It's one of my goals to figure that one out. In all the jumping and bumping around Travelers do between dimensions, they never run into themselves. That's the big myth of time and dimensional travel; that running into yourself creates some tear in the fabric of the universe. It can't happen; or, at least, it doesn't happen. The one traveling in seems to have precedence over the one already in place, and the one in place gets bumped."

"Bumped? Bumped where?"

"Not sure, but we assume another timeline, another universe in another dimension; at least we hope so."

"So," she continued, "if Tommy and the men change history on their way back home, as they plan to do, will I meet some version of Tommy here?"

"I would normally say no, but because they're going to attempt to change history in this timeline, which pre-dates all of you then, well yes...it's possible. In fact it's likely."

"But, if I understand what you're saying, is it also possible that if they're successful..." Suzanne hesitated, almost afraid to ask the question, "... that we might possibly...not exist at all?"

"Well, no," said Rollins. "Don't think of it that way. You already exist; probably in many dimensions, as do I and everyone else on the planet. Not existing here is not the same as not existing. You have one beautiful soul, my dear, and it shines brightly in many, many places." She accepted his logic, as best she could, but was deeply troubled by the prospect of losing the first man she ever felt completely in love with, and she was equally troubled about her own fate as well. It was too difficult to contemplate for very long. Suzanne was quiet again and Dr. Rollins knew why.

The road widened to four lanes and was surrounded by concrete barriers. The imposing entryway to the border crossing looked like a giant half-pipe storm drain. It was designed with security in mind. Massive lights on 100-foot towers illuminated the night sky ahead.

Suzanne's nagging inner dialog expressed itself as a new round of questions. "If I jumped backward into Tommy's timeline, if I went with them, what would happen to his Susan?" she asked.

Rollins involuntarily hit the car's brakes. He looked at her sternly.

"You must not. First of all it's not really backward, it's more like sideways, with small shifts forward and back, but regardless, you mustn't ever try, Suzanne. Their multiple crossing was rare. This is your Birth World. This is where you belong. If you tried to jump with them...God only knows what might happen. You'd probably end up in yet another timeline, further out. Remember, no one originating in this timeline has ever been reported in ours back home. Maggie and Hank went somewhere, but it wasn't home, we looked. I know this much, if you were somehow successful, which I very much doubt, you would probably displace his Susan, which you must understand...is you. That's reason alone not to do it. It's too dangerous and ... it's just not right. It's one thing for Margaret and me, and the boys, to have done it accidentally, but quite another to do it intentionally. You would never be able to live with yourself, trust me, I know."

The conversation awkwardly ceased as they approached their first checkpoint.

"Remember, you are Sadie Hawkins from D.C.," said Rollins, finally.

"You're my assistant and we're going to Asheville, North Carolina, for geological research."

"Got it," she said as Rollins rolled down his window to greet the first set of armed Fed-Stat border guards.

"Good evening sir," said the young Sergeant, in full battle gear. "I.D.s please." He shone a flashlight at their faces while two other guards circled the car with flashlights of their own, running long-handled mirrors under the car's carriage.

"Kind of late to be traveling?" said the guard. They both handed their laminated passes to him and he studied them closely.

"Yes, tell me about it," said Rollins. "It's a long haul to North Carolina and we need to be there by morning," he continued with a friendly smile.

"What's your business in North Carolina?"

"Oh, just more of the same. Geological research. This time we're looking for gold."

"Mind if we look in your trunk?" asked the guard, though it wasn't really a request.

"Certainly, no problem." Rollins pushed a button on the dash and the trunk released, popping up in the air, surprising the guards, who jumped back.

"That's quite a trick," said the Sergeant. "How'd you do that?"

"I rigged it myself, to save time," said Rollins with a big grin. "It's just a simple cable release."

With their noses in the trunk, the guards found pick-axes, shovels, buckets, testing equipment, a spare tire, and a jack. Satisfied, they closed the trunk, commenting on the automatic release and what a good idea that was. Rollins could have easily made billions in this new world with everyday, simple inventions that had just not yet been invented. Rollins chose not to capitalize wantonly. He was a simple man of science and needed only to be comfortable. His supposed nose for finding silver and gold came from Margaret's research during her days at the Library of Congress. She simply located mines that had not yet been discovered and didn't exist in Henry's universe. It was just that easy, and they vowed to do as much good with the money as possible.

"Okay, Dr. Rollins, Miss Hawkins. You two be safe." He handed them back their passes. "There's another checkpoint at the bridge. It's your next left-hand turn."

They thanked the guard and drove on. Suzanne was doing her best, but she couldn't hide an obvious flop-sweat and growing anxiety. Rollins slowed the car.

"Suzanne. You need to relax. We mustn't look that nervous when we approach these borders. The guards are trained to smell fear. Breathe in long, slow and steady." Together they inhaled deeply and she patted her forehead with his handkerchief, regaining her composure.

They were stopped for a second time, 100 yards in front of a ten-foot steel fence. There were at least 20 guards and military personnel engaged in a variety of activities. Again they were asked for their I.D.s and this new set of guards wanted to see 'that trunk thing' that the first set had radioed ahead about. Rollins complied, much to their impressed amusement, and then they checked his I.D. against a list of approved, MGV's (Multi Government Vendors) and found him on the third page.

He leaned into the car and looked at Suzanne. "Sir, Miss Hawkins is not on our approved list."

"Oh my," said Rollins. "She's my new assistant and I guess my secretary hadn't gotten the paper work in on time."

"You know we're under a level 2 terror alert?" asked the guard.

"Yes, I heard. Awful business about that. Have they caught anybody yet?"

"Not yet, but I'm sure we will. You two can pass, but get that approval in before your next trip, okay?"

"Absolutely," smiled Rollins. He rolled up his window as they were waved forward. When they approached the gate it slid open sideways, allowing passage over the quarter-mile bridge. The walls were high enough on either side that all they could see was straight ahead toward another set of checkpoints. They followed the same procedures on the Con-Fed side and were allowed to pass. They turned onto the highway and were just 40-minutes from the truck stop and the very distressed brother of Sadie Hawkins.

•••••

Tommy Fuller couldn't sleep. As tired as he was, there was just too much running through his brain. "You snore, too, Mike," he said half-aloud in Phillips' direction. He got up to head to the bathroom and noticed a light on in Margaret's room. He assumed she was reading. What he really wanted was a good stiff shot of whiskey and a half-dozen Extra 'C' Cokes. He hated to bother his hostess and was a little embarrassed about asking for booze, so he thought he'd take a quick peek on his own for a liquor cabinet.

He crept down the mercifully non-squeaky stairs. On his way through the living room toward the kitchen, he passed by the den; he couldn't help but be drawn to it. He stood at the doorway looking in and imagined an identical den in another house, in another world, just through that wall, or in another dimension, or somewhere he couldn't understand. He stepped closer, but not too close, and waved his arm tentatively through the air like he might detect a force-field or electrical charge, or some physical sensation. But there was none. If he hadn't seen Margaret vanish with his own eyes, he wouldn't have believed it.

"I wonder if we'll ever make it home," he asked himself, quietly. He worried about Suzanne and Dr. Rollins and how she would take the news with which Rollins was about to surprise her.

•••••

Highway 17 on the Con-Fed side of the border was also extremely busy, and this too worried Suzanne.

"I hope Joey is all right," she said. "I've never seen this much military and police traffic. He's not exactly patient."

"What kid is?" asked Rollins. "We're almost there. I think I know right where it is. I stop there for coffee frequently."

At 2:50 a.m. Rollins pulled his car into the parking lot of the Fuel and Drool and pulled up to the nearest gas pump. For some reason, self-serve fueling had beaten the other world by 20 years and while everything else seemed antiquated, this system seemed almost up to date. They exited the car and spotted Joey's Marathon 200 feet away, toward the back of the lot.

"There he is!" said Suzanne. "That car has to be the loaner. It must be him." She began to run, when she felt a hand on her shoulder.

"Suzanne!" shouted Rollins, stifling his voice the best he could. "Let me go to him. Remember, they're looking for you. Please, get back in the car. You can watch me from here. We have to look as natural as possible." Just then a convoy of Con-Fed jeeps displaying the Confederate Stars and Bars National flag rumbled past them making his point, and she reluctantly complied. She sat back in her seat watching Dr. Rollins walk toward the Marathon.

Joey awakened with a start when Rollins tapped on the window, a little harder than he needed to. Joey rubbed his eyes and tried to figure out where he was and what was going on.

"Young man, I'm Henry Rollins, a friend of Suzanne's. She's with me, in that waiting car."

The boy rolled down the window, still rubbing his eyes and looked suspiciously at him. He then looked toward the car being fueled and Suzanne dared a small wave in his direction.

"Pull over to the pumps and you can talk to Suzanne." Joey complied and wheeled the big car around, slowly making his way to the row of gas pumps with Dr. Rollins walking closely behind. When he parked and got out, Suzanne was there to meet him with a big hug and kiss on both cheeks.

"Joey, Joey. I'm so sorry about all this. What have I gotten you in to?" A tear formed and slid down her cheek. "What happened to your hand?"

"No big deal. Just a cut," he said. Suzanne began to cry, the pent up emotion stirred with every glance at her brother.

"Don't cry," he said. "We'll be all right, Sissy."

She put a hand on his shoulder "Well, we're going to park this car of yours and you'll come back with us," said Suzanne. "We need to stick together."

"No. I'm afraid you won't be coming back, Joey," said Rollins. "You either, Suzanne. You are both going home to Gettysburg. I'm taking Tommy's phone and crossing back over the border alone."

"What do you mean?" she asked.

"It's time for you to part company with your friends, Suzanne. This is at Tommy's insistence and the others too. We all agree. They, we, have endangered you too much. It's the only way to keep you safe. We've already involved you well beyond what you deserve. This is just too dangerous, and you're already a wanted fugitive. It's not too late to make a clean break. Both of you."

Defiance formed on her tear-stained face. "No!" She grabbed Joey's hand to lead him to the car like he was a toddler.

"Joey, you know this is what's best for both you and your sister," pleaded Rollins. "We'll never all get back over the border, you know it. And even if we did, then what?" He looked at Suzanne and knew the pain she was feeling, but had to make his case. "Are you going to make Joey a fugitive, too? Please don't make this any harder than it has to be. I'm sorry. It's the only way." He reached in his pocket.

"Here. This is from Tommy." Rollins handed her a folded piece of paper and she read the hastily scribbled note.

Suzanne, I'm sorry it had to be like this but know I love you and how sick I am about how this is all playing out. This was the only way to get you home, because I knew you'd never leave willingly. Trust Dr. Rollins. I can barely figure this thing out myself. But we'll see each other soon, find each other again, start that family. I'll never let you out of my sight again. You are my one and only. I love you. T.

She slumped against the car, leaned her head on her forearm and wept.

"Suzanne, please get in Joey's car," said Rollins. "We'll be seen. We're not safe out in the open. Joey, I need the radio device and the battery. Quickly m'boy." The teenager went to his trunk and opened it with his key.

"Where do you want me to put it?"

"Here," answered Rollins as he popped his own trunk open.

The transfer was made without incident or apparent suspicion. To anyone nearby, it looked like a kid putting a car battery in the trunk of an old man's car, nothing more, nothing less. The black phone and the tangle of wires were hard to make out from a distance.

Suzanne, dejected, opened the Marathon's door and slipped into the passenger's seat. She looked straight ahead, as if in a trance. Joey got in behind the wheel, pulled out of the Fuel and Drool, and headed back to Gettysburg without another word spoken to Dr. Rollins.

•••••

Rollins topped off his tank with gas and walked inside to pay.

"Hey Doc," yelled the women behind the counter. "Haven't seen you in awhile."

"Hello, Wanda," he said, forcing a smile.

"Why the sour puss?" she asked.

"You don't want to know."

"You got that right. The whole Con-Fed Army has been rumbling in and out of here all night, some kid sleeping in one of my booths, nutballs on the phone, been a crazy night."

He paid for the gas, ordered a coffee 'to go' and hit the road with Tommy's phone safely in the trunk, a full tank of gas and with one less passenger. "Oh, Suzanne..." he whispered. "How the daughters of Eve do suffer..."

With the unpleasant task behind him, Rollins was back on the road with a cup of coffee and a long trip ahead. He had already decided he couldn't attempt to use the same checkpoint so soon after having crossed. He'd be especially obvious and it would be hard to explain the absence of his assistant. It would be much better to drive to the D.C. border, 45 miles further, crossing there to work his way home from the east. It was an extra 90 minutes of driving, but the choice made sense. Though tired and ready for some rest, he found his resolve and drove on into the night.

Chapter 28

As Tommy Fuller walked quietly through the house, he noticed for the first time, family photographs on the wall. He thought about how difficult it must be for the Rollins' to feel like they were living a lie. They must have spent years trying to re-learn family histories, the likes and dislikes of friends they had never met, not to mention dealing with those back home they'd miss, and for Dr. Rollins, especially, having not been able to cross back over.

"It can't be easy," Fuller said quietly gazing at a photo collage. But he also knew life back home would be fraught with troubles a mile thick if they ever made it back, and since meeting the Rollins the possibility had never seemed so close. Henry and Margaret Rollins seemed to have as clear an understanding of their plight as anyone he could imagine.

He walked to the kitchen and began thinking about Suzanne. He wondered if Dr. Rollins had yet told her she wasn't returning with him. He hated to leave her like that. He knew she'd be devastated and would feel betrayed but he felt it was the only way. He hoped his letter would help ease her pain.

•••••

Suzanne cried for the first 20 minutes of their ride back toward Gettysburg, but eventually just settled into silence. Though he had a hundred questions for her, Joey, too, was tired and upset and didn't feel like talking. He worried about explaining a few things, such as Suzanne's whereabouts for the past 36 hours, and her sudden return. He hoped the break-in at Fuller's Auto would take care of itself and that they'd be back in their apartment before anyone knew he had gone, but Suzanne's reappearance would be problematic. They'd have to have a plausible explanation...what it might be, he had no idea.

•••••

Tommy Fuller found what he was looking for. Under the counter to the left of the sink, a small cabinet stored a half-dozen bottles of various liquors. "They're not teetotalers," he said to himself. The Jack Daniels caught his attention. He pulled the bottle from among the others accidentally knocking it against another bottle. It sounded like a glass shotgun echoing through the tiled kitchen. He froze, listening for movement, and, hearing none, took a long swig of the smoky, brown Tennessee Sour Mash. He looked out the window; the moon lit up the rolling hills. He thought again about how peaceful it seemed in the country and how clean the air was. He could see more stars than he thought was possible.

"It's not all bad, here," he said aloud.

"No, it's not," agreed Margaret who had come into the kitchen, adept at making sudden appearances. "I'll have a short one of those, if you're pouring."

Tommy turned and didn't even bother explaining the bottle in his hand. She knew why he was in her kitchen, and what he was doing.

"That's imported, you know?" she said, pointing to the familiar, square bottle with the antiquated black & white label. He retrieved two small glasses from the cabinet and poured each of them three fingers of the whiskey.

"Imported? From across the border?" asked Tommy.

"No, no," she laughed. "Farther than that, across the universe. I have to bring this from home. It's illegal here in the North."

"It tastes wonderful, like I'd never had it before," said Tommy, though he wasn't drinking it for its flavor. She walked to him and patted his back.

"I know you're struggling with this 'should I stay or should I go' issue. You're not the first, and you don't have to go. You can stay here, you know. I can get you a new identity, you and Suzanne could find a place far from the mess you're in now and you'd probably live happily ever after. But I don't think you will stay."

"Oh, no?" he asked.

"No. Because as much as you'd like to stay here, you know you have a responsibility somewhere else. And you're a good man, Tommy Fuller. And if you're lucky enough to have the opportunity to fix things, you will do what's right, hard as it may be."

The ethics of the choice weighed heavily upon him, but so did the fine points of a return trip.

"I'm worried about the going back process. We didn't just pop over like you and Henry and what's his name, Kay, the radio guy. We skipped universes, went backward 150 years in time, then forward before arriving in this place. How are we going to get back without repeating the process in reverse? Will we end up back in some version of the Battle of Gettysburg? It was horrible. We barely made it out alive."

"I know it must have been horrific," said Margaret sympathetically. "War is hell. Getting back will be tricky and I just don't know how exactly it might work, and I don't think Henry knows either, though he will pretend to. We've talked about this some, and there are endless possibilities." She paused and took a sip of the whiskey, clearly not her first taste of the spirit. "You know life back home is moving along just as you knew it four days ago. By the way, the Atlanta Braves lost to the Yankees in the three-game series."

"Too bad," said Fuller. "Damn Yankees."

"We think, Tommy, that if we can get you all through your portal, which is clearly at Emmitsburg Road in Gettysburg, that you will simply reverse the process. You'll jump back to 1863 in our universe here, and yes, you'll probably end up on that horrible battlefield. The Lord willing you'll then cross over to your original universe arriving back in the present, more or less. Remember, I lose 10 minutes every time I jump. You may lose or gain 10 minutes or ten hours, or ten days, we don't really know. These things are not nicely tied up with a bow for us. But where you have to be careful is what you do with your time when you're back in 1863. If you change things dramatically when you're back there, you'll change everything in this timeline from that point forward. You must not interfere with this history you've already created 150 years ago."

"But why?" he asked.

"You see, I can cross back over and be safe. But Henry can't." She took his hand to make sure he understood her. "I won't lose him again."

They turned to see Greg Jackson entering the kitchen.

"Why can't Henry cross over, Margaret?" asked Jackson, who had heard a good part of their conversation.

She took a deep breath. "His portal was destroyed, or collapsed, in your timeline. It doesn't exist anymore, and you see, his being stuck here is the quandary you're, we're *all* in. If we're successful in sending you back and if you go back to 1863, as we suspect you will, you may affect the outcome of this battle, the change in this timeline could....," she couldn't bear to say it aloud, but forced it out. It needed to be said, "it could end Henry's life."

Margaret paused and looked at Jackson. "We might lose him, Greg. He didn't want me to tell you this. He didn't want your decision to be based on his welfare, but rather for the good of all."

"What decision?" asked Jackson.

She paused and took another sip. "The decision on whether or not to try to correct, as you see it,...history."

This new worry hadn't even been conceived of yet and Jackson sat quietly contemplating the challenge that lay before them all.

"Where did he jump, originally?" asked Fuller.

"That's something you need to take up with him. He really should be the one to tell you that tale. But I can say that he was a part of the Philadelphia Experiment. Heard of it?"

"I have," said Mike Phillips, the last insomniac of the house arriving in the kitchen. He'd been listening at the door.

"Why is everybody sneaking up on me?" asked Fuller with a half smile, turning to see Phillips approach the counter.

"You started the sneaking around, buddy," said Phillips. "I heard the distinct sound of a whiskey bottle rattling down here. Stealth may not be your strong suit."

"For sure," said Fuller sliding the bottle and a glass across the counter towards Phillips.

"Isn't the Philadelphia Experiment some hoax from the 40s?" asked Phillips, pouring himself a small glass of the well-traveled Jack.

"Depends on who you ask," said Margaret. "The Navy said it never happened. Eye-witnesses claim otherwise. It was part of a covert project Henry was involved in as a field researcher. It was called the Rainbow Project, but again, he really needs to be the one to tell you." Finding seats at the island they all sat in the darkened room, thinking a million thoughts, waiting for the return of the one man who best understood their predicament, the one with a predicament of his own.

•••••

Henry Rollins was getting closer to the crossing point and he could not remember a time when the border had been so thick with military and police personnel. He guessed there might have been ten times the normal number of troops and vehicles, and each person in uniform gazed at him with an unusual intensity as he passed by. He found it very unnerving and couldn't wait to get back home.

He arrived at the first checkpoint as he neared the bridge to D.C. Con-Fed troops stopped him and he showed his papers. They didn't like him. They were very suspicious of these people from the North who came and went as they pleased. Here was a foreign enemy in their country with complete impunity. Had he not been such a sweet, kindly man they would have enjoyed hassling him. The guards did ask him to open the trunk and called him from the front seat to explain what they were looking at.

"That?" Dr. Rollins asked, pointing to the car battery and cell phone. "That's just a new wireless radio we're working on."

"We'd like to see it work," said the guard.

"So would I, my dear boy, so would I," said Rollins. "I'm afraid it never worked very well and now has stopped working altogether."

"Why are you returning so soon? You just got here a few hours ago," said the guard, looking at the time stamp on his travel visa.

"It's hell getting old, young man. I know I just crossed, and trust me this has been a long night. I left all my surveying equipment in my D.C. office, so I'm headed back for it and will be back down this way probably later today."

They accepted his papers and his explanations and waved him through. He made it through the final Con-Fed checkpoint and crossed the bridge to the first Fed-Stat guardhouse. There the guards went through the same endless questioning about his short stay and asked him to open the trunk of his car. He complied and he could hear them rummaging around not too gently. They called him out of his car and asked about the strange device attached to a car battery. He finished the same story about it being a non-working radio device and they seemed satisfied. Just before closing the trunk Tommy Fuller's cell phone lit up, began flashing, and then played *Dixie*. The soldiers reacted immediately and two new guards came by to check on the commotion.

"Bomb! Bomb on board!" yelled one of the men. The third border guard took a quick peek in the trunk and, upon seeing the car battery attached by makeshift leads to the cell phone, started yelling "I.E.D!, I.E.D!" a term Henry had only read about since the beginning of the Iraq War. These men should know nothing of Improvised Explosive Devices, a new phenomenon of the Mid-East wars, but yet, one man seemed to.

Sirens wailed, lights flashed, guards grabbed Rollins and dragged him behind a protective barricade 40 yards from his car. All Fed-Stat personnel and vehicles scattered like rats, leaving Dr. Rollins' Chevrolet alone in the middle of the bridge with his trunk echoing and repeating the first four bars of *Dixie* – "*Oh, I wish I was in the land of cotton, old times there are not forgotten, look away, look away, look away, Dixieland.*" Someone's messages were waiting.

•••••

Joey and Suzanne had arrived at their apartment after an uneventful, quiet drive home. They found the lights on and Anthony asleep on the couch. Two bottles of Extra 'C' Coke and five empty beer bottles sat on the table, while the radio played softly.

"I'm going to bed," said Joey who disappeared into his room. Suzanne looked at the sleeping form of her friend, Anthony, a boy who loved her, and whom she once held great affection for, and still did. She snuggled up close to him and wrapped her arms around his body. Somewhere between sleep and waking he began to try to talk. She put her finger across his lips.

"Shhhh. Go back to sleep. Go back to sleep."

He stroked her hair and returned her hug.

"I'm glad to see you. I really missed you," he said.

"Me too, Tony." They lay in each other's arms while the radio played songs they knew.

•••••

"He should be back by now, I'm beginning to worry," said Margaret to no one in particular. They had moved to the living room and were sitting, dozing, talking and sipping on the Tennessee whiskey and a few snacks Margaret had prepared.

The phone rang, startling everyone, and Margaret immediately picked up the receiver. "Hello?" she said.

"Mrs. Rollins?" came the unmistakable voice of authority.

"Yes. Oh my God what's happened? Is Henry alright?"

"Yes, he's fine, Mrs. Rollins, but he is being detained for questioning. Where was your husband headed, this morning?"

"Where is he? Let me speak to him." She was shaking and her voice trembled. Mike Phillips went to her, standing by her side.

"Please answer the question," came the dispassionate official.

"He was headed to North Carolina on a geological and mineral study," she said, "funded and approved by both governments, mind you." That was the perfect answer.

"Thank you, Mrs. Rollins. Someone will be in touch." He hung up abruptly before Margaret had a chance to respond. She looked at the phone and then at the others in the room.

"He just hung up." She stood motionless before almost falling back into her chair.

"I'm sure he'll be alright, Margaret," consoled Phillips.

"I'm really worried. This has never happened before," she said. "His heart is not good. This is not good for him. I wish they'd let him call me."

Across town a radio DJ, battered and bruised, stirred to life.

•••••

Billy the Kay was used to working late and rising early. As the Zoo Crew host, he regularly got up at 4:00 a.m. and this day was no different. He had been rising earlier than normal for the past few months, as his newest endeavor had to be worked under the cover of darkness. His portal for crossing universes was in the Madison building on F Street and doubled

261

as his office at the radio station. Like Margaret, he, too, had to be careful not to draw too much attention to his comings and goings. He'd had a couple of close calls.

An encounter with a late-night DJ, who thought he would borrow Kay's office, almost sent two people into therapy. The DJ brought his girlfriend into the radio station for a private dalliance. They had been locked in an embrace on the floor when, at a most inopportune moment, Billy The Kay appeared, in full living color, just 15 inches from their prone, naked bodies. Everyone screamed; the DJ, the girl, and Kay. The two lovers scrambled for their clothes and the door, and were convinced that Kay was a spirit who could walk through walls. The shaken DJ never showed up for his next shift. Kay was careful to double-lock his door from that point forward.

The double-duty Kay had been pulling in both universes for nearly 10 years had been wearing on him. He decided 'enough was enough,' and money was much easier to make in this timeline. In his Birth World he was a small-time traffic reporter in a mid-size station, earning $31,000 a year. He lived in a small apartment in Bethesda and just barely eked out an existence. But there was a purpose for the sacrifice. In preparations for his final push from millionaire into billionaire status he had been stealing and installing Microwave Vertical Array ELF (extremely low frequency) systems, cell phone relays. These were the miracle machines that made cell phone conversations possible.

He had been disguising himself as an electrician and had been placing the relays in his new world on strategic tall buildings throughout D.C., and in the Philadelphia area. Over the years he had learned enough about the basics that he was ready to launch a cell-phone revolution and corner the market before the low-tech wizards of his new world even had time to dream about pirating such a product. He already had stolen and reinstalled 100 cell phone ELF systems, and had them powered up. He'd brought over enough computer power and stolen software to handle 10,000 customers, initially. He had purchased 275 cases of a basic model Nokia cell phone, brought them one case at a time through his portal, and had them stored in a warehouse in D.C. How they were "Made in Japan," he wouldn't be able to explain.

Planning to distribute half of the phones for free, and sell the other half to a few gangsters in town, he knew he'd start a feeding frenzy in a portable phone, text-starved world. Though they didn't know it yet, he assumed these people here needed to tweet, text, and talk with mobility, joining the rest of his Birth World in their attachments to the one piece of technology no one could seem to live without. He could eventually license the technology to an electronics manufacturer, who would reverse-engineer the phones, making him a multi-billionaire within two years. That was his plan.

He woke up on this particular morning bruised and swollen from his encounter with Tate. But he was hard working, if not exactly honest. He would place his final array before making the cell phone network public in a few days. His small sports car had just enough room in the trunk for the final ELF array he would install on the roof of the Capitol Parking Garage, in D.C.

•••••

Agent Tate had just picked up his partner and they were on their way to the West Wing Diner, for a quick breakfast. Their plan was to head into Gettysburg to meet with Joey and Anthony and to try to learn the whereabouts of Suzanne and the fugitive strangers.

Chapter 29

The bridge was closed and non-essential personnel were evacuated while the bomb squad removed and examined the device in Henry Rollins' car. The doctor was sitting in an interrogation room, by himself, at a table, when a guard came to remove the handcuffs and speak to him.

"Your story checks out, Dr. Rollins," said the guard who returned his ID and helped the Doctor to his feet.

"Thank you, sir," he said. "You were one of the first guards at my car earlier, weren't you?"

"Yes, I was. You gave us quite a scare," he said.

"I can imagine so," said Rollins. "The device must have looked especially suspicious after doing combat duty in Iraq or Afghanistan?" The guard looked at him and raised an eyebrow.

"I don't know what you mean," he said unconvincingly.

"Iraq?" quizzed Rollins. "That's my guess. How many tours of duty did you have to endure?"

"Let's walk outside, Dr. Rollins. They're preparing to release you," said the guard. "The two men left the confines of the interrogation room with its two-way mirror and audio monitoring system. Once outside and away from earshot of prying officials, the guard spoke.

"How did you know?"

"You shouted I.E.D. several times," said Rollins. "Only a soldier who'd worked in Iraq or Afghanistan would know that term. I read the *USA Today*. I know all about Improvised Explosive Devices. I was just surprised when you did as well."

The guard was speechless.

"You're not crazy," said Rollins "You're a Traveler. You've crossed over, that's all. You're part of an elite club that's larger than you might think. Look, here's my number, call me and we'll work through this together. Don't worry, your secret's safe with me. By the way, didn't you recognize the cell phone?"

The man hesitated as if still not quite sure about what Rollins was telling him. "I did, and that's why I shouted. The damned insurgents used cell phones all the time to detonate their shit. And when I saw it rigged to a car battery, I assumed the worst. Instinct, I guess. But it wasn't a cell phone was it?"

"Yes, actually it is and I can see how that would look funny to anybody. Wasn't too smart of me, I guess." They arrived at his car and traffic was already moving. The checkpoint had re-opened.

"Thank you Dr. Rollins. Sorry for the trouble."

"No harm done. My elbow is a bit sore. You guys are kind of rough."

"Sorry, again. I *will* call you. I'm looking forward to talking with you."

"Just give me time to get home and take a nap, then call later." Rollins got back into his small car, his 83-years catching up with him. He regained his composure, started the car's motor, and headed back over the bridge, back toward the road that would lead him home, to a very worried woman.

•••••

Tate and his partner arrived at the West Wing Diner at 4:40 a.m. They ordered a full breakfast and coffee and waited in silence for the food. Billy Kay arrived five minutes later and almost walked out when he spotted the agents. He decided then and there, he wasn't going to let them intimidate him. In a matter of days, he would own them. Kay slapped Tate on the back, a little harder than necessary and Tate spilled a little of his coffee.

"Fancy meeting you guys here!" he said, faking enthusiasm. The diner was busy and Tate didn't feel like putting on a show for the crowd, but the slap on the back tempted him.

"Yeah, Kay. How are you? Feeling alright?" he asked.

"Funny you should ask. I've had a stiff neck for three months now and suddenly I'm cured. I've never felt better, it's like I've been to the Chiropractor, thanks for asking."

"The Chiro...what?" asked Tate.

"Never mind, you wouldn't understand," he said, still goading the agent. He went to the other end of the counter, ordered a coffee with 'wheels' and made his way back toward the door.

"Stay in town, Kay. We may need you again."

"You got it, fellas. I'll be on the air in 25 minutes. Be sure to tune me in."

"Oh yeah, we'll be listening," said Tate who turned toward his just arriving eggs and sausage.

•••••

Henry Rollins pulled over to the first phone booth he could find and called home. Margaret, relieved to hear from him, just barely managed not to cry. They both knew the risks involved with helping those who crossed over, but this group of Travelers posed a greater risk to their safety than any before. Rollins and Margaret both wished cell phones did exist; it was the one piece of technology Margaret couldn't import and make work in the new universe.

Moments after finishing the call to his very relieved wife, Rollins was back on the road toward home. Tired as he was, he looked forward to telling them about his ordeal at the border, and how calm and cool he had been, and about a new Traveler he'd met.

At 5:15 a.m. Rollins pulled his car into his own driveway, having completed his mission, like the good soldier he was. He'd retrieved Fuller's cell phone and facilitated the safe send-off of Suzanne. They greeted him on the porch and he was glad for the welcome and the friendly faces. Margaret cried and they hugged, and she moved inside to get coffee going.

"How'd she take it?" asked Fuller, his mind always on Suzanne, and to his surprise, less on Susan. He couldn't explain the subtle shift, and shook off the unsettling feeling.

"As you would suspect," said Rollins. "She's become very attached to you, Tommy. This will be hardest on her."

"Why couldn't Margaret get in touch with Susan, somehow, on one of her trips home?" asked Fuller.

"Normally she could, and she would," said Rollins, "but, as you may recall, we've recently discovered that we don't share a Birth Earth. You all are aliens to us, and visa-versa. You, or a version of you, is likely in our old universe. Anything we could say wouldn't make any sense to you, or any Susan we may find there."

He shook his head in disbelief at the entire premise, at what he was being asked to believe. His thoughts returned to Susan, and his messages.

"Did you get my cell phone?"

"I did. It's in my trunk." When he told Tommy the car was unlocked and where to find the trunk release button, Fuller dashed off to reclaim the item he'd been obsessing over for 36 hours. When he saw the phone his heart skipped a beat. The power was on and battery indicator was full, so he unclipped the leads. He tried to make a call, ignoring the 'No Signal' message on the screen. He took the phone into the house and rejoined the group who had settled in the living room.

"Here it is," said Tommy showing the phone to the group, a little less enthusiastic than they had expected him to be. "I've got five new

266

messages. Are we ready?"

"When your phone played "*Dixie*" at the border crossing, you'd have thought it was the end of the world," said Rollins. "They were sure it was a Con-Fed bomb. I guess it could seem a bit suspicious."

Fuller pushed the 'SPKR' button, and hit the 'MSGS' button, and what they all heard sucked the air out of the room.

A muffled digital recording played back the entire horrifying scene from three days earlier, universes away. It began with footsteps, faster, then running. Then came Tommy's moans and desperate narration.

'Oh no. Not now – not dressed like this.'

They listened in horror as the music of a subwoofer distorted the small speaker, and then a car's tires scream and burn. They listened to the laughter and taunting of the teenagers, of Tommy telling them 'Stop, or I'll shoot.' They heard the mailbox being bashed by an aluminum baseball bat, and Tommy grunt as he ducked away from the swinging weapon. They heard the metallic 'snap' as Tommy clicked the bayonet in place. Then they heard, as clearly as if it were happening in their midst, the click of the trigger and the blast of Tommy Fuller's musket, and the shot that ended a 17-year-old life.

Suppressing gasps for breath and approaching hysteria, Tommy pressed 'PAUSE,' and the others looked up at him.

"You know this goes a long way toward proving your innocence," said Phillips. "Tommy. We'll win with this."

Tommy Fuller collapsed on the couch, putting his forearm to his eyes. He cried uncontrollably for 30 seconds before gathering his composure. The conflicting emotions wrenched him, and screamed, bouncing around his skull: 'Stay with Suzanne, go home to Susan, go home to a murder trial, though one he might now stand a chance to win.'

"Tommy, dear – this is all too much for one day," said Margaret, with a hand on his knee. "Let's please listen to the rest tomorrow. None of us need any more surprises. Ok, sweetheart? Please, Tommy."

Tommy flipped the phone shut, and placed it on the coffee table. "You're so right. I need sleep," he said.

"We all do," she added. "You boys need to get some sleep and so does this old man, and so do I. I'll wake you if it gets too late." They made their way to their respective bedrooms and crashed hard.

After lying in bed for three hours, still unable to sleep, Tommy Fuller again snuck down the stairs and picked up his only link to his life back home. The phone was still fully charged and still displayed "No Signal." He slipped it into his shirt pocket and quietly crept outside into the cool night air. The sky was just turning from black to a deep, dark blue, indicating an oncoming sunrise; one that would signal day four in this strange new place.

He walked around the grounds of the Rollins' home trying to get the worries off his mind, and find a safe, quiet place to listen to the rest of his recorded messages, and break down in private, if necessary. It was beautiful country and Tommy always felt better when communing with the natural world. Trees and lakes and streams and ponds were the things and places that helped him sort out his troubles, and they were in abundance in this universe. A 30-foot rise, just south of the house, might afford a better view, he thought, so he hiked up the hill.

From the top he could see a few scattered farms, but nothing he could see would indicate that he was less than an hour from Washington D.C. Further to the west, not very many miles away, lay Sharpsburg and Antietam. Gettysburg was just to the north and Fuller realized he was standing in the midst of many of the Civil War's bloodiest battlefields, yet on this night all was quiet. Quiet is always preferred to war, he thought. "God, don't make me go back there..."

With his heart almost beating out of his chest, Tommy opened his phone and pressed 'PWR' and then 'MSGS' and held the phone to his ear. He fought back tears as he again listened to the worst single moment of his life, in real time. When he reached the point in the recording, where he'd pressed pause earlier in the house, just after the gunshot, what he heard almost made him pass out. The voices of the screaming boys morphed into that of soldiers, circa 1863. Bass and sub-woofer notes changed from rhythmic hip-hop music into erratic artillery shelling and faded back to Tommy slamming his truck door shut. "END OF MESSAGE," said the robotic voice, abruptly.

His accidental seven-minute recording, made through a tiny microphone, through a series of microchips to an SD card, had recorded his first transfer through a Schwarzschild Wormhole - possibly the first-ever audio recording of a theoretical event. What Tommy couldn't know was that 12 hours after the shooting, the police found high-definition video footage from a nearby security camera, which had captured most all of the event in detail. Besides watching the clear self-defense of the Civil War reenactor, the police were stunned at what they saw next. The shooter seemed to vanish and reappear three times in the course of the event, before finally getting up and leaving the scene in his vehicle. They watched, and re-watched, not trusting what they were seeing, but it was unmistakable, and unexplainable.

The science and importance of the accidental cell phone recording was lost on Tommy. He was multiple universes away, sitting atop a hill in some version of a Maryland countryside, wrapped up in the content of what he'd just heard. He looked down at his phone, which was daring him to play the next message. He took the bait.

The second message was from Susan. "Tommy! Tommy! Please call me back, or answer your phone. The police are at the front of the house." "END OF MESSAGE." Tommy pressed 'NXT MSG, 3' "Tommy! Where are you? The police are in the living room. They need to talk to you." "END OF MESSAGE." NXT MSG, 4, "Tommy...I don't know where you are, or if you're getting these messages. You're in a lot of trouble if you don't turn yourself in. Please." "END OF MESSAGE." NXT MSG, 5, "Hi Mr. Fuller? This is Detective Tate of the Federal Bureau of Investigation. It's imperative that you contact our office, right away. Thank you...." Tommy couldn't believe what his ears were telling him, as the detective finished by leaving his phone number, and then he heard someone who must have been nearby, strike a match. "END OF MESSAGES."

•••••

"Couldn't sleep, either?" Rollins asked Tommy as he walked back into the house through its side door.

"No. But hey, thanks for getting this phone for me," he said holding it up. "I listened to my messages. Not really much help. Sorry I was so worked up over it."

"No matter, my boy. It could have been important. I'm almost afraid to ask. What were the other messages like?"

"Mostly my wife, wondering where the hell I am, telling me I'm in trouble. And one...this one blows my mind... from the other version of the guy, that Agent, Tate, who's chasing us. Looks like that dude is after me everywhere I go, or have ever been."

•••••

Agent Tate and his partner were at the D.C. Border checkpoint, just 30-minutes after Rollins' had been allowed to leave. With information traveling slowly, by 2013 standards, they had been unaware of the emergency border closing until they heard it over their radio as they were pulling into the parking lot at the guard station.

Tate flashed his credentials at the approaching guard who invited them inside the small building.

"What happened here?" asked Tate.

"Oh, false alarm," said the guard. "Some old geezer had something in his trunk that looked an awful lot like a bomb and a couple of my men overreacted. We were only down about 30 minutes. The guy checked out alright."

"Which way was he traveling?" asked Tate, not yet suspecting anything too unusual.

"He was inbound; coming in to Fed-Stat. He's a Yank."

269

"Was he alone?" asked Tate. His partner lit up a cigarette.

"Yep. By himself. Turns out he's a pretty high-level guy. We were a little embarrassed but he was nice enough about it. He has All Access and Level Two clearance from both North and South."

Neither agent made the connection between Tommy's phone and what the guards had called a "radio bomb." There was nothing overly alarming in the border closing itself, as they were not uncommon, happening once or twice a month. Only the raised Alert Level had everyone a little more on edge, but a growing indifference to government alerts had already sapped much of their usefulness, and citizens and law enforcement both, were beginning to question their significance and utility. The agents continued their drive to Gettysburg, unaware that once again they had just missed their quarry.

•••••

Later in the morning, Margaret and her houseguests were surprised to find Dr. Rollins and Tommy napping in the living room, and they quietly made their way past them to the kitchen. The smell and sound of sizzling bacon coaxed the nappers from their chairs and again they all gathered around the island counter in the Rollins' kitchen.

"Good morning you two," said Margaret. "Our beds aren't good enough?"

"Oh no, they're fine, Mrs. Rollins," said Tommy, who couldn't bring himself to call her Margaret. "I just haven't been able to sleep too well. I do have some news, though."

He told the group about retrieving his messages, and that besides that which they'd heard, they contained little of any interest. Jackson suspected Fuller was hiding something, but couldn't place it.

"There's a young lady that would benefit from hearing from you," said Margaret. "Breakfast will be another 15 minutes, so use the phone in the living room, if you like." He got the distinct impression from her tone that this was not a friendly suggestion, but something more along the lines of a motherly directive.

He slid his chair out from the island and walked from the kitchen. He had no idea what to say to Suzanne. He knew she'd be heartbroken at the separation, possibly furious, and would feel like he had rejected her, but he also knew he had to talk with her. He knew Margaret was right.

"Dr. Rollins, where did you crossover?" asked Phillips. "Do you have any idea why you can't cross back?"

"I think I can answer both of those questions," said Rollins thoughtfully. "It started two years after Margaret had accidentally crossed over and barely made it back. That was in the early 1940s. I couldn't stop thinking about the physics involved in such a feat, and when I made enough noise about it to Dr. Einstein, he brought me on board as his assistant. I crossed over in 1943, quite by accident, when I was on board the USS Eldridge. So there I was, a 20-year-old civilian working with Einstein on the Rainbow Project."

"The *Rainbow* Project?" asked Jackson. "Wasn't that a Gay Pride float in the 2013 St. Paddy's Day Parade?"

"Not quite, Greg," he answered with a slight smile that acknowledged a pretty good joke, and a pop culture reference that even the old Doc could enjoy.

"You might know it as the *Philadelphia Experiment.*"

"I've heard of it, but don't really have a clue. You've lost me," said Phillips.

"The Navy denies it, of course, but it's been rumored for years that the Government was involved in teleportation experiments, and that in 1943, the *Eldridge*, a Navy destroyer was made invisible and teleported from Philadelphia to Norfolk, Virginia. Dr. Einstein himself worked on the project. Well guess what? They did it...sort of. And I was on board and I assisted. But the teleportation wasn't exactly a complete success. Fifty-three men died, three went missing, and they unceremoniously canceled the Top Secret project. I am one of the three missing men. I've never been able to locate the other two." He took a deep breath.

"Immediately after we activated the device, which turned the entire ship into the world's largest electro-magnet, I woke up in water, floating two miles out to sea, my hair still smoldering, the metal shirt buttons sizzling in the sea water, and burning into my chest; I still have the scars. I saw the lights of what I guessed was Norfolk off in the distance and I treaded water, steaming, for a minute, trying to get my bearings. Luckily I had on a life vest and the sharks weren't hungry that evening. I didn't know exactly where I was at first, but I assumed the invisible ship was in the harbor, where we had tried to direct it through a series of receiver radio magnets. I later found out the ship had vanished and reappeared right where she was berthed, but without me on board."

"Amazing," said Jackson, who was well acquainted with the legend.

"I swam toward the shoreline with the help of the tide," continued Rollins, "and I saw something very strange. The Norfolk NAVY yard where I arrived was flying the Confederate flag, which I figured had to be some sort of prank. Crossing over hadn't even dawned on me. The more I looked around, the more I realized something was very wrong. Remember the feeling you had when you first arrived here? You question your sanity, you feel nauseous; it's horrible. I hid out until daylight and hitchhiked, soaking wet, to Maryland and tried to find Margaret, Professor Einstein, or any of my teaching associates. None of them were here. The College was here but that was about it, so I hitch-hiked to my hometown."

"Then I was really confused when I read about my own disappearance in a newspaper I'd never heard of before. Supposedly some version of me had been sorting mail one minute and was gone the next. I now realize that I pushed poor Hank right out of the Post Office into, well, who knows? I was very worried about my Margaret, who was back home in our original universe. I was sure she'd have no idea where, or how, to find me."

"The whole Rainbow Project was so shrouded in secrecy and subsequent cover-ups that she didn't even know I was ever on board the *Eldridge*. I learned my lesson. Never keep those things from your wife, even if you're sworn to secrecy." Tommy Fuller thought of how hard it was to explain to Suzanne what they'd gone through, and how great she'd been, and what a relief it was to have said it aloud.

"I eventually made it to our old home, actually Hank's old home," said Rollins, "which we are now sitting in. I walked right into this house and started taking over Hank's life here. I felt guilty as hell, but it would have been harder on the people here for me to have disappeared, especially after they'd lost Maggie. The Police here suspected me of murder for a while. And anyway, I didn't have a choice. I didn't know how to get back. Two weeks later Margaret, my Margaret, walked back into my life. She found me, right here, in this house."

"How?" asked Jackson.

"I spent days and days frantically digging into the things Henry was involved in," said Margaret. "I was desperate. I went to Princeton, NJ, to talk directly to Henry's boss, Mr. Einstein. He denied knowing anything about it at first, but I was relentless, and because he was a good and kind man he broke down and told me what had happened with the Eldridge and his theory about wormholes. I understood none of it, of course, but I knew then and there that Henry might still be alive somewhere, and that I'd have to look for him. And through providence, I found him."

"Incredible," said Phillips. "And Henry, you can't get back because of...?"

"The *Eldridge*," answered Jackson who already knew most of the story from a conspiracy theorist professor he loved to listen to back at Harvard.

"That's right," said Henry. "The *Eldridge* was never even built in this timeline. That was problem one. And back home they covered up the disaster the best they could and eventually sold the ship to the Greeks. Some claim she was decommissioned by Greece and sold for scrap, others claim she still exists as a Greek Navy vessel under a new name. I don't know. I've never been able to get to the bottom of it. Interestingly enough, the *Eldridge* regularly traveled through a part of the Atlantic we all know as the Bermuda Triangle."

While her husband was telling the unbelievable tale, Margaret placed five plates of eggs, bacon, toast and orange slices around the island, and went into the living room to check on her youngest charge. He was just finishing his call.

"She's very upset," said Fuller. Margaret placed a hand on his shoulder. "She really doesn't want to, or can't talk. I couldn't quite figure out which. I think her ex-boyfriend is there."

"Come to breakfast. You'll feel better after you've eaten."

Chapter 30

Agent Tate and his partner arrived in Gettysburg at 9:15 a.m. and went straight to Fuller's Auto. Two local Gettysburg Police patrol cars were parked in front, and the agents stretched the crime scene tape to make their way into the vandalized garage.

"This is exactly the way we found it," said Bob Fuller to one of the officers who turned to see Tate and his partner walking in.

"Hey! This is a crime scene, you guys can't come in here," said a middle-aged, big-bellied Sheriff, walking over to the agents with plans to escort them out. Tate showed his credentials.

"Big friggin' deal," said the cop. "You have no jurisdiction here whatsoever."

"Look closer," said Tate to the cop as he pushed the I.D. in his face.

"F.S.C.-S.C.I. Federated States / Confederate States Cooperative Investigators," the Sheriff read aloud. "What's this shit?"

"Don't you guys ever read a memo?" asked Tate. "It means I work for your redneck government, Bocephus, and that I'm authorized not only in Washington, D.C., but in Richmond, too. It means I'll have your fat ass imprisoned if you don't back the hell up and move out of *my* crime scene."

A toothpick hung from the corner of the big cop's mouth, and he kicked a small pebble on the garage floor.

"Have it your way, Tate," he said with a fake smile. He nodded slightly and tipped his hat.

"Bye, bye," said Tate, oozing sarcasm. The two local cops walked away from the service bays.

"What the hell happened here?" asked Tate, looking at the twins.

"Some fool broke in last night," said Bob Fuller, trying not to show his anger at how the agents had just bullied his friend, the Sheriff. "You know you really should have let my boys here help us out. This is just a local deal. They don't take kindly to being pushed around, either."

Tate ignored the admonition. "What makes you so sure this is a 'local deal'?"

"Looks like some kids did it. Probably broke stuff just for the fun of it. Stole some tools, a couple of car batteries…"

"And how about our friend's radio device?"

Fuller scratched his head.

"Huh?" He hadn't even realized it was missing until he looked at the work bench where it had been the night before. "Well I'll be damned. They took that, too."

Tate looked around and smelled a staged crime scene. It was little things, a gut feeling from years as a detective who relied on intuition and observation. He looked at the broken skylight and examined the broken glass on the floor. He picked up the largest piece and saw dried, red blood smeared across the corner. He surveyed the rest of the garage and noticed a bloody paper towel on the floor near the sink. "No burglar alarm?"

"Hell no."

"Who knows you're without alarms?"

"Probably everybody in town. No one has alarms except the bank and the Post Office."

"Call my office in D.C. if anything comes up," said Tate, handing Bob Fuller his card. "Come on lets go visit young Anthony, see what he has to say."

·····

The knock on the door was intrusive. Everybody in the apartment had been fast asleep. When Tate kicked in the locked door, which had just been repaired from a similar, recent forced entry, Anthony and Joey nearly ran into one another coming out of their bedrooms, half dressed.

"What the fu…?" Anthony asked, before Tate slapped him across the face.

"Do you think we're fools?" demanded Tate. "I guess you must think we're stupid and that we don't know you've been playing us?"

"What do you mean?" cried Anthony, hurt by the implication, and the slap.

"The radio device. Where is it?"

"It's over at Fuller's."

"Don't play stupid with me kid." Tate raised his hand to strike him again.

"It's there, Mr. Tate. We left it right there until you got here. Just like you said." Tate saw the kid's expression and decided he was telling the truth.

"Who else knew it was there?"

"Just the twins. Bob and Billy... and Joey and me." Tate turned toward the younger boy.

"Well 'Hi' Joey? How you been?"

"Fine," he said, not looking up.

"You wouldn't happen to know where the device is, would ya?"

"No." Joey's hands were in the pockets of the jeans he had thrown on. Tate grabbed Joey's left arm, wrenching his hand from inside his pocket. The agent looked carefully, and saw nothing out of the ordinary.

"Let's see the other one, Joey?"

The boy slowly pulled out his right hand to reveal a large, bandage.

"Aww, poor Joey. You cut yourself?" He didn't answer. "Did you cut yourself on a skylight?"

"No. I broke a glass." He pointed to the sink where pieces of the water glass they had broken in his fight with Anthony still lay. Tate moved his face to within inches from Joey's own.

"Are you sure?"

"He didn't do it. I did," said Suzanne, walking into the room. "Leave him alone. I broke in, I stole the thing for Tommy, and I gave it to him. We snuck back over the border into the North and he's long gone. Joey and Anthony had nothing to do with this."

"My, my, my," said Tate. "What a den of thieves and liars we have here. We've been looking for you and your pals, you know. Now tell me what you've been up to, little lady. You and your Freedom Fighters have a little surprise planned for the Capitol of the Federated States of America?"

"No," Suzanne said, looking straight into Tate's eyes.

"We know your friends are plotting something big; the question is where?"

Suzanne didn't answer. Tate walked toward her. "I'm really getting tired of playing games with you little punks! Where are they and what are they up to?"

When she didn't answer Tate reared back to slap her across the face with the back of his hand. She cringed as the powerful man's hand swung in a perfect ark toward her jaw. He was stopped when Anthony dove for him, knocking him to the ground. Tate's partner reached for his gun and Joey dove at him like a flying Ninja, knocking a lit cigarette out of his mouth.

A single gunshot reverberated through the room. No neighbors came to investigate. That just wasn't done.

The four of them lay in a pile in the middle of the living room. Suzanne screamed and pulled her brother, like a limp ragdoll, from underneath the rotund agent struggling to get up. Tate and Anthony scrambled to their feet. They were all in a bit of shock, the noise of the gunshot still ringing in their ears. Tate's partner stood, the smoking gun in

276

his hand, a smoking cigarette on the floor. Tate pulled his revolver from its holster and yelled at Anthony to lie on the ground, hands behind his head. Suzanne fell to her knees and rocked her brother in her arms, crying, stroking his hair.

"What happened?" came the weak voice of the teen. "My head. I hit my freakin' head on something."

Suzanne laughed and cried simultaneously. "Joey. You fool. Don't ever do that to me again. Are you shot?" He sat up feeling his body for gunshot wounds and found none. Tate's partner had missed him and, in fact, hadn't intended on firing at all. The fat man picked up his still smoldering cigarette, and seemed as relieved as anyone in the room, to see the youth unharmed.

"All of you, up on your feet, hands behind your head," Tate commanded, gun pulled. "Tape or rope. Where is it?" No one answered. "Now!" he screamed. Anthony pointed to the pantry above the washing machine where a few odd tools and a roll of Con-Fed government brand duct tape were visible. Tate's partner retrieved the tape and bound their wrists with several tight wraps.

"You're going to the safe house until we get this sorted out." The agents marched their prisoners out of the apartment and into their car, shoving the three into the back seat. When they arrived at the safe house and were inside the garage, Tate turned to look at them. "I don't know what kind of heroic crap you think you're pulling, but this freedom fighting isn't kid's stuff, and you're all in way over your heads. I will find out who those guys are and what they're up to. I always succeed. Always."

They made their way down the familiar stairway of the safe house and the shorter agent used a pocketknife to cut the three loose.

"Let's sit down and figure this out," said Tate, trying a new, softer approach. "Things got out of hand back there and there's no reason for that. I'm just trying to figure out what happened to our…our relationship. I thought we had an understanding here."

Joey, Anthony and Suzanne suddenly realized the irony of having traded spots with the three men they'd met four days earlier.

"They kidnapped her and brain-washed her, Mr. Tate," said Joey, suddenly fessing up. "They made me fake a break-in to get their radio thingy and meet them near the border."

"Joey!" yelled Suzanne, rolling her eyes.

"And then they traded her for the thing and we came back here. That's it. That's everything."

Tate thought about the revelation and looked at the boy.

"Okay, now we're making progress. Thank you, Joey, for finally telling me straight. Look, we need you guys. We like you guys. But we've gotta know that we're on the same team, and I gotta be honest, I'm not really feeling much mutual trust. We're on the same side, right?"

"I thought we were," said Anthony, "until you decided to shoot at us."

"I am sorry for that," said Tate. He looked angrily at his partner, who knew the stern look was an act. "But we've just got to be sure, so…you're going to be here for a while. We've got to sort some of this out and we need to know where the three of you are and can't have any more nonsense. We'll be back."

The agents left the safe house, locking the solid steel door behind them. As they pulled out of the garage, Tate's partner spoke. "Sorry about the gunshot, boss."

"I'm sorry you didn't kill the little bastard," said Tate. "Let's go over to the surveillance room and listen in on these stupid kids. Maybe we'll pick something up; Joey seems to want to talk."

They drove less than five minutes straight across town to a small, unassuming house, just like every other house on the block, and once again fired up the machinery that would allow them to listen in on their captives, if they were dumb enough to talk.

•••••

Filled with home-cooked comfort food to the point of being overstuffed, the four men helped Margaret with the dishes and then walked out to the porch. The summer day was warmer and clearer than the past several and they all welcomed the change.

"Maverick is very happy when the sun shines," said Dr. Rollins. The dog was entertaining himself by throwing a stick in the air and fetching it. They sat watching his enthusiastic antics and felt their hearts lift slightly.

"I've been giving this a lot of thought," started Rollins, looking over his glasses, "and I know you have as well. I would like to offer up a plan of sorts, and hear what you think."

"Hell yes," said Jackson. "This is what I've been waiting for."

"I think there's a chance I can get you home, and here's how. First, I'm afraid, we've got to get you back to Gettysburg. Our best bet, I think, might require that we match up, as much as possible, with the day you crossed over: that means the same hour of the day, in the same clothing, at the exact spot, that's most important. That will give us our best chance. It's just a chance. Tommy, your cap. May I look at it?"

"Sure," said Tommy as he handed over the relic.

Holding the artifact was electric. Rollins had only to close his eyes to see into the past, imagine the man who wore it, hear the gunshot that took his life, and envision the carnage that was this great and bloody battle. He took a deep breath.

"I think this cap may be the key. Like Margaret's dress, this cap may activate the wormhole. This is not a reproduction, right?"

"No, this is the real deal," said Fuller. "I bought it at an antique store about five or six years ago. Get this, we think it might have belonged to Thomas Grissom, the brother of the guy who led us away from the explosion."

"I didn't realize that," said Rollins. "That's remarkable. And way beyond coincidence, if you ask me. Where are your costumes, anyway?"

"Uniforms," corrected Phillips, with a smile. "Our uniforms are probably still at the place they were calling the 'safe house'."

"We may need to get those back as well – I don't know, but it could be important, especially if we end up in...," he couldn't bring himself to say 'battle,' so he compromised. "...in 1863." No one liked the thought of re-entering the hellish nightmare that was The Battle of Gettysburg, but it was becoming more likely by the minute. "We've got one shot at this and have to match everything we possibly can."

"Oh great," said Jackson. "I was hoping it would get more difficult."

Rollins continued. "Once over the border, we get to your uniforms, head to the battlefield and try to make the jump. If my guesses are right we'll simply reverse the order in which you arrived. We'll go back to 1863 first, and then you'll crossover to your home Earth and I believe you'll arrive sometime in 2013."

"What about you, Henry?" asked Jackson.

"Well...I won't live in a world without my Margaret, and I'm hoping that traveling with you, who are already proven to be multiples, that the cosmos will land me in the right place, home with Margaret, the place I'm supposed to be. It's not in your universe, or here in this one, it's somewhere in between."

"You definitely want to try this?" asked Jackson.

"I mean to try, if you'll allow me," said Rollins looking at the group, and smiling at Margaret. "My portal is gone. It can't be accessed. If I am to ever travel home it will be as part of a group, as a Multiple. You, my friends are such a group, a rare group of multiples. The first I've ever known personally. And this corner of the planet seems to be primed for multiples, but I've never before known any first hand, and known the exact spot of the crossing, until you all arrived."

"Is this region really that busy with this kind of stuff?" asked Jackson.

"Yes, absolutely. It's really the whole eastern seaboard. The first reported multiple disappearance was the lost Colony of Roanoke Island in 1587. It's fact. One hundred people disappeared without a trace. And I hardly need to tell you about the Triangle."

"As in Bermuda?"

"Is there any other? Christopher Columbus had troubles there, and that's just where its history starts. Hundreds of ships, dozens of planes, thousands of people have all disappeared, mostly on calm seas and in clear skies. In 1948 a DC-3 with 31 passengers and crew vanished without a trace, just after the pilot radioed he was making his final approach into Miami. They were minutes from landing and within sight of the airport. No wreckage, no May-Day, nothing."

Rollins leaned forward and continued recounting all the disappearances he could think of. "Between 1920 and 1950, in Bennington, Vermont, dozens of people disappeared before the eyes of very credible witnesses. Three women and their car disappeared in New York after going through the Lincoln Tunnel. Construction crew witnesses saw the car go in, but it never came out." Rollins took a breath.

"Yes, this area is very busy. It's a rabbit's warren of worm holes and inter-connecting time tubes. And if you still aren't convinced, consider yourselves. You all and your truck are proof of a multiple crossing."

"So how will this all work?" asked Fuller.

"Margaret will go first through her portal. If we somehow change the history in this timeline, I want her where it's safe. And, as much as I hate the thought of it, I think I owe it to Billy Kay to let him know as well. He won't like it, but I've got to tell him what we're up to. Once Margaret and Kay have crossed over, we'll time our visit to retrieve your uniforms and make it to Emmitsburg Road no later than 10 a.m.

"Why 10:00 a.m.? asked Phillips.

"Because that's just before the explosion originally took place. History books are wonderful things. You should read them sometime." He winked at Phillips. "Well, that's the best-case scenario. The hard reality is that we have to sneak across the border when the whole world seems to be looking for you. Then we have to retrieve your uniforms without these agents or anyone else knowing. Then we have to get to Emmitsburg Road, and if we're lucky, jump back in time 150 years. God, I hate to think about that mess... and then cross over, back home into who knows what? I'm afraid that's my best offer."

"When do we go?" asked Greg Jackson. "And trust me, we are going to fix this mess. We made it, we'll clean it up."

•••••

"What do we do now?" asked Joey. "We're locked in." He plopped himself down in the big easy chair and put his feet on the table. He smiled unexpectedly, a random thought just entering his head. "You know, so far I've missed every day of school this week. That is *so* great." He was genuinely pleased with himself.

"This ain't good, you guys," said Anthony, ignoring Joey's levity. "They're playing hardball and we better come up with something."

"Like what?" asked Suzanne. "We are not going to sell those guys out. Tommy and his friends are about the most harmless men I've ever known. They don't have guns, they're not even Freedom Fighters. All they want to do is get home."

The boys looked puzzled.

"Why did they send you back to Gettysburg?" asked Joey.

"Because... because I was in their way."

"So where is their home? Where are they trying to go?" asked Anthony.

"I'm not really sure, but it's a long way from here."

•••••

Margaret, who had finished with the last of the breakfast dishes, entered the sitting room, wiping her hands on a dishtowel.

"I'm headed into the other library for a while today." She and Henry used 'other' to differentiate which Library of Congress she would visit, in which universe.

"Fine, sweetheart. We'll be here. See you for supper, and be careful."

Margaret had already changed into the only clothing that allowed for crossing over. She and Henry both referred to it as 'cross-dressing.' She lifted her compass from around her neck, set her course for due east, took three steps into the den and vanished in the blink of an eye. For her it was no different than going through any doorway between any two rooms.

"That is so cool," said Phillips. "It's real Captain Kirk stuff. I can't believe how easy it is for her."

"She's been doing it for so long that it's all very matter of fact to us; but I know what you mean. Every time I watch her disappear I'm awestruck. I do worry though, and, I hate to admit...I get a little jealous." They sat for a moment looking at the empty room that was much more than it appeared, hiding invisible secrets of the universe.

"Okay, so we're set for tomorrow?" asked Fuller, breaking the spell they were under.

"Yes, we'll leave around six. That should get us to Gettysburg in plenty of time," said Rollins. "Our first stop is the place you said you changed clothing; you called it the 'safe house'. We'll go there, get you guys in your uniforms and head over to Emmitsburg Road. Then we pray. I have no idea if it will work. Margaret will have crossed over by then, so she'll be safe. I'll call Kay tomorrow and give him 30 or 40 minutes notice. I don't want him knowing too far in advance. It's hard to tell how he'll react. If we're talking about changing this history, that will really screw him up. I'm assuming you plan to try, right? It's up to you, of course. This is your world, you made it, you can do with it as you please."

They hadn't thought of it in those terms before, but he was right. It was easy to see how people become seduced by power and this amount of power was staggering. While Tommy Fuller struggled with the options, for Jackson and Phillips the decision was already made.

"You bet your ass we're going to change it," said Jackson. "Besides, we're not really changing things anyway; we're setting them straight, fixing this mess, that's all."

Phillips nodded in agreement. Fuller sat silently holding his Rebel cap, feeling the scratchy wool between his fingers.

"Has it ever occurred to you guys that maybe *our* home, is an alternate from somewhere else, somewhere quite different?" asked Fuller to no one in particular. "Why should we assume that our world is the *best* world, and the *only* world? Maybe we changed this one to the way it was supposed to have been? Has anyone ever considered that?"

No one responded. The question was too loaded with emotion, politics, and concepts that were unfathomable.

"I feel like taking a walk," said Fuller. "You think it would be okay in the daylight with all the cops out there?

"I think probably," said Rollins. "The police seem to be concentrating on the borders and the highway. We're far enough out into the countryside where you'll be all right. Just stay off the roads."

"A hike sounds like a good idea," said Phillips. "This may be the last day we'll ever see this world. Mind if I tag along?"

Before Fuller could answer, Greg Jackson also spoke up. "I can't wait for tomorrow," he said. "You guys go. I'll stick around. Maybe I'll hide in the basement. If you see Harriet Tubman out there, send her my way."

It was obvious that Maverick wanted to go as well, so the two men and the Retriever set out in the cool morning air to enjoy the Rollins' farm and surrounding hills and hollows. They needed to muster strength and courage for the task ahead.

•••••

The July heat was warming the Maryland countryside, but it was still cool enough to make for a fine day of hiking. As Mike Phillips and Tommy Fuller walked through the fields, the younger man thought about how often he and Susan had hiked through the hills near Gettysburg and how much they had enjoyed the riverbank in the spring and summer. They shared their first kiss when they were both still teenagers while on a long walk. But he and Susan had grown apart. She was unhappy, and he felt powerless to change that. Though he couldn't prove it, he had it on pretty good authority that she had been unfaithful, more than once. Though they never discussed it, he had forgiven her, but he always felt she was so unhappy, and that he was the cause of her misery and infidelity. They'd both privately thought about divorce, but neither had the courage or strength to bring it up. He wondered how she was handling the shooting and his disappearance.

The patchwork of farms on the distant hills and the relative quiet was as peaceful a setting as at Suzanne's hunting cabin. They sensed an unusual and indefinable beauty in this place, and something about being outdoors and in nature soothed and emboldened both men for the task ahead. As content and calm as they were at that moment, Maverick was beside himself with enthusiasm. He acted as a tour guide, as if he'd roamed every square inch of the bucolic landscape, which probably he had. Once Phillips had made the mistake of casually tossing a stick, Maverick was relentless in his insistence on playing fetch, man's best friend, indeed.

"This was a good Idea, Tommy – this hike," said Phillips.

"Yeah, I do feel a little better. I'm still scared about going back, though. What in hell do we face if we pull this off?"

"Damn good question. We don't even know if this is going to work, so let's just get home first. Then we'll deal with your troubles, and our disappearance, once we've made it back. I think we have to stay focused on getting back."

Fuller was quiet.

With a stick still in his mouth, Maverick barked clumsily at Phillips. The dog was feeling ignored and he would have none of it. Phillips took the now soggy branch and hurled it like a boomerang and the dog was off.

Phillips began counting off the conditions of success on his fingers. "We've got to cross the border, get to the safe house, put our uniforms on, get to Emmitsburg Road, go back in time, stop the detonation in the middle of 200,000 troops actively engaged in battle, then go forward in time and cross over into our original universe, drop Doc off at some other universe while we're flying by... sounds easy enough." It was preposterous and monumental, and hearing it aloud created a renewed sense of dread. It was hard not to consider the plan anything but pure fantasy.

"Would you have ever imagined, in your wildest dreams, those words coming out of your mouth?" asked Fuller.

"Never," answered Phillips. "I'm still not 100 percent sure we're not dreaming."

They walked to the top of the ridge, the same ridge from which Tommy had retrieved the last of his phone messages. In the light of day they could see for many miles. Six miles to the southwest, snaking its way through the countryside, stood a 30-foot tall fence. This was the visible portion of the same fence that divided a nation and ran for thousands of miles, from the Chesapeake Bay all the way to the Rocky Mountains.

"There it is," said Phillips. "That damned border." They stood gazing at it. It was like viewing a smaller version of China's Great Wall. "I'd never imagined *that* in my wildest dreams, either. It's disgusting. That wall stinks to high heaven. I feel badly for these people." Fuller didn't comment.

Staring at the fence in the distance they silently took inventory of the changes in this world as a result of one battle 150 years earlier. Maverick, who had returned with the same soggy stick, sat still, quietly sniffing the air, sensing the sadness felt by the men as they looked at an international border, which should not be there. The border separated two nations, once whole, once filled with immigrants and refugees from around the world, united with the common cause of freedom for all.

As was true during the American Revolution, where "united we stand, divided we fall," became the rallying cry for 13 British Colonies seeking a better way of life, the new cry of the unification movement "UBD," "united is better than divided," promised a better, stronger land of the free, home of the brave.

But this was no longer the land of the free.

"We're so close to home we can't even imagine," said Phillips. "This has got to work, Tommy. We're going to make sure this works." They turned and walked back toward the house. Maverick followed quietly, sensing playtime was over.

Chapter 31

The safe house was well equipped for guests, or captives. Suzanne thought about calling Tommy, but she was too upset. Joey turned on the radio and tried to relax; he'd had a long night. After too many Extra C Cokes, Anthony was keyed up; the waiting was driving him crazy. Suzanne slept off and on in the recliner, too tired and too troubled to really sleep, or eat, or do much of anything but wait.

The agents were tired of waiting, too. "They're not talking," said Tate. "Let's flip the recorder on and get something to eat." The big machines hummed and came to life while giant reels of tape spun slowly. Each could hold 10 hours of non-stop audio, so Tate and his partner made their way to the nearest diner.

•••••

Margaret arrived home and was preparing a large meal for the men, and they again gathered around the kitchen's large island. They discussed the plan, but they were underfoot, so Margaret kicked them out of her kitchen into the living room. There the men found they were in general agreement with one another. The border was the biggest and first obstacle; crossing into a parallel universe seemed to pale in comparison.

"I can cross by myself at the border," said Rollins, "and you all take the footpath tunnel that Suzanne was talking about and I'll pick you up on the other side."

"What footpath tunnel? We don't know where that tunnel is," said Jackson. "Do you?"

"No, I'm afraid I don't. I thought you knew," said Rollins. The phone rang and Margaret answered.

"Henry – for you," she said, and he went to take the phone from her hand.

"Henry Rollins here."

"Yes, ahh Dr. Rollins this is…this is the guy you met earlier today." Rollins recognized his voice.

"Right from the…from Iraq?"

"Yes, it's me. I'd rather not talk on the phone."

"Yes, yes, quite right. How far are you from D.C.?" asked Rollins.

"I'm 30 minutes west of the city, more or less," said the border guard.

"*Bob*, you must know where the *hungry* like to eat?" said Rollins, hoping the less than cryptic code for Hungry Bob's restaurant was not too silly and yet was obvious enough to get the message across.

"I do," said the soldier, understanding the laughable attempt at stealth.

"I'll meet you there in 30-minutes," said Rollins, "and you can come meet some friends of mine and have dinner with us."

"That's…wow…okay. If you're sure?"

"Yes, of course I'm sure. We'll see you in 30 minutes." He hung up the phone and turned to the group who couldn't help overhearing the conversation. "I think I may have solved our border dilemma."

Dr. Rollins and Mike Phillips left the house and Rollins jingled his keys in the air. "Let's take my old Marathon. Who knows, it may be the last time I get to drive her." They went into the barn and Rollins slipped a canvas car cover from the mint condition 1985 Nashville Marathon. "She's my pride 'n' joy. Only 625 miles on this baby." They got into the car and after a few sluggish, groaning attempts, the engine turned over and the big car rumbled to life. They hurried down the driveway on the way to pick up their dinner guest. "I haven't finished telling you about the border guard," said Rollins. "He'll enjoy meeting you. He crossed over about three years ago and managed to work his way back into the military. Pretty resourceful. I think we need to offer him an attempt at crossing over with us."

"Is that wise?" asked Phillips. "Don't we need to keep the number down?"

"It really shouldn't make any difference if three or 23 try to cross. In a multiple crossing it takes the one with the X-Factor to act as the leader with the key, and I'm pretty sure that's Tommy Fuller. Everyone else in close proximity just follows. The trigger could be one of you others but, based on what you've told me, I think Tommy's the man. I think he's got X-Factor flowing out of his pores. I believe he had a number of crossings in the matter of an hour or two: the first on that street near his house in the midst of that tragic shooting affair, again when he was in his accident on the way to the reenactment, that's why his truck is here. The third time was during the battle, and you all were lucky enough to follow him over, and finally, I believe it was Tommy who brought you all here with him. With any luck we're going to follow him again," said Rollins with a friendly smile.

"With any luck you'll get us all back home, Dr. Rollins," said Phillips. "Via 1863, but back home nonetheless." He looked out the window at the passing countryside, lost in thought.

"You really think we'll be thrown into the middle of that damned battle again?" asked Phillips.

"I'm afraid so. It seems to be the logical progression. The first wormhole is time-linked. What I presume will happen, is that we'll actually stay in this dimension, this universe, and travel back in time to 1863. The first wormhole is like a high-speed tube connecting two points in the same timeline. You estimated that you were in the actual Day-Three of the Battle of Gettysburg for maybe 20 - 30 minutes. I think we'll have to endure the battle for about that same length of time, before crossing back into our home universe, jumping ahead to more or less July 6th 2013, but that could be off by days weeks, or months."

"Whatever you say, Doc." Phillips shook his head, seriously doubting any of this was even possible. "But what about you?" he continued. "Didn't you tell us you're not from where we're from?"

"Yes. But my theory, my hope, my prayer, is that I'll go back to my home universe in the crossing."

"How? Why?" asked Phillips.

"None of this is hard science, but I think the Cosmos, Fate, God, whatever you'd like to call it, will get me home to where I belong. I have a gut feeling on this."

"Sound's risky," said Phillips, always the pragmatic one preferring facts to feelings.

"It is. But it's a gamble Margaret and I are willing to take. We need to be home, together."

•••••

Fed-Stat Border guard Sergeant Clay Sullivan would later tell the men a story that proved he was indeed resourceful. He said he'd crossed over in Baghdad in 2004 while returning to the Green Zone after a firefight in Fallujah. He jumped off the truck in full battle gear and turned a corner toward his barracks. When he looked up again he thought he had gotten off at the wrong checkpoint. He found himself in the middle of what looked like 18th century Persia, which at first was not terribly unlike 21st century Iraq. Sullivan had recovered an ancient pendant that had been stolen from the National Museum of Iraq during the fall of Saddam Hussein and hid it in his backpack. He didn't know he'd found a key and it was waiting for him to arrive at a lock, a time-space portal. When he finally stumbled on the right spot, he crossed over and never figured out how to get back.

In Sullivan's new world he'd found things quite different. While the North American continent had seen its share of political and social shake-ups since the American Civil War, the rest of the world evolved on an equally skewed path. The Third Reich had essentially stopped its southeastern expansion at Turkey, living up to a treaty it signed with the Ottoman Empire. Iraq was called Babylonia and was a mix of French, Jewish, and English, and it was more than fifty percent Christian. The Islamification that should have taken place in much of the Middle East did not happen as millions of European refugees fled in the wake of the oncoming Nazi revolution, changing the population mix dramatically and quickly.

For the most part, many religions, factions, tribes, Mid-Eastern and Mediterranean peoples tolerated one another as they all lived in Hitler's shadow, united against his evil empire. Jews had no homeland, and the Arabic, European, and Muslim populations never learned to distrust one another with quite the same vitriolic hatred known in other universes.

Upon his crossing, Sergeant Sullivan, who did not fit anybody's idea of "normal," quickly had to shed his military attire for local garb before the Ottoman authorities hauled him off. Over the course of a year he managed to work his way, literally, back to America to find the U.S. dissolved and in a crisis he couldn't have imagined. With his knowledge of modern espionage techniques and technology, he managed to forge documents and find his way to the border guard position at the D.C. Checkpoint. He would later tell Dr. Rollins that it wasn't until their encounter and subsequent conversations that he even allowed himself to think about his past. He would tell Rollins he'd almost resolved that it was an over-active imagination and that he had suffered a psychotic break, but like a good soldier, held it together. His Post Traumatic Stress Disorder would have to wait.

Rollins pulled in to Bob's Hungry Boy Drive-In and parked in back. Phillips waited in the car while the Doctor got out and surveyed the parking lot. "I'll be back in a minute, Mike. I'm going to look for our friend."

No sooner had Rollins turned the corner when Phillips heard a loud rap on the window which made him jump.

"Hey! It's you!" said the almost too friendly manager from three days earlier. "Where are you coming up with these cherry Marathons? First you guys show up with one, then your friends show up."

"What friends?" asked Phillips, rolling down the window.

"You know, the serious guys in their dark coats. I sent them on to meet up with you in D.C. Did they ever find you?"

"Oh...ahh...Yeah, yeah they found us," answered Phillips, looking over his shoulder, hoping they weren't around the corner.

"Hey Bud," continued the bubbly manager. "I need to tell you about a racing association we're putting together." He became all-business while he told Phillips of his wildest dream. "It's nothing but hopped-up street cars and we drive on dirt tracks," he said. "There are already 10 tracks in North Maryland, Pennsylvania and Ohio. We're trying to organize. Would you guys with your Marathons be interested in a little racing action? We hear rumor that they're doing this in the Carolinas, too. You'd clean up with these beauties, could make some real money."

"I don't think so, but thanks," said Phillips.

"Suit yourself, but at least come to a race someday."

"Yeah, sure. Sounds like fun. What do you call your organization?"

"Funny you should ask. We can't agree on a name."

Phillips smiled. "How about NASCAR; the National Association for Stock Car Auto Racing?"

The manager stepped back with an ear-to-ear grin forming on his friendly, clueless face. "That's not bad. In fact...it's perfect! NASCAR! I love it. Thanks, Mr....."

"Doe, John Doe."

The manager walked off, almost skipping, just as Rollins returned with Sergeant Sullivan.

"Did I miss anything?" asked Rollins, getting behind the wheel.

"Not much. I just started NASCAR, that's all." Rollins looked at him with a puzzled expression. "I'll explain later."

"Mike, I'd like to introduce you to Clay Sullivan, formerly a Sergeant with the U.S. Marines, stationed in Baghdad."

"Hey, Clay. I'm Mike Phillips. Nice to meet you. Welcome to Crazy Land."

"Hi Mike. I've already been here a while, almost nine years."

Rollins turned the car around and was headed out to the highway. "We've got some catching up to do," he said. "I think I have some good news for you, Sergeant. I think I may be able to get you home."

They spent the next 35 minutes discussing the Multiverse, wormholes, time travel, the Civil War, Iraq, the execution of Saddam Hussein, the assassination of Osama Bin Laden, and the plan to get everybody back where they belonged. They pulled the Marathon into the barn and re-covered it with the heavy canvas. They walked toward the house and were greeted by Maverick, jumping, licking and whimpering in his excitement to see his master. Rollins turned to Phillips.

"Oh, I had almost forgotten, tell me how you just invented NASCAR, whatever that is?"

Suzanne, Joey and Anthony were sitting at the only large table in the safe house, eating soup she'd prepared.

"Are you going to tell us what's going on?" asked Anthony between slurps, forgetful of the hidden recording devices. "Like where you've been? What these guys are up to?" Suzanne said nothing. "Look at Joey, for God's sake. I mean he almost cut his hand off involved in your crap."

"It's not that bad," said Joey.

"That's not the point," he said, turning briefly to look at his friend. "You got him involved, Suze...in something that could have killed him and he doesn't even know what, or why he's doing it. You owe it to him. You owe it to us to let us in on what's been going on. If we're going to help, we deserve some answers." His verbal brow-beating finally got the best of her.

"Okay, okay...they're with the Unification. But they're not terrorists. They needed their wireless radio to communicate with their leader." Joey and Anthony looked at her, waiting for more.

"They got separated from their group near Richmond and were working their way back to D.C., where they have a headquarters. They needed my help to cross the border and that's all."

"That's all?" asked Anthony, still not satisfied. "What about that Japanese truck and those Civil War uniforms and that Tommy guy? That sonofabitch thinks you're his wife!" She glared at him.

"They were at an underground, high-level... costume party... in Richmond," she said, "trying to get information when all hell broke loose and their cover was blown. They had to leave fast and they didn't have any clothes with them. I don't know about the truck, and 'Wife' is a code word for a female operative who's helping the cause. Now that's all I know. Don't ask me anymore because I don't know anymore." Disgusted and frustrated, she pushed out from the table and threw herself on the couch, covering her face with a pillow. Anthony looked at Joey and they shook their heads. They didn't believe a word of it. Neither did Tate or his partner as they listened to the recorded conversation an hour later.

•••••

The afternoon waned and Sergeant Sullivan seemed like a new man. He told them that to be among people who knew about 9/11, David Lettermen, and George Bush was more than he had hoped for.

"You know this may be our last supper here, Margaret," said Rollins to his wife, taking her by the hand.

"It might be…with any luck," she answered, forcing a smile. They were all worried. This plan had so many holes, so many weak points that they all feared the worst.

"We need to reach Suzanne," said Phillips, looking at Fuller. "We've got to arrange to get those uniforms. No way we can do this without them, right Henry?"

"You had them coming in; I think you'll need them going out," he answered. "Remember Margaret's dress? We can't take the chance. It's about vibrations at the atomic level, or like taking two transparencies and lining them up together. The magic only happens when the alignment occurs."

"What about you and Clay?" asked Jackson. "Won't you need uniforms, too?"

"We weren't part of your original crossing. We're just tagging along."

"Is this fool thing gonna work, Henry?" asked Jackson, finally saying aloud what they had all been asking themselves.

"I don't know, Greg. But Gettysburg, Pennsylvania, is the location of your portal, that we know for sure, and it's there and only there where we have any shot at all."

"I'll call Suzanne's apartment, to find out about the uniforms." Tommy excused himself from the table and went to the phone in the living room. He returned a few moments later. "No answer."

"They could be anywhere," said Jackson. "Who knows if she even kept those ratty uniforms. They were filthy and stained with blood."

"We could call the safe house if we knew the number," said Phillips.

"I know the number," said Tommy. "I remember it because it was written on the phone, and kind of strange. It said 'Orchard-7-567' on the phone's receiver."

"Well that would be…," Henry closed his eyes before he spoke. "…let me see…672-5677, in whatever phone code Gettysburg is in."

"It's 843, I think," said Margaret. "Let's try it."

They walked into the living room while Tommy tried a direct dial with no luck. He called the long distance operator who was able to put the call through.

When the phone rang in the safe house the captives all jumped. Suzanne was closest and she answered. "Hello?"

"Hey Suzanne, it's Tommy. Are you alone? Can you talk?"

"Yes,… Mr. Tate…," she said with Anthony and Joey looking on and listening intently.

At the communications house across town Agent Tate and his partner both swiveled in the chairs at the sound of the ringing phone coming through a remote monitoring speaker. When Suzanne, protecting Tommy's identity, called him Mr. Tate, the real Agent Tate took special interest. He pushed the headphones tight around his ears and looked at his partner. "Did you catch that?"

"Yeah," said the shorter man. "She's talking to Mr. Tate on the phone. Only she ain't."

Tate scrambled to the machinery and flipped a switch labeled "Phone," and turned up a large volume knob, but only heard static. He could just make out hearing a voice, but the words were unintelligible. He flipped the switch several times, but there was no improvement in the sound quality.

"This piece of crap!" He pounded his fist on the table in frustration and flipped the switch back to "Microphone." The incoming call and phone tap was rudimentary and unreliable, but at least they could hear Suzanne's side of the conversation.

In the Rollins' living room, Tommy spoke to the only girl he'd ever loved. "Suzanne, I'm so sorry about all this." The others in Rollins' home looked a little embarrassed, like they were listening in on an intimate and private conversation, which they were. They excused themselves back toward the kitchen.

"I understand," Suzanne said calmly.

"I guess you're not alone?"

"That's correct," she said. "We crossed the border, and we met Joey, and saw Anthony at the apartment, then you brought us here to the safe house."

"You're with that creep?" Fuller asked, still not liking the idea of hot-headed Anthony being anywhere near her.

"No. He's not. I think you have that part wrong."

"Okay, okay. I get it," said Tommy, realizing she wasn't free to talk. "Are the Civil War uniforms still there?

"Yes, I think we have enough food."

"We need them tomorrow morning."

"Well, I don't know if it will last that long." Joey and Anthony looked at one another. There was enough food for a month.

"We will be there at 9:00 a.m., tomorrow morning."

"I know, sir. But you've got us locked in here. How are we supposed to help?"

"Are you guys locked inside?"

"Yes."

"Are Tate and his goon in town? Are they hearing this?"

"Probably."

"Well, we've got no choice Suzanne. Tomorrow is the day."

"I understand, I'll tell Joey and Anthony."

"Does Anthony have his gun?"

"No, sir. I don't think we'll have any problems."

"Okay then, if you're still there in the morning, I'll see you. If they move you, or you guys leave, hide the uniforms in the cabinet under the sink. Suzanne, I love you."

"I understand." She almost started to cry. "We only want to help you, sir. Goodbye." She hung up the phone and curled up in the recliner.

"Tate?" asked Anthony, doubting that it was.

"Yes," said Suzanne.

Anthony didn't believe her. He knew she had been talking to Tommy Fuller, but what he'd said to her would be impossible to find out, and he knew better than to even try.

Fuller hung up the phone and looked at his companions who were making their way back toward the living room. "They're locked in. They may be there tomorrow or not, she doesn't know for sure, but if they're to be moved she'll hide the uniforms for us."

"Good job, Tommy," said Jackson, with an uncharacteristic, sincere compliment. "I know that was hard. Good for you and good for her, too. That girl is something else."

"Tell me about it," agreed Fuller.

Sergeant Clay Sullivan had been listening to the conversations, trying to fit the pieces together, and seemed unusually quiet, though he did state that he was excited at the prospect of going home. Margaret jumped in and insisted that they all try to rest.

"Tomorrow is a very important day," she said. "For us and for this pitiful universe. Let's not screw it up because we're tired. To bed! All of you!"

Rest would come, but not before some last minute planning and confirmation of the details. She resigned herself to the fact that no one was going to bed anytime soon, so she excused herself and went to the kitchen to retrieve a box that she had been loading with photographs and various sentimental items from around the house. She turned on the kitchen radio, the music covering her soft crying.

Upstairs, Rollins met Sullivan in the hallway. "We'll get up at 6:00 and leave no later than 6:45," said Rollins. "Clay, your shift starts at 8:00?"

"Yes."

"And you assure me that I can cross at the D.C. border with Greg, Tommy, and Mike, hidden in my car?"

"I'm the ranking guard, and with our embarrassing treatment of you yesterday, I'll be able to convince the two check-points on our side to send you through without being bothered. Your papers are in perfect order and were verified authentic less than 12 hours ago. We have a pretty good relationship with the Con-Fed border patrol and it's generally understood that we wave through VIP's when alerted in advance, which I'll do the minute you arrive. And I'm to meet you all in Gettysburg at 10:30 a.m. in the parking lot of the Battlefield Memorial Park."

The discussion brought Phillips and Jackson out of their room and into the hall to join the late-night confab.

"How will you get through?" asked Phillips.

"I'll figure it out. We're always running diplomats and documents to Richmond. It shouldn't be a problem."

"Margaret and Maverick will cross over sometime in the morning," said Rollins, "long before 11:00 a.m. and I'll call Billy Kay. His show runs until 11:00, so I'll call him before we cross the border and give him the bad news."

"Here's something we haven't yet discussed," said Jackson. "How are you going to hide a 6' 3", 230-pound black man and two white dudes in your little car?"

"We're taking the Marathon," said Rollins," we'll need it once we cross the border, much less conspicuous. I'll put you and Tommy on the floor in the back, under a canvas tarp with shovels and buckets and such. And Mike, I'm afraid you'll have to ride in the trunk, also under a tarp and some other mining supplies."

"Great," the three men said in unison, clearly not excited about this part of their trip home.

"Once we're safely across the border, I'll get you all back in proper seats, I promise." Dr. Rollins calculated the timetable of events and laid it out one last time.

"We'll leave here at 6:45 tomorrow morning, we'll stop to cover you guys up and I'll call Billy Kay. We'll cross the border in D.C. at 8:15, arrive at the Gettysburg safe house at 10:00. We'll get the uniforms, you'll change clothes, and we'll meet Sergeant Sullivan at the Park at 10:30. We need to be at Emmitsburg Road by 10:45. Tommy, that's when you said you looked at your pocket watch and first started noticing things weren't right?"

"I think so, I was still in shock after...after the incident at home, wrecking my truck..." Fuller was still having difficulty admitting to himself or anyone else that he'd shot someone dead, though they'd all heard the gunshot accidentally recorded on his phone.

"That seems about right," said Phillips. "We all met at 9:30 and the thing started about 10:30."

"Okay then, that's the best we can do. We'll be on the old battlefield around 10:45, and with any luck, follow Tommy through the wormhole and hopefully back to our respective homes."

"Hopefully?" said Jackson. "Wha'chu mean 'hopefully?' You don't mean to say we might go somewhere else?"

"Anything is possible, but there's no reason to assume we won't just cross back to where we came from, just like Margaret and Kay do all the time. Don't worry so much. Margaret has crossed back and forth nearly

6,000 times, over the past 50 some years, without incident, if that makes you feel any better. These portals can be remarkably stable."

Margaret arrived back in the living room with an overflowing box of memories. She was fighting mixed emotions about crossing back over for good. Her two worlds were similar in many ways, but equally different, too, and she loved both of them. She knew she'd be leaving people and places that had grown near and dear to her. She also knew how much it meant to Henry to get back home and she couldn't deny him, she wouldn't deny him. They had discussed this possibility for years and decided that if they ever had the opportunity to choose, it would be their Birth Earth. That's where they were from, where they belonged and that's where they were going. She sat down, her box of memories at her feet, along with Maverick, who was begging for a head scratch.

"I just heard the weatherman," said Margaret to her husband, just coming back down the stairs to find her. "He said there was a fog warning for tomorrow for most of the area. I hope that won't be a problem."

"Fog is the least of our worries," said Rollins quietly. "In fact, it might help."

•••••

Agent Tate and his partner were in a quandary. Clearly the kids, or at least Suzanne, were not cooperating, and leaving them locked-up wasn't likely to gain them any new information. Letting them go and tailing them, they decided, would probably be more efficient and more likely to lead to something useful. In agreement they drove to the safe house and let themselves in through the door with three locks.

"Well, what did we miss?" asked Tate with a fake smile. No one answered. "Wow, you're a fun bunch."

"Pretty quiet here, Mr. Tate," said Anthony. Joey looked confused, wondering about the still unexplained phone call. Suzanne shot him a look that said: "Don't even think of opening your mouth." And he didn't. He was used to obeying his big sister.

"Well, we're sorry about all that mess back at the apartment, and for holding you here," said Tate, without an ounce of sincerity. "But everything seems to be okay, so you can go now. Just stay in touch with us. By the way, when was the last time you made it to school, Joey?"

"Last week, sometime," he hated school and hated talking about it even more.

"Well, don't you think you should get back there? Say, tomorrow?"

"Whatever…they don't really miss me that much."

"No, he's right," said Suzanne, getting up from the recliner. "School. Tomorrow."

The five of them made their way up the stairs and out into the garage. As Tate was beginning to relock the door, Suzanne pushed her way past him, remembering her mission.

"I've left the radio on. I'll be right back up." She ran down the stairs, grabbed the still unwashed uniforms from the hamper and threw them in the cabinet under the sink before Tate even had a chance to think about what she had said. She met him at the top of the stairs and they shared distrustful glances.

"I may have left something down there myself," said Tate, happy to play her game. They squeezed by one another and she stood at the top of the stairs. Her heart sank as she saw him go straight to the kitchen. He looked around the counters, opened the silverware drawer and then looked up at her. She looked away. The ridiculous game of 'hot 'n' cold' only lasted another minute with Tate really unable to detect anything out of the ordinary. He had not seen her with the uniforms, but it had been close. He walked to the large wooden radio and felt its top. It was almost warm enough to burn his fingertips. He made his way back up the stairs, locking the door before turning to watch his young quarry move out of the garage. Suzanne's heart was still pounding as she followed Joey and Anthony to their car.

"Let's stay in touch," yelled Tate, walking down the driveway to his own car. "Joey, school tomorrow."

Anthony, Joey and Suzanne rode in silence back to their apartment. Suzanne felt as if she was trading one prison for another and nothing either of the two boys tried would snap her out of a deep and profound sadness.

Chapter 32

The alarm clock was almost unnecessary, as no one in the Rollins' house had been sleeping. When it started its horrendous buzz, buzz, buzz everyone was eager to get started and get this day over with, whatever it may bring. Quick showers were followed by breakfast. Sergeant Sullivan was the first out the door, in a borrowed car of Rollins'.

Henry and Margaret needed some time alone. This was a dangerous mission, one for which they had been preparing most of their lives, yet facing it was harder than they could have ever imagined. Neither could stand the thought of a life, no matter how many or how few years were left, without the other.

They packed a few valuables and some papers and were leaving a house full of furniture and memories. They would both miss their lives in this universe but knew in their hearts they belonged home. They kissed and hugged and Henry watched his beloved Margaret and Maverick walk into the den and disappear through an unseen rip in time and space. Maverick never stopped wagging his tail and that gave Dr. Rollins some small amount of courage to go on.

Rollins walked into the kitchen where the men were finishing breakfast, and Phillips had begun washing up the dishes.

"No need to get too carried away there, Mike," joked Rollins regarding the irony of cleaning up a house they may very well never see again. "Well boys? Are you ready?" he asked.

"No," said Fuller "But I don't think I'd ever be ready for this."

"Very true," said Rollins.

"How about you, Greg? Mike?"

"Let's do it. I want to be home in time for the game," said Phillips. "The Yankees are starting a new pitcher tonight against Tampa Bay."

"Where are you watching the game?" asked Jackson.

"I don't know...MacAuley's?"

"Sounds good. I'll meet you there."

"That's the spirit," said Rollins, pounding his palm with a clenched fist. "We're thinking positive, and that has to help. Let's go."

The four men piled out the door and loaded a layer of pillows in the trunk of the Marathon along with two tarps and an arsenal of geological equipment. The men would ride together until they neared the border, and then pull off the road to take their places in hiding before the border crossing attempt at 8:15 sharp.

The day was not dawning cheerily. Light rain and patchy fog blocked the rising sun, and the sky swirled, mixing shades of blue and gray.

"What will happen to the people of this universe if we're successful," asked Tommy, out of the blue. Greg Jackson rolled his eyes, and they were all caught off guard by the awkward and difficult question.

"As I said earlier, I don't know for sure, Tommy," said Rollins. "It could be that this universe's time line was started in 1863 at the time of the battle, the explosion. If that's the case, and you're successful, then this universe will vanish, because you'd be erasing the event that caused its formation, and thus no branching from the original. If the timeline was started sometime before the battle, then I would imagine this universe will develop very much like our own."

"Yes, but you didn't answer my question. What about the people?"

"Again, I just don't know. If the timeline stays solvent, I'd like to think that it will be a start over, of sorts, from 1863 and that Maggie and Hank will meet in 1940. You and Suzanne will meet, and Mike and Greg will be partners in a law firm. But I just don't know."

They rode on, each lost in their own thoughts. When they neared D.C., Rollins turned on the radio just in time to hear Billy the Kay and his morning Zoo Crew. They were making crank calls and laughing hysterically at the confusion of the hapless souls unfortunate enough to answer their phones.

"I dread this call," said Rollins.

"Tell me again why we have to let him in on this plan?" asked Jackson.

"Well," started Rollins. "If we are successful and this universe vanishes and Billy Kay is still here, I think he will vanish with it and it's just not right to not tell him. It's almost like...murder, and since he has the ability to cross over, he can escape this fate, and live out his miserable life back home."

"If *he* can go, why can't we take one or two others with us?" asked Tommy Fuller. Everyone knew he meant Suzanne when he said 'others.'

"Because we can't take people of this universe back into ours," said Rollins. "First of all, I don't think it's even possible, and secondly, if it were possible we'd be displacing people who were already there and it's fundamentally wrong to knowingly displace someone. We're only taking those of us who crossed over from their origin universes: Kay, Sergeant Sullivan, Margaret, and those of us in this car."

"What about the hundreds, or thousands of others, around the world who may have crossed over through their own portals, who are stuck here, and who don't know that we're messing with their lives?" asked Fuller. "Is that fair?"

For that dilemma Rollins didn't have an answer. It was the elephant in the room that he was attempting to ignore. It was the most vexing question plaguing him and he didn't like thinking about it.

"No, it's not fair Tommy," said Greg Jackson, trying to inject logic and pragmatism into the conversation. "But is it fair to leave loved ones back home in agony? Is it fair to leave a world intact where some people are still considered property because of the color of their skin? Is it fair to deny Henry and me and Mike our homes and families? Is it fair to allow Europe to languish under Hitler's grandson and the Third Reich? None of it's fair. It's the lesser of the evils and I think a jury of our peers would acquit us. We created this mess. We can fix it." The car went silent until they saw their first sign for the upcoming border crossing.

'F.S.A.- C.S.A. BORDER 3 MILES AHEAD. PREPARE TO STOP.'

"Well, this is it, men," said Rollins. "We're right on time. It's 8:00." He pulled the Marathon into a gas station and walked in to use the pay phone just inside the door. After two tries he reached Kay's radio station board operator and call screener.

"Billy the Kay in the Morning, what's your question for the K-Man?" asked the chipper voice from the station's control room.

"I'd like to speak to Billy."

"What's your question please?"

"It's personal."

"Isn't it always, buddy? Call back after 11:00." The screener hung the phone up in Rollins' ear. He quickly loaded the phone with another 10 cents and redialed the number.

"Billy the Kay in the Morning, what's your question?"

"Don't hang up, please. This is an emergency. Tell Kay Dr. Rollins is on the phone and it's an emergency."

"Okay, hold on."

A minute went by and Rollins listened to the on-air hi-jinx played in the phone's receiver. Kay sounded happy and bright and Dr. Rollins felt a little badly about shaking up his morning. He was really worried about Kay's response to what would be a shocking revelation. The Zoo Crew announced a commercial break and Kay picked up the receiver.

"Rollins, what's going on?' he asked, annoyed.

"Hello, Bill. Are you sitting down?"

"No, and just get to it. What's up? What's the emergency?"

"Bill, I'm telling you this for your own good. You have to cross over before 10:45 this morning or you may never...well, just do it."

"Why? What are you up to, you crazy old fuck?"

Rollins hesitated and then launched into the plan, fearing it might be the only way to convince him.

"We're changing the time line and I'm attempting to cross over. This will probably be your last chance to go home. If we manage to pull this off, then this universe is history – it's not even history – it may be gone forever and if you're here...well, you get the picture."

"Why in God's name would you mess around with the universe like that?" Kay was furious. "Are you insane? We've got a good thing going here, Doc. Is that Mike Phillips guy involved in all of this? Ask him where the hell my car is."

"That's unimportant. A few other Travelers and I will be going back around 11:00 a.m. this morning. Margaret has already returned. Look, Billy, I'm giving you fair warning. This may be your last chance. You've got to go. At least cross over and then try to cross back later if you like, we may not pull this off. But if you don't go and we *are* successful and you're still sitting in your Zoo Crew chair, you're gone, vanished, poof."

"You sonofabitch, Rollins. You just can't stand to see me make a dollar," Kay sighed. "And just how are you going to do this fool thing?"

"I can't tell you that. Well, I could tell you, but I don't trust you. Let's just say we're going to fix this place or spin it out of existence...or maybe die trying. One way or another, there will be no more Confederate States of America...look, I've got to go and I'm done talking to you. I've given you fair warning. No later than 10:45, not even by a minute. If I were you I would go now. Good luck."

Rollins hung up the phone and left Kay standing in his office, two feet from his portal, shaking his head and cursing. "That sonofabitch..."

Rollins returned to the car and quickly pulled back out into the road before spotting what appeared to be an abandoned warehouse. He drove behind the building and turned off the motor.

"We've got to hurry. That took a little longer than I expected. It's 8:10."

The men maneuvered into position, getting as comfortable as possible. Fortunately the oversized Marathon left plenty of room for Phillips in the trunk, and Fuller and Jackson spooning on the floor behind the front seat.

Dr. Rollins covered them with tarps and placed the shovels and boxes of equipment carefully on top. It was a fairly convincing, nondescript car full of survey and geological equipment. They reached the first checkpoint at 8:16.

"Good morning," said the guard. "Papers please. And open the trunk."

"Certainly," said Dr. Rollins. "You boys gave me quite a time last night," he said smiling and showing off a bruise on his wrist.

"Oh, Dr. Rollins. Yes, sir. Sorry about that. A misunderstanding," said the guard, waving to the guards at the final Northern checkpoint on the bridge. "You can go ahead. Sorry, again."

"No worry, you were just doing your job," said Dr. Rollins, smiling. He rolled up the window and pulled forward.

"One down, three to go," he said to his hidden passengers.

He pulled to the next checkpoint and Sergeant Sullivan walked to the window, waving the car to stop.

"Good morning, sir. Papers please," said Sullivan with a deadpan delivery. "Yes, everything's in order here. Thanks for breakfast, you may go." Sullivan quickly went to the phone in the guardhouse and made his call.

Rollins drove across the bridge through the giant border fence reaching the Con-Fed border checkpoint where he simply held his papers in the air and was waved through. He was again waved through at the final checkpoint and they were on their way.

"Well, that was easy. Sullivan came through for us," said Rollins, clearly relieved. "I'll pull over in about two minutes," he said, turning his head to speak through the layers of junk covering Fuller and Jackson.

"Hurry please," came an urgent and muffled request from the trunk.

Rollins pulled off the main highway and drove on looking for a suitable place to stop and help the men from their hiding places. An old barn in the countryside seemed to fit the bill and behind it the men were uncovered. They returned the supplies and tarps to the trunk and took their seats.

"That *was* easy," remarked Phillips, smiling. "Nice job, Doc."

"It will be safer to take the back roads into Gettysburg and we've got time. I don't want to run into any trouble," said Rollins. "Greg, we're in Corn Fed now. I hate to tell you, you may need this." He opened his glove compartment and pulled out a red, knit cap with a license stitched to it behind a clear piece of vinyl. "Hopefully, you'll never have to put it on, but keep it nearby just in case."

"Yez, boss," Jackson said with a grin, high on the possibility of getting home, and out of this upside down hellhole of racism. It was 8:25 a.m. and they were a little ahead of schedule, making their way along parallel routes to Gettysburg, the Alpha and Omega of this most unusual adventure.

Chapter 33

In the studios of 1560-WKDC, Billy the Kay stomped out of his office and into the control room. "You guys finish the show. I got some business," he said.

"The boss is going to shit, Billy," said one of his Z-Crew. "He hates it when you don't finish."

"Too friggin' bad," Kay yelled through the control room mic. "My...my mom's sick in New Jersey."

"I thought your mom died like 10 years ago?"

He pressed the button marked 'Studio Mic' and yelled. "Just finish the goddamn show."

He stormed into his office, slamming the door shut behind him. He sat as his desk and put his head in his hands, still furious at Rollins and his meddling. He dug through the top drawer of his desk, producing a business card. 'Agent Archibald Tate. National Security, Washington, D.C.' He dialed the number, holding the phone in one hand, and pounding his fist on the desk with the other.

Tate's office forwarded the call to the agent's listening post in Gettysburg and Tate picked up on the last ring, just as they were arriving back.

"Yes," said Tate into the receiver.

"Yeah, Tate. This is Billy Kay. I've got some information for you."

Kay carefully recounted bits and pieces of Dr. Rollins call, changing much of it but getting the names, and locations pretty well covered. He was hell bent on stopping Rollins from interfering with the launch of his new cell phone business, there was a fortune to be made. Kay made it his business to not let 'Rollins and his do-gooder, time-traveling, universe-hopping flunkies,' as he was thinking of them, meddle with a plan he had worked on for more than three years. His final words to Tate were enough to persuade the agents to call in Con-Fed reinforcements and alert all the local Gettysburg police.

"Something big is going down around 10:45 or 11:00 in Gettysburg," said Kay. "And my guess is it will be at the Battlefield Park, near Emmitsburg Road. Take some fire power, they're armed."

Tate and his partner made a few calls, raced out of the house and headed back to the apartment hoping to intercept the fugitives or maybe gain new information from the kids. As the agents turned down Main Street they passed a green Marathon just coming into town headed in the opposite direction.

"That was Tate that just passed us," said Phillips, sinking into his seat.

"Are you sure?" asked Rollins.

"Absolutely. But I don't think they saw us. They looked like they were in a big hurry, though."

"They're headed for Suzanne's apartment. I know it," said Fuller. "Turn around! We've got to get there first!"

"No!" said Phillips. "This may be our only chance to get our uniforms back. We're almost there. Suzanne, Joey, and Anthony can take care of themselves. They'll be alright. They don't really know anything, anyway. Let's keep it that way, for their sake."

Rollins stepped on the gas, picking up the pace for the last mile to the safe house.

"We'll be less obvious if only one of us goes inside," said Phillips. "Tommy, you want to go?"

They parked about half a block away and Tommy walked quickly to a door on the side of the garage. Finding it locked, he looked around, hoping he wasn't being watched, and then kicked it hard with his booted foot, popping the door with a snap and a crunch.

Inside the garage was another locked door; this one made of steel, and it was triple locked. He kicked this one too, and only managed to slightly dent the heavy door and jar his ankle in the process. His eyes darted around the four corners of the empty garage. He saw a few household tools: a shovel, a hammer, and a screw driver. None of those implements gained him access. In the far corner of the garage, next to a set of tires and rims, he spotted a crow bar. If that didn't work nothing would. In a matter of 30 seconds he pried the wooden doorframe away from the locking mechanisms and was able to kick the door open.

Downstairs he found the bundled uniforms stuffed under the sink, just as he had asked. "Good girl, Suzanne," he said to himself. He ran back up the stairs and out to the waiting car.

"Got 'em," he said as he entered the rear door, throwing the foul smelling garments into the back, onto Jackson's lap.

It was 9:50 and they had 40 minutes to kill before meeting Sullivan at the Park, which was only a few minutes from downtown.

"Do you think they're on to us?" asked Jackson.

Phillips turned to his friend. "How could they be? Sullivan wouldn't say anything."

"Billy the Kay," said Rollins, sick at the thought. "I knew it was a bad idea."

"What do you mean? What did you tell him?" asked Phillips.

"Not much. I knew better than to give him any details, but maybe he put two and two together. I told him we were going to try to fix things and get home. I told him it was our goal to reunite the North and South by fixing the Civil War. He knows it all went bad in Gettysburg and he knows about you guys. He'd rather stay here profiting on stolen ideas than to do the right thing."

"We should have let him vanish into...wherever these people go," said Jackson, not too thoughtfully.

"Is that what happens, Dr Rollins?" asked Tommy. "They vanish? They turn to dust? We can't let Suzanne and Joey and even that punk, Anthony, disappear into nothingness!" he cried, on the verge of grabbing the steering wheel from Rollins' hands. "It *is* like murder and I won't be able to live with myself, knowing what we've done."

"Tommy, it's nothing like that at all," said Rollins. "Suzanne *is* Susan and Susan *is* Suzanne. They're one and the same. Joey and Anthony and all the others are back home living out their own fates. These people we know here are the same souls, inhabiting different dimensions. That's all. You're not turning anyone to dust. If anything you're reuniting them, making them more whole. Suzanne is at home waiting for you, you just know her as Susan. She's the girl you love. We've got to set things right." He stepped on the gas and sped away from the safe house, hoping the matter had been put to rest, and fearing that it hadn't.

•••••

The town was unsettlingly quiet. The tourist-driven economy, that was the Gettysburg the men knew, had never materialized in this place.

"You've got to change into those uniforms," said Dr. Rollins. "...without drawing too much attention to what we're doing."

"Maybe the motel on the way to the Park," said Phillips. "I saw it on our way into town the other night."

They hurried down Main Street, passing the road leading to Jackson's neighborhood. They passed Fuller's Auto, which they knew as MacAuley's Irish Pub. They drove by the library and an old house that had three days earlier been the small office that housed the law firm of Phillips, Gilder, Bailey & Scott.

The Gettysburg Haven Motel had a few cars in its lot and a permanent 'Vacancy' sign, which they commented on, Phillips joking that that "can't ever be a good thing." Rollins pulled in and parked out of sight of the front desk. He hurried in and rented a room from a fortunately disinterested clerk. He checked the road and signaled to his passengers. They made a beeline to the door he had just unlocked. Inside, the tiny room was cramped for four grown men. The three reenactors struggled to each find room to change.

"These things smell god-awful," said Jackson, as he sorted through the uniforms trying to determine whose was whose.

"Try not to think about it," said Phillips. "With any luck you'll be taking a hot shower at home in less than 45 minutes."

"You are an optimistic one," said Jackson, pulling off the borrowed shirt and replacing it with a white cotton Civil War era reproduction, stained by the blood of their dead comrade, Brad Lake. Jackson touched the dried blood on the sleeve. "Really, Doc…what are our odds?"

"You don't want to know," Rollins answered truthfully. He had put his life, career, and freedom, as well as that of many others, in jeopardy. If they weren't successful they'd probably all end up in some dank Con-Fed prison. Even if they were successful, they might still end up in prison. Though the responsibility weighed heavily upon him, he pushed on, focused on the mission. "It's 10:05. We meet the Sergeant in 25 minutes. Help me think men; what if Tate is on to us and he's rallied the troops? How are we going to avoid the Feds, and cops, and who knows who else?"

"Maybe we should try to sneak in from the back-side, instead of all meeting at the parking lot," said Jackson.

"Yes, yes. Good idea," said Rollins. Just then the sound of cars moving at a high rate of speed rattled the windows of the room and they peeked through the curtain to see four Confederate Army vans speed down the road, headed in the direction of the Park. Their hearts sank.

"This is not good," said Jackson. "They know."

"Kay," said Rollins, sinking onto the bed. "If I ever see him again I'll wring his neck."

"Well," said Fuller, buttoning the Rebel uniform jacket, also stained with blood, sweat, and the debris of real war. "Since we're moving forward, we should take the back road along the west side of the Park. We ended up in those woods after we ran from the explosion and the fighting. It's a good mile or so from the parking lot. Might be our best shot."

"You mean you were off the battlefield when you jumped into 2013?" asked Rollins, having missed this piece of information before.

"I think so," said Fuller. "When we wandered back out of the woods to the battlefield, the Memorial markers were already there."

"My, my. That's interesting. Those woods *have* to be our first stop, then," said Rollins. But what about Sullivan? We can't hang him out to dry. He's the only reason we made it this far."

"Yeah," said Jackson. "What about Sullivan? Where's a damn cell phone when you need one?"

•••••

"I can't stay cooped up in this apartment any more," said Suzanne nearly flinging herself off the couch. "I need to go out."

"I'll go with you," said Anthony, who had been reading a gun magazine. Suzanne thought about arguing with him, really hoping to be alone, but she couldn't face another showdown and she felt badly for him. "I'm going too," said Joey, appearing from out of his bedroom. Suzanne rolled her eyes.

"Okay, well let's go then. I'm losing my mind sitting in here. Maybe we could get something to eat. I've got a few bucks."

"Yeah, you owe me $10. Remember? And a car..."

The three had been gone for less than five minutes when Tate and his partner flew into the complex's parking lot, screeching to a halt. They ran to the door and found it swinging free, unencumbered by a working latch. It had been kicked in twice, making entry easy, though they were too late. Once again they had missed their targets.

Chapter 34

Sergeant Sullivan, after falsifying orders to deliver a diplomatic pouch, signed out an official vehicle and was well on his way to Gettysburg. With military precision he had timed his arrival to be within minutes of the agreed upon 10:30. The same Con-Fed vehicles that sped past the motel had already passed Sullivan 20-minutes earlier, clearly in a hurry to go somewhere. When he arrived on the outskirts of town and noticed unmarked cars and local police racing around like Keystone Cops, he was pretty sure Rollins' plan had been uncovered. He stayed the course as he hoped his official vehicle would go mostly unnoticed, which so far, it had. Even at the parking lot rally point, his would be just one more official car among the dozens probably on their way. He wondered if his new friends knew about the scores of law enforcement and military on their tail.

Kay had, fortunately, not known of Rollins' Marathon and told Tate they were probably driving his Ford Atlantic or Rollins' Chevy Rambler. Though the authorities had accurate physical descriptions of the men, they weren't looking for a Marathon, and this had given Rollins' crew one small advantage, along with the patchy fog, in getting through town. Rollins and the men, who had finally changed into their Rebel uniforms, snuck back out of the motel's lot and out on the road.

They sank down low in their seats. To the outside world it appeared to be just one old man out for a drive. They left the main road as quickly as possible, but not before passing a car driven by an attractive, young blond woman. Fuller gave Rollins' directions without the benefit of seeing; he knew the roads that well. Once they were off the main road, Rollins' passengers reemerged from their hiding places. Where the fog cleared in spots, they could see the Park through the trees. The men tried to estimate a good jumping-off point, near to where they may have been while within the perimeter of the woods. A fence blocked access along the road, but didn't appear to be too difficult to cross over, at least for the younger men.

•••••

"Suzanne, what's wrong?" asked Anthony.

"I thought I saw someone, that's all."

"Who?"

"Just a guy. He looked familiar...in that green Marathon we passed back there."

"Yeah," said Joey. "I saw it too. It looked an awful lot like..."

"Dr. Rollins," said Suzanne and Joey together.

She slammed on the brakes and wheeled the big car 180 degrees. "Shit, Suzanne!" yelled Anthony. "Don't kill us!" She sped back down the road and the fog had broken just enough to allow them to see no more than a few hundred yards, but no sign of the shiny green Marathon appeared.

"He must have taken the Old Post Road." She slammed the brakes on again, nearly throwing Anthony through the windshield. Turning the car fully around, she sped back down the main road, turning left at an unmarked intersection. Though she didn't know it, she was less than a mile behind Rollins' car full of Rebel soldiers, one of whom she'd fallen hopelessly, madly, mysteriously in love.

•••••

Furious at not finding the kids in their apartment, Tate and his partner raced to the safe house. When they found that it had been broken into, they knew their fugitives were close by.

"They've been here," said Tate, fuming. "I knew that bitch was hiding something."

They got back into their car and drove on toward the Gettysburg Memorial Park. Tate, along with a growing posse of local and Federal authorities, fell in behind Sergeant Sullivan, who by now figured the plan must have changed. The authorities behind him blew their horns, pulsed their sirens and lights to get around. Sullivan slowed and pulled to the right to accommodate.

•••••

"That's got to be near the right spot," said Tommy Fuller, pointing out to his left. "Find a spot to park." Rollins pulled off the road onto a non-existent shoulder. Going a little too fast, the big car bounced once, and slid sideways down a five-foot embankment, slick with dew and the moisture from heavy fog. The car came to rest with a soft thud in the mud and wet grass.

"I guess we're here," said Rollins. "No moving this thing, I'm afraid – even if we wanted too."

"We better go. Cops could be here any minute," said Fuller, glancing at an old watch, borrowed from Rollins. It was 10:30 exactly.

"How do you propose getting through that fence?" asked Rollins.

"We'll go over it," said Jackson.

"The hell we will. I'm 83-years-old. You might go over it, but I certainly won't." Rollins went to the trunk and produced a pair of pruning shears.

"Not exactly designed for a chain-link fence, but they might help."

"Let me try," said Jackson, taking the long handled shears from the Doctor. They waded through the tall grass toward the fence, 10-yards away.

"This fog is ridiculous," said Phillips. It had gotten so heavy that the water vapor molecules hung in the air, unmoving except for soft, moist swirls that followed them as they walked through the tall weeds.

That same fog suddenly slowed Suzanne's car to a crawl. It was particularly heavy, but she crept along with just a few feet of visibility.

The men reached the eight-foot fence and Jackson put the curved blades of the shears to a link and promptly broke the steel blades into pieces.

"That fence is made of galvanized, zinc-coated steel," said Rollins. "I'm afraid that's my fault. I invented it in 1956. Well, truth be told, I had help from back home."

"Sorry, you're going to have to go over, Henry," said Phillips. "Greg, you go over first. Tommy and I will hoist the Doc up and over, and you'll be on the other side to catch him."

"Catch me?" questioned Rollins, sure this was a bad idea.

"We're running out of time, Doc. It's the only way," said Phillips.

Jackson hauled his large frame to the top of the fence with a fair amount of difficulty. He balanced precariously on his hands, with his upper body hanging over leaving his legs dangling in the air. The fence shook beneath his weight. As he tried to steady himself the shaking became more pronounced until a six-foot section of the fence simply crumbled, sending Jackson and the nearby support pole crashing to the ground.

Rollins smiled. "Who's gonna catch Jackson?"

"This is your lucky day, Henry," said Phillips. "Keep it up. We need all the luck we can muster."

"I don't believe in luck," said Rollins.

Jackson picked himself up, unhurt, and the four men moved through the collapsed fence section and into the foggy woods.

•••••

At the Gettysburg Battlefield Memorial Park, 30 law enforcement personnel had gathered in the parking lot. Tate and his partner arrived to find general chaos between Federal agents from two governments, Park Police, local Police, County Sheriffs and State Troopers, all without a single command authority. Not being shy, Tate took what he felt to be his rightful place. He jumped on the hood of his car, put his middle and index fingers together, inserted them into his mouth, and whistled loudly enough that Tommy Fuller, nearly two miles away, turned his head.

"What was that?" he asked of the others, the group already 100 yards into the woods.

"What was what?" asked Jackson.

"Did you hear a whistle or something?"

"No. Maybe it was a bird, or a squirrel?"

"I don't know…" Fuller scratched his head. "Oh shit."

"What now?" asked Jackson, annoyed at all the chatter.

"My cap. It's in the car." They all stopped dead in their tracks.

"Tommy, you've got to go back to get it," said Rollins. "Your Rebel cap may be the key to the whole crossing. It was on your head every time you crossed."

"I know, I know…I just…I'll be right back. Don't lose me." He ran back through the fog in the general direction of the break in the fence, hoping he was headed toward the car, but between the lack of visibility and the unfamiliar woods, finding his way was a challenge.

"Hurry, Tommy!" yelled Rollins, though he could no longer see Fuller. "It's 10:40! The time of day could be key."

"Let's spread out," said Phillips. "Twenty yards apart, back toward the car. It will make it easier for Tommy to get back. You, stay here Doc. Don't move."

"Please don't get lost," said Rollins. "And for God's sake, hurry…"

310

Chapter 35

Tate's piercing whistle instantly got the attention of most who had gathered, including a Border Guard and Official Driver named Sullivan from the Federated States of America.

"Listen up. I'm Agent Tate with the Fed-Stat National Security Division." Tate couldn't believe he actually heard a few laughs and a muffled 'Boo' from the back of the crowd. He ignored them. "I'm the one who called this thing in. I've been tracking these guys back and forth across the border for three days and…"

"Good job, Tate!" came the interrupting and jeering voice of the same Gettysburg cop who'd been berated in Fuller's Auto a day earlier. "You're quite the law-man!" Scattered laughter filtered through the parking lot and Tate was visibly thrown. His partner tried in vain to light a cigarette in the heavy, damp fog.

"I'm not sure what these guys are up to, but the best we can guess from our intel is that for some reason they're coming to this Park with some big plan, and my guess is, it ain't good. There are at least four of them, maybe as many as seven…"

The cop interrupted again.

"Well, which is it? Four or seven? You Yankees can count, can't you?" This time the laughter was louder and was answered by insults hurled back at the cop from Fed-Stat authorities. The back and forth was getting to a point where an all-out, North/South street brawl was seconds away.

Over the yelling, Tate offered one more piece of the puzzle. "We think they blew up your Supreme Court in Richmond, a few days ago." The sobering comment stopped the bickering and the jabs and this time everyone seemed to be listening. Sergeant Clay Sullivan, who had never been to the Park, took advantage of the attention-diverting speech and slipped quietly to the back of the crowd. He had studied a map available to him in the Security Office that morning and found the Park to be an elongated rectangle with the city on one side, forested land on the other and Emmitsburg Road more or less situated in the middle, about two miles from the parking lot. He disappeared into the fog, unseen and unnoticed by anyone.

•••••

Tommy Fuller, alone, found the fence, but that was only the first step. He rattled the intact fence not knowing if the opening Jackson had created with his fall was to the left or right, or how far; five feet or five hundred feet. The fog was just too thick to tell.

"Shit. Shit. Shit," he said. He found a large tree limb and propped it up against the fence as a reference marker and began running to the right. He covered 20 or 30 yards and found no opening, so he propped another branch up at that point and ran back the other way. He passed his first marker without slowing and in another 20 or 30 yards, still finding no opening, stopped again. While he caught his breath he heard the unmistakable low rumble of an idling car engine and then a voice he knew so well.

"I can't see a thing," Suzanne said, sticking her head out through an open window, trying to make her way in the fog.

Tommy stood silent, shocked. "Suzanne," he whispered, her name floating through the fog.

"Well, just keep it slow. You're still on the road," said Anthony.

Their voices started to get quieter as the car slowly inched its way farther down the road. Tommy was still in shock. He had already said his goodbyes and couldn't go through this again. He was committed to the mission, and yet, here was the voice of the woman he loved, tempting him. His broken heart raced.

A third voice came through the fog from the road.

"I see something!" yelled Joey. "It's Rollins' Marathon! It's there in the grass! Stop."

"That's it!" Tommy thought, snapping out of his own fog. The car, the break in the fence. He stumbled toward the voices and saw the Marathon. He had been only 30-feet away. He went to the side of the car best hidden from the road, quietly opened the door, and retrieved his cap. His intention was to slip unseen into the fog.

"Tommy?" Suzanne's voice was soft and quivering and he dared to look up. Her face came in and out of focus as she seemed to hover, suspended off the ground. She was beautiful in the mist and he stood frozen. Joey and Anthony came to her side. Their faces, too, came in and out of focus as the mist swirled around them, these three souls that he felt so responsible for. Suzanne started down the embankment as the fog cleared between them, and surrounded them like a soft white cocoon. She moved forward, toward him.

"No! Suzanne, don't come down here." He couldn't look at her any longer. He knew that up close her face would be beautiful and tormented, full of the pain he was causing her.

"It's okay, Tommy. I understand."

He looked up and saw not the face of tormented rejection, but of courage and understanding and deep love. He saw the face of Susan. He turned to run, but thought of something he needed to say.

"You may have saved us, you know," said Tommy holding his cap in the air. "I had to find the car and couldn't, but then I found it because of you. If all goes well you guys won't remember any of this and in about 15 minutes the United States of America will be whole again." He laughed at what he was about to say. "You're actually gonna know me. I'm an auto mechanic and, sorry Anthony, Suzanne really is my wife, but you've got a great life planned out for you somewhere, and Joey you'll be in school tomorrow morning talking to your guidance counselor about college." His tone turned serious.

"Stay away from the Park for a few minutes, it could get ugly. If I were you I'd get back in your car, turn on the radio, close your eyes and…relax for a while. You might just wake up in a new and better world. Thanks for everything – all of you…I'll see you again, I hope, very soon." He turned to walk back into the woods and Suzanne ran down the embankment and threw her arms around the only man she had ever loved. They kissed passionately and rocked in each other's arms.

"I promise, it's going to be all right," he said to Suzanne. The others looked down the embankment through the fog at this apparent 19th century Rebel soldier embracing a modern, strong young woman, and yet the two seemed like a perfect pair.

"I believe you," she said. They kissed again and stopped only when a voice came from the distance. It was Greg Jackson.

"Tommy! Have you found the car? Tommy, come on. Hat or no we've got to move now! It's already 10:45!"

"I've got to go. We're late," said Fuller. "You know, Suzanne, I'm the luckiest man in the world. I've loved you in two universes."

"I'll see you in a few minutes," she said. That was all Tommy needed to hear. He knew that, succeed or fail, she understood the mission, the Multiverse, the Universal Soul, and Quantum mechanics as well as any of them, maybe better. He turned, and without looking, ran toward the sound of Jackson's voice.

In the studios of DC-1560, things were going badly. The Zoo-Crew were a mess without their leader, and they stumbled and bumbled through every bit, embarrassing themselves and the station in the process. The station manager was furious at Kay for abandoning his show, yelling obscenities as he stormed into Kay's office. Kay sat, unfazed by the name-calling. He'd heard it all before. He calmly looked at his watch, the only digital watch in Fed-Stat. It said 10:44.

"You know what boss?" he asked rhetorically. "That crazy old bastard Rollins just might pull this off."

"Rollins? What the hell are you talking about, Kay? Have you lost your mind?"

"Unfortunately, no. But you're about to lose yours." Kay stood, pushed his chair under his desk, turned his back to the station manager, shifted slightly to the right, and walked through the wall. The exact spot was precisely between the photograph of Kay posing with Jimmy Hoffa, the former Mayor of D.C., and a poster of Lynyrd Skynyrd, with "Alabama Rum Runners" written across it with a question mark.

•••••

"They're supposedly headed out to Emmitsburg Road," said Tate to the assembled crowd. "It's about a mile or so from here to the northeast. We'll go on foot. We have reason to believe they're armed, and planning terrorist activities." The small army of police and military walked slowly through the fog, following a deteriorating concrete footpath the Park Service had laid out in the 50s and had not maintained. They all had guns drawn and were spreading out across the field as they approached Cemetery Ridge.

•••••

Fuller and Jackson found Phillips, and together they all met back up with Dr. Rollins. They walked forward another 20-yards and came to the edge of the woods at the tree line. "We were back this way, further into the trees," said Phillips. They spread out slightly and Jackson stumbled on the remnants of an old wagon wheel and called out to the others who joined him. Nearby, leaning against a tree, they also found the two guns they had left behind five days earlier.

"We're on the right track, Doc,' said Phillips. "We were exactly in this spot a few days ago. This is where we woke up."

"What do you mean 'woke up'?" said Rollins. "Explain it to me."

"We found ourselves in the firefight, ran from the explosion and ended up here. We were kind of knocked around from the big bang."

"My ear's still ringing," said Jackson.

"There was that Rebel soldier, Billy Grissom," said Fuller adding to the details. "He was here with us and then he wasn't... it's all kind of fuzzy."

"This might be *the* portal or *a* portal," said Rollins. Tommy Fuller's cap was on his head, right where it belonged. "Okay, now follow Tommy closely and walk back and forth near this spot. Pick up your guns." They did. Only inches apart from one another the four grown men felt foolish playing the follow-the-leader game. Like a snake, lost in the woods, they systematically started walking an invisible grid, quickly covering 30 square feet of the forest floor.

"You guys look pretty ridiculous." The voice of Sergeant Clay Sullivan surprised them all. "I risked my life for this?" He smiled and the men waved to him, thrilled he had found them and made it, but Sullivan backed away awkwardly.

"Good to see you, Clay!" shouted Rollins. "I thought we'd lost you. Our plan got changed up a bit as you can see. They're on to us, I'm afraid."

"Yeah, there are about 30 or 40 idiots, one-and-a-half clicks, ahhh sorry, they're about a mile that way." He pointed out to the east. "They seem to be pretty fired up. They think you guys blew up the Con-Fed Supreme Court, and they have itchy trigger fingers."

"Why would they think that?" asked Rollins.

"Because that's what Tate told them. I know you didn't do it though." Sullivan had something other than the mission on his mind and had a peculiar look on his face that made the men uneasy.

"You know we didn't do what?" asked Rollins.

"The job down in Richmond." He smiled with a smug, broad grin they hadn't seen before.

"What's going on, Clay?" asked Rollins.

Sullivan smiled. "Yeah, I know you didn't pull the Richmond job. I'm sort of good at wiring suicide bombers and the rednecks pay really well. I've been working for them for the past five years. That job was supposed to have been a hell of a lot worse, but the kid panicked and blew too soon." The men looked at him with utter disbelief.

"Look, I can see you're confused. I've got some bad news for you guys. Sorry to do this, really." He pulled his holstered weapon and pointed it at the men. "I had to see what you were up to. Sorry about the little charade. You know you were really screwing up our operation and the heat was headed in our direction. Tate will be glad to see that I...killed the terrorists. Nothing personal, you understand."

Rollins' face drained of its color. "Clay, what are you talking about? You're one of us."

315

"No I'm not, actually."

"What do you mean? Clay, don't you want to go home?"

"I am home. I like it here better. Less bullshit. I'm smarter here. I've got five hot girlfriends in D.C." The smile was gone from Sullivan's face. "On your knees, hands behind your heads, all of you, now!" The men knelt down on the forest floor. "You guys should be proud of yourselves. You idiots accomplished what the entire Confederate Army couldn't–you won the goddamn Civil War! Civil War reenactors! Give me a fucking break." He laughed and circled behind them and the men feared their impending executions.

"I'm sorry men," said Henry. "I trusted Sullivan and Kay. I'm just an old fool."

"Shut up Rollins," said Sullivan.

"You're a piece of shit," said Jackson.

"You could have learned a few things from the niggers around here, but I can see you didn't. You don't know your place." He kicked Jackson in the kidneys, sending him slumping forward with a muted cry of pain.

Phillips, thinking fast, tried to engage Sullivan in conversation. "I don't understand you blowing up your own beloved Con-Fed supreme court?" asked Phillips.

"You don't know about the reunification talks going on behind the scenes, do you?" asked Sullivan. "Those weak, Jew judges have got to go. We're just speeding up the process. Yes, this is the way it should have happened. It's just too bad I didn't arrive 75-years earlier to see slavery still legal. Man I would have owned me a mess of them…"

Jackson jumped up in a suicide move to take down the racist, mercenary, turncoat Traveler, and Phillips seized the moment to spring to his feet. Together they tackled the Sergeant, caught off guard. They wrestled on the ground, Sullivan easily pinning Phillips underneath him and before anyone could make the next move a gunshot punctuated the air. The men stood motionless, knowing this monster, this gun-for-hire, had snuffed out the life of their friend.

Jackson stood back and they waited for Sullivan to get up.

"Well, are you going to help me?" asked Phillips. "Get this shit head off of me." Sullivan's body was limp and Phillips struggled to work his way out from underneath.

"My God, Mike. Are you all right?" asked Jackson, smiling at his friend's apparent resurrection.

"Oh, peachy, thanks."

"That was the coolest thing I've ever seen," said Fuller. The gun was still in Sullivan's hand. He'd accidentally shot himself.

"I don't know what to say," said Rollins. "I had no idea about him."

"It's okay, Doc," said Phillips. "He had us all fooled."

"To think I had him in my home." Rollins would have ruminated about his own poor character assessment, but knew the importance of timing and turned his attention back to the mission. "That shot won't help keep us secret, that's for sure. They'll be on us. Get back in line and stay close. Let's get going."

Are you sure about this?" asked Jackson, as they resumed the absurd parade in an ever-widening square.

"No, I'm not, but the portal could be anywhere. The exact spot could be right here under our noses. We've got to check everywhere you were. Keep walking. Faster!"

Chapter 36

Tate assumed command of the multi-national, impromptu militia and within minutes they arrived at the Memorial sight. The 30-foot tall statue of President Jefferson Davis looked out with steely eyes across the vast expanse of the Park, lording over the huge crater, as its gruesome trophy. The small army of men had been wandering around the Memorial, almost forgetting they were looking for armed terrorists until a single, gunshot emanated from the woods. A group of ten or so, led by Tate, turned in the direction of the shot and began to approach the thicket of trees. They were less than a quarter of mile from the fugitives when Tate's partner suddenly launched into a tar & nicotine-driven coughing fit.

Tommy Fuller stopped suddenly, causing each of his friends to crash into the one in front, sending them all to the ground. Phillips grunted when the bulk of Jackson's mass fell on him, knocking the breath from his body.

"Tommy, what are you doing?" yelled Jackson in an automatic response to Fuller's sudden stop and the resultant pile-up. He'd been just a little too loud.

Tate heard Jackson's voice and the commotion coming from the woods.

"That way." He pointed his gun in the air and whistled again. "They're this way! Watch the fog and watch where you shoot. Follow me."

This time the four men in the woods all heard the whistle and most every word of Tate's chilling order. "Come on Tommy, get up!" yelled Rollins. "Do those rifles work?"

"No!" cried Phillips. "They're wet and we don't have any powder or Minié balls anyway!" The men stood together and could hear the footsteps of the approaching military.

318

"Then I guess Sullivan's gun will have to do." Rollins retrieved the .45 caliber, 12 shot revolver from underneath the lifeless body of Clay Sullivan. "Tommy, keep walking, we're right behind you. Try over to the left! We haven't been over there yet. Watch your ears, I'm going to try to slow them down." He fired the gun twice into the air and the shots rang out in the relative stillness of the foggy July morning.

•••••

Suzanne, sitting in the middle of the large front seat of the Marathon, clutched both Anthony's hand and her brother's as they sat in the old car with the radio playing softly. They heard the shots ring out and she closed her eyes tightly, knowing it had begun.

"Come on, come on. Please Jesus, just get this over with."

Tate and his men fired blindly into the fog in the direction of the shots they had heard. The four men could hear bullets whizzing through the trees. One came close enough that a three-inch branch disintegrated before their eyes.

"Keep walking, Tommy, faster," said Rollins with both clarity and urgency. Through the fog they had to be careful not to bump into trees, which seemed to appear out of nowhere.

•••••

When the shots stopped echoing and their ears recovered they heard new noises, thundering hoof beats in the distance, then gunfire. They looked at one another not daring to think it, but it had happened; they had made their first jump. When they heard the deafening boom of a Yankee artillery barrage and the distant shouting of countless soldiers on a battlefield, they knew, they were certain they had crossed over. The many days of planning and the lifetime of Rollins' quantum physics study had paid off. Just as Rollins theorized, they'd slipped into 1863, reversing the trip through 150-years of time.

This first wormhole did not connect parallel universes, but two separate periods in the same timeline, in the same universe; any interference here would most definitely change the future, and that was part of the plan. The portal had been firmly attached to the present and to The Battle of Gettysburg and they had arrived just prior to some of the fiercest fighting. When Confederate Captain Billy Grissom came running into the woods, they feared they had missed their chance to stop the detonation and the only opportunity, to not only fix the timeline, but to get home as well.

"We're too late," said Phillips, seeing Grissom, knowing the

319

detonation was minutes away, and well out into the battlefield.

"Stay down, you cowards," Grissom yelled at the deserters. "I want you to survive this blast so I can watch you hang."

They had to think fast and it was all coming at them at light speed. Phillips took the lead. "We're not deserters, Captain Grissom." He grabbed Dr. Rollins by the forearm. "We followed this Yank into these woods and almost lost him in the fog. How long before the explosion?"

Grissom looked at the strange crew and especially hard at Greg Jackson.

"One, maybe two, three minutes. I don't know. It almost didn't work. I shot a couple of Yankees who found the fuse and put it out, but I relit it. My brother's dead. Here's his cap, that's all I got."

Grissom reached into his belt looking for the cap, which had, unknown to him, fallen out on the battlefield. Tommy instinctively put his hand to his head and felt the very cap Grissom was looking for upon his own head.

"It was just here." He searched frantically for the missing Kepi, his only link to his beloved brother. He slumped to the ground, fraught with emotion and fatigue. The young Rebel never saw it coming. Mike Phillips circled behind him and slammed the butt of his rifle into the back of his head.

"He'll live another day if I didn't kill him," said Phillips. "Come on, we've got a bit of work to do."

"What do you mean?" yelled Fuller.

"We've got to stop that detonation. You heard Grissom. The fuse is burning."

"No!" yelled Fuller. "We'll never make it!"

"We've got to try, Tommy. And anyway, we don't have a choice. The next portal is down there at Emmitsburg Road, not 20 feet from the bomb. You want to go home? You want to see Susan again? We've all got to go. If you thought this universe was bad, try it here starting in 1863 for the rest of your natural born days."

"He's right," said Rollins. "If we don't move on, we're stuck here. Grab Grissom's side arm, Mike." Phillips had been hovering over the body of the Captain noting he was alive but certainly not feeling well.

"He's going to come-to any minute," said Phillips. "Let's get the hell out of here."

•••••

History had not yet changed even though the men had made their first jump. Like all timelines, this one, too ,was directed by sequence and logic, ones and zeros: a binary code of cause and effect that could not be altered by events that *might* happen, only by events that *have* happened. As far as the timeline was concerned, the explosion on day three of The Battle of Gettysburg had gone off as expected, so the present had remained, thus far, unchanged.

One hundred fifty years into the future Tate and his men were still seeking the four fugitives, not realizing they had slipped through their net once again, a net weakened by unseen wormholes. Tate and his men spread out, quickly working their way into the woods. They found no sign of their terrorists, though they did find Sullivan's body.

"He's a Fed-Stat Border Guard," said Tate, leaning down to check the man's pulse and I.D. "What the hell was he doing out here? Looks like they took care of him. He's dead."

Tate moved on toward the fence line and his men followed him, cautiously looking behind every tree. Somewhere ahead through the fog a radio played softly. They approached the source of the music.

•••••

"That thing could blow at any second," said Rollins. "Tommy, we still need to follow you. You and your cap are the key. Move out. This is it, boys! Good luck!"

They ventured into the open battlefield, dodging horses and cannon balls, Rollins dressed in modern clothing, the others in uniform. Had they not been in such a hurry to get to the cave, they might not have made it through the fighting. Facing death or mutilation from a bomb able to vaporize a small town seemed motivating enough so that the bullets flying around their heads did not sidetrack them. Phillips and Jackson each held an arm of Rollins, and they were moving so fast that the Doctor's feet hardly touched the ground. Speed was their only hope, and their beeline straight to the rock outcropping may have saved them.

This group of four men, one very young, another quite old, from the rather small to the rather large, black and white, rich and poor, represented the Nation they were trying to preserve, a microcosm of American society. This truth was lost on them in the moment, and they couldn't take time to reflect upon the symbolic cultural and generational mix; it was not a high priority, given the circumstances.

At the top of the ridge the noise was horrifying. Screams and pleas from the wounded mixed with retreating Rebel Yells from the Confederate Soldiers, and hoof-beats from 300 mounted cavalry. During the brutal hand-to-hand combat, bayonets clashed against one another with metallic scrapes sounding more horrible than a thousand fingernails on a thousand blackboards. The enormous din generated by cannons and thousands of troops firing their weapons was sickening, a stark contrast to the relative quiet of the past few days. Being chased by Tate and his goons was nothing compared to this nightmare. At The Battle of Gettysburg, the smell of gunpowder and death permeated the air.

Yankee soldiers poured over the ridge by the thousands. Most of the Rebels had already retreated, as planned. If not for the smoke lingering in the humid air, the Travelers would have been picked off in seconds. As it was, they barely escaped several attempts by Federal troops passing by. Rollins proved to be a decent shot having saved them more than once. They felt badly about shooting these men and hoped the wounds were not lethal, but their fate was out of their hands. Once again, as with most wars, they found themselves forced to choose between the lesser of evils.

Tommy Fuller was first to reach the cave.

"There!" He pointed to the obvious camouflage of scrub and tree branches protecting the wagons from view.

"We've got to get to the fuse!" yelled Jackson. They pulled at the branches to try to find the burning end and, though the smell of the magnesium and clay mixture was choking, they could not see where it was coming from. Galloping horses flew overhead followed by more Yankee infantry. While they could not find the burning end of the time-fuse, they clearly saw the three large wagons piled high with a deadly and massive cocktail of annihilation.

"I see it!" cried Jackson, bending low and scrambling to reach the still burning canvas-covered fuse. At the rate it was disappearing and turning to ash, he figured he had 10 seconds, at the most, before it vanished under the wagon's tarp and they would become a part of the cataclysm.

Chapter 37

A gust of wind and the late-morning sun began to burn off the heavy fog and Suzanne and her passengers appeared to Tate and his men at the top of the embankment.

"Up there!" Tate shouted. They ran toward the car and Suzanne cranked the engine. It only moaned. The radio had drained an already weak battery and the engine wouldn't fire. She pounded her fist on the wheel as she saw Tate no more than 50-feet away, and closing. Tate fired his weapon in the air and the rest of his bloodthirsty gang took that as their authority to shoot to kill.

•••••

Tommy Fuller had to crawl on his knees and elbows, as the fuse was climbing up the backside of the nearest wagon. It took him a few seconds to reach it and he hesitated for a moment. "I could run, slip back through to 2013 and live here with Suzanne," he thought. "I have options. No troubles, no rap music, no gangs, no bills, no arrest warrants…"

Mike Phillips yelled under the wagon Tommy was underneath. "Do you see it? Tommy? Please. We need to go home." His plea was wrenching, his voice full of emotion and fatigue.

Tommy watched the fuse burning closer and closer to the clump of detonator material just under the tarp. He had no death wish, so it was either run immediately, or stop the detonation. He pictured Suzanne, humming along to some new song she liked on the radio. Then he heard her voice in his ear, remembering her smile and her last words to him: 'I'll see you in a few minutes.' He grabbed the burning white-hot magnesium fuse with his hand and ripped it from beneath the tarp.

•••••

Tate's militia fired at the car, bullets shattering the rear windows, penetrating the doors.

"Get out! Run!" Suzanne yelled to Anthony and her brother. She slid to the passenger side of the car following the boys out of the door and down the other side of the embankment. They tumbled head over foot, with Tate's private army closing fast. Anthony threw himself between Suzanne and the hail of gunfire and engulfed her body with his own. They fell together, tumbling.

•••••

Tommy Fuller screamed in pain as the still live magnesium burned within his clenched fist. Jackson pulled him out from under the wagon by his boots and pried his burning hand open, scraping the still-sizzling chemicals from his blackened palm. He screamed in pain as they helped him to his feet. Above them a rider-less horse jumped the unseen cave and tumbled to the ground, throwing a Yankee canteen over the head of Rollins. The old man braved the 10-yards to retrieve it, and poured the cool water on Fuller's badly burned hand, bringing him momentary relief.

"You did it, Tommy. By God, you did it," said Jackson. But they had no time to admire his heroics. They were still in peril.

"One more, boys. We have one more hurdle to jump," said Rollins, and they helped Tommy to his feet.

Fuller led his three companions in their bizarre, tight formation. His pain was severe, though they were so close to success and in such danger that pure adrenaline kept him moving.

"We were farther back, toward the Rebel line, down the hill a little!" yelled Jackson over the tumult of the battle. "That way!" He pointed and Fuller managed to work his way through the final remnant of the advancing Yankee troops and they stumbled across the body of their fallen friend, Brad Lake.

"Oh my God! Brad!" Phillips was shocked at the sight of his companion. "We're taking him with us," said Phillips.

"No," said Rollins. "He's dead. You can't help him. Taking him back won't revive him. It doesn't work that way. His wounds are permanent. Unless...."

They wandered the hillside near Lake's body and recognized that they were at the vantage point where they had, just days earlier, so enjoyed watching the historic reenactment. All around them the battle raged and they could see in the distance the vulnerable and helpless Confederate troops being slaughtered where they stood, and it was about to get much worse. General Lee had placed every hope in three wagons filled with high explosives and the two brave brothers from Tennessee. It was a good plan, they were good men.

"It could have worked," Lee thought, as he turned to Major General George Pickett, and Lt. General James Longstreet, ordering some 13,000 troops on a suicide mission, later known as Pickett's Charge. A reporter once asked Pickett, many years after the war, why the charge had been unsuccessful. He replied with wit, "I always thought the Yankees had something to do with it." None of the Confederate commanders could know that one time, in one universe, they had been successful in a secret plan that came within seconds of working, forever dissolving the Union that they felt was oppressing their beloved States Rights.

Exhausted, no longer able to stand the pain and the shock, Fuller fainted and collapsed. The others followed as he rolled a few feet down the ridge. Rollins knelt by his side. They were in the very spot where they had started their adventure five days earlier. The battle was fully engaged around them, and a soldier they recognized appeared out of the smoke, musket in his hand.

Billy Grissom looked down at the four strangers, one of whom had recently given him the butt end of his rifle. He saw Tommy holding his injured hand. He looked at the wagons, just as he and his brother had placed them, and he knew the fuse was no longer burning. He looked to his left, down toward the ground and the body of a Rebel soldier, Tom Grissom, a fallen hero, his brother.

"Yankee spies!" he screamed, through blood and tears as he raised his rifle. He took aim first at Tommy Fuller, but then swung the rifle 90 degrees, taking a bead on the center wagon carrying the nitro. Fuller, coming to, saw what was happening, turned toward Dr. Rollins and grabbed the pistol sticking out of his belt.

A single shot rang out, amidst the chaos. It hadn't come from Grissom's rifle, but rather his own stolen sidearm. Tommy Fuller shot Billy Grissom, a young man about his own age. The brave Confederate soldier fell to his knees, dropping his rifle, a Minie ball round still packed into the long barrel. Fuller struggled to get up and took three steps to the left.

As softly as a ghost fluttering in the moonlight, Tommy Fuller disappeared before their eyes. Henry Rollins grabbed the sleeves of the remaining Travelers, and, pulling them with him, dove for the spot where Fuller had vanished. The three were a fraction of a second behind Fuller and together they soared through time and space, traveling the distance of a universe in a split second. Fuller, his X-factor, and his Confederate cap acting as the key, again unlocked a door connecting universes that were briefly agreeable to letting Travelers experience its mysteries first-hand.

Earlier in the day Greg Jackson had asked Rollins how far apart the universes had been, and Rollins answered: "How far is up from down, or left from right?" While those questions would stay with each of the men for the rest of their lives, the pressing question on their minds, at that moment, was, "Are we home?" There were no guarantees.

Chapter 38

By the time Jackson could focus his eyes, the sounds of war had vanished. Rollins was gone, and Tommy Fuller and Mike Phillips stood, unable to speak. Fuller struggled to stand, then turned to his friends, and spoke to them for the last time. "I love you guys. Thanks for everything, I'm not staying. This is my do-over." He took two steps forward and vanished. He was headed back.

Stunned, Phillips and Jackson looked at each other, unsure of what to say or do.

"I don't believe him. That crazy Rebel," said Jackson. "What's he think he's going to do?"

Phillips had an idea, but kept it to himself. "I think we made it home, Greg."

They surveyed the battlefield—no crater, no 200-foot granite monument honoring Jefferson Davis.

"Yes. We made it." Phillips wanted to shout, but couldn't find the strength. "I think we made it, but where's the Doc?"

The two men made their way toward the Park's picnic shelter, where they filled their bellies with ice-cold, clear water from one drinking fountain.

"That's a good sign," said Jackson, looking at the simple, unmarked fountain. His last drink here had been from a 'Whites Only' spigot. They walked toward the empty parking lot and noticed immediately their cars were gone. A bone-chilling wind was cutting through in a way uncharacteristic for July.

"Well," said Jackson, scanning the parking lot for his BMW. "It's either way after the reenactment, and it's been all cleaned up, and our cars towed off somewhere...or..."

"Or, we haven't been here yet," said Phillips. "Remember what Rollins said? About the time variations? It could be days, even years before or after the event. That means...Brad!" For the first time in several days Mike Phillips held out hope for his fallen comrade, Brad Lake.

"We're charting unknown territory here, Mike. Let's take it slowly, and let's take comfort in knowing we've spared an entire earth population a life with Europe ruled by a Hitler and a United States split in two, not to forget a dozen other atrocities. We changed it all for that world by stopping the detonation, and we've made it home, and we're alive to talk about it. It's one for the history books, but no one will ever read about it. No one would ever believe it. Hell, I don't believe it."

"Yeah," said Phillips, still pondering Fuller's sudden change of heart, and return to the unknown. "I hope Henry's OK," he said, changing the subject.

They walked on for another few minutes, their long shadows coming and going as the sun intermittently peeked through the clouds. They were glad to be dressed in wool, as a bitter and cold wind blew over the ground and into their faces.

•••••

Tommy Fuller arrived back on the Gettysburg Battlefield assuming that only a few moments had passed. Thomas Grissom lay dead on the ground, and he looked for the body of Billy Grissom, who should have been there beside him, shot by Rollins' stolen side arm; but his body was gone. Though war raged around him in its full fury, Tommy Fuller turned to survey the cave and the "Yankee Surprise" within. His thoughts turned to Suzanne. Finding her safe and whole, just the way he'd left her, was his only hope and his clear mission. He knew of only one way to ensure it.

Crawling under the center wagon, Fuller saw the magnesium fuse still burning, with around half-a-foot of canvas-covered fuse left before reaching the detonator clay. He had actually arrived several minutes earlier, than when he had left. He couldn't stop to ponder the insanity of the fact, but the fuse was still very definitely burning, though not for much longer.

When he stood, two Yankee soldiers barreled over the hill and fell dead at his feet, shot by a very healthy Billy Grissom, dressed in a Yankee uniform.

"You! Soldier! Help me," said Billy to Tommy Fuller. "We got to slow that fuse down. It'll blow too early." Billy Grissom was following his brother's final dying order to extinguish the burning fuse, wait a few minutes, and then re-light it, once enough Yankees were in the trap.

Fuller was stunned, unable to speak. The sensation he felt was that of déjà vu a thousand fold, mixed with a healthy dose of nightmare, and paralyzing fear.

"Never mind. I got it," said Grissom, disappearing under the wagon. "Where's your gun?" Fuller didn't answer. Grissom threw him his side arm. "Stay down, and cover me."

By this point the mass of the Confederate A.N.V. were retreating, and were chased by tens of thousands of Yanks, right up the middle, flanked and squeezed, just as Lee had hoped. They waited an agonizing four or five minutes in the midst of the carnage, before Grissom reemerged from under the wagons.

"Okay. It's relit. If you wanna live, come with me."

The two men weaved and dodged oncoming cavalry and infantry, all while stepping over the bodies of the dead and dying. When they were almost at the woods' edge, a flash in the sky and a detonation wave from an exothermic reaction, traveling at four miles-per-second, knocked both men to their knees. For the second time in less than five days, Tommy Fuller endured what should have been a crippling, if not deadly, explosion. How many more times he might tempt and gamble with Fate, and win, he dared not guess. He struggled to his feet, cap in hand, and this time knew exactly where to go.

•••••

When Henry Rollins could finally catch his breath, he dared to let the world around him take form. He was standing on the shoulder of a paved road. A van whizzed by, filled with tourists, who, in air-conditioned comfort, were enjoying a historic tour of Gettysburg, Pennsylvania. Rollins' jaw dropped. The van was electric; it said so proudly on its side. Overhead a Boeing 787 Dreamliner was making its final approach into D.C. and its enormous shadow momentarily blocked the sun, while Rollins struggled to focus on its massive size.

"Oh my. Oh my…" was all he could manage. From a distance, amid modern sights and sounds he'd only ever witnessed on video, thanks to Margaret, he saw something that pre-dated even his substantial 83 years. From a block away he could just make out something old, something out of place in a sea of modern machinery, the silhouette of an old car, coming toward him. He could hear it coming long before he could see it clearly. As the rat-a-tat-tat sound of the small engine got louder, and the car moved closer, he stood in disbelief at what was taking shape.

A car from the early 1900s, looking very much like a Model A Ford, rolled down Emmitsburg Road, puttered toward him and let out an enthusiastic Ahh-ooh-gah! Ahh-ooh-gah!, as it slowed. A slender arm waved from the driver's side window, before the car pulled to the shoulder and stopped.

"Hello, you old dog." It was Margaret.

For the first time in decades, the normally verbose Dr. Rollins was physically unable to speak.

"Aren't you going to say hello?" she asked.

"Margaret," said Rollins. "I...you... you never cease to amaze me."

"I have never seen you at such a loss for words," she said with a small chuckle, wiping a tear from her eye. "If you hadn't shown up here....I don't know what I would have done," she said. "I would have hunted you down and killed you, that's what. Well, get in. This car is your early Christmas present."

Rollins was still unable to form words. As he walked to the passenger side of the car, he noticed Maverick sitting in the front seat, wagging his tail. He shared the seat with his dog and closed the door, while Margaret pulled back out into the traffic, which was moving much too fast for his taste. He looked at a brass plate on the polished wooden dashboard.

'Marathon Motor Car, Southern Motor Works, Nashville, Tennessee.'

"I went all the way to Nashville," said Margaret, and had to beg the owner to sell it. At first he wouldn't budge, but ultimately he couldn't turn down three-quarters of a million dollars. It's one of only four left in the world. He was such a nice man. And you know he was the grandson of a Civil War soldier. After the War he actually worked the line at Marathon Motor Works, in 1906. This, Henry, is your 1914 Marathon. It was the last year they ever made a car. It's a wonderful machine, don't you think? I drove it here from home just this morning."

"From home?" asked Rollins, still in shock.

"Yes. You're home, finally."

The couple had finally achieved the work of a lifetime, and it was sinking in. Rollins looked at a very modern Gettysburg, but with plenty of care given to its historic past.

"What was the man's name?" he asked, "the grandson you say you bought the car from?"

Margaret smiled with the knowledge and anticipation of how the information she was about to share, would surprise even her un-surprise-able husband. "William "Billy" Grissom the 4th. I remember, because he gave me a tour of the old Motor Works. A picture of his great-grandmother and great-grandfather hung on the wall. The great-grandfather was wounded right here on this battlefield. He was a Confederate soldier who had once lived in Tennessee; the brother of the boy behind the failed Grissom Plan. The great grandmother's name was Elizabeth, I think."

330

The puzzle pieces swirled in Rollins' head as he tried to make the connections. The same William Grissom that had been laid out by Fuller's gunshot from 20-minutes earlier, actually in 1863, had survived his wounds, made it back to Tennessee and married Elizabeth Robbins, the girl both Grissom brothers courted in their youth. This same man had had a hand in assembling the car in which he was currently riding.

"How did you know...? Rollins began to ask the obvious.

"I didn't," said Margaret. "I hoped...I prayed that the timing, as in my jumps would be close. I of course knew the plan, that you were headed to Gettysburg, and about when you would arrive, and about when that horrible explosion was to occur. I've been driving around town for an hour with all the tourists. Waiting. Praying."

"Always full of surprises, Margaret," said Rollins. "Oh, how Mr. Einstein would have loved all this." He turned to her and placed his hand on her cheek. "Thank you."

"You're welcome," said Margaret. "It's good to have you home."

Chapter 39
July 3, 1863 10:57 a.m.

Billy Grissom lay unconscious at the woods' edge, while fallout from the detonation rained down around him. A nearly fully formed wagon wheel crashed through the canopy of the forest, still smoldering, narrowly missing Fuller, as it hit the ground.

Fuller stood to get his bearings. With his cap in hand, he looked for the familiar landmarks that represented his next portal. It only took him a moment to find the hill he had rolled down five days earlier, and the exact spot that would bring him to 2013, and he hoped a waiting girl named Suzanne.

With a few dance-like steps at the foot of the hill, Fuller knew he'd made the jump, when the sky flashed, and early July sunlight turned to clouds, wind and winter snow.

"Oh crap," he said, as the sudden chill set in. "Where am I now?"

He no longer had his companions to help attempt to make any sense of all the Traveling madness. This time he was on his own. He crunched over the frozen ground as the wind began to pick up. He made his way toward the Battlefield, but the snowfall was too heavy to see much further than 20-feet or so. As he got closer to Emmitsburg Road he saw a ghostly figure that appeared to be floating in the snowy swirls, some 30-feet off the ground. It was Confederate President, Jefferson Davis, who seemed to look down upon him, smiling. Fuller breathed a sigh of relief as the statue became clearer. He flipped up the collar of his wool jacket, and pulled his cap down tightly upon his head. When he did so, he felt the sharp prick of a pin, or something equally sharp, and adjusted the cap.

"It's not July, I guess," he said aloud.

"No, I guess not," said a teenage boy, laughing. "It's December, three days before Christmas!"

Fuller spun on his heels to see a bundled-up kid, attempting to make a snowman from the newly fallen, wet snow. Across the Park younger children were engaged in a snowball fight. Fuller moved closer to the boy.

"Hello," he offered.

"Hey," said the boy. "Is that a Civil War outfit?"

"Oh, ahh… yeah. It was the warmest thing I could find to wear." Tommy spoke to the back of boy's head. The kid was putting the finishing touches on his misshapen masterpiece.

"What's the date?" Tommy asked.

"I told you," he said, turning to look at the man. "December 22nd."

Tommy paused and took a deep breath of the cold winter air.

"What year?"

"It's 2011," answered the kid. "Hey, are you okay? You'd better keep that Civil War stuff on the L.D., they don't really allow it here."

Tommy looked at the boy's face when he turned.

"I think you mean the D.L., the 'down low'," he corrected. He couldn't help but smile as tears welled in his eyes.

"Yeah, I'm okay," said Fuller to Joey Michaels, a younger version of Joey, but unmistakably the younger brother of Suzanne Michaels, the girl he loved.

THE END

At a small AM radio station in Philadelphia, the traffic reporter signed on. "Billy the K here with your noon traffic update," said the timid voice. Kay had crossed over, as had been strongly suggested, and would later apologize to Dr. Rollins, who categorically told him to get stuffed. Kay would never earn more than a fraction of his accumulated wealth from the other side. He tried in vain to cross back over and find a new portal, but was never successful; Kay's old boss would see to that. He'd had Kay's office emptied of its furniture, and exorcised by a local priest.

The Rollins' would enjoy their years together living in their old home in Sugarland, Maryland, which had become engulfed by the urban sprawl of D.C. Theirs was the only farmhouse not leveled during the housing and retail boom of the 1990's, Margaret having successfully lobbied the Historical Society for 'Landmark' status.

The house sat, happily enough, wedged between the Super Wal-Mart and the Home Depot, which they got used to, and found that it actually came in quite handy. They hoped Tommy Fuller would find the note they'd folded, hidden and pinned to the inside of his Kepi.

Tommy, we have a feeling that you and Suzanne may yet still find a way to stay together – just a hunch. If so, we'd like you to have a fresh start. You'll find gold bullion hidden in the basement of our home. Get it quickly, and quietly, as our disappearance will soon cause trouble and investigation. Use the money wisely and generously – it's as much a burden as it is a blessing. We won't be needing it anymore. Be good, do good things. Love, Henry and Margaret

Margaret eventually threw away the age-worn, old dress that had played such a big part in their lives, and she put her small compass in her jewelry box. She knew her 'cross-dressing' days, as they joked, were over, and though she would miss many parts of her other life in a simpler, quieter place, she had an enormous sense of accomplishment in helping her friends and her husband get home. She knew this was where they both belonged.

Suzanne carried no knowledge of her first adventure with Tommy Fuller, having met him for the second time in December, 2011. Their first encounter in 2013, to her, never occurred. When her kid brother Joey brought Fuller home, like a stray dog, she thought the young man was mysterious, and kind of cute, if not a little old for her.

Pre-dating his first arrival by 18 months, and with a full foreknowledge of events yet to occur, Fuller was able, with one phone call, to thwart the bombing of the Con-Fed Supreme Court building, and, by making an anonymous tip, have Clay Sullivan arrested. He was also able to persuade Suzanne, her brother, and a troublemaker friend of theirs named Anthony, to steer clear of the Freedom Fighters and the unification movement, even though Suzanne's father and Unka George were small-time border jockeys.

A universe away Mike Phillips and Greg Jackson would find their arrival home, also time-skewed, but only by six months. When reenactor Captain DiCarlo called Phillips at his office about the upcoming reenactment season's schedule, Phillips and Jackson both found excuses to not attend, their reenacting days behind them. Before DiCarlo hung up, he had one more question.

"About that Fuller, kid." said DiCarlo. "His wife filed a missing persons report, and nobody seems to know where he is. Have you seen him around?"

"No, we sure haven't," said Phillips. "But I'm sure he'll turn up somewhere."

The conflict had many names in the press and among the citizens of the United States: the War of Northern Aggression, the War Between the States, the War of Southern Independence, the War of the Rebellion, or, as some well-heeled bluebloods of Charleston, South Carolina, still refer to it, "that minor unpleasantness." To most Americans, then and now, it was known simply as the *Civil War*. It was the first modern war incorporating military advancements including: submarines and torpedoes (yes, that's true), machine guns, aviation (also true), and the use of massive explosives. It was also a war of brutal hand-to-hand combat and a war where a soldier was twice as likely to die from disease, malnourishment, the elements, or normally non-lethal wounds, as he was a bullet.

Military tacticians in the 1860s hovered between the ancient and modern. Like unsure adolescents, leaders from both sides were often reluctant to embrace new technologies, even after they had proven their efficacy. Case in point: aviation. Manned, tethered hydrogen and hot air balloons were employed for reconnaissance by both sides, and spotters high above the battlefield could electronically telegraph, via 500-foot cables, the positions of their enemy to commanders on the ground. Though moderately successful in several campaigns, the Balloon Corps was dismantled by 1863, two years before the end of the War.

The Confederate Navy scrubbed its submarine program even after the *H.L. Hunley*, the world's first practical submarine, successfully sank a Federal blockade ship, the *USS Housatanic*, just off the South Carolina coast. The Hunley earned a place in history as the vessel behind the world's first successful submarine seek-and-destroy mission. The 40-foot long 4-foot wide, hand-cranked "torpedo boat" itself became a victim of her own success, sinking shortly after the Housatanic. She went down with all eight crewmembers aboard. After retrieving her, intact, from the bottom of Charleston Harbor in 2003, the Confederate sailors' remains were interred, accompanied by a full military funeral at Charleston's Magnolia Cemetery. Eight horse-drawn caissons transported the crewmen in a procession through downtown Charleston that lasted most of the day.

Fifty-thousand spectators attended the memorial service, and for the first time in over a century, press from around the globe were once again reporting on the American Civil War. They called the spectacle the 'Last Confederate Funeral.' Ten thousand Civil War reenactors participated in an official role in the service.

While the 1860s kept the Americans fully engaged in this form of not quite modern, not quite ancient warfare, individual thinkers from around the globe were making exponential leaps forward in the sciences and humanities. These scientists, philosophers, and authors from virtually every continent, had fully evolved from the repressive dark ages of dogma and were in the midst of an information explosion. In an era before the automobile, men (and for the first time women) set about describing to the world, complex theorems that had actually been hinted at for centuries. Though they hadn't yet developed language to describe them, the most forward thinkers were considering advanced concepts such as spacetime, Edgar Allan Poe having written about it in 1848 saying: "Space and duration are one." H.G. Wells, Jules Verne, and Mark Twain had already considered time travel. Wells, in 1890, coined the phrase "Time Machine" in his book titled as such. Einstein's Theory of Special Relativity was a mere 30-years removed from the Civil War, as was the introduction of a polished Unified Field Theory, a combination of all known physics and quantum mechanics theories that had been considered as far back as 1820.

Despite these advances in understanding, and rapid development in the sciences, our great-grandparents, still living in the age of kerosene lamps, would have been hard pressed to have fully imagined wormhole travel, parallel universes or time travel. Within one generation these concepts, thanks to both popular fiction and the scientific community, were widespread and spurred the imaginations of those who would split the atom, land a man on the moon, and build particle accelerators. In the short 150 years since the 1860s, mankind has experienced unparalleled technical advances. Each generation since has witnessed exponential growth in the sum of these ideas, based on the sacrifices and work of the previous.

•••••

The first Civil War reenactment I attended was on December 1st, 1989 in Franklin, Tennessee, which was at that time, a sleepy, small town 18 miles south of Nashville. Franklin of the late 1980s was still a decade shy of the urban sprawl and building boom it knows today. The 125th anniversary of the Battle of Franklin took place on a cold, gray December day, not unlike the first days of the original bloody battle.

Along with thousands of spectators, I watched the reenactment unfold across the open farmland of the mostly still undeveloped Williamson County countryside. The spectacle of thousands of men in authentic reproduction uniforms, hundreds of mounted Cavalry, dozens of cannons and a commitment to authentic portrayals in both the civilian encampments and on the battlefield, was gripping.

I was suddenly, and quite unexpectedly, overcome by an unsettling, adrenaline producing sensation. I considered, albeit briefly, that maybe I wasn't witnessing a reenactment, but instead the actual Battle of Franklin. I felt like a spectator on the sidelines of history, looking on the carnage through some mysterious crystal ball, blurry around the edges, but focused in the center. For a fleeting moment, full of both wonder and trepidation, I had no doubt that I was standing on a ridge in 1863 watching history unfold in real-time. The reenactors had accomplished their mission.

Twenty years later, I would, myself, become a living-historian, a Civil War reenactor, and join the 4th New Hampshire / 7th South Carolina reenactors group based in Conway, South Carolina. To date, I've participated in 12 reenactments and living history events around South Carolina, Tennessee, and Georgia's historical battlefields, in front of thousands of spectators, who, hopefully, were just as moved as I was standing on that ridge in Franklin, Tennessee, two decades earlier.

Made in the USA
Charleston, SC
19 August 2014